The Whole Fam Damily

The Whole Fam Damily

or
Round and Round and Round She Goes
And If She'll Stop, Nobody Knows
—Anne Onymous

Anne Cameron

HARBOUR PUBLISHING

HARBOUR PUBLISHING
P.O. Box 219
Madeira Park, BC Canada V0N 2H0

Published with the assistance of the Canada Council and the Government of British Columbia, Tourism and Ministry Responsible for Culture, Cultural Services Branch.

Cover illustration and design by Sean Murphy, Mobius Graphics
Back cover author photograph by Dianne Whelan
Typeset in Adobe Garamond and Kabel
Page composition by Vancouver Desktop Publishing Centre
Printed and bound in Canada

Canadian Cataloguing in Publication Data

Cameron, Anne, 1938-
  The whole fam damily

  ISBN 1-55017-134-8

  I. Title.
PS8555.A48W3 1995   C813'.54   C95-910736-3
PR9199.3.C34W3 1995

for my kids
Alex
Erin
Pierre
Marianne
Tara

for my grandkids
Sarah
David
Terry
Daniel
Sheldon
Jenelle
Andy

Lloyd Anderson did my farm chores while I was lost in the ozone, working on this. Thank you, Lloyd, your help is very much appreciated.

And a huge thank you to Alan Cook, computer systems analyst extraordinaire, who saved this manuscript when it looked as if the machine was going to send everything into the ozone. I think we agreed I'd write "Couldn't have done 'er without you."

My physician, Bruce Hobson, has kept me on my feet long after my back decided to dump me on my gluteus maximus. Thank you, Bruce!

Eleanor has held the rest of me together with her love, her loyalty, her honesty and her lists, and, perhaps most important, her self-sufficient ability to not feel threatened when I'm more involved in "the story" than in my own life. I love you.

1

They were sitting in the King's Hotel, both of them starting to feel unaccustomedly emotional. It wasn't often the siblings expressed affection for each other, except perhaps by teasing or pretending to argue. But something, and not just the beer, was swirling in each of them tonight, and each had already told the other how glad she was to have the other for a sister. Tammy's husband, Steve, had just paid for their fifth jug of draft when someone yelled from the middle of the room that it was his turn at the pool table. Steve filled his glass, picked up his cigarettes and left quickly, laughing and calling something about kiss it all goodbye, boys, the champ is comin'.

"Jesus," Tammy frowned. "That's it for him tonight. He gets on that damn pool table and just stays there until they close the place. Go over to talk to him or something and he shoos you away like you were a fly."

"Too bad." Cindy tried to sound sympathetic but couldn't see what Tammy had to complain about. After all, Steve worked, and he worked steady, or as steady as anyone did when they were a faller in the bush. He made real good money and sent most of it home, too, and never asked questions about how Tammy filled her time while he was in camp. So what did she have to complain about?

"I guess he's entitled, right?" Tammy had that way about her, as if she could read your mind or something. "Anyway, it gives us a chance to visit private-like, right?"

"Right," and Cindy smiled, took a good swallow of her beer and looked around the King's beer parlour. The same old dead animal heads were up on the walls, dustier than ever, their glass eyes staring well over the heads of the crowd, but seeming to look at you. Like the eyes of the guy on the Quaker oats box. No matter where in the kitchen you went, that guy in the weird hat was somehow always looking at you. Same with these dead, dust-encrusted, glass-eyed animals.

Someone fed coins into the jukebox but god in heaven alone knew what tunes had been picked. There was so much noise and laughter from the overload of bodies in the place that the music got lost. Only the heavy drums made themselves heard, and then it was more like you felt them than heard them.

The round-topped tables were jammed too close together. You couldn't push your chair back without bumping into someone else's chair, and getting between the clutter of furniture to go to the can was like an obstacle course or ballet.

"Wish the waiter would change the cloth," Cindy grouched. "It's soaking wet. Whoever sat here before we did musta spilled a gallon of beer."

"Just pray it's beer and not something worser." But Tammy stood up and waved, then yelled, "Anybody workin' here tonight?" until the waiter came over, not amused by her wit. "Maybe you could take this soakin' wet rag with you?" she smiled, but there was no humour in it. "The damn thing's drippin' a puddle on the floor."

The waiter glared, but he did this thing where he moved all the glasses and the big jug to one side of the round-topped table, then slid the terrycloth cover over, too. He moved the glasses and jugs to the bare side, hauled off the cloth and walked away without wiping up or putting the glasses where they belonged.

"Cranky bugger." Tammy fussed until she had the glasses sorted out and refilled, then she dumped the ash tray onto the floor under the table and put it back empty, in the middle, between them. "If he doesn't want to empty it now, he can sweep it later. I can't stand the way they treat you. I mean without us there'd be no job for them, right? So how come they act like you're ruining their lives by comin' to the place?"

"Yeah. And look at you like they were better or something."

A woman on her way back from the Ladies suddenly started yammering at another woman, wearing a red dress and sitting with a balding blond guy. The one in the red dress seemed caught off guard, said something about not knowing what the other woman was talking about. The one doing the yelling said if Red Dress didn't understand words, she'd bloody *show* her what she was talking about, but before she could get started the waiter and the blond guy got in there and stopped it.

"Bloody moron," Tammy muttered. "Every damn time I come in here that woman is going on about something. Someone ought to clue her in. We should phone Barb," she grinned. "Can't you just see what would happen if Barb hadda been sittin' where the broad in the red dress was sittin'?"

"Like right now," Cindy agreed.

"Right now for sure! Were you there the time she . . . Nah, you weren't. I remember now. You were in Vancouver that time. Livin' with good old stinkfeet."

Tammy recounted the legend of sister Barb and the Broad in the Bathroom and made it sound so funny they both wound up laughing. That reminded Cindy of the time their brother Frank had said something to someone and that led Tammy to a rehashing of Brother George and the Cab Driver.

Halfway through the next pitcher of beer, they realized it had been years'n'years since all the siblings were in the same place at the same time. Before the waiter brought the next ice-cold jug, the idea had given birth to itself. After all, Hallowe'en was well behind them and Poppy Day had passed practically unnoticed. Grey Cup was staring them in the eyeballs, although none of them really gave a toot about that, it was just something the radio, papers and TV yammered on about for a week or so. But it did mean Bah Humbug was coming again, and wasn't that supposed to be a time for family? Well, then, there you have it, and why don't we think about it.

Steve wasn't the least bit ready to leave, so when they'd finished their jug they each got a case from the Off-Sales and headed back to Tammy's place to get on the blower and start arranging things. Tammy took the car, because by the time Steve was ready to leave he'd be lucky if he could see the For Hire light on top of the taxi parked outside the pub. He'd had his licence suspended so many times it sort of hung in mid-air all on its own. He had to haul it down out of the clouds for the cops whenever they pulled him over for driving with two wheels on either side of the yellow line.

Heaven must have been in favour of the idea, because by two-thirty in the morning they'd managed to get hold of all the others. Cindy supposed Steve would have a fit when he saw the phone bill, but with any luck at all it would come after he'd gone back into camp. Then he wouldn't get to open the envelope and have one of his world-famous temper tantrums.

Steve's temper tantrums scared Cindy but didn't seem to faze Tammy the least little bit. She just shrugged and told him to stop whining so much, what was money for anyway if not to spend? Each time she said that, he had another explosion and cut loose with his routine about savings accounts, interests, down payments on houses and stuff like that, and each time that started, Tammy yawned.

"Hey, John D," she would say, acting bored stiff, "save it for your banker, okay?"

"You watch your mouth, okay?" He had a voice that could rattle the dishes in the cupboard, but no matter how often he threatened to dump Tammy on her ass or shake her till her teeth rattled, he never did it. Tammy was lucky. She'd never had to get her eyebrow stitched shut or stay in the house for more than a week and a half waiting for the bruises to fade. Cindy had. She knew what that was like. Knew all too well what that was like, thank you.

At least it was behind her. She'd have to try to get back there to get her stuff, but maybe George or Frank would go with her. Just love to see Jack try something with those two backing her up. She would gladly pay for the chance to see that!

As it happened, she got her chance. She didn't even have to pay, although she did have to wait until Bah Humbug time. The wait wasn't bad because she and the kids stayed with Tammy—once Steve had gone back into camp there was plenty of room. Once or twice she thought about getting a place of her own, but knew she'd be lonely, and knew too that it was too easy for Jack to find her. If she was all by herself when he did, all hell would bust loose and she'd be lucky if all she wound up with was a black eye. Besides, she told herself, Tammy could use the company, and the help. Getting things ready for a family reunion was a lot of work. Sometimes Cindy wondered how Tammy did it. And why. Steve made good money, there wasn't any real need for Tammy to have a job, minimum wage wasn't going to inflate the old savings account or buy tickets on a cruise ship. But Tammy just laughed and asked how in hell Cindy thought a person could fill her days with nothing to do but wait for someone else to come out of camp? "You might try it yourself," she teased. "You never know, it might do you the world of good. At least you wouldn't have to eat shit so much."

"I don't eat shit," Cindy protested.

"G'wan, anybody who's on welfare winds up eatin' it. And you never know, maybe if you'd'a had your own money, old stinkfeet wouldn't have started to think he owned you."

"I've got better things to do with my life than sit at a phone and call people and try to talk them into signing up for a new freezer and a load of frozen food to put in it! I don't even like getting those kind of calls, you can be sure I wouldn't like making them."

"Like? What's to like? You don't have to like anything. That's why they call it work, dough-head. If you liked it, they'd call it play. What I like is having a paycheque, having my own money."

"You don't make enough money to buy your beer and pay the phone bill!"

"Bee ess I don't. I support myself every inch of the way. I buy my own clothes, I buy my own grub, I've even got money put away so's I can buy my own car soon. You'd be surprised how much better you feel about yourself when you know you aren't sitting there like some poor beggar with a tin cup, waiting for someone else to have an urge to put a few measly pennies in it so's you can maybe go for Chinese food once in a while. I can probably get you on the same shift as me, if you want."

But Cindy wasn't the least bit interested. She wasn't crawling to some boss, not for anything. She watched Tammy head off after supper, and tried hard not to let it show on her face that she thought Tam was a fool, or if not a fool, the next best thing to one. Phoning people she didn't know, people who didn't want the call, some of them probably got nasty about it. And doing it until nearly ten at night, too. And some days she went in at noon, and didn't get home until eleven. The hours were crazy for sure, almost as crazy as the job and the people doing it.

But once in a while, instead of going home, Tammy went to the pub and joined Cindy, and they had a good time until closing, talking about their plans for the get-together, remembering old times, laughing now about things that hadn't been the least bit funny when they happened. Maybe if they'd all been put in the same foster home it would have gone better for them, but they'd been split up, put in different places, and it sometimes seemed as if they'd all been trying to get back together again ever since. Well, they would this year! She knew it would be wonderful, a dream come true. Finally!

George showed up with his kids, but not with his wife Maria, who was being detained at the pleasure of the Queen. A little problem with a john, his wallet, and the police. "Nah, she'll be fine," George laughed. "I mean it. The guy's one of those who can't just get it off, okay? So he says he'll pay her double if she'll humiliate him. So, okay, she says. They go to his place, which is prob'ly gonna turn out to be his big mistake and her lawyer's biggest weapon, and she does the usual, you know, call 'im down, tell 'im he's a bad boy, slap him a few times, then she ties 'im to the bed. Uses tape on his mouth so's he can't yell. Calls him all kinds of names and each of them gets him more'n'more into the mood until finally he manages to accomplish a woodie. And then, instead of doin' a blowjob or somethin', she stiffs him. And he's on the bed wrigglin' around, tryin' to get loose and she's swipin' stuff and callin 'im a fool, askin' how he's gonna feel when they find him, stuff like that. She leaves and an hour or so later she calls the cops, tells 'em about it. Didn't want 'im to starve to death, right? But the guy not only gives a good description, he cruises the strip every night until he spots 'er, then calls the cops and lays charges. *But*—" and George started laughing so hard he had to take a break from his story and gulp some beer— "he admits to the cops he paid 'er to humiliate 'im, and she *did*, right? Besides which, she's the one told them where to find him. So the lawyer says she'll get off on prob'ly everythin' except maybe soliciting, and that's a chickenshit charge anyway."

"Too bad she'll miss Ex-Mess," Tammy said.

"Yeah, but that's okay, I mean it's for the kids, right, and they're gonna have a good time all the same, and we'll have our own wingding when she gets out."

Easy for him to talk. Wasn't him sitting in the public safety building. But he was right, it was all for the kids anyway, and the whole bunch were having a great time, racing around outside, hooting it up on the little playground area. It wasn't much of a playground, but what can you expect, they treat you like you're no good anyway.

There was a time Maria wouldn't have had to work the strip, or bother herself with a jerk who wanted to be shamed. There was a time she made real good money without that kind of stuff. But time and kids and the crap she shoved in her arm had changed things. And the hepatitis-B. Even so, she made enough that combined with the welfare cheque, they got by just fine.

Was a time, too, George had made good money, but no more and never again. A good bouncer can always find work, but George had got a bit carried away and the court came down on him like a ton of bricks. With the conviction on his record nobody wanted to hire him, because the last thing a place needs is the publicity they'd get from hiring someone who'd already turned one guy into a turnip by kicking him in the head. It's not as if that's what George had in mind from the get-go, the guy was drunk, and nasty, a big bugger, used to pushing his weight around and getting his own way. But he hadn't run into anyone like George before. When dumping him flat on his ass a couple of times didn't cool him off, and when trying to make it seem as if it was all a joke anyway didn't slow him down, George decked him. The guy got up with a hunka chair leg in his hand and swung it like a baseball bat. He had the bad luck to hit George on the shoulder, so George let fly and sent him backside over appetite, then gave him a good solid kick behind the ear to take the starch out of him. And it sure did, but it took more than the starch. These days the guy spent his time slumped in a chair staring at nothing. The judge was a rangitang old fart, too. Hit the club with a fine almost guaranteed to send them bankrupt and put George away for a year and a half. So no more bouncer work for him. It was too bad, he'd been a good one. But he liked being the one looked after the kids and all. Or at least he said he did. And without him to back her up, Maria probably wouldn't have been as safe as she was, and she probably wouldn't have made as much as she did.

Frank came with his girlfriend Ruby and the kids. Ruby's son Tom was a total pain in the ass but little Frank was cute, even if he didn't look the least bit like his dad. Pray to god he didn't wind up looking like his mom or his brother, because the both of them might look okay from afar but were far from looking okay. Who would ever be able to figure out why Frank had bothered with Ruby, let alone stayed with her. Well, stayed with her on-and-off, as they say.

With Ruby, about the only thing anyone could go along with was that even if she never seemed to do anything about the way Tommy behaved, at least she didn't have a fit if someone else took a hand. Half an hour into the visit, Tommy pulled a typical stunt and Tammy just grabbed him by one arm and whacked his butt for him. He yelled and whined and snivelled and howled, but shut up when Frank asked if he wanted a really good excuse to make all that noise.

Tammy had a humungous pot of chili ready when the kids came drifting in, complaining about being cold. "No damn wonder," Tammy laughed. "The whole lot of you's soaked to the knees. Haul off the wet clothes and find something dry to wear because you're not waltzing all over my place in squishy dirty socks."

Which was fine except they dumped their wet things in a sodden heap just inside the door. That meant that when Jack came busting in halfway through supper, he tripped in the tangle of jackets, jeans, gumboots and muddy socks. That made him mad. So things didn't even start out okay and go downhill from there, they were already about as low as they could go before he opened his mouth. And when he opened it, everybody knew.

"Listen, bitch," he said. "Get your coat and their stuff and say goodbye to this zoo."

Cindy's head was full of things she'd like to say to him. She'd had so many daydreams and fantasies about telling him to go take a hike that she almost actually told him that. But he scared her. So she just sat and looked at the food on her plate and went to that place where even if he did hit her, she wouldn't feel anything. Darelle started crying—she was that scared of Jack—and Donny did what he always did when he knew his dad was in a bad mood. He just slumped down in his chair and shook.

When Cindy didn't say anything, Jack got real mad. It always made him just about crazy when she couldn't bring herself to answer. And Darelle crying didn't help. She wasn't Jack's kid so he didn't have a lot of use for her at the best of times.

"Hey, why don't you calm down and join us?" Tammy sounded so quiet and so reasonable, as if someone standing in a pile of wet kids' clothes and yelling was a normal everyday happening.

"Mind your own business."

"Well, hell, I thought I was doing exactly just that, what with this being my place and all. Come on, we're having chili and garlic French bread."

"Shove it up your ass."

That's when George looked at Frank and Frank looked at George and they both looked at Jack and laughed out loud.

If it had been anybody else laughing at him, Jack would have just booted arse until the ambulance arrived. But it wasn't anybody else, it was George and Frank, so Jack made himself eat more than just a bowl of chili and a couple of slices of bread. Darelle even stopped crying, thank god for small mercies. Jack told Cindy to wake up and join the real world and do something about the pile of wet clothes, and she figured she'd better do what she could to keep him in a good mood. As soon as she finished eating her supper, she went over and started picking stuff off the floor, hanging the jackets on the hallway hooks, putting the socks and jeans in a heap to take to the washer.

She was bending over and scooping up the pile when the door opened and Barb hurried in with Real and the kids coming behind her. The door hit Cindy in the bum and staggered her forward, and everybody laughed and made jokes about really getting into her work. She didn't like being laughed at but nobody cared, they were too busy fussing over Barb and pretending to be friends with Real, the crazy bastard. While Tammy rushed around laughing and saying how happy she was they had been able to make it, getting bowls and more

French bread, heating the water for tea, and fussing over them, Cindy got the wet-kid smelly clothes into the washer.

Of course nobody noticed, they were too busy helping shove the Chrissy prez stuff under the plastic tree, trying to get their two bits' worth in and pulling jackets and mitts off the latest troop of kids. By the time Cindy got back to the table Real was sitting in what had been her chair, shovelling chili into his buck-toothed mouth and talking around and between the beans.

Even without a mouthful of food, even without a bellyful of beer, you weren't always sure what the crazy fool was talking about. Real had this thick Quebecker accent and a head full of off-the-wall ideas. Since the age of ten he hadn't been any closer to Quebec than watching the Montreal Canadiens play on TV, but the damn accent hung on and wouldn't you think people'd make an attempt to talk the bloody language properly? Cindy couldn't stand him, but she tried to be polite for Barb's sake. Maybe what he was going on about tonight had to do with the TV or something, because he seemed to be yammering about aliens and a spaceship which had been seen up near Egmont. Six people said it came down out of nowhere and one of the mountains in the watershed opened up like an automatic garage door, and the thing flew inside. Then the mountain closed itself up again. Real was about smart enough to buy into that shit. Once he'd spent most of a weekend going on about how there was this thing living in the ocean, bigger'n the monster in that lake in Scotland. To hear him tell it, one of the captains on the BC Ferries had seen it, not only on the radar but with his very own eyes. He'd called out and pointed, and no fewer than six crew members, including the purser, had seen it too. A tourist from Kansas had even taken some pictures of it. Real insisted a friend of his had a spyglass set up in his living room, aimed out the big picture window, and had seen this monster three or four different times.

But now he'd put the monster on the shelf and was going on about life from other planets, bright lights in the sky and mountains that opened up like garages, with automatic doors. Next he'd be trying to convince everyone there were aliens disguised as humans, maybe living right next door. Well, maybe there were, maybe the ferry captain and the crew were really aliens. Maybe the bus driver was from some other world. You could tell Real that and he'd believe it. Cindy wasn't sure why Barb had ever got mixed up with the crazy hooligan, or why she'd stuck it out with him for so long. It wasn't as if Barb was homely, she was real good looking, and could probably have had almost any guy she wanted. So why did she want this loonytoon?

Barb acted as if they'd seen each other only a couple of minutes ago, just a smile and a hi and that was it, not even a how-are-you. Well, two could play as easy as one. "Nice trip?" she asked, moving to the sofa and claiming a place on it before everyone else left the table and took all the spaces.

"Not bad. Ferry was so crowded we didn't even get in for a cup of coffee. Line-up practically went around the whole boat twice, and then those who did get in just sat talking forever, as if buying a bowl of soup meant they'd bought the whole boat and could do what they wanted. When'd you get here?"

"I never left."

"You mean you been livin' here with Tammy since you phoned? Kinda crowded, isn't it?"

"No, we're fine," Cindy said. Tammy didn't say anything, so it looked as if she agreed with Barb and that ticked Cindy off too. But she didn't let on, and when the rhythmic noises from the washer stopped, she went in and put the kids' gear in the dryer because some of them would need stuff in the morning. Leave it up to the others to do anything about it and you might wind up waiting a long time. Cindy was starting to feel a bit put upon, but maybe it was just that since Jack had walked in she'd been coiling tighter and tighter, expecting a godawful fuss to erupt.

After a while they hauled the mattresses off the box springs and set them up on the floors in the bedrooms. As the kids got tired and cranky, they got sent off to sleep, and when the adults started getting heavy-eyed, they moved kids to the living room where sheets had been put over the carpet. Once asleep, the kids couldn't have been wakened by bomb blasts. That left the box springs and mattresses for the adults. Cindy tried to make sure Jack was asleep before she finally gave in, but she knew it wasn't going to last, and sure enough, it didn't.

He'd been drinking steady since before he got his feet tangled in the clutter of clothes, and he'd been mad since before she tucked the kids under her arms and tiptoed from the house with most of his paycheque in her pocket after he'd shoved her around the last time. He waited until she was nearly asleep before he grabbed her and started shaking her, telling her she was all kinds of a slut and whore, whispering sick promises of what he was going to do to her as soon as he got her alone, telling her she'd better make up her weak mind she was going back home with him, no trouble or argument or she'd be sorry.

She just started screaming. Even before he got a chance to hit her, she was screaming. She'd been waiting for an excuse to scream since he came in the door, and she didn't have to think about it, she just opened her mouth to say I'm Sorry and out came the noise, like a cat when someone steps on its tail.

She was still screaming when George and Frank came running in, bare feet poking out from the legs of their jeans. Real came, too, but seemed to know the best thing he could do was just mind his own business because this was a family thing and he wasn't family any more than Jack was.

Only a couple of kids woke up, and they went right back to sleep as soon as the noise stopped. And it stopped. Once they'd dragged Jack off her and out of the bedroom, and hauled him out the door to the blacktop that served as roadway, parking lot and play area, she was able to let screeching give way to crying. Tammy got her some toilet paper, Barb got her a beer, Ruby settled the kids who had come half-awake in the uproar, and Cindy just let herself enjoy the good cry she'd been trying to have for more than a month and a half.

She could hear the thumping and grunting outside the bedroom window, and she knew Jack was collecting it for all the other times, too.

Of course some snoopy damn neighbour had to go and call the cops, there's one in every crowd. So when Steve arrived home from camp there were flashing lights all over the place and Mounties outside the house asking questions.

"Hey, hey," Steve laughed, "don't ask me, I just got here, I know nothing, nothing at all," and he pushed past them into the house.

When the cops left, they took Jack with them, clothes and all. They drove him to the Emergency to get his face fixed, and warned him if he went back he'd find himself in the Crowbar Hotel for the holidays. The hospital decided he should stay in a day or two because of the cracked ribs and the cuts on his face and head. So Tammy loaned the car and Cindy caught the ferry to the mainland with George and Frank, and went to the house in Richmond to get her stuff. She took as much as would fit in the trunk and back seat but had to leave the furniture, which was a shame, especially Donny's crib, which Jack's mom had bought. But she got all her photo albums and her music tapes, the clothes and most of the bedding. She even managed to get a box of kitchen stuff.

They got back the same night, and Darelle quit crying right away, which was nice because Tammy looked like she was about ready to give the kid what-for.

"Jesus, Cindy, you gotta do somethin' about that kid. She must have a dee-formity, like her bladder sits behind her eyes or something, she hasn't quit all damn day."

"Yeah, well, she gets scared when I'm not around. And when she gets scared she cries. I was that way myself, if you remember."

"If I remember? Jesus. But just because you were that way doesn't make it the way to be, okay? I mean she's a drag to have around when she's like that."

"Why'n't you smarten up, Darelle?" Cindy said mildly. "I told you I'd be back, and I'm back, so give us a break, okay?"

There was even time to head off to the stores for one last fling before they had to put out the cookies and milk. George and Frank had taken most of the cash out of Jack's wallet before the cops arrived and it was a sizable chunk, a real windfall, enough to guarantee some nice gifts for every kid, not just her own. She got Tammy a whole raft of nice bath stuff, as a thank you for letting them bunk in with her. Tammy was a real sucker for bath stuff. The kids were in a frenzy, they'd found a couple of packages of icicles and were hanging them on curtain rods, over the backs of chairs, they even picked some winter grass for the reindeer.

"No, I mean it!" Barb yelled a couple of times. "You go to bed and you go to sleep because you know very well he won't come if you're awake, and he won't come if you're bad!" Then Real went in and clued in his own two, which settled down the rest of them quick enough.

Tammy had a couple of big plastic milk jugs filled up with the eggnog she made herself. She wouldn't tell anybody what was in it, but Barb said she guessed not all those brown flecks were nutmeg, ha ha, and Tammy laughed and rolled her eyeballs, sort of agreeing without saying anything.

They got the rest of the presents from where they'd been hidden and stacked them under the little white plastic tree. It looked real pretty with nothing but blue bulbs on it. They took a couple of pictures of just the tree, then the rest of the roll was different combinations of people, this one with that one, these three with those two because it had been so long since they were all together at the same time. They took one without the in-laws and one with, then took one of only the in-laws and made jokes about it being the outlaws on parade.

They finished the eggnog and started in on the beer, everybody took a cookie and Steve swilled down the milk. Then they checked on the turkey, almost thawed, enough they could get the big lump of liver and that other stuff pulled out of the body cavity. Cindy didn't like that part. There was something gross about shoving your hand inside a big dead bird and hauling out this glob of still-frozen guts stuck to a big neck. The guys all had to make jokes about how when you looked at the neck your stomach started to ache and maybe it was a tom turkey, and did any of the women want to save it for a cold and lonely day? "And those are the same mouths you're gonna eat with?" Tammy said mildly.

She got everyone working on vegetables and stuff, and Cindy sat breaking bread into small hunks and complaining because after all you can buy crumbs at the store just as easy as loaves. "Yeah, but the dressing is, like, soggy," Ruby argued. "Every time I've made it with those crumbs it's just gone kind of, I don't know, like it packs back together or something."

"I never had that problem."

"How would you?" Barb teased. "You haven't stuffed anything except your own face for a hundred years."

"What a thing to say! Listen to *you!*" but she was so happy to be away from that nasty bugger Jack, and so happy to have her own quilt to sleep under again, and happy too because George and Frank had made sure they'd emptied Jack's wallet before the cops got it, so she'd ended up with lots of money to get stuff for the kids.

She'd been afraid all she would have would be the welfare cheque, and because she was staying with family and not paying rent, it hadn't been very big, not hardly worth getting at all. Cheap buggers, anyway. Telling her what they did, saying that because the kids were old enough for school they expected her to start looking for a job right away. What right did they have to say stuff like that anyway? Whose business was it but hers if she got a job or not? Made it sound like she was a bum. Well, she'd had a job, just before she got pregnant with Darelle, and she held it down for a full three months, too, and paid taxes on every cent she earned so what was their beef? But she hadn't said that to the worker, she'd nodded, and made herself smile, and said she was already looking, and had a line on a job as a telephone sales representative for a freezer-and-frozen-food company. The whole thing had insulted her, but she hadn't said anything to Tammy about it because she didn't want to hear any I told you so's. Well, maybe she'd just show them all, and soon, too. Maybe she'd go see if they needed anybody at the bingo hall. She liked bingo, and being the one calling out the numbers might be fun. She'd think about it, and see.

2

Darelle didn't even think about crying until long after everyone was up and busy with the camera. That wasn't until past noon. But before they started lining kids up and setting off the flashes that made your eyes see little changing-colour dots afterward, they had to gather up the crumpled and discarded wrapping paper and fold it around the ripped-open boxes and packages.

"Just a minute," Real blurted. "Hang on there, will ya?" and he shifted his younger ferret closer to the tree, then tipped the candy-smeared face to the angle he wanted. "Now pretend like you're openin'er for the first time. Make out like you had 'er about half open when someone spoke at you, so you looked up, smilin' and happy." The ferret nodded, Real lurched out of the way, Tammy aimed the camera and said "Now." The slant-eyed suspicious look vanished and for a moment the ferret looked like the most angelic, happy child on the face of the globe. If the mean-minded little christer survived, he might make a fortune as another Brad Pitt. But miserable as he was, he could wind up hanged for the good of the world.

"Got 'er," Tammy smiled. The ferret leaped to his feet and raced off to join the others. Within seconds he and his older brother were rolling in a heap, kicking, punching, and biting at each other.

"This is the only warnin' you're gonna get!" Barb shouted. "Next voice you hear is gonna be your old man." She might as well have threatened her umbrella. The boys didn't waver in their seeming intent to slaughter each other. "Real, do somethin', will ya?"

"Ah, hell, it's Christmas," Real growled. "Don't I at least get a chance to have a cup of coffee or somethin'?"

"How's anybody gonna enjoy their coffee with *that* comin' down on us?" Barb snapped. So Real got up off his chair and went over to haul the boys apart. One of them got a whack on the side of the head that made his ear ring for over an hour, the other was sent hurtling across the floor to land on his belly, a *whoosh* of air forced from his lungs by the crash landing.

"Listen to your mother next time," Real roared. The boys began to cry. "And if you don't shut the hell up, I'll give you somethin' to cry about, believe me!" They shut up, their faces red and getting redder as they fought their sobs.

Tommy had a mountain of Ex-Mess stuff and would ride to hell in a wet bucket before he'd share a single thing. He sat well out of everyone's way, not quite but almost behind the sofa with his heap of loot. Ruby didn't hardly drink and made sure Frank didn't climb into the bottle very often, so she had lots of money to buy presents. Besides, Frank was working steady because Ruby had said she sure the hell wasn't going to be the only breadwinner. "If I was going to do that," she said clearly, more than a few times, "I'd do it for me'n the kids, and only me'n the kids. He eats about three times what the two of them together do, so it'd be a helluva lot cheaper for me to just open the door and point him outta it." You'd think someone like Frank, who was not bad looking by anyone's standards, would tell someone like Ruby to hit the pike. But Frank seemed ready to bend over backwards to keep her in a good mood. It wasn't just because of Little Frank, either, because he had other kids with other women and wasn't doing much for any of them. It's a puzzle sometimes, the people other people hook up with. And a bigger puzzle why it is the most mismatched and unlikely pair don't split up while others you'd think had at least a half a chance are going different directions in no time flat. Saying he was pussywhipped didn't explain anything, it was only another way to ask the same question: Why *her*, for cryin' out loud?

Between Frank working and Ruby working they had a near-new

car, and maybe it was one of those little ones Tammy called JapCrap made out of recycled Coke cans but it was cheap on gas, the inside of it didn't look as if the dog had ripped everything apart, and the radio played. They had a rented house all to themselves, with a yard and a swing set for Little Frank, and Tommy-the-Creep had his own room, with a toybox made out of an old wooden trunk Ruby had bought at the Goodwill, then sanded down, varnished and done something, god knows what, so the tin on it looked like brass.

Tommy also had loot from his real dad. Every month the real dad sent money, and for Christmas he sent extra, then the parcel delivery guy had come with a great big cardboard box inside which were enough presents for an orphanage. And Ruby's mom had bought for him, and both her sisters, and the real dad's parents and the real dad's sister, too. You could hardly see Tommy for all the stuff he had. And what did *that* mean? How come the real dad stayed involved? Most didn't, hell, look at Darelle's dad, out of sight, out of mind for years, and his damn family, too, as if they'd never set eyes on her, never fussed over her and said Oh, she's so beautiful, just like a little angel. So when had she stopped being their little precious, and why hadn't Tommy's real dad's family taken the stroll, too?

Maybe it was the sight of the unfriendly little christer sitting there with his plastic bazooka and all his little action-figure soldiers, or maybe it was the thought of a real dad who sent money and stuff, or maybe it was all those grandparents and aunts and uncles who thought to remember him, or maybe it was just that she hadn't had as much sleep as she needed, but something ticked it off and Darelle started to cry. She stood, arms hanging at her sides, face lifted slightly, mouth open but soundless, tears pouring forth.

"Notice something?" Barb said scornfully. "Every time that whiny little bitch starts to blubber, she makes sure she's turned toward you so's you don't miss any of it."

"Ah, jeez, Darelle, give it a rest will you?" Cindy said. "Do you got to cry *all* the time?"

Darelle didn't answer. She just stood and let her opinion of everything slide down her face.

"Had about a gutful of that," Tammy said, dangerously quietly. And the next thing Darelle knew, almost a quart of cold water was tossed in her face. She gasped and went silent in horror. Tammy smiled widely. "If you feel better with your face soakin' wet, darlin', you can have it like that any time you want. Just let me know and I'll be glad to oblige you." Darelle took a deep breath, all set to let rip and bawl the house down. Tammy turned on the tap and, still smiling, held her hand under the stream of water. "Do you prefer it warm, cool or cold as ice?" she said quietly. "There's a lot of water in the tap, and I'm sure ready to help you get your face as wet as you want it."

Darelle turned away, puzzled and angry. She knew Tammy would do it. "My shirt's all wet," she whined.

"If you don't want your shirt wet, go put on a dry one," Tammy said coldly. "Similar, if you don't want your hair soaked, go in the bathroom and use a towel. Use the hair dryer if you want. And while you're in there, look in the mirror. Take a good long look. See what you look like, Pouty Face. And know somethin', too. Any time you start snivellin' for no reason, this is what's comin' down." She grinned. "Don't worry about the floor, I'll wipe 'er up this time. Next time," and the grin vanished, "you'll do 'er."

"Hell, Tammy, that's a bit much," Cindy said mildly. "I mean jeez, eh."

"I spent years of my life puttin' up with you blubberin' at the drop of a hat," Tammy said, "and I couldn't do a thing about it. But damned if I'll have that same whinin' and sulkin' ruin Christmas in my own house."

"Ha ha, Darelle, ha ha!" Donny chanted. "Lookit you!"

"You stop that, now," Cindy told him. "Don't tease your sister."

"Old wet-head, wet-head, wet-head," Donny chanted, "Nothin' but a wet-head. Got water on the brain!"

Real leaned slightly, and swung. The back of his hand rapped against the side of Donny's skull. Donny yelped and started to cry.

"You stop that!" Cindy yelled at either Donny or Real, it was hard to tell which.

"Shut up, Donny, you had it comin'," Barb said, and she grabbed him by the shoulder, aimed him down the hallway, and gave him two on the butt to get his feet moving. "G'wan in the bedroom if you want to cry."

"I can wet *your* face too, you know," Tammy offered.

"That's right," Steve laughed, "everybody gang up on Donny. Come on, everybody, all at once, let's jump on Donny."

"Oh shut up," Tammy laughed, "or we'll all gang up on you."

Darelle put on a dry shirt and used the blower on her hair. She knew the other kids weren't sure if they should laugh at her or sympathize. Well, they'd better not laugh!

Phoebe came in the bathroom and sat on the edge of the tub, watching as Darelle fussed with her hair. "I hate your mother," Darelle hissed. Phoebe shrugged. "Did you hear me? I said I *hate* your mother."

"Hate away, I don't give a shit." Phoebe stood, opened the little window, then pulled a crumpled package of smokes from under the waistband of her faded jeans. She took out a cigarette, rolled it between her fingers to straighten it, then lit it and blew the smoke out the window.

"You'll catch it if you get caught," Darelle warned.

"How'm I gonna get caught unless you snitch on me. And if you snitch on me, I'll beat the shit out of you. I can do it, too."

Darelle didn't need to be told Phoebe could beat the shit out of her. She knew that. She had always known that. Phoebe was older, Phoebe was bigger and, as Phoebe herself had said more than once, Phoebe asleep was ten times tougher than Darelle was wide awake. Phoebe's younger sister Linda, who was only a few months older, could beat Darelle up too, and had, more than a few times. But Linda didn't go out of her way to find an excuse to hammer on any of the other kids, the way Phoebe did. Phoebe seemed to get some kind of real kick out of bullying other people.

"I'm not gonna snitch," Darelle promised. "But someone could smell it."

"Everyone in the damn house is smoking. As long as I don't fill the bathroom up with smoke so's the next one in sees it, I'm fine. Besides, when I'm finished, I'll brush my teeth." She held out the lit cigarette. "Want to try?" Darelle took it, puffed, even inhaled without choking. Phoebe stared at her, not exactly impressed, but certainly more approving than any time either of them would easily remember.

"So you think your mom's gonna move back in with your dad?" Phoebe asked.

"He's not my dad. Not my really one."

"You know what I mean."

"I don't know. She don't much like him now. He's pretty cranky."

"Yeah, I heard. Broke her jaw one time, right?"

"I guess. And her arm, once."

"My mom says he's a fuckin' animal."

"He's pretty mean." Darelle didn't want to talk about it, she didn't even want to think about it. Every time she was reminded about Jack, or the way he behaved, she felt as ashamed as if she herself were responsible. On the other hand, where did Phoebe get off talking about other people being mean? Everyone knew she was just about as vicious as a sack full of weasels. Darelle wished her own really dad would come back. She couldn't remember very much about him, except that he'd loved to dance and thought nothing of just turning on the radio or the music channel on TV and boogying in the living room. And he didn't slap people around or yell, either. He'd been gone so long she couldn't even remember what his face was like, but she remembered the dancing. And then, poof, as if he'd been made of the smoke from his own cigarettes, he was gone, and it was some other guy living with them. Then that guy was gone and Jack was with them. Poor Donny, to have that for his really dad!

Phoebe handed Darelle the cigarette a second time and watched as she took another drag. She knew Darelle was afraid of her, knew all the kids were scared spitless. It didn't bother her one little bit. In fact, she liked it that way. Their fear meant they did what she told them, and that made the damn babysitting a whole lot easier. And it was always Phoebe got stuck running herd on the other kids. Who knew, maybe one day someone would even think to pay her for it, but probably not. Last time she'd suggested it, she'd been told she got paid. She got her meals, clothes and a place to sleep, didn't she? And after all, they said, someone did it for you when you were young. Sure, but the ones who did had gotten paid for doing it. And nobody had done it for a long long time. Phoebe could clearly remember waking up and finding nobody else in the house with her except Linda, and it was Linda crying and wailing had wakened Phoebe. So how old was she then, because Linda still needed a bottle, and it was Phoebe had to get it for her. Well, figure it out then, there was only two and a half years between them. Linda had been able to stand up and walk around but still wore diapers so Phoebe was what, four and a half, maybe five at the outside. And no babysitter that time. Or any time after if the truth were to be told.

Darelle handed the cigarette back and Phoebe finished it, then flushed it down the toilet and turned on the fan. She gave the fan a few seconds to do its job, then turned it off and gave the room a couple of zaps of underarm deodorant spray. Darelle grinned and for a moment Phoebe almost liked her.

"I'd never have thought of that," Darelle admitted.

"'Course not," Phoebe agreed. "You're dumb and I'm not."

"I'm not dumb!" Darelle's eyes flooded with easy tears and her bottom lip quivered.

"Oh stop that baby stuff! My god, you're boring," and Phoebe headed for the door. As she passed Darelle, who was dabbing at her eyes with some toilet paper and sniffling away again, Phoebe grabbed at the soft skin just above the elbow and pinched cruelly. Darelle gasped with shock and pain and got all set to wail. "One sound," Phoebe hissed, "and I'll rip a hunk right out, Blubberguts."

The turkey had been in the oven since before everyone went to bed, and wonder of wonders, someone had been able to figure out how to set the automatic oven timer. Things were looking up in the working brains department. The scent of roasting stuffed bird was starting to fill the kitchen. Donny was half bent over, peering at the big foil-covered mound on the other side of the glass. His hard little butt was there right in front of her, and Phoebe didn't even try to resist the impulse, she just gave a bit of a kick sideways. She had only meant to get a rise out of him, make him yelp and straighten quickly, but either he was more off balance than she'd thought or she'd kicked harder than she intended. He went forward, his face rapping sharply against the oven door. The sound of his wail of pain was covered by the sound of Frank's hand against the side of Phoebe's head.

"What the fuck's wrong with you!" he yelled, and he hit her again, harder, on the other side of her face.

"Hands off my kid," Tammy yelled.

"See what she did? You think she should get away with that? Look at his face! Be lucky if he doesn't get a scar from that."

Tammy hadn't seen what happened, but Frank told her and she believed him. Impossible not to believe him, there was Donny, hurt so bad he couldn't even holler, the middle of his forehead and tip of his nose bright red and starting to raise up in a blister. Cindy was yelling and hollering she needed someone to drive them to the Emergency, and Barb was yammering they didn't need a doctor for cryin' out loud, don't just stand around like a pack of know-nothing idiots, get the kid to the sink and run cold water on the mess.

Real was all for smearing the burn with lard. "Oh, bright bloody idea," Barb sneered, "then instead of just having a bit of a burn there, he can get barbecued and fried. Jesus, you're so stupid you must have to call in Handyman-for-Hire just to get your ass wiped. If you wipe."

"Talk to me like that, slut and I'll knock you flat on your ass."

Frank drove Cindy and Donny up to Emergency. Darelle sat in the living room blubbering hysterically until Barb told her either she put a cork in it or she'd find herself out in the yard with a bruise on her ass. That didn't stop the tears, but it did stop the *wah wah wah* and the *hoo hoo hoo*. Real and Barb kept nattering at each other until George told Real to watch what he said and did or he'd wind up saying ouch and doing nothing more than lying on his back seeing tweety-birds. Ruby told Tommy he'd better occupy himself amusing little Frank and to stay out of everyone's way for a while. "They're pretty upset, and you know how they get then," she said calmly. "They're halfways up the wall at the best of times, the whole damn lot of them."

"You be careful how you talk about my family," Barb yelled, "or I'll clue you in, too."

"Don't try anything with me," Ruby said quietly, and Barb shut up and glared.

Linda went over to play with Tommy and little Frank. She wanted to sit like Darelle and just howl, but she didn't want to look like the kind of sucky jerk everyone thought her cousin was. She didn't know what was worse, the way she felt thinking about what her sister had done to Donny, who was, after all, just a little guy, and probably a few bricks short of a full load, and who hadn't been doing anything to deserve getting hurt, or the sounds coming from the bedroom as Steve beat the living Christ out of Phoebe, while Tammy yelled and cursed at the both of them. Sometimes Phoebe was just too stupid for words.

Bad enough what she'd done to Donny, but you'd think she'd have caught on by now that the worst thing she could do when the crap hit the fan was refuse to cry. She'd bite holes in her own arm before she'd cry. And until she did, Steve would pound on her. "That's enough," Darelle heard Tammy scream. "You're gonna kill her if you don't stop."

"Can we sit with you guys?" Georgie asked, wide-eyed and scared.

"Sure," Tommy shrugged. "You want to play soldiers? You and Melanie could take these ones and Linda'n'me could take these ones. We can set up mountains and stuff. Or we can set up the battleship game if you know how to count. You throw dice, see, and move your boats, and see, there's squares where it says Direct Hit With Torpedo and stuff like that."

"Yeah. Yeah, that sounds good." Georgie probably would have agreed to almost anything at all. The sounds from the bedroom were pretty awful. Linda was just about ready to vomit and then big George got up and went into the bedroom. She didn't hear what he said, his voice was low and quiet, but Tammy came into the kitchen and stood by the sink, face pale, hands shaking, and then big George came out, holding Steve by the arm, and talking quietly. He led Steve to the kitchen table, gave him a gentle push into a chair, then patted his shoulder and went to the fridge for three bottles of beer.

It was so quiet in the kitchen you could hear the grease crackling in the turkey pan. The sound of the dice rattling in the little brown plastic cup was like the crack of thunder on a hot summer night. Barb ran some water in the sink and that sounded like Niagara Falls, and when she started to peel potatoes the *click click click* of the peeler where it fits through the hole in the handle onto the little rod-shaft in the middle was annoyingly loud.

"And look," Darelle whined, holding up her arm and displaying the purple bruise. "She pinched me and left a mark."

"You shut your mouth or I'll leave more than a mark," Barb invited.

"Might just come over and give you another pinch," Tammy offered. "I know how she felt and why she did it. I've wanted to pinch you more than once or twice myself."

"Start cryin' again," George roared, "and so help me god, Darelle, I'll use the belt on you myself."

"I wish she'd shut up once in a while," Tommy hissed. "Every time she whines like that everyone gets mad."

"Yeah," Linda agreed. "And as soon as everyone's mad, Darelle starts bawlin' again and that just makes them madder."

"I think," Georgie said timidly, "you're supposed to sink my boat now. I think you landed . . ." His voice trailed off and he looked puzzled. Linda checked the board and laughed.

"Nah, you got it wrong. You're supposed to sink *my* boat."

"Oh. Okay then," and he laughed happily. "Bang you're dead I guess, eh Linda."

"Bang I'm dead, Georgie. Or at least everyone on that boat."

When Barb had the potatoes peeled she put them in the big pot, covered them with salted water so they wouldn't turn pink, cleaned the peelings from the sink and then told the kids to quit what they were doing and line up for paring knives. "Put yourselves to work," she laughed, "It's time to peel the greenies."

"Shoulda got frozen ones," George yawned, draining his beer. "It's a pain in the jaw peeling those."

"Frozen ones taste like frozen ones," Ruby answered. "And what else did you have planned?"

George grinned and made a little kissing gesture. Ruby laughed, as easy as if it were George she was married to instead of Frank. If Maria had been there, instead of in the Crowbar Hotel, George wouldn't have done what he did and Ruby wouldn't have taken it as easy. But then, nobody was easy when Maria was around, she was too much like an explosion waiting to go bang.

The greenies were done and waiting in their pot of cold water, the turnip was peeled and cut into cubes, the carrots were sliced and in with the turnip, and the cranberry sauce was made and in the fridge before Cindy and Frank came home with Donny. He had some clear goo smeared on his face and a square patch of flesh-coloured Elastoplast stuck to the middle of his forehead. He also had a big sucker shaped like a Santa Claus. "They gave it to me," he bragged. "They said I was brave."

"Go to hell," Linda hissed. "Because of you, Steve beat up on Phoebe."

"Steve beat up on Phoebe because of Phoebe," Ruby snapped.

Linda blushed and looked down at the floor. She hadn't known Ruby could hear, or she wouldn't have said anything.

"All this fighting and squabbling and pushing and shoving and pinching and nagging had better stop right now," Ruby continued, her voice hard as nails, "or the whole damn lot of you are going to wind up in bed and hungry as wolves while the rest of us have a nice supper. And don't think I'm just pushing air over my teeth, okay? I mean it. There's no excuse for this kind of behaviour!" Which would have been fine except at the time she was saying it, her own kid was busy agitating with the ferret and the weasel, and the next thing they knew all three were rolling on the floor kicking and punching, squealing like piglets. Ruby walked over, grabbed Tommy by the shoulder and the weasel by the hair, and hauled them to their feet. She shoved the weasel into the closest chair and gave Tommy a push that sent him across the room and onto the sofa, then she hauled the ferret up by his ear and sat him on the stool in the kitchen. "Not a word," she told them. They sat sticking their tongues out at each other until Steve gave the ferret a rap on the chin which caused him to bite his tongue. "Shut up," Steve said. All three did. For about two minutes, and then the faces started again.

Steve went to the drawer, brought out three supermarket bags and dropped one over each head. "There, nobody can see anybody and you can pull all the faces you want. But if you take off the bag I'll use my belt."

"Not on my kid you won't," Ruby argued. "Nobody's using a belt on *my* kid."

"Shoot your kid instead, then."

"No. You whale the snot out of the other two, then give me the belt and I'll leave stripes on my own," she said, as calm as if she were discussing the weather. "I can't stand it when someone else is havin' all the fun." She winked at Steve as if she hadn't heard the uproar, as if her stomach weren't still churning, as if she didn't have ghosts of her own brought awake by the sound of leather on flesh. "Why bother havin' a kid if someone else is going to have the fun of beating it to a livin' pulp?"

Steve forced a grin, but looked like someone who wasn't sure if he was being agreed with or called down.

Phoebe didn't come out for dinner and Steve wouldn't let anybody take anything in to her, either. The Spirit of Good Will must have come down the chimney by then because the kids didn't fight, argue or complain that someone else had a nicer, bigger or better piece of turkey, they just sat stuffing themselves. They were so well behaved Steve thawed and loaded a plate for Phoebe. He took it into her room himself.

And came out seconds later with the plate still in his hand. "Window's open," he said quietly, "and the room's empty."

"Oh god," Tammy looked as if she were suddenly twenty years older.

"She'll beg before she comes back in the door," Steve promised.

It was such a nice dinner, everything cooked just so, and more cranberry sauce than you could shake a stick at. The only fly in the butter was when Maria phoned from the remand centre, and even that didn't start out as a downer. She talked to the kids, she said Merry Happy to all the in-laws and outlaws, then talked to the kids again. It wasn't until she was getting ready to tell George bye-bye for now that things went a bit to hell. George kind of leaned against the wall, the phone to his ear, listening, and nodding, and looking as if he were about to pass out, although his voice, when he told her not to worry, everything would be fine, just fine, sounded firm and confident.

He hung up the phone, shook his head, walked across the kitchen, hauled out a bottle of whiskey, popped the top off it and took a swig. "Don't nobody drink from this bottle," he tried to grin. "We might have us a bit of a problem here." He shook his head as if he knew his grin looked like something you'd see on a corpse. "Maria's got that Hepatitis-B thing again. So me'n'the kids have to be tested for it, too."

"Well, Jesus!" Barb sounded as if she didn't believe him. "How in hell would she get *that?*"

The police brought Phoebe back Boxing Day, past midnight. Steve was very quiet for as long as the cops were on the doorstep but once they left he went up like a hot air balloon.

"Joy riding?" he yelled. "*Joy riding?* Car thief, more like it!"

"I didn't steal anything," Phoebe whined. "I was just minding my own business and some friends asked did I want a ride and I said yes and then the cops pulled them over."

"Minding your own business my aching ass! You don't *have* no business out there for two days and two nights! *Your* business, bitch, is to do what you're told and you were told to stay in your room, and by god you will stay in your room, believe me."

He took off his belt and used it on her until she was welted and striped from top to toe, then he took a length of yellow nylon rope and tied one end to her ankle, the other end to the bed. "Chew on that if you want," he snarled, cuffing her on the side of the head so hard her ear ached like fury.

She tried. She worked at the knots with her fingers but had no luck at all. Steve knew how to tie spaghetti noodles together and keep them tied. She gnawed on the rope until her teeth ached, but she might as well have sucked her thumb. When she had to go to the bathroom, she yelled until Steve went in, undid the knot from the bed and stood outside waiting for her, the rope passing through a crack at the bathroom doorway. "And don't bother lookin' for razor blades or scissors," he taunted. "You don't got a hope in hell, sister."

Every mealtime Phoebe had to come out of the room, the rope still fastened to her ankle, and sit at the table with the others pretending not to notice the bruises and welts, the increasingly raw spot on her ankle, the rage and insult simmering in her eyes.

They sat still and quiet, awed by the fury in both Steve and Phoebe. "Two of a kind," Tammy said quietly. "One of 'em's stubborn and the other of 'em's bull-headed, and I'd be damned if I could say which one was the which." She thought of how it used to be, when Phoebe was a toddler and Steve thought the sun rose and set in her eyes. He took her with him just about everywhere, and nothing was too good for her. And then, bit by bit by bit it began to erode, until here they were like pit bull terriers, their teeth sunk deep into each other's most tender parts, locked in mortal combat, neither of them able to say how it had happened. Sometimes Tammy half expected to wake up at night hearing a *thunk thunk thunk* as Phoebe sank an axe into Steve's skull. Other times she expected to see him taken to jail for breaking Phoebe's neck. At best it was armed truce, with her caught in the middle.

New Year's Eve they decided to do the town. Except for Frank and Ruby, who chose to stay home and watch the parties on TV. Frank hardly ever took so much as a beer, having quit boozing and partying when Ruby made it clear she would be over the horizon with the kids if it started up again. Nobody could figure out what it was she had that pulled Frank into line and kept him there. George always said it was just old-fashioned pussywhipped, but Real said one was like another so maybe she had something hidden away.

Steve didn't say anything, maybe because he didn't have much room to talk the way he put up with Tammy's goin's on. Besides, he was a tiny little gomer, and probably knew the women weren't going to line up for the chance to hang out with him if Tammy dumped him. As soon as you said "faller," people got this idea you were talking about Paul Bunyan or Billy Beaujean or Big Joe Maquero, but Steve was more like Dopey the seventh dwarf. He had this dipshit moustache he had copied off Emiliano Zapata or Juan Valdez the coffee guy, and his idea of a haircut had got stuck back in the sixties. He had that kinky blondish hair that he wore in what he called a natural and anyone else would call a bird's nest, and the only times he came close to being taller than Tammy were when he was wearing his caulk boots or dressed up with his feet stuck into those damn hippy-looking platform shoes. But small as he was, he was tough, and probably only George could afford not to be careful what he said when Steve was in one of his furies.

They left by seven-thirty, not even ticked off at Ruby for saying nobody was using *her* car if they were going beering. They had Steve's car, anyway, and if it fell apart and the pieces rolled off down the hill, they could squeeze into Real's old junker. Ruby only said it to try to get a rise out of them and let them know what a low opinion she had of boozers.

At nine Ruby went to the bedroom and stood in the doorway looking at Phoebe, who was lying on her side, glaring at a paperback book and pretending she didn't care she was being punished.

"If I let you up will you give me your word you won't make me sorry I did?"

"What do you mean?" Phoebe tried to sound tough, but her voice was shaky.

"If it was up to me I'd take that damn rope off altogether. It isn't up to me and I don't want to wind up in a go-round with your dad. But I'll untie you and you can come in the living room and watch TV, have some popcorn, pretend you've got something to celebrate tonight. It's New Year's Eve, after all."

Phoebe just nodded, hopeful. But Ruby wouldn't come out of the doorway until Phoebe said the words. "I promise there won't be any problem, Auntie."

They made a huge bowl of popcorn. Frank peeled off to the store to get a mountain of chips and an ocean of dip. He also got a great big bologna roll for sandwiches because the turkey was long gone and the ham wasn't cooked yet. After all that bird and stuffing and other rich food, the bologna tasted like spices, and with mustard smeared thick the sandwiches were heaven.

Ruby noticed how raw Phoebe's ankle was, and she got a basin of warm water with some Epsom salts in it and tried to soak the sore spot. But the rope got in the way and finally Frank muttered something under his breath and pulled his jackknife from his pocket.

"My dad'll raise the roof," Phoebe said, trying hard not to cry.

"Fuck your dad," Frank grumbled. "This is bullshit, if you ask me," and he cut the rope. Frank wasn't afraid of anyone, certainly not afraid of some half-pint tree-cutter. Frank was bigger than most guys, even if he didn't have muscles layered on top of other muscles like George. Frank said the only reason George got muscles like that was he got sent to the pen. and had nothing to do but lift weights. But George had been layered with muscle even before that.

They soaked Phoebe's foot, then Ruby smeared antibiotic salve on the big red raw strip all the way around the ankle. The rope was marked with blood where it had gone twice around her leg. Where the delicate bones were close to the skin, there was a groove rubbed raw and tender, with little pockets of yellowish stuff. Ruby was especially careful around those little holes, smearing lots of the clear ointment. She put a thick padding of gauze, then some adhesive tape, and patted Phoebe's knee"Hey, kid, I happen to know you aren't stupid, okay? So why act like you are? All you get out of it is grief."

"I didn't mean for Donny to get hurt," Phoebe sobbed. "I thought he'd just, like, you know, look funny when he stumbled."

"You didn't get tied up for what happened with Donny." Ruby sounded so calm, so logical, the other kids just gaped. "You got tied up for taking off and getting brought back by the cops. You got tied up for joy riding. Keep it clear in your head what it is you got tethered for. Otherwise," she said sadly, as if she really knew what she was talking about, "you'll get all mixed up about what came first, the chicken or the chickenshit, and you won't know what is and what isn't. And once *that* starts to happen, you'll end up in crap so deep you won't believe it."

Ruby sat on the sofa next to Phoebe and cuddled her, and Phoebe stopped trying to pretend to be tough and snuggled right back, sighing sometimes, a deep, broken sound that was almost like a sob.

"What you should do," Ruby said softly, "is wait until everyone's at the table tomorrow, then you say right out loud to your dad that you're sorry, you didn't mean to make so much trouble. Then he'll bluster a bit and tell you to smarten up, and yammer yammer yak yak, and then you say again that you're real sorry. And probably by the time he's filled his belly with ham and pineapple sauce, he'll be over his mad."

"Screw him," Phoebe said clearly.

"Well, if you want to stay in hot water forever, that's your choice," Ruby laughed. "I didn't say you had to *mean* what you said; I only said that if you play it right you might even get to smell fresh air before you turn nineteen."

At midnight they all went out on the porch, even Phoebe, and they yelled and hollered and Frank shot off Steve's rifle a few times, aiming at the face of the moon. Everyone on the TV was singing "For Auld Lang Syne" so they sang along, what words they knew, and then went back in to pig out on more sandwiches and popcorn. All the chips were gone and the dip too, and the smaller kids were more asleep than awake, but nobody told them to go to bed, they just drifted off by themselves, one at a time.

The ham was in the oven, the potatoes and vegetables were peeled and waiting and Frank and Ruby had four big mince pies cooked and cooling before any of the celebrants dragged themselves into the kitchen to sit, bleary-eyed and suffering, over cups of coffee.

"Where's my mom?" Darelle asked, all set to start crying.

"She'll prob'ly show up later," Tammy yawned. "And if you cry, so help me Jesus, first I'll pound the tripe out of you and then I'll stuff your head in the toilet bowl and flush until you're wetter than you ever dreamed of being. Catch my drift?"

Darelle nodded and packed her blubbers away for a time they might do her some good. "Where is she?" she repeated.

"Met up with some guy in the bar." Tammy pushed at her cup, hinting she wanted a refill. Darelle wanted to know more so she took the cup, poured and doctored coffee, and took it back to her aunt.

"Who?"

"Oh, shit, I don't know. Some young guy." Tammy's tone was casual but something in the look on her face told Darelle the best thing she could do right now was shut up about it.

3

Isa McRae thought for sure she'd found a sure-fire hit idea for a feature film script. "After all," she reasoned, "for twenty-seven days a month I swallow a little red Premarin pill as part of my estrogen replacement therapy. And all you have to do is write that name down on a piece of paper and you get the hint. *P, r, e* as in pregnant, *m, a, r* as in mare, and *in* as in urine."

"You're kidding!"

"I'm not kidding. It's made out of pregnant pony pee."

She figured Bette Midler would be a good choice for female lead, with maybe Tom Berenger for the love–romance–sex interest. Although sometimes she remembered the commercials with James Garner and what-the-hell-*was*-her-name, and thought they'd do wonders with it. James was starting to show his age, but somehow, on James, age didn't seem to be a detriment. And it might add a bit of irony to the story, although just exactly how, she wasn't yet sure.

She could see entire scenes already. The somewhat off-beat frustrated and dissatisfied city-raised woman, someone who had perhaps been trained for a job and then seen that job just sort of vanish. A printer maybe, put out of work by desktop publishing, or something similar, she'd have to check out which jobs had gone into the black hole. And this person is working at a job she hates, and then oh, a second cousin or a far-flung aunt or something dies and our person inherits this farm, or ranch, or—have to look into that, too. And since farming is something else which is on its way out, she is bitterly aware that what once might have been a stroke of good luck is now a hollow joke. Maybe she even says something like: A farm is just a piece of ground you stand back and throw money at until it breaks your heart.

But through a set of circumstances not yet figured out, this woman realizes the truth about hormone replacement therapy and where the fundamental ingredient comes from, and she decides to have a pregnant mare farm.

Any good screenwriter can tell you the best way to do your research is to actually *do* what you're going to write about. It can draw the line between a script which works and one which just makes money. Hacks can hire researchers, but a good script doctor will find a way to *do*.

Isa already had two mares, so she had some idea of what was involved in the care and keeping of horses. Even so, she was all set to take the money she'd put aside for the tax department and use it to buy mares otherwise destined for dog meat cans. She figured to get draft mares, the bigger the better; lovely placid grey Percherons, great gentle Clydesdales, gorgeous docile Belgians. She figured the bigger the animal, the more it would pee.

She knew there'd have to be some way to catch the urine, and that it would be less than pleasant, but what is there about farming that isn't just a tad distasteful? She guessed the process would involve a catheter, and she had visions of huge mares grazing in the pastures, their red rubber catheter tubes poking demurely from beneath their tails, running along their huge back ends to plastic bags hung from some sort of custom harnesses. They might look a bit funny, waltzing Mathilda with a several-gallon plastic bag more or less full of piddle attached to one side, but Isa was quietly convinced the mares would adapt, and if they could get used to it, so could anybody watching them.

She would probably have to invest in sturdy shipping containers, too. Probably something along the line of those five-or-so-gallon blue plastic barrels in which the juice concentrate people used to ship their syrupy glop. That stuff the restaurants then mixed with tap water and called "fresh re-constituted."

Caught in the daydream of her own making, Isa saw herself going out to the barn every morning, changing full pee bags for empty ones, turning the mares loose to graze contentedly all day, then coming back to the barn to empty the catch-bags into the plastic jugs. She would probably put the catch bags in a big tub of water with disinfectant added, then take the plastic jugs down to the depot and put them on the bus to the city, where they'd be picked up and shipped off to the people who made hormone pills and birth control pills. She was a bit foggy about that part of it, but figured a bit of research would clear the air and give her a good idea of the process.

She had gone so far as to find out the names and addresses of several slaughterhouses and the going price of horseflesh. If she was willing to give them as much for the animal alive as they were going to get for the same animal dead, she could save money on stock and save a few lives as well. She had even talked to the owner of a prize-winning quarterhorse stud. And then she had pontificated to a sweetie who just sat shaking her head in disbelief, "We'll have to sell these baby horses, we can't just have them cluttering up the pastures, more and more of them every year."

"Isa, darling. Please, check this out before you jump in with both feet and wind up with the tax people chucking you into the pokey."

"Who can I check it with? If I breathe one syllable of it in public every patch-knee poverty-stricken farmer for a hundred miles is going to jump up and beat me to it. You *know* each and every one of them prays to god every night, hoping to win the lottery so they can go on farming for another three years."

"But Isa, darling . . . who's going to want these huge mutty foals?"

"What I had in mind was crossing big mares with a quarterhorse stud to try to get something which would qualify for Sport Horse registration."

"Oh, Jesus, Isa, really!"

"What's wrong with that idea?"

"There has to be *somebody* who will know. Ask the vet."

"The vet? Why would the vet know?"

"Who do you think inserts the catheters? Who do you think is going to come out regularly to change them for you?"

"I don't know. I thought maybe I could learn how to do it myself."

"Isa. Listen. I am the woman who loves you. I am the woman who loves you completely and utterly and, I'm told by many, in spite of the laws of god and man. I want for you only the best of what you want for yourself. Please. For me. Check with the vet before you buy every large-bodied mare in the slaughterhouse feed lot. Please."

So Isa got on the blower and called the vet's office. The receptionist said she'd give the vet the message and she was sure Laurie would phone as soon as she could.

Instead of phoning, Laurie dropped by when her barn calls were done. She sat at the table, a mug of hot tea cupped in her hands, and listened quietly as Isa outlined her idea from start to hopeful finish. To Laurie's credit, she did not bust out with a hoot and roll on the floor laughing.

"It's not a very nice business," she said gently.

"Neither is all the manure, or killing everything for meat. All those fluffy chicks become broilers, all those hopping bunnies become hasenpfeffer, and the big-eyed calves with the long lashes grow up and become steaks and roasts and washtubs full of entrails which have to be buried. Not much nice in that."

"The places I've seen—and I've seen quite a few because we have to do our internships, too—used draft horses. You figured that one out right, the bigger the mare, the bigger the bladder. And they keep them in tie-stalls. They just stand there all day, being fed as little as possible, so of course they fill up on water because they're hungry. Which makes them pee even more. They never go out because a moving mare can slip her catheter. And many of these places don't want to be bothered with foals so they either abort them in the last stages of pregnancy and get the mare pregnant again as fast as possible, or they kill them as soon as they're born."

"You're kidding!"

"A few keep the foal a month or so, then wean it early and sell it to other people who raise them up for meat, same as with beef."

"Wouldn't it work if it was done differently? I mean, if they got out in a pasture and got to live like horses, and had their babies and . . ." Isa's voice trailed away. She managed to filter through her brain the reality of profit and loss. Obviously, if you wanted to collect pee, you didn't want the horse cavorting. A pint spilled is a pint lost, is money you don't get to see. A baby kept is money out, and there was too much of that already. A farm with a two-hundred-thousand-dollar gross take-in was a farm which actually paid the owner forty thousand in wages. The rest either got eaten by the stock, or went back into upkeep.

"Wouldn't work, huh?"

"You want the truth or something that will make you feel better?"

"Okay." As easily as that, Isa dropped the idea of personal experience. She'd keep the idea, though. It could be made as hilarious as all getout what with mares getting loose and running down the road with their pee bags sloshing and splashing. Maybe our character starts out with the idea Isa had put forth and then gets so into the whole horse trip she can't get rid of the babies, and she knows so little about training them that they are the most bratty pack you could ever find, and she makes her mark in life raising rodeo stock, although the animal rights people would shit a brick over that idea.

"Another cup of tea?"

"Love one."

"Thank you," Carol said quietly. "I thought we were going to wind up living on a raft, floating in a sea of mare piss, watching the horse buns bob past us while this dear lunatic sat gazing moon-eyed at all the lovely little baby hay-burners."

"The lovely little baby giant hay-burners and their year-old siblings and their two-year-old siblings and their—"

"You've got it."

That's when Isa started to laugh. "I better go get me some 6/49 tickets. Think of the script you could write, someone who wins, oh I don't know, five or six million and *thinks* she can fulfill this lifelong dream of owning a farm, and once she has it she gets the idea about the estrogen but she can never quite pull it off, she's a soft touch for geriatric cast-offs and—"

"*Shut up!*" Carol pretended to lose it and Laurie cracked up and said something about beginning to suspect Isa spent at least half her time in fantasyland.

Isa and Carol owned fifty acres, thirty of it in hay. They kept their first crop for their own use and sold probably half the second right out of the field. Depending on the size of the harvest, they might or might not sell some of the rest. Fifty acres in farm terms is nothing. Mention fifty acres to farmers in Ontario and they nod politely, thinking of a medium-sized chicken pen. Say fifty-acre farm to someone in Alberta or Saskatchewan and if they're polite, they will try hard not to laugh. Mention fifty acres to someone from Manitoba, they'll think of the corner of Portage and Main in downtown Winnipeg. But fifty acres on the coast is a good-sized chunk, especially if it has soil. Surrounded by the most expensive real estate in the country, Isa and Carol lived on what developers would long ago have turned into a golf course if it hadn't been for the Agricultural Land Reserve.

Every morning they were up by six. With a cup of coffee making a warm lump in her belly, Isa went to the barn to feed the horses and throw down hay for the cows. After she left the barn she hand-rolled and lit a cigarette, and went in search of the duck eggs. The ducks had decided to live near the barn since the night a coon got into the hen yard and killed the white India runner. That meant the eggs might be anywhere. With duck eggs in her pockets and smoke spiralling around her head, Isa went to the shed and let out the dogs, who immediately raced around in circles pretending to growl and fight with each other, then took off to go see if Isa had missed any eggs. While Isa moved to the chicken shed to check the layer pellets in the hanging feeders, the dogs sucked eggs. With the chickens taken care of, Isa fed and watered the rabbits, then went back to the barn, curried and fussed the mares, and let them out into the pasture. Then she went back into the house for another cup of coffee.

Usually about the time Isa was having her coffee, Carol headed to the barn to do her chores. By the time Carol was finished wheelbarrowing horse buns and cow pies to the enormous manure pile, Isa was working at her computer, and it was time for Carol to hurry to the house to get cleaned up and dressed for her job.

Carol had to get into real drag to be ready for work. No jeans for her, no Nike sneakers, nothing as comfortable and casual as that. She headed off to work looking like the cover advertisement for an L.L. Bean catalogue. Some mornings, Isa would look up from the glowing screen, see Carol coming in the doorway to the Hell Room, and her stomach would tighten, then turn over. Isa was sure there were probably one or two women on the face of the earth who were better looking, and sure, too, she had never seen them.

Carol got to do the un-fun stuff, the horsebun cowpie stuff, because Isa's bad back acted up if she did any of it. Isa supposed her back was giving her the message. The one which says Over The Hill. For a couple of years the dull ache had been kept at bay by a couple of aspirin, but then Isa had to turn to Tylenol, and now she was taking acetaminophen with codeine. And when the sole of her foot went pins'n'needles and she began to drag her toes when walking, the physician sent her to a specialist who gave her the bad news. Among the many things he told her was the bright idea sitting for hours in front of a computer was known to be tantamount to destroying the human back. He seemed to think it would be the second easiest thing in the world for Isa to find some other way to support herself, a way which didn't involve sitting, writing TV scripts or cashing cheques for doing so.

"Sure, and wind up living on tofu burgers and yum-yum bulgur wheat like a couple of do-nothing go-nowhere hippies." Isa had no use for hippies. Given half a chance she could go into a long rant and rave about gimme-gimme-Jimmys who yap on against the system while making sure the system feeds, clothes, and educates their seemingly endless string of socially crippled kids. "I've been working since I was eleven years old and paying taxes since I was seventeen so a pack of grasshoppers could spend their entire lives sitting on their flabby bums smoking wacky tabacky and spewing out babies like they had assembly lines inside them instead of ovaries. The whole useless lot of them ought to be put to work. Digging ditches, maybe, or building these bicycle paths they keep yammering on that we ought to have."

People who had heard Isa talk were surprised when they found out she had graduated from high school. They didn't think she sounded like someone with any education at all, let alone twelve years of it. Isa talked low-rent Vancouver Island. When she first got out of school she moved to the city and ran head-first into the realization she lived in a society still divided by class. By every definition, she sounded low class, so she saved up some money and signed on for elocution lessons. She concentrated for months and eventually learned to put the "g" on jumping, hopping, skipping and running. She learned there were hundreds of thousands, maybe even millions of people who had never

heard anyone use "amn't" instead of "aren't." She also learned the city
is full of the most colourless, bland, boring speakers she had heard in
all her life, people who say the same things in the same way, probably
because they think the same unquestioning thoughts.

Isa stayed a year in the city, then went back to the Island without
bothering to kiss the bright lights goodbye. She also went back to
talking the way everyone around her had talked for most of her life.
On some level, one she had explored very little, she felt it had to do
with culture, and she figured hers was as good as anybody else's. She
also had a very clear analysis of colonialization and what it means
when everyone from here wants to pretend they're really from
somewhere else. Slowly she realized that not only did a lot of people
want to pretend they were really from somewhere else, most of them
actually were. Where once you could sit having coffee in the Scotch
Bakery or enjoying your lunch at Lindsay's, and know pretty well
everyone who walked past on the sidewalk, now a person was lucky if
she recognized someone once a week. The old-timers, and even those
who were not yet thirty thought of themselves as old-timers, met in
groups, like endangered trumpeter swans, to bemoan the influx of
outsiders. The outsiders in turn tried hard not to let their scorn show
too clearly. These hillbillies, these next-best-thing-to-crackers had no
idea what a gold mine they'd been sitting on, no idea of the possibil-
ities. And so those who had come from somewhere else attracted by
the clean air, clean water and open beaches set about systematically
turning the place into what they had left behind—mostly treeless,
fenced and semi-obscured by smog.

When one too many tidal marshlands were turned into trailer parks
and a few too many rivers became lined with high-priced condomin-
iums, Isa realized the inevitable. She also realized if she felt bereft it
wasn't because The Goof had been given the door or the kids had
gone off to forge their own futures; she was bereft because entire
mountain slopes had been clearcut and there was no longer an
oolichan run. And she set about looking for a place which would
replace what had been taken.

She didn't find the place until she had found herself and found
what she really wanted in life. She figured all the luck she would ever

have had got used up when she found Carol and then, together, they found the farm.

"Now I lay me down to rest, I promise Lord I've done my best, and while I sleep please pull a switch, let me wake up filthy rich."

"You'll go to hell for things like that, Isa. It's blasphemy."

"From lapsed Catholics and reborn Pentecostals may the good Lord make us all safe," Isa teased.

"You forgot the things that go bump in the night."

Isa knew about those bumps, and the ghosts of the past which made them. Often she lay in her bed at night, her mouth dry from the codeine she took every four hours, visited by scenes she had spent years trying to forget. If she wasn't wrestling with the past, she tried to think of something she could do to get her away from the computer and the hours of sitting which only made her back worse. She tried hard to limit the stretches of time she spent working on filmscripts. She even set the dinger so she could be pulled out of wherever it was she went when she worked and hie herself to the pool for some of the swimming the specialist said might help.

The back didn't get any better, though. Hours and hours of sitting in an office chair in front of a glowing screen, trying to put daydreams into words—if it wasn't murder on a person's back, it was at least mayhem. Not to mention what it does to the head to spend so much of your life in a world which doesn't exist.

"You're different about it," her daughter Jennet said quietly, pouring thick cream into Isa's mug of coffee.

"How do you mean?"

"I don't know how to put it but, well, it's as if you're calmer about it somehow."

"Oh, I'm probably calmer about almost anything you'd care to name. I'm older, my dear. And, some might think, wiser. Besides, I used to *have* to make it all work out, *have* to carve out a reasonably lucrative career. I had you rotten kids, remember?" She laughed. "Now I can write more of what I'd like to write—not that any more of what I'd like to write gets produced, it's just I don't have to buy shoes and pay dentist bills, so I can waste more time now."

"Oh, mea culpa, Maw, mea culpa. What is it, really?"

"I guess I no longer think the world can be set on fire, or even changed, by any film anyone is going to make. I used to think we could push the edges and get some improvement. Open their eyes, touch their hearts, all that good stuff. I believed that the way some people believe in religion. And I thought If Only . . . If Only we could find a producer with integrity, If Only we could get a director with commitment, If Only, If Only, If Only."

"And now?"

"They pay good money. It's something I enjoy doing, so I'm good at it. Because I'm good at it, I enjoy doing it. And they pay good money."

"That's kind of sad."

"Nothing sad about it at all. It's a business. It's a dirty, cutthroat, shark-infested, maggot-riddled, filthy business. What's sad is there are so many idealistic people still think they can change the world."

"You don't think they can?"

"Hey, we're talkin' about an audience that lines up in the freezing snow to see blood'n'guts'n'gore'n'violence. We're talking about a voting public which stays home in droves to watch Tough-Guy Tuesday on TV."

"Yeah, but—"

"Darlin', we're talkin' an industry that made not one, but two blockbuster money-making hits out of the foul crap done by the same mass murderer. We're talkin' an audience which goes *tsk tsk* over street violence while at the same time drooling over a film about some guy who fries up other people's livers and eats them."

"I think I'd rather sell real estate to those who are heavily into conspicuous consumption," Jennet winked. "After all, they're going to buy their ugly over-sized, over-priced, over-financed status symbols from some dumb crumb, might as well be this one." She looked out the window at the concrete slabs of the city and shrugged. "You never know, I might even make enough on commissions to wave bye-bye to this shitty and get myself thirty or forty acres of farm. Raise chickens, live a healthy life, get back to the land, get in touch with my karma and dharma by working with my hands . . ." and then they were both laughing.

Gus didn't have any questions. He just nodded when Isa told him sore back or not, she was staying in the same old cold water which had supported them all for so many years. He sipped his Sprite and smiled often. Gus seemed to meet anything the world threw at him with a smile. But at least he was out of his religious phase. That one had been hard—frustrating, almost enraging. Isa could have handled it if he'd shaved his head and dressed in an orange nightgown, then rang bells and danced in the street. She'd known any number of people who had come out of that one with a sort of untouchable calm and good yoga skills. She could even have handled it if Gus had joined the Jehovah's Witnesses and gone door to door warning of the imminent Armageddon. If he'd done that, she could have contacted the group behind that intermittent newspaper ad, the one promising the real scoop on that particular cult, and had them send Gus their data. He'd have read every word of it, she knew, if only to prepare himself to argue them out of their misbeliefs. She would have been only mildly alarmed if he'd got himself involved with the Seventh Day Adventists or the Worldwide Church of God. But not Gus. Dear me, no, not Gus, nothing so trendy and New Age for him. He'd taken a header into Roman Catholicism and could recite the names and specialties of any saint a person would want to name. Carol had told her time and time again to relax, but it was easy for Carol to say that, she'd moved herself beyond the clutches of the Church. The saints weren't threats to her, the rituals weren't bugaboo to her. To Isa they were mysterious, sinister, a fate almost worse than death.

But Gus had come out the other side. God in her heaven only knew what he was working on now. Isa prayed it wasn't Scientology or one of those crystal-collecting channelling cults. She wasn't sure she could contain herself if Gus began to speak with an accent out of a B-grade British Raj movie. How in hell had this happened?

The first odd thing in which Gus had plunged himself had been herbs. Books on herbs, more books on herbs and still more books on herbs, which were, let's face it, weeds. And Gus more and more and more convinced that if we all just added them to our diets we could conquer cancer, leprosy and anything else you would want to name. Then horoscopes. God, the horoscopes! Years of having your every move and opinion explained by this planet being on the cusp of something else and the other planet in transition. The horoscopes were followed by numerology, which somehow led to a fixation on the theories of Adelle Davis and the appearance of huge boxes of vitamin pills, especially the Bs and Cs. Only once had Gus given anything close to a comprehensible answer to Isa's repeated "*Why?*" He had looked at her and smiled—of course he had—and said he was researching everything he was going to need for his novel. "I don't want to write film scripts, Mother, I want to write something *real*." Isa was used to that kind of phony intellectual superiority from other writers, and usually she just guffawed when someone tried to pull it on her, but to hear it from her own son was a tad much.

With religion behind him, at least for the time being, Gus was researching dreams. The meaning of dreams, the cause of dreams, the symbolism of dreams, the interpretation of dreams. Well, at least it wasn't the Catholic Church. Isa could have told Gus more than he wanted to know about dreams. Not just about dreams, but about nightmares and how strongly tied they are to memory, and how sometimes, it's impossible to tell where the one stops and the other begins.

People sitting around a table in a kitchen, and they were playing cards. Counting wrong too, didn't they know how to count? It wasn't fifteen–two it was fifteen–sixteen. Then they said fifteen–four, and that was wrong too. When she said it was three–four, not fifteen–four, they laughed, softly indulgent laughter, and someone, she wasn't sure who, told her it was a new way of doing things, and when she was older he'd teach it to her.

They had bottles of beer. Brown bottles with long necks. The women poured little bits of beer into glasses and sipped, the men lifted the bottles and drank, their Adam's apples bobbing, and she could hear the *glub glub* of the beer leaving the mouth of the bottle.

Fifteen–two, fifteen–four, fifteen–six and a pair is eight, they said. If she counted like that at school the teacher would make her stand in the corner with the idiot cap on her head. The men laughed and talked, joked and teased, the women chatted quietly to each other, their soft voices running counterpoint to the loud, confident rumble of male voices.

One of the women had bright red fingernails. Isa wasn't sure how you got bright red fingernails like that, but she'd like some. Maybe when nobody else was around she'd ask her mom about it, although you'd think if her mom knew, she'd have hers like that too. And all the women were wearing perfume. That was nice. That and the smell of the powder they patted on their noses. Well, that's what they said when they left the table and headed for the toilet, pardon me I have to powder my nose.

There were some plates of sandwiches, cut catty-corner into little triangles, they looked real pretty and Isa could eat as much as she wanted. Chopped egg with green onion and chives, her favourite. There was a big plate of sliced garlic sausage, too, the men seemed to like that more than the women did, although Isa ate her fair share. "You keep that up, toots," her dad laughed, "and you're gonna smell like the bride at a Polish wedding," and everyone laughed. That didn't make sense either. Why laugh? What was so funny about that?

And then the inner movie switched. Same kitchen, same people, same clothes, probably the same night, but the cards were back in the Bicycle package on the shelf, the table was moved aside, flush against the wall, the chairs were out of the way, and those people were dancing to music from the radio. *Dum de dum de dum-de-dum, dum de dum de dum-de-dum*, with a string of pearls out of Woolworth's, *ta dum de dum de da daah* . . . and her mother was smiling up at her dad who was smiling down and everything seemed so nice and then her dad had her and was carrying her to her bedroom, she could smell beer on his breath and cigarette-smell, too, and he had something nice-smelling in his hair. *Brylcreem, a little dab'll do ya . . . look so deb-on-air.* And what was that anyway, deb-on-air? Have to ask Mom, she'll know.

But then it was pitch black outside, and only a dim light showing in the hallway, and no music, no smiling. She could hear sounds and they scared her, and mom was crying and saying oh Jesus, does it always have to wind up like this, please, for god's sake, at least tell me what I've done to make you angry. And him roaring You know goddamn good and well, and then the sound of a slap and Mom screaming, not so much because she'd been slapped and hurt, but because she'd come to the end, her nerves had frayed until they snapped. Just scream scream scream and him saying Oh shut the hell up, what's the damn matter with you anyway.

Isa had the youngest mom of anybody she knew. Some kids had moms who had lines in their faces already. Not Isa's mom. Isa's mom looked like those ladies who worked in the Emporium selling fancy clothes, or at the desk in the dentist's office, those smooth-faced soft-skinned shiny-eyed women. Except Isa's mom didn't work in those places, she worked at the bottling plant and lots of times she brought home half a dozen bottles of the pop they were turning out, case after case of it, loaded onto big trucks and driven to stores and cafes and gas stations for people to buy and drink when they were thirsty. Dad worked too, and sometimes he'd get real mad about Mom working and tell her to bloody quit, and Mom always waited until he cooled off then said Oh, darling, you *know* sooner or later there's going to be a strike and at least this way you won't have to apply for strike pay so the union will have more in its war chest. He'd mutter and mumble but then he'd grudgingly nod, and that one would be over for that time.

But you knew there'd be a next time. There was always a next time.

4

Tammy had been beering for almost two weeks, and Phoebe was just about fed up with being the one stuck babysitting. She might not have minded so much if all she had to worry about was herself and Linda, but Darelle and Donny were still underfoot and it was beginning to look as if they'd never leave. As near as Phoebe could figure out, there wasn't a reason in the world for Cindy to look for a place of her own. Horning in the way she was, she had everything she needed, even someone to babysit her brats without getting paid. Donny wasn't much trouble. He was easy enough to get along with, happy playing by himself or with the others and quiet most of the time, but Darelle was a pain in the ass. Not just the snivelling at every little thing, you could almost get used to that, but the snitching and tattling was enough to make Phoebe want to pound the snot out of her. You didn't dare, though, because she'd yap to Cindy and Cindy would yap to Tammy and Tammy might or might not holler about it. No telling whether she'd pull down the roof or just shrug and say Hell, I'd give her a whap every ten minutes on general principles if it was me stuck with her.

Some nights neither of them came home. If it was just Cindy who didn't come home, Tammy would make some joke about Ah, love in bloom I suppose, or Get as drunk as she was last night and even the greaseballs look good. If Cindy came home and Tammy didn't, Cindy would merely press her lips together disapprovingly and make some remark about married women who thought they were still single. When neither of them came home it was pot-and-kettle time. No remarks got made except in Phoebe's own head and she might as well keep the remarks there, because all she'd get for saying them out loud was a crack on the ear.

Sometimes she lay in bed stiff with anger at being left alone in charge of the other kids, and she'd dream of walking up to her dad and saying Look, I kept a record this time, and she didn't come home this night or this or this, and twice she came home and brought some guy home with her. But it was no more than a dream. Phoebe knew she wouldn't do it. While there was a good chance her dad would believe her and lay a good hiding on her mom, there was every bit as good a chance he'd call Phoebe a troublemaking streetwalking little slut and lay the hiding on her. And if he did believe her and walloped Tammy, Phoebe would pay for it the next time he went out to camp. No matter how she looked at it, she couldn't see a way to win.

The guy Tammy brought home was called Dick. Phoebe thought of him as Dick the Prick, even though he wasn't. He seemed like a nice enough guy. Funny as hell right up until he was so drunk he made no sense whatsoever. He was a bit creepy sometimes, though, because when he got to the point you weren't sure what he was going on about, he was as apt as not to lie down. You'd think he'd passed out, and the next thing you knew he'd be talking away, arguing with someone nobody else could see, holding forth at great length in what Phoebe thought was a foreign language. But when she asked, he said no, he only spoke English.

"And crazy," Tammy said, but her voice wasn't sarcastic, just sort of teasing.

Dick worked on again off again with his brother, who had a front-end loader, a skidder, backhoes and some other stuff. The work wasn't steady but it paid reasonably well, and probably if Dick had been more on the ball and less inclined to go swimming in a sea of beer, he'd have worked more often.

It came out one night, when they were sitting around drinking beer and watching a TV movie about life in the slammer, that Dick had been behind walls for two and a half years. "What did you do?" Phoebe asked. He didn't answer at first, then he looked at Tammy, did this thing where he tipped his head and shrugged, and said, "Oh, I was a pretty bad druggie." For once he wasn't laughing. "And I got bent out of shape about it, broke into a pharmacy in town and started scoffing everything I could get my mitts on. The security alarm had gone off, but I was so nuts I didn't care, and when the cops came I got in a big fight with them, right up until all that stuff I'd took started to work, and then I passed out. They thought I'd been cold-cocked by the cop I was fighting with and they threw me in the cells. But later on they checked, and I was in pretty bad shape so they whipped me off to the hospital and pumped my gut. I came out of it three days later, just in time to wash m'face, brush m'teeth, and go stand in front of the judge and say I'm guilty, thrash me with a wet noodle. And he sent me off to the Crowbar Hotel to contemplate my sinful ways." He grinned, and it was hard to tell whether he was laughing at himself or the system.

Linda stared at him, then turned her attention back to the TV and tried to ignore Darelle, who was sitting on the floor beside her, fussing with nail polish. Darelle with any kind of make-up was hard to ignore, though. She kept nudging Linda and holding out her hands, asking "What do you think?" and "Is this better?" until finally Linda had enough.

"What I think is you're way too young for that stuff, and anyway you chew your nails so bad you've hardly got anything to smear that glup on unless you want to wear it on your fingertips."

"You're just mean!" Darelle whined.

"You start snivelling and I'll slam you flat," Tammy warned. "You know what I told you. If your feelings get hurt that easy, don't make other people snap at you."

"She's just jealous!" Darelle pouted.

"Oh sure," Linda yawned, "I'm so jealous I can hardly stand it. Because you, of course, are just perfect. Eight years old and a movie star or something. I guess *not!*"

A car drove up and stopped right outside the house. They heard a door slam, and footsteps heading up the walk to the steps.

"Maybe that's Dad!" Linda blurted.

"Naw, if it was your dad he'd come in a cab and the car didn't drive away. And if it was a cab and he didn't have the money to pay, the driver would walk to the door with him and there's only one person coming up the steps." Tammy rose and moved toward the door.

"Sherlock Holmes herself," Dick teased.

"If you used your loaf you'd be able to figure it out for yourself. Besides, he always calls on the radiophone before he leaves camp. Always."

Tammy opened the door before there was a knock and the cop stood with his hand up, surprised for a moment. Then he lowered his hand and used it to pull a little book out of the breast pocket of his uniform. He asked a question, Tammy answered, then he said something in a low, steady voice and Tammy was still, trying to absorb his words. Then she leaned against the door frame and very quietly said, "Ah, no. The poor guy."

At least they knew it hadn't hurt. When a cable snaps, whips back and rips a man's head off his shoulders, there is no time for pain.

Steve was brought back in a body bag and cremated immediately. Nobody in the family, not even Tammy, saw him. Linda was never convinced it was her father had been killed. From what she overheard, eavesdropping obsessively, the mess was so complete it could have been almost anybody. But she couldn't imagine why her dad wouldn't have preferred to come home, walk in the house and yell *Surprise, surprise!* She invented dozens of scenarios, Steve loaning his boots and belt to some poor guy who had lost his own, someone stealing Steve's wallet so it was found in the pocket of the corpse. But however complete she constructed the fantasy, she couldn't pretend Steve was coming home. And even if he had decided he'd had a gutful of Tammy screwing around, he wouldn't walk off and leave Linda. Phoebe, well, anybody would gladly leave her. But Steve had always called Linda his little buddy, had introduced her as "my daughter and best friend." And he'd have shown up when Sandra was born just to check and see if she really was his.

Sandra made her appearance four months after Steve's memorial service. You'd think a new baby would have slowed Tammy down some, but no, not a chance.

Steve had insurance, and Workers' Compensation came every month, so much for Tammy, so much for each kid as long as they were living at home and going to school. "Great timing," Cindy said, watching Tammy change Sandra's diaper. "Just think, you get orphan's allowance for her for the next eighteen years.."

"You're just jealous," Tammy answered calmly. "All you get is straight welfare, and it's cheap compared to orphan's pension."

"Shame it was Steve who had to die. Should have been that damn Jack, but I guess *he'll* live to be ninety."

Whatever else could be said about Tammy, she knew her own potential and her own limitations. She knew how easy it would be to let the insurance money dribble away, the way every other speck of money in her life had dribbled. She looked at houses and studied the prices and knew she had a good down payment but not enough to cash out, and she didn't want to be nose-to-nose with mortgage payments for the next twenty years. She bought a brand new double-wide trailer, a near-new car, and paid pad rental two years in advance. That left enough for new bikes for the kids. Linda was delighted. Phoebe looked at hers and shook her head. "Oh, wow, golly gee, why not a trike, instead," she sneered.

"Hey, you want a trike, take that down and exchange it."

"I'm not a baby! What in hell will I do with a bike?"

"Push it up your nose for all I care."

"Can I take it back and use the money for clothes, instead?"

"No."

"Why not?"

"Because you're so fuckin' miserable I think *I'll* be miserable too. You want to be hard to get along with, fine, the rest of us will be hard to get along with too. You don't want the bike, fine, don't ride it. No skin off my nose."

"I *hate* you!"

"Good. Feelings should be mutual."

Phoebe tried to take her bike back for a refund but Tammy wouldn't give her the receipt, so instead of getting the full price of it, she got about half what it was worth when she sold it, unridden, to someone who didn't care if it was hot or not. She got enough money for a new pair of jeans and two tops she thought were nice and everyone else said looked like they belonged in Sal's place on Fraser Street. Tammy didn't say a word about the sale of the bike. Until Phoebe asked if Tammy would drive her to the municipal pool. "Ride your bike," Tammy said quietly. "And you can ride your bike to softball practice too. And the movies. And anywhere else you want to go."

"What a bitch."

"You don't know the half of it."

"You'll be sorry."

"I probably won't be. And if I am, I won't be the only one."

Maybe the best part of moving into the trailer was that Cindy, Darelle and Donny didn't. Cindy got an intent-to-rent form from the welfare and with it found a basement suite, two bedrooms, kitchen, living room and little bathroom. She hated it, but she didn't have much choice. The trailer wasn't laid out the same as the house, and anyway, with a new baby there wasn't much chance they'd have enough room.

Darelle was glad they had their own place. Cindy didn't tell her off if she cried, the way Tammy did, and while she missed Linda, she sure didn't miss Phoebe one little bit. Donny didn't seem to care one way or the other. As long as he had his shoebox full of little cars, he was happy.

If Cindy went out by herself, she got a babysitter, and whatever guy she brought home usually paid the tab. If Tammy came over and they went out together, Linda and Sandra came too, and Linda was in charge.

"Don't see why they put *you* in charge," Darelle groused. "You're only a year older'n me."

"Yeah, but I don't cry all the time. And a year is a year, Darelle."

Tammy's relationship with Dick the Prick was on again off again and seemed to depend on whether or not she had someone else on the string. If she did, Dick hit the road and when whoever-it-was got fed up and left, Dick was back again.

"You got no hold on me," Tammy told him. "I can do what I want, see."

"Whatever you say," he shrugged.

Sometimes when she'd had a few too many, Tammy would get herself worked into a fury and start yammering at Dick. He'd yammer right back, and usually he could out-talk and out-smartmouth her. Then Tammy would get bent right out of shape and go at him, hitting him on the head and shoulders, calling him all kinds of gutless bastard, and Dick would just bring his arms up to protect his face, hunch over, and take it. He never raised a hand to her. When she'd slapped and whapped him half a dozen times, Tammy would back off and glare.

"And don't you forget it," she warned.

"Oh, I don't forget," he answered. "One day you'll get yours."

"Not from you I won't!" She was all set to go at him again.

"No, not from me. But you'll get yours all the same. People as hit other people wind up gettin' hit, it's a law of nature."

Cindy's landlady said she didn't think it was right for a nine-year-old to babysit an eight-year-old, a three-year-old and an infant. "It makes me feel as if *I'm* supposed to make sure they're safe," she scolded.

"I don't expect you to look after them."

"And if there's a fire? I suppose I can just get myself out and not worry at all about getting them out, too? Or if one of them gets sick, or hurt, or . . . whatever, I just turn a deaf ear? No, and I won't have it in my place."

So either it was a paid babysitter or Tammy came and got them and drove them to her place, and they stayed there. Which was okay except Phoebe was there, and Phoebe didn't care who said what or that Linda was supposed to be in charge. "That'll be the day I take any orders from a tit like you!" she yelled, and she slapped Linda's face so hard the mark was still there the next day, fingers and all.

"What happened?" Tammy asked. Linda told her. Tammy got the belt and went into the bedroom where Phoebe was still asleep. Dick shook his head at the noise but Linda was glad. She didn't even care that Phoebe would pay her back the first chance she got.

And then Cindy met Gus and brought him home with her.

He was bent over the pool table, expertly sinking balls, when she bumped him without meaning to and cost him the game. "I'm sorry," she blurted, inwardly cringing and bracing herself for the explosion. "I didn't mean it."

But he just shrugged, and grinned. "I know you didn't mean it. It's okay," and he crossed to the blackboard to chalk his name at the bottom of the list of those waiting for a chance.

He went back to his table and sat down with a half dozen or more others, who laughed and hoo-rahed and told him he'd been lucky to have any time at the table at all.

"Usually," one of them said loudly, "you can't even see to find the cue."

"Now, now, don't talk mean to me, you know I get scared paralytic when you do," Gus laughed.

Cindy paid for a jug of beer to be taken to the table, as an apology. Gus filled his glass, then brought it over to Cindy's table. "Mind if I join you?" he asked, polite and quiet.

"Please do." She tried to be polite and quiet, too. He was younger than she was by maybe five or six years, probably closer to ten, and they both knew it, but he didn't seem to care. He bought a jug for their table and talked easily with Dick and Tammy, but mostly he talked to Cindy. He didn't even try to flirt with Tammy, and that made him different from most.

When the waiter hollered for last call, Tammy reached for her purse and stood up, shaking her head when Dick suggested they still had time for another jug.

"I'm going home," she said flatly.

"Well then, I'm getting a case at the off-sales," Dick answered, standing up and swaying noticeably.

Somehow, between the table and the car, Gus had joined them with his case of beer. He accompanied Tammy to her place and helped carry Donny out to the cab, then went back to the trailer and got Darelle and carried her, too. And just as slick as that, he had his opened case tucked under his arm and was in the cab with them. As the cab pulled away, Tammy laughed and yelled, "Have a good time! Don't do anything I wouldn't do!" and Cindy pretended to be shocked, and shy.

Gus carried Donny into the basement suite, Cindy carried the beer and Darelle walked on her own, snivelling every step of the way. Gus paid the driver and even said thank you, which Cindy thought a good sign. They sat in the living room, Gus on the sofa, Cindy in the big chair, sipping beer and pretending he was only visiting briefly, and then Cindy went to the bathroom, and when she came back she sat on the sofa instead of back in the chair. And it was easy after that.

In the morning Gus was up first, and had found the coffee fixings and cereal before the kids were awake. Donny stumbled into the kitchen and stopped dead, staring at the stranger.

"You want cereal?" Gus asked. Donny nodded. "You like nanners on it?" Donny nodded again.

Darelle didn't even bother whining when she got up, she just sat down to cereal with bananas and started to eat. Gus drank another mug of coffee and told the kids to be quiet, let their mother catch up on her sleep. "If you're real quiet," he said, "and if you can get dressed without waking up your mom, I'll walk you to the store and you can each have a peach."

"I want candy." Darelle said, smiling as sweetly as she could.

"Well, I'm buying peaches," he answered, and he imitated her smile so she knew he knew what she was trying to pull.

She gave up on the phoney-baloney charm and decided if it was peaches or nothing at all, she'd take a peach.

Tammy was in a lousy mood. Everybody knew it, but nobody knew what it was had set her off this time. She snapped at Linda, she took a swing at Phoebe and whacked her on the ear, and all Dick got were foul looks and stony silence. Dick cooked supper, Linda and Phoebe did the dishes and tidied the kitchen, then Dick started getting Sandra ready for bed. Still Tammy glared and glowered.

The baby was in bed, sucking on her bottle and almost asleep, Dick was sitting on the sofa, Linda and Phoebe were sprawled on the floor and Tammy was busy ignoring them and the TV program they were watching. The girls were nattering quietly, each insistent and refusing to give an inch.

"They're lizard people," Linda insisted. "Just look at the mouths."

"They aren't lizard people, you goof, they're snake people."

"Snakes don't have arms and legs, Phoeb. Lizards do."

"You're both wrong," Dick yawned. "Just look at the pattern on the chests of 'em; they're some kinda turtle people. See how they've got their costumes padded so's to make it look like plates or something?"

"Yeah? You really think so?" Phoebe was slowly but surely thawing toward Dick, mainly because he seldom put her down and never took a swat at her, and more than once had stepped in to defuse Tammy's anger, even when it meant she came down on him.

"And they're like cold-blooded, right, and don't see things the same way as the humans do. Well, turtles wouldn't, even if they grew up here instead of out in space somewhere. They're cashing in on the Ninja Turtle thing, and instead of heroes with a shell they've got villains with chest plates. See, when that guy stands up, look at his chest. See how—"

"Oh for cryin' out loud will you idiots give it a rest?" Tammy exploded. "Who needs a university course on what kind of creepy-crawly they're supposed to be. It's a lousy TV show is all, and they aren't turtle people, they're actors! You bunch are gonna drive me bug-house."

"I know they're actors," Phoebe said, and something in the tone of her voice let them know she was taking a stand. "I'm just trying to figure out what those actors are pretending to be, is all. It might be important sometime. They ask about stuff like that in school, what things in a story represent."

"Don't be so stupid."

"Stupid?" Phoebe turned her head slowly and stared at Tammy. She didn't say a word, she just stared for exactly the amount of time guaranteed to tip Tammy over the edge.

"Don't you look at me like that!" Tammy was up off the chair and swinging. Phoebe rolled out of the way and the crack on the ear intended for her instead hit Linda, who yelped.

"Hey!" Dick got up and stood between Linda and Tammy. "Just cool off, okay? You got something up your nose, fine, but don't bash the kids for no reason."

"Who are you to tell me what to do in my own house? Especially about my own kids."

"Me?" he grinned. "Why madam, I am absolutely nobody whatso-ever." He sat down again, but the kids knew Tammy wouldn't be going any further with it. Dick had done it again, taken the heat.

"I don't want to hear another goddamn word about are the Cardassians snakes or lizards. Don't even think about dumb crap like that, you hear?"

"Right," he agreed pleasantly. "And you kids take heed, okay? The thought cop says no thinking about Cardassians. Not even little thoughts. You be careful, now, I'm warning you. Save those thoughts for other things. Heaven and hell and international economic downturns and important stuff like that."

Tammy was so mad by now she walked away from them, her back stiff. She went into the bedroom to take the empty bottle away from the sleeping baby and pull the covers up snug and warm. Sometimes she felt as if she was going to start yelling and not stop until there was no voice box left in her throat. Seemed like all she had to do was look at Phoebe and she wanted to whap her. And Linda, well, god in heaven alone knew what was going on in that kid's. Not even ten years old and already she could talk about the news and what was going on in other countries as if she had invented it all herself. She and Dick would get going and you'd think they were talking a foreign language. As if any of it was important.

Dick just lolled back on the sofa and turned his attention back to the Cardassian Ambassador and the stunt he was working overtime to set up. Phoebe moved back to her original spot next to Linda. They didn't say anything, just looked at each other and shrugged.

The program ended and while the commercials blared away at twice the sound level of the program, Dick made a pot of tea, Phoebe cut slices of cake. She even put one out for Tammy, as if there were no hard feelings. Anyone who knew her would know she was seething inside, but she took the cake to the bedroom where Tammy was sitting on her bed, knees jacked up, smoking a cigarette and leafing through an old magazine.

"You want a cup of tea?"

"No thank you." Tammy wasn't giving an inch. Whatever was gnawing on her bones was still working on her nerves. But she took the cake, and that was a start.

They were watching some stupid show that was supposed to be a comedy, people swapping insults and put-downs, coming in one door and going out another, none of it making any sense, and suddenly Dick was on his feet, pointing his finger at Linda and yelling at the top of his voice, "You're still thinking about Cardassians! You don't fool me, it's written all over your face, you've been thinking

Cardassians for a good five minutes!" He turned to Phoebe. "Isn't she? Can't you just tell by looking at her?"

"Yeah, she is, she's thinking about Cardassians for sure," Phoebe agreed, just to see what Dick was going to do next, the crazy fool.

He grabbed Linda and lifted her to his shoulder, her legs hanging down his back, her head near his chest. He started to jump up and down, jiggling her belly on his shoulder. "Well, you were warned, missy, no thinking Cardassian around here."

Linda had the giggles so bad she couldn't even tell him to stop. He bounced her, he jounced her, he jiggled and shook her, then lowered her to the rug and started to tickle her. "Gimme a hand here, Phoeb, she's gonna get us all in trouble with her Cardassian obsession."

Phoebe got into it, too. They rolled on the carpet like a litter of puppies, then Dick grabbed one under each arm and hauled them up, swung them around and dropped to the sofa, with one on each side. He was puffing and pink in the face, all of them laughing like loonytoons.

"That'll learn ya," he managed.

"*Learn* ya? Where'd *you* learn to talk? That'll *teach* you!" Phoebe pinched his arm gently. "You want to grow up ignorant? Get a grip, eh."

"Atta girl," he said softly. He gave her shoulder a gentle squeeze, pulled her tight against him in a friendly hug, and didn't hold onto her too long. "You're a lot of fun, Phoebe," he said.

She waited for him to add something typical like When you're not a pain in the ass, or Especially when you're asleep, or something, but he didn't say it. After a while that part of her insides which had gone tight with expectation began to relax again.

"Hey, sweetheart," he called. "Want some ice cream? We'll whip down to the store and get some. What flavour would you like?"

"Don't matter to me," Tammy answered, but her voice wasn't as cold and distant as it had been. Maybe she'd get over whatever it was before someone inadvertently kicked off an explosion.

As they were piling into the front seat of the car, Phoebe nattered an imitation of Tammy. "Don't matter to me, don't matter to me."

"Then we'll get Cardassian Turtle Supreme," Dick laughed. "And no matter what it says on the carton, you just remember every bite you take is Cardassian Turtle Supreme. You got it?"

They bought a big carton of ice cream and a package of marshmallow puff cookies. Then, while eating, they didn't dare look at each other because otherwise they'd explode into loud, long laughter and they didn't dare tell Tammy what was so funny. And if that happened, she'd go into orbit.

Tammy ate her ice cream slowly, feeling like a total goof. She didn't know what was bugging her. Maybe it was just she wasn't used to having someone around so much. There's a lot to be said for being married to someone who is off in camp three-quarters of the time. When he's gone you do everything your way, and when he's home it's party time and honeymoon and knowing that before the cell walls start closing in on you, he'll be back in camp turning first-growth forest into the next thing to desert. Dick was okay, and he did more than his fair share of stuff around the place. When he had money he handed it over to her, more than enough to cover his expenses when he wasn't working. He wasn't weird around the girls, which was a big bonus. It was just that he was *there* so much of the time. Well, at least it wasn't ready–aim–fire between him and Phoebe the way it had been with Steve. Two of a kind that had been. Linda, now, she could get along with just about anybody at all. Phoebe looked like a good mix of Steve and herself, whereas Linda didn't look like anyone else in the world except her own self. Unless she looked like one or more of her grandparents, but no way of telling that, Tammy's parents were both pushing up daisies and Steve's parents lived too far away for anyone to visit anyone else, not that Tammy was interested, thank you, not after the way they'd behaved at the beginning, telling Steve he was all kinds of a fool and far too old to be getting involved with an under-age kid. Was it their business? Not likely. Well, Steve had been lots older, but so what, they'd got along good from the start. A few sparring matches, sure, but didn't everybody? And so what if she'd stepped out when he was in camp. She never rubbed his nose in it, just as he'd never rubbed hers in what he did.

Dick, now, well, he was a horse of a different garage. At least with Steve you knew what he was thinking. Dick, he kept pretty much to his own self. She knew there were plenty of people, her own sister included, who privately entertained the notion Linda wasn't really Steve's daughter, that Tammy had got caught when Steve was in camp and she was cat-assing around with someone she'd met in a bar. Tammy herself wasn't certain. Except Linda was real smart, and Steve, well, he'd been the smartest person Tammy had ever met in her life, probably borderline genius. No telling who or what he might have turned out to be if he'd had even half a chance, but when you're the umpteenth kid in a poor family living in an area known to be poverty-stricken at the best of times, you don't get many opportunities of any kind, especially not for education. They say it's free, but it isn't. They say it's there for the taking, but just try taking some of it without paying tuition and student fees and books and lab costs. Free for the taking? Sure, and you could finish your course in jail if you went about it the wrong way.

Tammy figured Linda was at least as smart as Steve had been, and she couldn't remember any of her one- or two-night stands being especially bright, so she figured none of them had been sperm donor. Linda would have lots more chances than Steve had ever been given, he'd made sure of that, what with his insurance policies and all. Phoebe, now, she was no slouch, either. If you could get her to sit down and apply herself, she could probably do just about anything, but she was as apt as not to speak out of turn or something and wind up in hot water. Make you wonder, that one.

Another who'd make you wonder was that young guy Cindy was effin' around with. Seemed at least as smart as Steve, but very definitely strange. Tammy herself didn't have any firm opinion about past life regression or reincarnation or any of that weird stuff. Some people believed it, most didn't, and she wasn't sure because there had been a few little things in her own life that made her wonder, but nothing you could call proof either way. Déjà vu, well, pretty much everybody had one or two episodes like that, and lots of people said it didn't mean anything.

Gus, though, he was some hot on it all. He didn't push it on you, give him that much. If he'd had a few beer too many he might say something about the karmic wheel, and how it had turned and he and

Cindy were getting another chance. She'd asked him about it once. Well, she should have damn well known better, what with him being pretty well packed at the time. She asked and he'd told her.

"You're kidding," was all she could think of to say.

"No, I'm not. That time around you weren't her sister, you were my aunt, and it was Phoebe was her sister, but basically, we're all connected."

"And we got killed, huh?"

"We were engaged, Cindy and I, and we were having a big party at my parents' place, everyone having a good time, singing and dancing and toasting each other, and then the Cossacks arrived and wiped out pretty well the entire village." He smiled and looked over at Cindy, who wasn't paying any attention because she was so busy working on her second or third gallon of beer. "But we're together again, and all that other is in the past."

"Jews, huh? All of us."

"All of us."

"You'd almost think if we'd been Jews back then we'd at least know a few of them this time around."

"Not necessarily."

As if that wasn't enough, Gus went on to explain that he had been the intended bride and Cindy the intended groom. She was a rabbi, a teacher.

"*Cindy?*" Tammy couldn't help it, she burst out laughing. "Hell, she couldn't teach a duck to swim. Not in this life or any other."

But Gus just smiled, and she knew he wasn't going to let go of his own ideas about that. Well, let him have them, everybody is entitled to their own damn opinion. Or as Steve had said often enough, opinions are like assholes—everybody's got one.

5

The sound of the old air horn fractured the evening. Isa was in the barn brushing the mares and trimming their halter paths, just behind their ears where the webbing rubbed their manes into tangles and tats. "Fifty acres," she muttered, "and you still can't wrap it around you and find peace and quiet."

"Maybe they're celebrating. Getting a head start on next New Year's or something."

"There it goes again. Last night it went on for an hour. If it isn't those dogs up there barking hysterically at each other, it's kids on those awful snarling trail bike things. Or else it's whoever-it-is out there with no sense of rhythm at all and a big dream about learning to play the drums. Wouldn't you think you'd need to be able to hear the difference between bum-tiddly-um and rat-a-tat-tat before you could call yourself a drummer?"

"Well, at least with that horn going you can't hear the dogs."

"With that horn going you can't hear yourself think."

She finished grooming the mares, then she and Carol walked up the long driveway to see for themselves what was going on with the air horn. The cooling air was thick with the smell of yellow-flowered clover, and big fat bumblebees lumbered through the air, working overtime. They were out in the morning hours before the honeybees and still at work hours after the tame ones had gone back to their hives for the night. Their low, steady drone was soothing. Isa always connected it with the scent and taste of blackberries warm on the vine.

A car moved slowly down the road, the mutty spaniel-type white-with-liver-coloured-blotches yapper rushed screeching from his porch. Immediately, in response, the black lab and the touch-of-collie rose to their feet and joined the chorus. And from the front yard of the house across the street, the air horn began to wail. At the sound of the horn, the blotchy spanielly-thing yelped, pelted back to his porch and lay down, shaking with fear. As soon as he shut up, so did the rest. Moments later the air horn subsided, too.

The door to the spaniel-type's house opened, and one very angry middle-aged man in satchel-assed jeans came stomping out, the undone laces of his work boots flapping. He marched purposefully down the walk, opened the gate just enough to let himself out but keep all the dogs in, then started across the road, already hollering.

"Gettin' damn sick and tired of this!" he shouted, his face red, his throat swelling.

The front door of the house across the street opened and a beer-bellied man who could have been twin to the one working himself into a fit of fury came down the steps laughing. "If you don't like the sound of my horn," he suggested, "you might think of doin' something to shut up that yappy mutt of yours."

"What do you expect me to do about it? Dogs bark, you moron."

"Yeah, dogs bark. And air horns blow."

"I'll have the cops on ya!"

"You do that. Want I should loan you a quarter for the phone call?"

"Take your quarter and *push* it, fella! I'm warnin' ya—"

"If a leaf falls off a tree that useless mutt starts yammering, and as soon as he starts he sets all the others off too. You put him out when you get up in the morning and he raises Cain until ha'past ten when you take him in for the night. I don't know how come you can't hear him but you can hear the horn!"

"Punch out your lights."

"Do that. I'll sue you for everything you've got. And when I've got it the first thing I'm gonna do is take that splotchy nightmare to the vet and get his voice box took out so's I don't have to listen to him. Take the others in, too."

"The guy's crazy," the spaniel's owner said to Isa and Carol.

"Maybe he's got a point about getting the dog's voice box

removed," Isa suggested quietly. "Be better'n a big fight in the neighbourhood."

"Oh, sure," Beer Belly sneered, "and I suppose *he's* gonna pick up the tab for it."

"I'd pay half," the laughing near-twin agreed. "Of course, if you have him put down permanent I'd pay the full shot. I hate that damn dog."

"I'm not havin' him put down. He's a good bird dog."

"He doesn't have to bark to be a bird dog," Carol said quickly. "All he has to do is go fetch the bird."

"Won't *be* any pheasants with that horn goin' off all the time."

"Horn's gonna go off every time the dog goes off."

"Gee, maybe I should go home and get the heifers to bawling or something. We could all get into this one." Carol was laughing, but neither of the workies was getting angry with her. She could do that so easily, joke and get everyone else doing it, too. "Put Isa on the bagpipes, maybe pound some pots and pans with big spoons or potato mashers, see if we could get Samuelson's kids out yelling and hoo-rah-ing and letting off firecrackers or something." She turned to the dogs' owner. "Maybe you could load up your expensive shotguns and start firing at the moon," Then she turned to the laughing neighbour. "You, I think, are doing enough with the air horn, we don't want you getting overtired."

"How much you figure the vet would charge? Coupla hundred bucks, I guess, eh."

"Sixty-seven fifty," the neighbour answered quickly. "In at eight in the morning, home before supper. I can make the appointment if you want, and I'd take him in and pick him up afterward, what with you bein' at work all day and me sittin' here livin' off the fat of the land on retirement pension."

"Sure. About time you did something besides sit on your duff and drink beer, you lazy fart. Boy, some guys've got 'er made; you shoulda been ashamed'a yourself on payday all those years you stood around chewin' snoose and doin' nothin'. And now, well, see how much use you were to them, they're glad to pay you to stay th'hell home and leave 'em alone."

"Eat your heart out," the neighbour mocked and both men laughed.

Carol turned and started back down the driveway, Isa following. "You're slick," Isa said. "Should run you for politics. They'd have been punching and kicking if you hadn't turned it all into a joke."

"Stupid, both of them," Carol laughed. "Like a couple of kids. G'wan ya did, g'wan I never, did so, did not, did so, oh yeah, yeah," she chanted, and then she was skipping and Isa was laughing and feeling very lucky in her life.

So why was it, less than a half hour later, sitting in the big easy chair, unwinding before bedtime, somewhere between reading a magazine article and watching a not-very-good TV movie, she began to see images behind her eyes. She was used to the internal cinema, knowing it helped her make good money writing scripts. All she had to do was stay on track and transfer the mental pictures to the laser-printed page. But sometimes, like now, what she saw was different, not something she had created, more like those gas bubbles which rise slowly to the surface of a swamp—*blurp*—their methane leaving a brief but bitter stink.

A wedding, and the six-year-old child didn't know what wedding meant,

what is bride, what is groom, and why is the best man best, and at what? But they were all laughing, some of them dancing,

some men standing together at one end of the big hall, standing up on a thing someone called a stage, but no horses, no cowboys, just a floor higher there than the rest of the room, and the men up there

playing music for the dancers.

Along one wall big tables with platters and trays of food, green-looking things with red stuff in them, Mom said stuffed olives but there were other things, purply-black with pits inside and Mom said they were olives too. Maybe like cats, some grey, some black and white, different colours, still cats. Olives didn't taste all that good at first, but once you got used to them the green ones were okay and the black ones were too mushy when you chewed. Little pickled onions, Isa's favourite, and sliced meat of every kind. Someone had tried to make potato salad without potatoes. Maybe they didn't have a garden and couldn't afford spuds at the store, because they used macaroni and it wasn't very nice, too much stuff in it with no taste at all, cold macaroni, yuck. One potato salad was nearly yellow with egg yolk and maybe mustard, bits of grated carrot in it and chunks of celery, and the spuds mashed, not cut into cold gooey hunks. And salad with crab meat in it, and big hunks of smoked salmon, and bowls, whole bowls full of smoked oysters. And when you'd had enough of all that, one of the big tables was covered with desserts, cream puffs and coconut bars and lots'n'lots of what Mom called snowballs. She made them with mashed spuds, added all kinds of stuff, then dipped them in chocolate and rolled them in coconut.

The man they said was groom was also the man they said was Dad's brother. He must be, Dad even called him little brother, but it didn't sound much nice when he said it, and little brother–uncle–groom said big brother but it didn't sound all that nice either. Maybe they didn't like each other very much—

The child had a new dress for the party, and new socks, too, white ones, the kind that came up to her knees. Usually she had dark blue socks or brown socks because, Mom said, they didn't show the dirt as much so you didn't have to scrub them hard, the way you did with white ones, and that meant they lasted longer. But tonight she had knee-high white socks and a new dress. Most of the kids had new shoes, too, but the child hadn't had to get new ones. Dad just shined and shined on her Sunday school ones and they looked just fine, you could see your face in the gleam on the toes. Some of the kids with new shoes were starting to squirm in them, but the child was past that with hers, they were as comfortable as shoes could be.

She was tired, because it was long past the time she would ordinarily have gone to bed, but she wasn't sleepy. There was too much to watch. Some of the kids were starting to act up, to race around yelping and shoving. The child might have liked to do that, too, but Dad had laid down the law and you didn't get him mad, especially not when he was drinking. Mom was trying to get him to switch to beer but he smiled and told her to shut up, he was a big boy and able to run his own life. So she shut up and smiled and said Oh, I know that, I just thought maybe you'd like a nice cold beer, is all, and then talked about how all the dancing made her thirsty and there was nothing like a cold beer to quench your thirst.

The child found a nice quiet place to sit on the three little stairs going up to the stage-thing. The tall man playing the funny guitar looked over at her and winked. She couldn't help it, she smiled at him because of the wink. His guitar had a big metal plate over the top of it, and it sounded different than the other guitar, it sounded sharper. The winking man smiled and nodded and the child sat watching the band. They had little signals to each other, not the same as when the big kids played softball, but almost the same, little nods of the head, or long hard looks at each other.

The child liked to watch what people did around each other. The Observer, Mom said. Honestly, she said, she must be going to grow up to be a newspaper reporter or something. Just sit for hours and eat things up with her eyes. And, she laughed, you have to be careful what you say, little pitchers have big ears and hers are longer than you would believe possible.

And then Mom was there, and Dad, and they were just checking up on her, was everything all right? If she got sleepy there were places for the kids to lie down in the coat room, all she had to do was just say so and Mom would take her there, sit with her until she fell asleep. Before the child could say she was fine, thank you, a man was there. He was nobody the child knew, he looked like a big man, but not muscle big, more like beer-belly big. "Who's this, then?" he laughed, and Mom looked at Dad. "That's our daughter," Dad answered, and the man stuck out his hand, same as if she was a grown-up. "How do you do," he said. The child did what she had been told to do. She stood up and reached out to shake the man's hand.

Something zizzled her hand and all the way up her arm. She yelped and jerked her arm away, and the man laughed and laughed and laughed, and turned his hand palm side up to show the little buzzer-thing. "Gotcha!" he roared, still laughing.

She did not want to cry. She absolutely did not want to cry. The man with the guitar with the tin top stopped playing and glared at the beer-bellied man. Several people said Tsk tsk and What a shame and It's a dirty trick to play on a wee girl. "Shake again!" The man stuck his hand out but the child wouldn't shake hands. Then he touched her bare arm, and she jumped again, yelped, and could not stop the tears. And that's when Dad punched the beer-bellied man, *whap* on the jaw.

The images became fractured, bits and snatches of things. Mom in the coat room with her, rocking her, but she couldn't go to sleep. She wasn't crying any more, she had actually hardly cried at all, and her stomach felt funny, but not from too much cream puffs, from the touch on the arm. Then the child was back on the steps and the man with the guitar with the shiny top was playing and singing, and looking right at her, and he winked again. She felt better after that, he knew it wasn't her fault. In the car going home, Grandmother was saying something angry about fighting at your own brother's wedding, shame on you, and Dad was being cheeky to his mother, saying Any time some drunk pulls a thing like that on one of my kids I'll uncork the old short-swifty. At your own brother's wedding, Grandmother repeated. At my own if it happened there, Dad snapped, or at yours, Madam, if you ever decide to get married. They all shut up. The child felt it was all her fault, she should have just laughed when the man buzzed her arm, after all, it hadn't really hurt, it just surprised her. Well, it *had* hurt, but not enough to kick off all this trouble.

She was asleep when they got home, and half-wakened as he lifted her from the back seat and carried her into the little shingle-sided house with fruit trees in front and in back. The clamshells on the driveway crunched under Dad's feet and she could see the moon looking like Grandpa's little grass-cutting sickle. Frogs were singing in the slough, everything from big gronkers to little squeaky tree frogs, *bor'k bor'k bor'k.* Dad smelled of cigarettes and aftershave, of whiskey and something else she couldn't identify, and he hummed as he walked to the house.

Mom helped the child off with her shoes, her coat and her dress, then covered her up to sleep in her socks, petticoat and underwear. The pillow felt soft under her cheek and her eyes felt heavier than her legs, she drifted cozily, but could not fall into the warm and welcoming dark. Some part of her was still awake enough to hear the sound of their voices as they got ready for bed. Time shifted and twisted on itself, the spaces between words seemed longer than they could have been, and then there was a crash, louder than if a chair got thrown against the wall, and footsteps, not running, more like shuffling, and screaming No, don't, dear god what have I done this time, stop it, for god's sake don't, not again, you promised, and slapping sounds, and worse, heavy *whump* sounds, each one followed by the dull thump as Mom hit the wall, and the child was out of bed and running, screeching No Daddy, no Daddy, no, and it was as if she had only taken two or three steps, she remembered running from her room but didn't remember running down the hallway, but there was their door and she opened it, No Daddy, no Daddy no, and ran into the room. Mom was in the corner, against the wall, her nose bleeding, her lip bleeding, wearing only her slip and underwear, the front of the slip spotted with blood from her face, and he was in his suit pants, no shoes, no socks, no shirt, no Daddy no and then he half turned and everything went bright orange, then red, and finally black, black, black and as the black closed she heard Mom yell Oh damn you to hell look what you've done this time.

The mental movie jump-cut to Grandmother's kitchen, Mom and the child, and they had been there quite some time. Been there more than minutes or hours, been there days and maybe lots of days. Mom and Grandmother were canning fruit, the kitchen was steamy, there were probably twenty or thirty bright clean bottles waiting and twice that many already filled and sealed, standing on the counter side-by-each, lovely colours catching the late afternoon sun.

The child got off her chair and went to the bathroom. In the mirror there she looked at her face and knew it hadn't been weeks or even lots of days, because the swelling was still there, and the big bruise still there, her top lip looked like an inner tube, her nose like a big purple plum and both her eyes were black down past her cheekbones. When she sucked, her front teeth felt loose. Not loose enough to fall out, but loose. Every time she blinked her eyes they hurt, and her whole face ached. A voice in her head, a voice she didn't recognize, said Boy you sure look ugly. She might have argued but the proof was in the mirror, staring back at her. No sense arguing with what is obvious. Boy, you sure look ugly.

6

Gus brought Cindy and her kids to Isa and Carol, to visit for three days. He was working, he said, on the outline of his novel, had pretty much decided on his characters and their names. He showed Isa a chart he had made, and he explained how the marked-in vertical bars showed the chapters and the coloured horizontal ones showed the development of the several subplots. Isa had never drawn a diagram in order to write and wasn't the least bit sure what purpose one would serve, but she said nothing. She didn't want to discourage Gus, who could be very touchy. He had put on some weight, had his hair cut and styled and was talking about buying a secondhand car. "First we're going to get a bigger place," he said easily, "so we'll need some extra furniture. After that, I think I'll look for a small station wagon, or maybe a hatchback." He swooped up Donny, pulled up the kid's tee shirt, then did a horse laugh on his belly. "Maybe just get half a car, the half with the engine and front seat, and we'll put these kids on skateboards, drag 'em behind us with a rope. Then, if someone I know doesn't behave, just untie the knot and let 'im drift," and he blew another horse laugh while the kid howled with laughter and kicked his legs.

Any hesitations Isa had about Cindy, and Isa had a host of them, were overshadowed by the fun she had with the kids. She and Carol took them to the beach, to the river, to the park. Gus seemed easy and happy and Cindy seemed just about ready to jump out of her skin the entire time. The kids helped set the table, helped make salads, helped gather eggs and stood, round-eyed and frightened, when they saw the horses and cows.

"They're some big," Darelle quavered, her eyes moistening.

"Of course they're big," Carol smiled, "they're supposed to be big. They wouldn't be much use if they were small enough to fit in your pocket. Unless, of course, you wanted to put them on your key chain."

Darelle looked at Carol and the incipient tears vanished.

"They'd poop in your pocket," she said gravely.

"Wouldn't that be yucky!" Carol took Darelle's hand and looked at it as if examining it. "Put your hand in your pocket to get your chewing gum and pull out a horse bun."

"Bun? Horse *bun?*" and the kid was laughing. "We could have a bake shop. Horse buns and cow pies."

Both Carol and Isa noticed right away that Cindy wasn't one to jump up off her chair to pitch in and help. Maybe she had been raised to believe she was so gorgeous she was mainly a decoration, and all she had to do was sit and smile. Maybe if there was some real life in the smile . . . but sometimes it seemed as if it had been drawn on with indelible marker pen, and just sat there on her face without ever being reflected in her eyes. Isa tried to tell herself it was just an advanced case of Motheritis, and that probably she'd be finding fault no matter who it was her kid took up with. Later, when she and Gus were alone in the orchard, she came right out and asked him whether he and Cindy were planning to get married. He walked quietly for a few moments, then shook his head.

"I've thought about it, but I don't think I'm ready," he told her. "I have a bit of trouble with relationships, I don't seem ready, or I can't relax. Oh, I'm okay when it's like it is now, no strings attached, here for a good time but not necessarily a long time. But as soon as I start thinking about happily ever after, I just sort of shut down. And, well, I guess it's no secret that Cindy has had a hard time finding her way though interpersonal stuff too."

"I know she was either married or involved before, the kids are proof of that."

"Yeah, they are for sure. They've got different dads, did you know that?"

"No. I don't think I did. Does it matter, though? I mean, for all the time it takes to get pregnant . . . it doesn't mean there was a full-time relationship."

"No, except she was trying for exactly that. She's been . . . involved . . . with quite a few guys, and she says each time she thought it was what they call the Real Thing. And I think I'd rather not get tied down until I have more of an idea what it is I'm signing on for. Maybe the old-fashioned extended courtship is a real good idea. When people were 'intended' for years and years."

Cindy seemed to think they were already married, every way but officially. "Darelle, go find your dad and ask him if he's got a cigarette, I've run out." "Donny, ask Daddy if . . ." It was when she started referring to Isa and Carol as Grandma that Isa could feel the noose being slipped over her head and around her neck. "See if Grandma wants a cup of tea, will you, Darelle? Donny, you be a good boy and put some water in the kettle."

"Which grandma?" Darelle asked.

"Either of them. Both of them," and Cindy laughed softly.

"Oh, you don't have to call me Grandma," Carol said quickly, "You can just call me Carol, that way there won't be any mix-ups."

"And I'm Isa," said Isa, but nobody paid any attention. She was Grandma.

She drove them to the bus depot feeling as if the car was jammed, and when they were finally in the bus, waiting for it to leave, the kids kneeling on seats, their noses pressed against the windows, waving and grinning and throwing kisses, Isa felt pounds lighter. She got into the car thanking whoever is in charge of good luck that Carol was at work, because she would finally have some time to herself. No need to make conversation or listen while someone else did.

She drove to the beach, parked well above tide line and walked down the slope, past the enormous tree which would have been the ideal place to sit, except that the ground was pocked with little pencil-sized holes, with long-bodied wasps or hornets crawling in and out. Isa had looked in every bug and insect book and these creatures weren't mud-daubers or yellowjackets or anything else in the books. Whatever they were, they stung with no excuse at all and the stings were agonizing. Isa knew the municipal guys had come at least twice covered with protective gear and soaked the area with some spray that killed everything, but after a brief pause, the white-striped black horrors had reappeared. Were they some kind of mutant wasp, created by the dioxins, furans and who-knew-what-elses spewed into the air and water by the local pulp mill?

The place was undeniably gorgeous—no oil-covered rocks, no stained sand, no festering flotsam or jetsam, no gasoline rainbows in the tidal pools—but the wasps weren't the only odd thing Isa had noticed. The cancer rate in town seemed off the map, and so did birth defects. You weren't supposed to eat the shellfish, and local salmon had been found to have tumours. What Greenpeace had to say was about enough to make a person wake up in the middle of the night with cold sweats.

Isa often wondered what it was like for the guys who worked at the mill when they heard evidence about the risk to their health, to their children's lives. The frying pan or the fire, damned if you do or don't, better poached or roasted? And really, when you came to the beach, sat on a log and stared out at the chuck and the islands, what truly clean job could you think of? Everyone knows half a dozen stories about sick people who got sicker after being cared for by medical professionals. Teachers have to follow a government-dictated curriculum but half the kids in grade eleven can't fill out a job application. People who work in supermarkets sell over-packaged poisonous junk, and the ones who traffic in so-called health food seem not to know that every aquifer on the continent is contaminated with fertilizers, insecticides and pesticides. People who build cars and highways and who work in gas stations help the rest of us kill ourselves with car pollution, and nobody has a good word to say about journalists. So who has a clean job?

She knew she and Carol would never make a living from farming if they had to depend on what they made from their hay and their calves. The only ones making it were large-scale farmers with crowds of animals—and they were just barely getting by. They had to use steroids and growth hormones and enough antibiotics to make your head spin, and they had to treat their animals horribly just to compete.

Isa laughed then. She sat on the log and just let 'er rip, mocking herself along with everyone else. She drove home and parked the car, reminding herself to say thank you to Carol for taking the pick-up to work instead. Little things like that could touch Isa deeply, and she still wasn't used to someone being quietly considerate of her. She hadn't even had to ask! Carol had noticed that they would be jammed together like sardines if they went to the bus in the pick-up, why not exchange vehicles, and she had handed over the keys as if they were just keys, rather than thousands of dollars' worth of payments.

Two hours before it was time to start making supper, Isa put on her lace-front boots and walked the fence line, checking the posts, adding staples, and pulling long grass away from the electric wire that kept the cows from simply putting their heads down and pushing fence wire, posts and the whole shittin' show flat on the ground.

The dogs sniffed and prowled, tails wagging, nuzzling at her hand, pressing against her leg. The cows drifted over and grazed nearby, following. She wondered if they were watching to make sure she didn't overlook anything. It was hard to tell how smart cows were or weren't. Just when you were convinced they were the dumbest things on four feet, one of them would do something that left you standing, jaw ajar.

Satisfied that the fence would hold and the cows wouldn't get out and trample the neighbours' lawns and gardens, Isa put away the fencing tools, went in the back door, and sat on the chair near the boot rack. She had to grab the leg of her jeans and haul her leg up so her ankle sat on her other knee, and then untie her laces. Damn back. Damn disintegrated joints. She didn't mind getting older, it was the fear of getting useless kept her awake some nights—when the ghosts of the past weren't keeping her awake first.

Just before Christmas, Gus phoned and said the kids wanted to come for the holidays. Isa had some real doubts that it had been the kids' idea, but whomsoever's idea it was, it suddenly sounded very good to her.

"Are you and Cindy coming, too?" she asked, her voice carefully neutral.

"Nah, we'll just put 'em on the bus and tell 'em to stay sat or else," he laughed.

"Aren't they a bit young for that?"

"Nah, Darelle is Miss Common Sense herself. They'll be fine."

Isa didn't figure Darelle for much common sense, and said so to Carol, who shrugged and shook her head slightly. "Maybe compared to the rest of them she is," she suggested. "Whose bright idea was this? Why don't we go down, pick them up, and head back with them the same day. Just whip in, grab 'em, blurt out the sorry, no, really, not even one cup of tea, we've got to hit the road or we'll miss our ferry connection and—*zip*—we're out again. If the kids get tired or we get tired, well, the highway is lined with motels from Gibsons to Madeira Park."

It worked. It worked so slick a person could have been excused for starting to believe in divine intervention. The kids were waiting, quiet but so eager, their packs by the door. Carol smiled widely, said a brief Hi, how are you to the adults, and lifted the packs from the floor. "Will you help me with these?" she asked, and both kids were up, opening the door, holding it open, fuss fuss fuss.

"Sure you don't have time for a cup of tea?" Gus seemed disappointed.

"I wish we did," Isa fudged, "but the way they have the ferries scheduled, if we miss the one we're trying for there'll be a long wait at Earl's Cove."

"I thought they went every couple of hours." Cindy's voice was tight and mistrustful.

"Oh, they do; from here to Gibsons," Isa explained, smiling. "But after Gibsons we have an hour's drive to the next one and that's where everything gets bizarre. Oh, here, I almost forgot, I picked up an extra schedule for you, just in case you change your mind and decide to bring in the New Year on the farm."

Cindy looked at the card before tacking it to the wall above the phone, and Isa knew she was checking on what Isa had told her about the schedule. Isa also knew that she would be able to skate around the truth with this woman, but not too far from it.

Gus hugged Isa. "We put a couple of their Xmas presents in their packs. Nothing noisy, though."

"Did you take pictures of them with the tree and all?"

"Yeah, I'll send you copies when they're developed."

The kids sat quietly in the car, wide-eyed, caught somewhere between glee and uncertainty.

"Will we stop for pees?" Donny asked, his voice not quite shaking.

"Oh, you bet we will," Carol said, as she drove easily through the city traffic. "We'll stop for pees and we'll stop for hamburgers and we'll stop for good looks at things. We might stop so many times it'll take us six years to get there. We might stop for so many things we forget where we're going."

"Did Santa come to your place?"

"Santa left a note on our tree. Wait until you see it. The tree, I mean, not the note. I bet you haven't seen such an eensy-teensy itty-bitty tree before in your life."

"Does it gots lights?"

"It hasn't got lights. There's no room for lights. Our tree isn't even really a tree. You'll see."

"What did the note say?" Darelle demanded.

"The note said 'What kind of a joke of a tree is this? Those kids will make you get a real one'."

"Did Santa leave you a present?"

"Just a note."

Isa turned to smile at them in the back seat. "And the note also said, 'Nothing for you until you have a real tree'."

"Las' year we went to our auntie's place and had a tree and everything but this year we didn't go because my mom hates my auntie's guts," Donny announced. Darelle jabbed Donny in the ribs with her elbow. Donny glared. Darelle frowned. Donny slumped back and didn't say a word for over half an hour.

On the ferry they had hamburgers and yogurt. They wanted to go out on the promenade deck so Isa took them. But they didn't stay long; the wind was cold and their jackets were not new. In fact, Donny's jacket was about ready for the dog's bed.

"It won't be long now," Isa said. "And when we get home you'll have lots to do. Eggs to gather and cows to feed and if it snows, which it looks like it's going to try to do, we can rig up a slider for you tomorrow."

"What's a slider?"

"It's a thing that isn't a sled but works like one."

The kids took one look at the decorated spider plant and burst out laughing.

"No wonder he left you a note!" Darelle giggled, "You're lucky he even came."

"That's what Carol said, too. Well, maybe tomorrow you can show us how to do it properly."

"You know how. Gus said when he was a kid you had a tree one time that touched the ceiling."

"That's true, we did. And we had to tie it to the back of the big chair so it wouldn't fall over on us. We don't want one that big again."

"Gus said you always have turkey," Donny said hopefully. "Will you have turkey?"

"Of course. If you want it."

"We didn't get no turkey yet. Mom said if we were going to be up here the lef'overs would just go to waste so we only had some hot wings."

"They were good!" Donny blurted. "But not turkey."

"You just wait until you see the turkey," Carol laughed. She headed for the freezer. "It isn't a great big huge one because, well, your mom was right about leftovers. But we got a *fat* one. Small and fat. Yum yum."

They stared at the frozen butterball, then looked at each other and grinned.

"We unwrap it, cover it with a tea towel and sit it here on the drainboard to thaw overnight. Then, tomorrow morning, we stuff it. And you guys have to help, okay? And when it's stuffed, we put it in the oven to cook and . . . see about that tree we're supposed to rig up."

The kids were borderline exhausted after the trip, but trudged to the barn to help with the chores. They brushed the mare's flanks until even the thick winter fur gleamed and glistened. They weren't nearly as afraid of the animals as they had been on their last visit.

When the chores were done there was spaghetti with Paul Newman's sauce, and then it was bathtime. Donny almost fell asleep in the tub, and Isa had to towel him dry so he wouldn't fall into bed soaking wet. Darelle lasted maybe ten minutes longer, and then was asleep, her face finally relaxed.

The next morning they were up at eight, and so excited their adrenalin kicked the day into overdrive. Everything had to happen at once, and their voices got increasingly shrill.

Over at the next farm the kids were in Junior Forest Wardens and had been selling trees as a fund-raiser. Luckily they had a few left over; the smaller ones, the scrawny or tatty ones with gaps in the branches. "Good," Carol pretended to sigh with relief, "it will fit. I was afraid they wouldn't have one we could tuck in the corner."

"Do you got dec'rations?"

"We have some. And we're going to make more."

"How?"

They cut the cups out of egg cartons, crumpled up aluminum foil, then smoothed it out and fit pieces over the little cups. They painted other cups, they strung cranberries on a thread, they strung popcorn, and cut stars out of styrofoam cups. While Carol played overseer on the assembly line, Isa whipped into town to look for strings of lights. She thought she'd have hell's own time, but the hardware store had tables of surplus decorations, and at less than half price. Buoyed by her luck, she bought some glittery stars and plenty of icicles and tinsel. She also took half an hour to hit the kids' clothing aisles where the prices were about half what they had been before the great day. When she got home with the booty, Carol looked so relieved Isa knew she had been starting to feel desperate.

"Oh, good on you!" she breathed.

"Aussie rules shopping," Isa laughed. "No helmets, no penalties for using elbows. Here, kids, have a ball," and she turned them loose with the decorations while she and Carol went into the bedroom, closed the door, hurriedly took off price tags, wrapped presents and, finally, blessedly, carried them out to stuff them under the tree. The kids stared.

Then it was into the kitchen, where Carol already had the turkey stuffed and in the oven, and before long the rich scent of roasting butterball was joined by the smell of fresh-baked cookies and mince pies.

"We'll get the spuds and veggies on to cook, and then . . . it's open-the-presents time."

"I'll peel," Darelle offered quietly. She looked at Isa, then at Carol, and finally at Donny, who was slowly and very carefully putting presents under the tree, his face glowing with excitement. "And thank you. He doesn't really believe in Santa Claus. Not *really*, but . . ."

"Oh, I think that's pretty normal," Isa lied. "I don't *really* believe any more, myself, but . . . you never know."

The clothes fit and the toys were an absolute hit. Donny sat on the sofa, togged out in new stuff from the skin out, putting on and taking off his Garfield slippers. It seemed to Isa his body language had changed, he was suddenly more confident, but maybe she just imagined that.

She had forgotten how much food a couple of kids can put away at Christmas dinner. The butterball wasn't going to drown them in leftovers after all, thank heaven. They ate until she half expected them to open down the midline, and then, when they finally announced they were stuffed and couldn't eat any more, they dove into the dessert.

Darelle helped clear the table, Donny stood on a chair and washed dishes and Carol dried and put them away. Isa scraped the scraps into the dog dishes, poured gravy on the dog food, and mixed the mess together before putting it down for the mutts. Then she headed out to the barn to do chores, and when she came back in, the kitchen was clean and tidy and the kids were in the living room playing with their new toys and watching television at the same time.

By the time the kids were in bed, wearing their new pyjamas and stuffed with food, Isa was closer to exhaustion than she'd been in years.

"You okay?" Carol asked quietly.

"I would be if I wasn't so depressed."

"Right. And a jolly ho ho ho to you, too."

They cuddled together on the sofa, Isa with her head on Carol's shoulder, and neither of them was the least bit surprised when, without even looking at each other they both said, at exactly the same time, in exactly the same soft and almost mourning tone, "Ah, bah humbug!"

Snow started to drift from the low-hanging clouds the day before New Year's Eve. And they knew they were in for a good one because the flakes were small and dry, and they stuck to the ground. By mid-afternoon the white covering was ankle-deep. By the time evening barn chores were done there was enough on the long downhill slope of the driveway that the plastic garbage can lid could slide quickly and easily. When the kids finally went to bed, the utility room smelled of damp wool and the clothes-drying rack was covered with wet socks, damp jeans and shirts. Sodden new jackets hung on clothes hangers, dripping onto newspapers on the floor.

Isa went outside for her last check of things, so tired she felt as if she could lean against the holly tree and sleep upright. The flakes falling now were bigger. They hissed as they fell to the ground, and she imagined a light *plop* when they landed. The dogs hadn't yet managed to stain the snow yellow, there were no muddy bits of cow manure-enriched goo, and in the light from the windows the white on the lawn fulfilled every promise of every postcard.

The movie screen on Isa's inner eyes began to run. She tried to turn it off, tried to have the film declared unfit for viewing, tried to call in the censors, tried to send it back to the editing room to be recut, but it was too late. All that takes time, and what might have taken hours in real time became but a few seconds of memory, with an effect that would last for weeks.

Snow falling then, too, and she wakened in a room made bright by clear silver moonlight. Strange noises, but not so strange she couldn't recognize them. And the grunting, the sucked in breath telling of pain, of shock, of fear. She didn't want to get out of bed, she wanted to crawl under her blankets, stuff her fingers in her ears, squeeze her eyes shut until she couldn't see things she knew were happening, and instead her feet were on the cold linoleum floor and she was running across her room. When she opened her bedroom door the cold hit her like a slap in the face, and at the end of the hallway the door to the outside was gaping open, flakes of snow coming inside, melting on the door lintel, on the shoe-wiping rug.

Nobody in the house, the noise on the porch, more grunting, more gasping, loud hollow thwacking sounds, then *thump-thump* and she knew someone oh please god not Momma was going down the fourteen steps to the ground and going the hard, hurting way

please, not my Momma

"Oh god, Fred, stop," and it was Momma's voice, but not a hurt Momma.

The snow on the porch burned her bare feet, and she knew she should go get her coat, get her lined boots, but she couldn't turn away, she could only stand there, shivering, feeling her eyes so wide she was afraid the eyeballs would fall out, feeling her face going stiff, stiff, stiffer. She wanted to pee, but not in her Christmas pyjamas. She pressed her thighs together, sucked in her belly, holding the pee inside, waiting for the urge-need-demand to stop.

Momma and another lady, a blonde lady, someone the child didn't know or even recognize, were at the bottom of the stairs, clutching each other's hands, the blonde woman weeping. And Dad and another man fighting, vicious punches, swift kicks. Droplets of blood on the snow and blood smeared on their faces, some of it coming from Dad's nose, most of it coming from the eyebrows and mouth of the man she didn't know.

"Stop! *Stop!*" the blonde woman screamed, and then she was running, running between the two men, neither of whom wanted to hit her. They stepped back, breathing as hard as if they'd been running for miles, and then Momma was there, her arms around Dad, not so much holding him back as just holding him, her face against his chest, her tears wetter on his shirt than the falling and melting snow.

And then Dad was looking at Isa and he shook his head, but not as if he was denying anything, more as if he couldn't believe what he was seeing. He put his big bloodstained hands on Momma's arms and pushed her away, not very gently. "Take your daughter back into the house where it's warm," he said. "Go on, woman."

"Please, no more—"

"Fine then, but take the child inside, she's going to catch her death of cold out here."

"Please . . ." and Momma was sobbing.

"For the love of Christ eternal," he roared, "will you do what I said? Get the girl inside or there'll be more than him nursing a thick lip. I said fine then, didn't I?"

Isa turned and went into the house, she didn't want to be the reason why the devil-light in his eyes flickered, didn't want to be why Momma fetched herself a thick lip.

She closed the door and padded to the big sawdust burner, gave the jigger thing a shake to knock down the ash, opened the draft to get the sawdust burning hotter, and only then noticed her feet were almost the colour of grape juice, with white blotches on the top. Momma came in, rushed to her, hugged her tight, stroking her hair.

"I'm fine," Isa-child said clearly. "I'm okay."

"Here, open the oven door, I'll put a folded towel on it so you don't get burned, then you put your feet here and get yourself warmed up. Oh baby, why did you go out in the snow like that?"

"I thought he was trying to kill you again." The child's voice was distant and matter-of-fact.

"You know your Dad would never hurt me," said Momma, who always told Isa god wanted us to tell the truth all the time, no matter what; said Momma who always told Isa telling lies was a sin; said Momma who until then had feet of gold and turned them to something less than clay. She smiled, but her face looked more like she was getting ready to scream. "Your dad loves us both very very much."

Sound of a car engine, revving, then fading. The front door opened and a blast of cold entered the house first, then her dad, smeared blood congealing on his face.

He moved wordlessly to the kitchen sink, ran water and splashed it on his face, then held his right hand under the flow. His knuckles were swollen, and one of them was cut. He looked closely at the cut, then laughed, a hard, harsh, triumphant sound. He used the strong fingers of his left hand to squeeze, as if the cut were a pimple or a festering sliver. Something came out of the cut and he laughed again, got a small jelly glass from the cupboard and dropped something into it—*clink*. He held the glass out for Isa to see. "Stupid bugger left his front tooth in m'hand," he laughed. "And look, see there? It was his gold-mended one!"

Fresh blood ran from the knuckle, but he didn't care. He just poured some peroxide on it, wrapped his clean hanky around his hand and went to the icebox for a fresh beer.

"Why were you fighting?" Isa asked.

"Never mind now, dear, it's bedtime," Momma said hastily.

"He was talking when he should have been listening," Dad grinned. "And what he was saying was disrespectful to this house and the woman in it."

"Oh please, no, he didn't mean it the way you took it," Momma blurted. Would she never learn when to shut up? "It was a joke, is all."

His eyes changed to chips of blue ice. "And was I laughing? And if you were laughing, woman, tell me why!"

"No, no, I wasn't laughing."

As the cold left Isa's feet and moved to the pit of her stomach, she promised herself that she would never—*never*, not in her whole life—end up like Momma. She loved Momma, loved her so much it sometimes left her shaking, but she also knew which side her bread was buttered on, and maybe, just maybe . . .

"He won't be in a hurry to do it again," she said, and made herself laugh as if proud. "He's going to look funny with eyebrows sticking out like cow horns."

"Bloody right!" and Dad was laughing, lifting her from the chair, holding her with one arm and kissing her cheek. "Here," he held the beer bottle to her mouth, "have a sip. And then you can't say I never gave you anything, right?"

When she went outside the next morning, the blood was still there on the trampled snow. There was more blood on the porch. And in the middle of it she could see the mark of her own little foot, where she had stepped in it and not even noticed. You'd think a person would know when she was walking on someone else's blood.

Isa never forgot what she had learned that night, even if she couldn't articulate it until later. There are only two kinds of people, the kind who get walked on and the kind who don't. Young as she was, she decided she wouldn't be the kind who got walked on, and if anybody tried, she was fully prepared to go for the throat.

7

The large, soft leaves filtered the sunlight, and the scent of salmonberry was rich and comforting. Where the sun hit the berries they seemed almost translucent, especially the dark-red-almost-black ones. Funny how salmonberries came in so many colours on the same bush, and most of them ripe. How did that happen, anyway? Whether light orange, dark orange, red or almost black, if they were soft, they were ripe. And they all tasted the same. How would a thing like that happen?

Isa lay on the ground in the little hole she'd made in the thicket. She'd made a hidey-tunnel, too. But not on the path side. Anybody would be able to see it on the path side. You had to go around the thicket, over a log, and come in the back, and that's where the little hidey-tunnel was.

To her right, the waterfall tumbled down the rocks. Not wide, but high, and the water white with foam before it leaped out from the stream bed and fell down to the almost-round pool at the bottom. The pool was deep and cold, with rocks around it and facing it, except on this side where the trees and the salmonberry thicket pressed close. A stream ran from the pool, diagonally toward the left, and the path stopped at the edge of the water, but there were boulders you could jump to and make your way across the stream to the rocks without getting your feet wet.

The rocks were warm, she knew, and by afternoon they would feel hot to the touch. But she probably wouldn't go to them, not today.

There was no place to go to from the rocks, the bluff slanted up and the tangle of windfall and blowdown was thick, the logs too high to just jump over, and he'd catch up to her before she could scramble away from him.

Most of the time she was safe here. Most of the time she was just fine here. But today he was mad, and he would be looking for her. So best to just lie here, and listen to the deep, steady drone of the bumbly-bees in the berry blossoms. And wasn't that something, that you could find blossoms, and unripe berries, ripe berries and overripe ones, all colours, all at the same time.

The buzzing of the bumblers grew louder, moved from her ears to inside her head. The sun through the leaves was warm, the dry yellow grass beneath her smelled of last year, and the spots on the back of the red ladybug began to grow, to throb. She yawned, then dry-sobbed, and the sound of the bees grew distant.

When she wakened, someone was in the water of the pool at the foot of the falls. An old woman, her white hair drawn back in a loose bun, her body naked. The woman's body was thick at the waist, her breasts drooped. Isa stared, but not at the woman's nakedness. It was what the woman was doing.

She was singing. Or chanting, or something. Then the white head disappeared under the water, and when it reappeared the old woman was facing a different direction.

Isa watched, fascinated.

And then the crone was walking from the pool. Just walking, not at all shy about being naked. She walked directly to the thicket where Isa crouched, and it was as if the salmonberry bushes parted to let her through. Wordless, she took Isa by the arm.

Isa couldn't have said no if someone had paid her to do it. And she couldn't make herself pull away. She just went with her arm and never afterward remembered her feet touching the ground. And yet the old woman was gentle.

Isa stood quietly, the sound of the bumbly-bees all around, as the old woman removed the threadbare tee shirt, the faded jeans, the tired underpants. She traced her finger, thick-knuckled with arthritis, over the welts and belt tracings. She made a sound in her throat and jerked her head disapprovingly. But not at her, Isa knew.

Now she was led into the pool. The water was so cold it burned her, especially on her inner thighs and across the small of her back where the wide leather belt had landed so many times. The old woman started her singing-thing again, then placed her hand over Isa's face, pinching her nose shut. Isa felt the woman's other hand on top of her head, and then she was pressed under the surface of the water.

In the water everything was green-tinged. Isa could see sunlight shafting in bars down to the algae-covered rocks. She could see waterbugs, shelled helgermites, and small-bodied bullheads. When she came back up out of the water she was facing away from the rocks. The old woman was doing her singing-thing, then down they both went again, back under the water.

Four times. And when they surfaced for the last time, they were facing the sun-warm rocks once again.

Isa had no memory of leaving the pool. She stood on the rocks, the soles of her feet warm, her skin goosebumped, as the old woman rubbed her with fern leaves, rubbed her with salmonberry leaves. Her touch on the bruises was soft, so soft Isa's eyes filled with tears, which dribbled down her face and fell onto the summer-hot granite beneath her scratched and calloused feet. The tears dried as soon as they landed.

And then, worse luck, she was home again, sitting at the kitchen table, listening to him give her the warnings. Any more bullshit from you, young bitch, and I'll give you something you won't be able to ignore, is that understood.

Yes, sir.

Take a bloody telling, you hear me.

Yes, sir.

And she didn't know what she had done to kick it off. She had no idea why he was so mad.

Just take a bloody telling or you'll wish you had, is that clear?

Yes, sir.

All she knew for sure was that it wasn't possible to walk softly enough, talk pleasantly enough or obey humbly enough to keep the wide leather belt from stinging, burning, bruising, hurting. She had tried to ally herself with the one with power and, like a dowser's stick, it had turned in her hands, turned and pointed toward her, bringing the fury down on her head.

She went to the waterfall and pool nearly every day after school, looking for the old woman. It wasn't until summer holidays, when she could get there early early in the morning, almost before anyone else in the world was awake, that she saw her again. And yet, in their first look, the bond was re-established. It was as if Isa had known that old woman since before she was born.

Without so much as one word spoken, Isa jumped from boulder to boulder, then, on the big rock, she stripped off her clothes silently and dove into the cold green pool, coming up beside the old woman, standing beside her, facing east. Isa didn't speak, she didn't know the words, recognized only the feeling. What the old woman did, Isa did. When the old woman ducked under the water, so did Isa.

Afterward, they rubbed their bodies with bracken fern, with cedar, with salmonberry leaves, drying themselves, purifying themselves, scenting their bodies so that for the rest of that day her own nose reminded her of the waterfall, the pool, the old woman, and the deep sense of peace.

The sutures in Dick's eyebrow were thinner than the thread Tammy used to sew buttons back on shirts and blouses, and the same funny blue as the gut leaders on fishing line. His eye was swollen but not black or blue, more like the colour of liver, and it looked sore.

Everyone knew Tammy was the one had done it, but nobody said so, especially not Dick. Nobody asked him what had happened, nobody even really looked at his eye or at the puffy lip. And Dick didn't seem to want to make any fuss about it either, he just went to work, same as always.

Tammy hissed when she got a good look at her car in the morning light. The driver's side fender was shoved back and the headlight was smashed. But she didn't say anything. She fed Sandra, gave her a fast bath, stuffed her into her clothes and told Phoebe and Linda to keep an eye on her. Then she got herself ready and left in the car. She got back in time to start supper, and the car had a different fender, not new and not the same colour as the rest of the car, but a good one. The headlight was fixed, too.

Who knew? Who even cared, really. This kind of thing happened every cheque week. Some weeks were just more—what, active?—than others?

Cindy showed up without Gus, but with Darelle and Donny in tow. When Dick got home from work they all had supper together, pork chops with applesauce, mashed potatoes with gravy, frozen French-cut beans and a big grated carrot-and-apple salad with mayonnaise dressing. They talked about TV shows they had seen, they talked about Barb phoning everybody in the middle of the week and talking for fifteen minutes, as if she was Missus ArBee and didn't have to worry about the phone bill. And then, while the girls did the dishes, Tammy bathed Sandra, put her in her nighttime diaper and pyjamas, and put her to bed with a bottle of milk. Sandra grizzled and whined a bit, but she was doing less and less of that since they'd all decided to ignore it.

Dick changed his clothes and Tammy got herself all tarted up and off they went, the Three Musketeers. When they came back, they brought probably a dozen others with them. Sandra was the only kid who didn't wake up. Once she had dropped off, she could sleep through an invasion of the brain dead.

Which was pretty well what was going on by three-thirty in the morning. The kids, who knew better than to sit around in pyjamas when the place was full of drinkers, had all put on their clothes and were sitting together on the sofa watching late late late late night movies and eating chips, cheezies and party mix from big bags. The TV sound fought with the noise from the stereo and the uproar from the houseful of drunks. You couldn't actually tell what the movie was about.

Cindy was real drunk, and like every other time she'd been pie-eyed, she had a bad case of the gab'n'gossips. She'd sit down next to someone and start talking, and after maybe fifteen minutes that person would have to go to the bathroom or something and would drift off and not come back, so Cindy would go sit and chew the ear of someone else. Eventually that person would need to go to the can too, and Cindy would move on again. Well, no wonder people needed to go to the bathroom. You couldn't tell what Cindy was yapping on about, the way she sort of jumped from subject to subject.

And kept bringing her mother into it too. Her mother had been dead for probably ten years, but give Cindy a few beer and it was I am the resurrection and the life all over again.

The noise got louder, Cindy got more chippy, and the next thing the kids knew they were all being told to put on their coats and come with her. "This is no damn place for kids," she slurred. "Not my kids, not anybody's kids."

"You go near that baby and I'll punch out your lights," Tammy laughed. "Let sleeping babies lie, you know what they say."

"I'm not going anywhere," Phoebe resisted. "It's raining out there for god's sake."

Cindy's hand flashed, and connected with the side of Phoebe's face. "Then stay here and get beat up or raped or something. See if I care. And watch your tongue around me, mung mouth."

They were only five blocks from home when the patrol car went past. Cindy had Donny by the hand, and he was crying. He'd been more asleep than awake when he got taken out into the drizzle, and all he wanted to do was find a bed and crawl into it.

The patrol car came back and stopped right beside them. One of the Mounties got out of the car and came over as the other talked busily into the radio.

"What?" Cindy chipped. "You gonna tell me I was speeding?"

"Easy, lady." The big cop sounded bored.

"Who you callin' easy? What business you got stoppin' me? It's a free country, isn't it?"

"Come on now, get a grip. You calm down and we'll give you a ride home with the kids."

"Take your ride and shove it," and she pushed the cop aside. He shook his head, exasperated, and might have let it go at that but Cindy had to take a swing at him too. When it missed, she fired a kick, and as luck would have it, her shoe connected with his kneecap.

The police station was brightly lit and there were no magazines or comic books or anything, not even a TV. They could hear Cindy yelling and raging in some other part of the building, promising all kinds of retribution and vengeance. Donny was as good as asleep, leaning against Linda, his head resting on her shoulder. Predictably, Darelle was crying. At first Linda gave her tissues from the big box on the counter, but after a while she got tired of it. If Darelle couldn't get her own snot rags she'd have to do without and leak all over her chin.

The lady cop moved the tissue box next to Darelle, and even brought a round wastebasket for the used ones. She was very concerned for a while, talking to Darelle, being nice to her to make her feel better. But the sniffing, snivelling, and snoffling finally got to her, and she walked off to sit at a desk and busy herself with a bunch of papers.

A man in a suit and a woman in nice slacks and a soft sweater arrived. They talked to the cop who'd been kicked, they talked to the lady cop, they signed some papers and gave some of their own to the cops to sign, and then they took Linda, Donny and the still-sniffling Darelle out to a beige-coloured car with writing on the doors.

"This isn't the way home," Linda told them. "We live on the other side of town."

"Yes, but we're taking you somewhere to spend the night."

"Why can't we go home?"

"I think you know why, dear."

Linda knew why. So did Darelle. Knowing pushed Darelle from sniffing and leaking tears right into sobbing and wailing.

"Will you *please* shut up?" Linda snapped. She would have cried herself, but she didn't want to look as sappy as Darelle.

They drove up to a house where the lights were on, and a sleepy-looking woman in nightgown and wrapper met them at the front door. She had fuzzy slippers on her feet, not the flip-flop kind, more like loafers, with crepe soles.

Donny climbed uncomplainingly into the bottom bunk and fell asleep immediately. The lady untied his laces, pulled off his shoes, put a blanket over him and let him sleep in his clothes. She had pyjamas for the girls, but Darelle, sobbing and howling, wouldn't put them on or even take off her clothes. The welfare lady said something to the lady in the fuzzy slippers and they both shrugged. Linda changed in the bathroom, went back to the bedroom, climbed into bed and lay down, yawning.

"How can you?" Darelle said loudly. "How *can* you?"

"Oh shut up, will you?"

"I want my mother!"

"Tough."

Tears weren't enough, sniffing wasn't enough, sobbing wasn't enough, none of it was working, so Darelle started screaming. Linda sat up in bed as if she'd been zapped on the butt by something hot and sharp. The welfare woman came running, the woman in fuzzy slippers came running, and still Darelle sat on the edge of the bed screaming. The welfare woman looked frantic, and the woman in fuzzy slippers just took Darelle by the arm, pulled her from the bed, practically dragged her to the bathroom, put her in the shower and turned the cold tap full open.

Darelle stopped screeching as soon as the blast of cold water hit her in the face. Linda remembered the time her mom had thrown cold water in Darelle's face. This was different and yet, somehow, it was the same. It seemed an awful thing to do, it made Linda feel she ought to protest, but what the hell else could a person do with Darelle when she started in on her blubberguts stuff? Darelle's screaming was as mean in its way as people shoving her in the shower. Linda figured they were both ways of pushing people around.

"Now take off your wet things, dry yourself with a towel, put on your pyjamas, get into bed and be quiet or you'll be right back in here. This has gone far enough."

Linda was asleep before Darelle got into bed, and she didn't wake up until past eleven in the morning. She could hear Donny chattering a mile a minute, in what sounded like the kitchen. Darelle sat up in bed, arms folded across her chest, glaring.

"How long you been awake?" Linda asked. No answer. "You hear me, what I asked?" No answer. "Fine, then. Be like that. And up your nose if you think I give a poop."

Donny and Linda had Rice Krispies with milk and sliced up strawberries. Darelle sat on her chair, glaring and refusing to speak. The fuzzy slippers were gone now, and the woman was wearing jeans and a faded blue shirt that looked like one of Dick's work shirts, only cleaner. She came to the table with a coffee, lit a cigarette and sat watching them for a few minutes.

"My name is Kate." Her voice was deep and sort of cracked when she talked. "You're going to be staying here for a few days. I don't know how long. You can either look on it as a holiday and make the best of it," she looked at Donny and smiled, "or you can go out of your way to have an absolutely miserable time," and she looked at Darelle. Darelle wouldn't look at Kate, she glared at the table until you could almost see daggers in the air, like in the comics.

"Can I phone my mom?" Linda asked, wishing her voice wasn't shaking. "To let her know?"

"Your mother already knows." Kate reached across the table and patted Linda's hand. "But for sure, you can phone her. I'm not your jailer, okay? The phone's not under lock and key and you'll probably feel better once you've spoken to her. And I'm sure she'll feel better, too."

"What about *me?*" Darelle yelled. "What about *me*, eh?"

"Well, I don't really know about you. We can try phoning the police station, to see if—" But Darelle was yowling again, mouth open in an unnaturally round O, and a monotonous *aaaaaaah* coming from her throat. When she ran out of wind she took a deep breath and went back to the *aaaaaah*, and everyone knew Darelle wasn't crying, she was just making noise.

Kate watched for a long few seconds, then got up, took Donny by the hand and made a come-with-us gesture to Linda, who rose eagerly. The three of them left the kitchen and went downstairs to the playroom, where there was a Sega with two paddles. For probably a half hour Kate sat reading a magazine while the *aaaaaah* continued, increasingly monotonous. Finally Kate put down the magazine and went back upstairs.

"You want to wind up back in the shower?" she asked, conversationally.

Darelle stopped the caterwauling and began to cry, really cry, not just snivel or whine or grizzle or screech. "Any more of that," Kate said, her voice hard, "and you'll be in the bedroom in the basement, with the door closed and locked, so the rest of us don't have to put up with your bullshit. I'm sorry things are the way they are for you, but none of us caused your misery, so don't take it out on us."

"Oh, she cries all the time, it don't mean nothin'," Donny said, coming into the kitchen. "Do you got any other toys?"

"I have toys. Boxes of toys. And games," Kate took him by the hand

and started from the kitchen. Linda came in as the other two were going out, got herself a drink of water, then decided she'd go too. She wasn't much interested in being with Darelle, not if all she was going to get to do was watch her sulk.

"You're supposed to phone your mom," Darelle whined.

"I'll phone her later."

"But I want to talk to her too."

"Then phone, dummy, you know the number."

Linda waited until Darelle was in the bedroom, sitting on the bed with all the pillows behind her, sulking and letting tears leak down her face.

"So what the hell happened?" Tammy asked, her voice sharp and thin with worry.

"Oh, Auntie Cindy mouthed off at a cop. Then she tried to hit him. And then she kicked him in the knee."

"So what are they going to do?"

"I don't know."

"Where are you? Did they say when you could come home?"

"I don't know where we are. There's a number on the phone dial here, but I don't know the street or anything. Other side of town, though. Donny's okay, but Darelle's being a pill, screeching and all that."

"Well, listen, I don't know what I can do on the weekend. Those damn suits only work Monday to Friday. But I'll try phoning, and anyway I'll be on their doorstep when they show up for work on Monday morning. You be good, you hear? You mind your manners, you be real polite, and if she says do the dishes, no back talk, just up and do the buggers, okay?"

"Will you phone me? I'm kinda scared."

"Don't be, okay? I mean, of course you're scared, but, like, well, don't get too into it, know what I mean? Nobody's gonna bite your head off, and you didn't do nothin' wrong so you're not in any trouble. You just be as good as we both know you can be, and I'll spring you as fast as I can." Tammy made it sound like a big joke. "I'll maybe bake you a cake with a hacksaw in the middle and toss it to you from a fast-moving car."

"Your cakes!" Linda tried to make a joke too, to show Tammy she was going to be okay. "Your cake would smash in the front of the whole house."

"Oh bee ess, kid, you know I make the best cakes in the world. And I'll have a big double-chocolate for you when you get back from your all-expense-paid vacation."

The other kids came back from soccer practice, some boys, some girls, some who lived there, some who fostered there. Kate made lunch but Darelle wouldn't eat any.

"What's the matter with *her?*" one of the kids asked.

"She's just sulkin'," Linda answered. "She does it all the time."

"Won't do any good. Kate don't care about that stuff."

Monday morning the welfare woman showed up after breakfast and said Linda was to go with her in the car.

Darelle got all set to wail. "What about *me?*"

"You and Donny will stay here a few days more, dear."

"Why?"

"Because, dummy," Linda snapped, "your mom has to go in court, okay? You can't go home by yourself."

"I could go with you."

"Well, you're not gonna. She already said, Darelle. Stop bein' such a baby. My *gosh.*" Linda almost started to cry.

When they got to the welfare office, Tammy was sitting under the No Smoking sign, filling the air with clouds of cigarette smoke. She grinned as if it was all a huge joke. "So, do I got to sign my life away to get my kid back, or what's the scoop?"

The scoop was, Linda could go home. Darelle and Donny had to stay with Kate for a month and a half. Cindy was only in the pokey fourteen days, but she had some hoops to jump through when she got out before the welfare would let the kids go back with her. By the time they got home, Gus and Cindy had made up, and he had moved back in. Cindy said to anyone who asked and even a few who didn't that she sure had learned her lesson that time. "Don't kick a cop in the knee," she laughed, "especially not in the wee knee."

8

The first time Isa phoned the welfare to report the kids had been left alone, Gus was off somewhere. Nobody knew where, really. He'd said he had to get some space, take some time, get in touch with what he was thinking instead of continuing to react to what was going on. He'd said a lot, but none of it told anybody how to get in touch with him if he was needed. Cindy seemed to think he was visiting Isa, and the tone of her voice suggested she didn't believe Isa when she said she hadn't seen him.

"If he phones you, will you let me know?" she said, disbelieving and suspicious.

"If he phones I'll tell him you're concerned," Isa evaded, "but I doubt he'll phone me. He'll show up at your place first. He's gone off on his own before, and he'll go off on his own again. Usually he lets his boss know and either takes holiday time or gives notice. Once he went hiking and backpacking in the Stein for three weeks, another time he did the West Coast Trail . . ."

"Well, if he does, you let me know, okay?" Cindy sounded like someone on the brink of either a good weep or a temper tantrum. "I don't know *what* to think. He just up and went."

"If he gets in touch with me I'll tell him to phone you."

"No, he won't phone," Cindy whined. And then Isa knew there was more to the story than she was being told. It sounded to her as if there had been an argument or a scene, and Gus had done what he always did when things took a nasty turn—up and offed, to wait it out until people cooled down. "If you hear from him, maybe you could phone me and let me know?"

"All right, I'll—"

But Isa didn't get to finish her sentence. Cindy was giving chapter and verse on how broke she was, she didn't even have money for milk for the kids. "And my cheque doesn't come for another ten days, so I don't know what I'm going to do. I tried to borrow some from my sister, but she's laid off right now, and so I was wondering if you could, like, you know, front me maybe fifty dollars? I'll pay you back."

Isa wanted to sigh, but didn't. "Do you have a bank account number? The way the mail is, it'll arrive about the same time as your welfare cheque. The only way to get it to you right away is one of those computer transfers." She wrote the account number on a piece of paper and put it in her wallet. She figured she'd probably need it again, and she didn't much feel like paying long distance rates to listen to dead air while Cindy went in search of her chequebook with the number printed on the cheques. She drove into town, transferred seventy-five dollars to Cindy's account and waited for the call saying Thanks, it got here.

When there was no call that day or by suppertime the next, Isa phoned. Darelle answered, and Cindy could hear the TV going in the background. "Hi, can I talk to your mommy?"

"She's not here."

"Oh. Well, this is Gus's mom . . . Isa. Do you know when your mom will be back?"

"No." Darelle sounded guarded, and ready to bawl.

"OK. Can you remember to tell her to phone me when she gets in?"

"I don't know when she'll get in." Darelle wasn't giving an inch.

"Oh. Well. How's things with you?"

"Fine."

"Good. Uh, do you think I could talk to Donny?"

"Sure," and the bang as the phone hit the top of the end table was loud. There was a scuttling and scurrying sound, then Donny took the phone.

"Hi," he said, and she could hear the little smile in his voice.

"Hi yourself, guy. How you doin'?"

"Good."

"Yeah? How was school today?"

"Didn't go."

"What's the matter, are you sick?"

"No. We didn't wake up in time."

"Sleepyhead, sleepyhead, lying there asleep in bed," Isa teased him. He laughed, and she repeated the silly chant. "So, are you going to school tomorrow?"

"I don't know. If my mom gets home, maybe."

"Wasn't your mom home this morning?"

"No. She went out."

"Did she come back for lunch?"

Sometimes it was hard to remember that Donny's developmental level was much below what it ought to be. Small-built and cuter than anyone had any right to be, he seemed only three or four years old when in reality he was six, heading toward seven.

"No," he said.

"Supper?"

"No."

"Is anyone there with you now?"

"No."

"Boy, you must be pretty awful kids if nobody will babysit for you," she tried to keep the teasing tone in her voice, and it worked, he giggled again. "Maybe I'll try to find a babysitter for you, okay?"

"Yeah. Maybe she could cook some real supper. We just had cold beans."

"I'll see what I can do."

What she did was dial the Child Help Line. They took the particulars and that was the last Isa heard from them. When she phoned Cindy's number again, there was no answer. She phoned the next day; still no answer. So she phoned the Ministry of Social Services, was put on hold, waited nearly five minutes, then got a receptionist who said she herself was not familiar with the report or the case, but she would look into it and get whoever was working the file to call Isa.

Isa waited until just before the Ministry office was due to close, then she phoned back. She got a different receptionist who knew nothing at all but said she would look into it.

"I've waited all day for someone to look into it," Isa flared, "and I don't much feel like waiting all night, too."

"One moment, please," and there was a subtle change in the receptionist's voice. The casual put-it-off-don't-sweat tone was gone and the get-the-lead-out-this-one-is-nasty tone was in. Two minutes of listening to bland on-hold music, and then Isa actually got to talk to someone who knew something. However, whatever that person knew was blanketed by some rule of confidentiality. Isa was assured the kids were fine, they were being well cared for, and the worker very much appreciated the concern and interest Isa had demonstrated.

"Can I talk to the kids?"

"I'm sure they'll be pleased to receive any message you would care to leave for them."

"I didn't ask if I could leave a message for them, I asked if I could talk to them."

"I'm sure you can appreciate that we are not at liberty to divulge the phone numbers of our support families, but I'll leave a note for their worker and I am confident she will convey your greetings to the children."

Isa blew. "Never mind conveying the goddamn greetings! I'm going to give you my phone number, okay? You're going to write it down on a nice new piece of paper. Then either you or the worker who is getting paid for supposedly protecting those kids will give that number to both Darelle and Donny and tell them—not request, or ask, but *tell* them—to phone their grandmother. Not next week, next month or next year, but inside the next hour. Now is there any part of that too involved, complex, convoluted or challenging for any of you people?"

Isa was never sure if it was her low-rent approach, her warrant officer tone of voice, or the magical word "grandmother" did the trick, but Darelle phoned less than fifteen minutes later.

"Are you okay?" Isa asked.

"No," and Darelle began to sob. "I want my mother!"

"Darelle, listen. Darelle! Put a sock in it and listen. This is not a bad thing, okay? We just couldn't find a babysitter to go to your place, so we had to line you up with someone who could babysit at her place. It's no big deal, all right?"

"But I want my mother."

"Sure you do. But whether you're at home all by yourself eating cold food, or staying where you are and getting real meals, your mother wouldn't be around. Is that right?"

"Yes."

"So why eat cold canned beans when you can have real meals?"

"But—"

"I know. It's not fair. Okay, I'll go along with that, it isn't fair. But it's how it is. And when things like that happen, all we can do is try to make the best of it. Now let me talk to Donny."

"Yes, Grandma," Darelle said meekly. Isa wondered just how smart the kid was, anyway.

"Hi." Donny sounded fine.

"So what's the place like?"

"Okay."

"Are there other kids there?"

"Yeah."

"Many?"

"Yeah."

"How many?"

"I don't know. Some."

"What did you have for supper?" Isa was reaching for straws, trying to get him past his one-word responses. He sounded okay, but spaced out, as if some part of him hadn't made the trip to the foster home.

"Supper? Uh, pork chops. We had pork chops. And the lady put applesauce on our plate too, but it wasn't dessert, it was to dip your meat in. I never had that before, did you?"

"Only one time and it was real good. You're lucky, eh, pork chops and applesauce and . . . what else?"

"Pie."

"What kind?"

"I don't know. Yellow."

"Lemon? You had lemon pie! Boy, wish I had some lemon pie." She said it, and probably sounded as if she meant it, but it would stick in her throat and choke her like the word *grandmother*. Isa knew what she wanted for her grandchildren, and there was nothing in this situation that fit with her hopes, her dreams or her coping ability. Trash is as trash does, and trashy is trashy.

The second time Isa called the Child Help Line, Gus was back from his search for himself but not living with Cindy. Isa had no idea what sort of low-rent soap opera had come down, but he'd rammed his stuff in a plastic garbage bag, stormed out and taken a bus up-country, where he got a job driving a gravel truck. By then, Cindy had borrowed over three hundred dollars and Isa knew she'd never see any of it again. Sometimes, delving into an increasingly deep and dark hole, searching for what was left of what had once been a damn fine sense of humour, Isa thought the reason her back was giving her so much trouble was that increasingly, some areas of her life were becoming complete and utter pains in the ass. She had said as much to her daughter Jennet and been given a half-joking lecture on a new book, based on some theory that what a person had wrong with them was, in large measure, due to something else that was going wrong. "Here it is, low back pain, and . . . well, here you have it, Mom, it says here the reason people have low back pain is that some things are so bad, and are such heavy loads, the person really can't stand up under it any longer."

"Does it give any hint what a body is supposed to do? Jesus, Jen, I can't just blink my eyes and pretend those poor little jiggers aren't in real trouble!"

"Yeah, Mom, I know. Got lots of codeine pills?"

"Yeah. Lots."

"Get more, I guess, eh? How much money has she squirrelled out of you? She's got about two hundred out of me."

"You? I didn't even know you knew her!"

"My phone number was in Gus's little book. See how easy it is to get sucked in? She got his book somehow, and phoned me . . . it's like spider webs, or syrup."

"So how's *your* back?"

"So far she's just a pain in the neck, so I'm okay."

Isa phoned the welfare because she had been trying for three days to get someone to answer the phone at Cindy's place. Nobody there early in the morning when the kids should have been having breakfast and getting ready for school, nobody there after school, nobody there at suppertime, and nobody there in the evening.

By then, Isa was practically on a first-name basis with the worker handling what everyone euphemistically called The File. He took the particulars and said he'd look into the situation immediately. Isa waited three and a half stomach-rumbling hours, and when he didn't phone back, she called his office. He was at his desk. He sounded tired and empty, and Isa wondered if he'd been sleeping. If he hadn't been, maybe he should have been. From the sound of him he was ready for a hospital bed.

"They weren't at the apartment," he said, his voice harsh. Probably living on cigarettes and coffee.

"Then they're probably at her sister's place," and she told him the address. "If they are, every adult concerned is probably sitting in the bar and the kids are bunched together looking after themselves and each other."

"I'll look into it," he promised.

George showed up with Georgie and Melanie. Nobody even asked about Maria, who had been out of the pokey all of a couple of months. All you had to do was look at George, most of the story was there. He was rake thin, with dark circles under his eyes. His hands were so skinny his fingers were like claws, and they were nicotine-stained practically to his wrists. All those bundles of muscles were gone, might as well never have been there. He was smiling, though, and had money in his pocket, lots of it, so whatever had come down was done with. Except for whatever it was with Maria.

Tammy sent Dick out looking for Cindy and found her in the Terminal with a table full of regulars who were determinedly working their way through a couple of pitchers of draft. Cindy drained her share quickly and told everyone else she'd see them later. The beer caught up with her in the car, and she was in a rare good mood when they dropped by her place to pick up Darelle and Donny. She didn't even rip strips off them for making a mess while she'd been gone. At least they'd been quiet enough the old snoop upstairs hadn't caught on to the fact they were alone. Nosey old biddy, anyway. Well, Cindy was nine-tenths of the way toward showing her a thing or two. She was at the top of the list for subsidized housing, and there ought to be an opening in a couple of weeks. None too soon! Bad as living with the damn nuns. She didn't have any idea at all what was going on with George, but it sounded as if he needed to be with family for a while. Good old Alexander Graham Bell had figured out how to make that happen.

Georgie and Melanie arrived with some new clothes and their Nintendo. That kicked off such a gimme-gimme Tammy threatened to take it away, box and all, and store it on the top shelf. Phoebe announced they'd take numbers, and one would play two, then the winner of that would play three and the winner of that play four, and so on. She, of course, would be one.

"Big deal, you just think because you're oldest you'll win and get to play and play and play," Linda argued. "If we take numbers, one will play two, then three will play four and then five will play six. And *then*, the winner of five'n'six will play the winner of three'n'four, and the winner of that will play the winner of one'n'two."

"Says who?" Phoebe yelled, and, of course, swung a roundhouse.

Tammy grabbed her by the wrist before the whack connected with anybody. "You settle down," she said coldly, "or they'll wind up taking you away in an ambulance."

They phoned Barb and tried to talk her into coming down, but she must have had something else on the go, because she didn't sound too interested. Frank showed up, though, without Ruby and the kids.

"What's the matter, she think she's too good for the rest of us?" Cindy griped, her good mood evaporating.

"So what you going to do, prove she's right by acting like that?" he answered, as proddy as she was. "*I'm* here, aren't I? What do you think I should do, drag her along on a rope? Anyway why do you care, you don't even like her."

"Because she doesn't like me!"

"Then why'n'hell d'ya want to go beering with her? If you don't like her and she don't like you, best you stay clear of each other."

"And who are you to tell me what's best?"

"Will you shut up!" Tammy flared. "If you can't stay in a good mood when you're drinkin' maybe you should quit drinkin'! We're lookin' for a good time, and we're not interested in crabbiness, okay?"

"Oh, listen to you," and Cindy might have got into it with Tammy but everybody told her to button it or they'd go without her. That ticked her off so much she sat glaring for over an hour, but nobody cared. Eventually she got up from where she was and wandered over to where the others were sitting around the table with beers, talking up the Good Old Days and Remember When. She slid into a chair and sucked on her beer. Nobody made any big deal about her change of tactic, so she didn't have to defend or apologize, and she could pretend nothing had come down, everything was fine.

Darelle found a bed and lay down on it. For a few minutes she looked at some comic books but even though she hadn't read any of them, she was too sleepy to do it now. Reading was hard work, and she didn't enjoy it, she seemed to get mixed up on some of the words, reading "the" for "then," or the other way around. Sometimes she would read every word in the paragraph just fine, except she had no idea what any of it meant. She knew the words one by one, but the sense of it all escaped her. She'd watched the eight o'clock movie on Channel 11, and that lasted until ten, then she watched the movie on Channel 6, it ran from ten until midnight madness came on, and after that she watched the start of the late late but had nodded off on the sofa before she could figure out what the movie was supposed to be about, and she might have slept until noon except Donny had started whining he couldn't find anything to eat, she should cook him some macaroni. She held off as long as she could, hoping one or another of the adults would lurch to the stove and cook, but they ignored Donny, as they were busy ignoring all the other kids. So finally, just to shut him up, Darelle did what he wanted. There wasn't any cheese for it but he liked it almost as well with just margarine and some pepper sauce.

Sometimes she wished he'd learn how to boil his own macaroni so she could sleep in once in a while.

When she wakened from her nap the adults were all gone and the kids were on their own. But at least there was lots of food. She had two big roast beef sandwiches with a bowl of potato salad. Everyone else had already eaten and there was no cake left, but Darelle didn't care. There was ice cream in the freezer. It was under a big thing of frozen fish, she supposed that was why nobody else had already scoffed it back, because they hadn't found it. She didn't tell them anything about it, she just took the little plastic Häagen-Dazs container into the bedroom, and sat with the comic books, spooning the strawberry taste into her mouth. She would have liked to eat it all but you can't have everything. She could eat it later. There was still some of it in the bottom when she gave up and put the container back in the freezer.

It wasn't long after that Phoebe found the ice cream. She went looking for juice and that was the end of any plan Darelle might have had about finishing it off later. Phoebe took the container to the living room and sat on the sofa, smirking widely and slowly spooning it in. The other kids glared enviously but knew better than to get into it with her. Phoebe was in a lousy mood, even for Phoebe. She finished off the ice cream, then took the container to the sink and washed it out. This was unusual for her, she most always left stuff at her backside for someone else to tidy. They all knew she was just making sure there wasn't one more lick in there for anyone else.

Donny played Nintendo a bit but got bored with it. He wasn't any good at it and got beat once too often. Rather than compete, he went into Tammy's bedroom, turned on the TV set and sat watching some dumb thing until he fell asleep, or next best to it. His face went slack, and even though his eyes were still open, he looked as if he had gone to dreamland.

Georgie and Melanie were the best ones at Nintendo. Sandra was too little to do anything except point and yelp excitedly. Phoebe could outplay Linda and Darelle, but she couldn't win against either of the kids who owned the game and that didn't improve her mood at all.

"Turn the stupid thing off and disconnect it, I want to watch TV," she growled.

"Go in the bedroom and watch with Donny."

"Go in the bedroom and set the stupid thing up in there, I want to watch TV *here!*"

"Mom said we should play it here," Linda argued.

"Yeah, well she's not here and I'm in charge so you do what I say or else."

"Boy," Georgie said in a loud whisper he wanted everyone to hear. "Poor you, gotta live with *that* all the time."

"You want a good slap in the face, maybe?" Phoebe offered.

"Of course I don't want a slap in the face," Georgie laughed. "I don't want a slap in the head, either. Matter of fact, I don't want no slap nowhere," and he turned his back on her.

Phoebe was on him in a flash. Georgie rolled in a ball with his arms protecting the sides of his head and his ears, his knees shielding his face. Hitting him wasn't doing any good, so Phoebe kicked him. He yelped. Darelle started crying, Linda scooped Sandra and raced for the door with her, Melanie grabbed the broom, swung it like a softball bat and hit Phoebe across the back of the head. Phoebe fell to the floor and when she tried to get up she couldn't get it together. Georgie was up and moving. He fired a kick to the side of Phoebe's head, then grabbed Melanie by the hand and headed after the others.

At least they had time to grab their jackets, so it wasn't too bad even if it was raining. Later, when Sandra stopped whining and started really crying, Phoebe let her in, though she wouldn't let anyone else through the locked door.

"Poor Don, I wonder if she's taking it out on him?" Linda worried.

"Donny wasn't even there, he's prob'ly still sleeping. Or watching TV. And anyway, he's got sense enough to stay out of her way."

They sat in the carport, where at least the rain wasn't pelting down on their heads. Darelle wished she'd had time to make a sandwich and bring it with her. She sniffled once or twice but the others told her to shut up or they'd push her out of the carport. She already couldn't go into the house.

A beige-coloured car moved slowly toward the house. Georgie hissed warning, grabbed Darelle and Linda by the arm and pulled them back into the dark end of the carport, behind some stuff Dick had heaped there. Melanie didn't need to be dragged, she was first one there.

"What?" Darelle wailed, her eyes brimming with tears.

"Shut up! Ssshhh," Melanie glared. "Can't you see the design on the door? It's either cops or whoofare. Prob'ly lookin' for my mom."

"How'd they know to come here?"

"Jeez, don't they got computers at your school? They know

everything, dummy! Who your relatives are, where they live, everything. Now shut up!"

Phoebe knew whoever was knocking on the door was no friend of hers. Donny might have been dumb enough to go answer, but she pushed him back down in bed and shook her head at him. She thanked god for small mercies. Sandra was sound asleep in her crib, the TV was off and the lights were out, so whoever was snooping around would think nobody was home.

The other kids watched from behind the pile of stuff. The guy knocked a few times, looked around as if expecting to see them dangling from the roof overhang, then got back in his beige car and drove off. Nobody said a word or moved an inch until he was out of sight.

"Why they looking for your mom, anyway?" Darelle asked.

"That's for me to know and you not to," Melanie snapped.

They were still in the carport, so cold they couldn't even shiver any more, when the grown-ups came home with great big newspaper-wrapped parcels of fish'n'chips.

"What'n hell you doin' out here getting pee-monya?" Tammy demanded.

"Phoebe locked us out." Linda tried not to cry but you could tell it was a struggle she would lose. "She got mad at Georgie for nothing at all and when Melanie wouldn't let her kick him, she hit her with the broom, and then she chased us out and locked the door and wouldn't even let us have supper or anything."

"Where's Sandra?"

"I grabbed her when I ran but then she was hungry and Phoebe took her in the house. But she said we could all *die*, she didn't care."

"Where's Donny?"

"Inside. He was asleep."

Phoebe knew she was going to catch it. They knew she didn't care.

"And she just sat on the sofa and gorped all the ice cream all by herself too," Melanie said, too angry to care about tattletale rules. She looked at her father. "Why'd you bring us here?" she shouted. "I'd rather be in a foster home. At least there they don't knock you on the floor and kick you all over like she did to Georgie."

"Jesus Christ, Phoebe, you got things rattling loose in your head?" George said mildly. "Now why'd you go kicking Georgie? He's your cousin."

"I don't care," Phoebe lipped back. "Doesn't mean anything to me."

"Oh, really? Well then, if family don't mean nothing to you, I guess it don't mean nothing to me, either." George smiled and shrugged, his voice soft and easy. And then he popped Phoebe on the side of the jaw and dropped her to the floor. "Keep your damn hands off my kids," he said, as pleasant as if he was telling her what time the bus came to the corner.

"Hey, speakin' of keep your damn hands off my kids," Tammy yelled.

"Settle down, settle down." Dick sounded bored. He was opening the fish'n'chips parcels, dividing it all up into equal piles, same for the kids as for the adults. "Get some plates or something, do I got to do this whole thing myself here?"

"Never mind putting any out for Phoebe," Tammy decided. "She probably isn't hungry anyway, bein' as how she ate all the stuff we left for the others and then hogged the ice cream."

"I never hogged no ice cream!" Phoebe screeched. "There was hardly any in it!"

"Oh bull, it was brand new yesterday." Tammy opened the fridge and looked in. "And not a speck of roast left, nor any spud salad either. You're gonna wind up the fat lady in the circus the rate you're going, Wide Butt."

Donny came out of the bedroom and went right to Cindy. He stood tight against her, his face buried against her belly, his arms around her, clutching. "That's my good boy," she crooned, swaying and almost dropping her fish'n'chips on the floor. "That's Mommy's good little boy. Here." She thrust the plate of food at him. "You take this to the couch and wait for me."

"You go to the couch and I'll bring it to you," Dick laughed, "or we'll be scrapin'er outta the rug for the next month."

Darelle got her plate and headed for the sofa to snuggle up to Cindy on the other side, but before she got there Cindy moved so she could put her plate on the arm of the sofa. Donny was stuck to her same as if someone had smeared him with Krazy Glue, so the best Darelle could do was sit next to him.

Phoebe just walked into the bedroom and slammed the door.

Everyone was talking at once, eating and laughing, filling each other in on who said what to whom, who did what, and when, and what about when that big goof started lipping off and those loggers got up from their table, went over, lifted him clean out of his chair and carried him to the door? Didja see the look on his face when he realized they were going to turf him? Laugh? I thought I'd get a belly ache.

They were just finishing off the food when two cars drove up, horns blaring. People outside were laughing and yelling, doors were slamming. The kids took their plates to the sink, piled them neatly and quietly, and did a quick fade. With their bellies full and the chill of the carport finally wearing off, they all fell asleep within minutes. They were so far in dreamland that by the time the noise started to rouse them, the fight was well underway.

Darelle screeched and rolled to the floor. She crawled under the bed while Donny headed for the closet. Phoebe came tearing into the room with Sandra and pushed her under the bed with Linda and Darelle, then Phoebe got into the closet with Donny. Georgie and Melanie were under the bed, too, squinched back against the wall, and when Darelle started to cry Georgie pinched her leg and told her to shut up or everyone would know where they were.

Something crashed and then they heard Cindy swearing, saying she was damn well leaving, she wasn't putting up with this kind of crap.

Dick laughed, but it wasn't a happy laugh. "You? Drive? You don't even have a licence."

"So? Least mine isn't under suspension!"

"No, you don't have one for them to suspend!"

"So? You think I don't know how?"

"You couldn't find your arse to wipe it, is what I think."

They heard the slap, then heard Tammy holler that nobody was gonna hit her old man and get away with it. Someone whose voice they didn't recognize said he'd damn well hit anybody he felt like and not all of them together could stop him.

Phoebe came out of the closet, went quick-as-a-cat to the dresser and started sliding it along the floor. "Gimme a damn hand here, will you?" she hissed. Darelle amazed everyone by getting out from under the bed and going over to help Phoebe. With the dresser in front of the door and the bed jammed up tight against the dresser, they were about as safe as they were going to be until this go-round was finished.

They heard a car take off, engine racing, and hoped it was some of the new people leaving. Then they heard some of the new people yelling and cursing about how someone had swiped someone else's damn purse. Heavy footsteps thundered to the front door and down the steps, but other crashes and bangs told the kids there were still people raising the roof in the house. Another car took off, going even faster than the first one.

Something hit their bedroom door with an awful smash and the door splintered. That's when Tammy started screaming. She just screamed and screamed, then they heard the horrible mind-numbing roar of Dick's hunting rifle. Three times it went off, the reverberations shaking the walls.

They were all under the bed by that time, clinging to each other, too scared to make any sound at all. Even the baby just clutched and shook, her breath coming in short gasps.

The sound of the gunshot was still echoing when what sounded like a herd of buffalo went out the front door and down the steps. Car engines roared, someone yelled Wait for me, and then Tammy quit screaming. "Where the fuck *is* she?" Dick yelled, his voice thin and tight with rage.

Another car started up and took off, engine whining. The kids stayed under the bed, Melanie shivering so badly her teeth were chattering. Phoebe reached from under the bed, yarded off the blankets and pulled them under. "Wrap yourself up warm before you get sick or something," she said.

"Thanks, Phoebe. I'm not really cold, I just . . ."

"Yeah, I know," Phoebe agreed. "I know. I'm just about ready to pee a lake here."

They heard the sirens coming down the highway, more than one of them, cutting the night with a fearful *eeee aaaa eeee aaaa*. "We better hit for the bush," Georgie said, slithering out from under the bed. "If the cops find us they'll stuff us in foster homes. Come on, Mel, they'll keep us this time."

It was so slick you'd have thought they'd practised. Everybody grabbed their jackets, and while Phoebe snatched two bottles out of the fridge, Linda got Sandra's blanket and Darelle sniped up two bunches of bananas from the fruit basket. Donny stuffed the apples and oranges down his shirt, and then they were out the side door and cutting behind the neighbours' houses.

Lights were on all over the place, and dogs barking like fools, trying to drown out the sound of the wailing sirens. They could see flashing blue lights coming up the road from the highway, and then a flashing red light that had to mean fire truck or ambulance. The salmonberry thicket crackled and snapped as they pushed through. Phoebe pulled the blanket up over Sandra's head so she wouldn't get scratched or cuffed. Behind the salmonberries, the alder trees, leaves withered and dropping, and behind them the fir and cedar, dark and gloomy, standing sentinel in the night.

When they couldn't see the flashing lights any more they slowed, and Donny found a place under a cedar where they could sit together, hidden from view by drooping branches. The ground was cold but not wet, and with a bottle stuffed in her mouth like a plug, Sandra calmed down. Phoebe peeled half a banana and got that into her, then gave her the rest of the bottle and she went back to sleep.

The cops surrounded the house and yelled things through a bullhorn. When nobody answered, they tried phoning from a neighbour's house. They waited for more gunshots, then four men in heavy flak jackets made their cautious way into the empty house.

The ceiling in the living room was pretty well gone. A .303 can make a substantial hole, whether in plaster or human flesh. The wood chopping axe was stuck in the wall next to a splintered bedroom door. There was blood smeared on the axe handle and the wall, and a spray of droplets stained the carpet in the hallway. One of the kitchen cupboards was pulled right off, the dishes, cups, plates, glasses and saucers fallen, most of them smashed on the counter, in the sink, or on the floor. In the living room the lamp was on its side, two coffee tables were overturned and the sofa was tipped onto its back.

"Well Jesus Christ," one of the cops sighed, "weren't we all just havin' a ball."

Cindy made it down the road to the highway, along the highway and partway up a side road before she lost it completely and the stolen car left the pavement. She had just enough of a survival instinct to fling herself sideways on the seat. The car ran along the edge of the road and hit a power pole dead centre, snapping it off just above the ground. The power pole hung in mid-air long enough for the car to push it aside and plough on by, then the pole slowly drifted down as the power and phone lines stretched, stretched, stretched until they could stretch no more. About the time the lines started to snap, the car hit the second power pole. It splintered and tip-tilted dangerously, but didn't crack off. Wires writhed like snakes, spitting sparks and snapping like a huge set of false teeth.

Cindy waited a moment. Then, reassured that she was not dead after all, she opened the stolen purse, found the wallet, opened it and took all the money. She stuffed the money in her jacket pocket, then eased open the door of the car and took a look at the pickle she'd got herself into.

It was like playing hopscotch, only what you would win or lose was a lot more than your special square-marker. But she knew she couldn't stay in the car. Sooner or later the cops would come to find out why half the town was without power or phone.

She jumped from the car and leapt over writhing wires until she was clear of the worst of it. She crossed the road and went into the bush where she could hide herself. At first she couldn't stand to look at the wreck, she stood with her back to it quaking with fear and telling herself what a dumb tit she'd been. She lit a cigarette, her hands shaking terribly, and when it was smoked halfway down she turned and took a good look at the go-round across the street.

The whole thing hit her the wrong way and she started to laugh. "Oh, my *gawd!*" she gasped. "Just look at what you've gone and done *now!*"

She figured the best thing she could do was stay in the bush so if any car came down the road she'd see the headlights and hunker down until it had gone past. If she could make it to the highway without being seen, she'd be fine. Except, of course, for fingerprints. Well, she could figure out a story for that. Maybe say the noise in the house had got to her and she went out and sat in a car for a while. If they asked her if she stole the car, she could just look dumb and say Me? Hey, I don't even have a driver's licence. And that was a true thing. She'd say Hey, if I knew how to drive don't you think I'd take my test and get my permit? Let them try to prove different, nobody had seen her drive off in the damn thing.

It was past daylight when she got back to Tammy's house. The cop cars were gone. There was a big yellow plastic ribbon with black writing on it strung all the way around the house but it was easy enough to duck under it and go inside. She could see neighbours peering at her from windows but she ignored them.

Inside, everything was a total wreck, and no sign of the kids. Well, maybe the whoofare had scooped them again. Best thing she could do was act dumb. She grabbed the phone book and found the number, then dialled and asked for her worker. "My kids aren't where I left them last night," she blurted, and she didn't have to be Katharine Hepburn, her voice was shaking without trying. "I left them with my sister, her oldest kid was going to babysit for me, and I come out today and there's nobody here and the place is a wreck! Do you have my kids?"

When the cops got back to the house, Cindy was doing housework. She had already swept up the worst of the broken glass, set the furniture right side up and sponged the blood off the walls.

"I can't find my kids," she sobbed. The cops looked at her as if she'd crawled out of a piece of bad meat, but she didn't care. She gave them the story about Phoebe babysitting, then elaborated a bit. "I couldn't get a ride and I had to hitchhike out here this morning and they're *gone* and the welfare doesn't know where they *are!*"

The cops gave her hell for crossing under the yellow tape and tampering with evidence, then they left. A half hour after they drove off, the kids came drifting back from wherever they had been hiding.

"I'm so glad to see you," Cindy yelped, trying to hug them all at the same time.

"Had to come back," Phoebe said coldly, "we were out of milk for Sandra."

Dick was the first of the others to show up. He came in the back way, about an hour after dark, holding his hunting rifle casually in one hand. He grinned and winked at everyone, looked at the mess he'd made of the ceiling and shook his head ruefully. Cindy tried to get him talking, but all he said was, "You better button your lip, bitch, you're the one kicked it all off in the first place, swiping that purse and all."

"Me? I swiped nothing."

"Nothing? *Nothing?!* What about that damn car?"

"Oh, that," she shrugged. "Well you don't think I was going to stick around here with everyone yelling about that purse, do you? The bitch prob'ly lost it, is all."

Dick shook his head again, then pulled a little bottle of some kind of black dusty stuff from his pocket. He got out his gun cleaning kit, oiled the inside of the barrel, then got the steel wool from under the sink. He wrapped a little twist of steel wool around the brush he used to clean the barrel of his gun, then sprinkled the black dusty stuff on both brush and steel wool.

"What are you doing, Dick?" Phoebe asked quietly. "Is this something I should know about?"

"What I'm doing is saving my own ass." He looked up, the anger gone from his eyes. "What it is, see, every gun's got what they call tooling or rifling marks on the barrel, and those marks can leave marks on the bullet. You've seen it on TV, prob'ly." Phoebe nodded, no trace of smart ass to be seen. "So I c'n pretty well bet they pulled the slugs out of what's left of the ceiling, right? So what I'm doing is altering the marks inside the barrel of this gun. Between the steel wool and the graphite dust, and with just a tiny pinch of Irish luck tossed in just in case, well, I think I've got a half-assed chance of staying outta jail."

He had to yard on the little string before the cleaning brush would come all the way through, and he muttered if the string broke he might as well throw the gun in the lake because nobody would get the damn brush out unless they used dynamite. When the brush finally came out, Dick sighed and nodded. "Now I lay me down to sleep," he joked, "a bagga peanuts at my feet. Please Lord hear me weep and wail, keep my ass safe and outta jail." He finished cleaning the gun, then got a spare blanket from the little closet in the hallway and wrapped the gun in it, safety-pinning the blanket shut around it.

"Now what?" Phoebe asked.

"They prob'ly looked all over the place for this gun. Now I have to try to make 'em think it was here all along."

Cindy sat sulking and watching TV while Phoebe and the other kids followed Dick. He lifted a little section of boards out of the wall around the back porch. "Didn't know it was here, did ya?" he said. "Well, it's access to the water shut-off valve, in case you ever need to turn the water off because of a bust pipe." He went in and they heard him fumbling with something, then he backed out again and his hair and shoulders were tasselled with old spider webs. "God bless mother spider," he winked, and he picked up a handful of the dry dusty dirt under the porch and tossed it casually. Some of it clattered against the boards. "Gonna look like it's been there since last hunting season," he said softly. "I hope t'god."

Dick was showered and wearing clean clothes, with his other stuff washed and already in the dryer, before the cops arrived back at the house.

"Quite honestly," he told them, "I will be goddamned and go-to-hell if I've got any idea at all what the fuck was goin' on here last night. But I betcha it costs me close to three hundred dollars just to fix the ceiling."

"Do you have a gun?" the big cop asked.

"Yessir, I sure do."

"Do you have a permit for your gun?"

"You betcha. I guess you'd like to see it, huh?" and he hauled out his wallet, dug in it and brought out a folded paper. "Here you go."

"Where is the gun now?"

"If nobody's took it, it's where I put it after hunting season," and he looked over at the kids. "If I tell you where it is I'll have to find a new place for it. Can't be too careful with kids around, you know how it is."

But they wanted to see it, so he showed them how to get the little square open. When he made like he was going to go in and get it himself, the big cop put his hand on Dick's shoulder. "I'll get it," he said firmly. Dick stepped back, nodding. The big cop waited until the smaller one, who was still the size of a football player, got a big flashlight from the cop car. Then he went under the porch and came out covered with spider webs, carrying the dusty, dirty, blanket-wrapped rifle. There were even some cobwebs on the blanket, from where Dick had taken a swipe at a particularly thick clump of them.

They took the rifle with them and Dick apologized for the mess the big cop's uniform was in. "I shoulda warned you," he said, sounding as if he meant it. "It's a helluva mess down there, I get filthy as a coal miner every year when I bring 'er out for hunting season."

Tammy and George drove up not two minutes after the cops had driven off with Dick's rifle. They yelled and shouted at Cindy for a while, but had to cut that short when the cops came back yet again. This time they had a thousand and six questions about the wrecked car.

"I don't even know what kind of car it is they're saying got swiped," Tammy said. "A whole buncha them showed up here, and yeah, they came in cars, but I don't know how many. They were drunk. And they brought booze with them and got drunker and then I went over to finish doing the dishes and I don't know damn-all what happened, but there were people I hardly knew all over the house, pulling the place apart."

"I was nearly asleep," George lied smoothly. "I know even less than she does because at least she was at the sink there. Me, I was in the back bedroom. Then all hell bust loose and I came whipping out to check on m'kids and ker-thunderin'-*pow*, some son of a bitch cut loose with what sounded like a cannon."

"I was outside," Cindy told them. "It was real smoky in here, and a coupla those people were in real ugly moods, and some woman who was with them was bitching on about how she couldn't find her damn purse. And I didn't like how she was looking at me anyway, so I went outside. It was kinda drizzly so I sat in one of the cars and, like, turned on the radio to listen to tunes, and then things in here got kinda out of control so I got out the car and took a walk down to the highway. And I thumbed down a ride and went home because I don't like it when things get rough."

"And left your children alone?" The cop gave her a hard look that had everything to do with the kids and not much to do with the wrecked car.

"Hey, what am I supposed to do? Wake 'em up and drag 'em off down the highway with me? I figured they'd be fine, nobody's gonna lay much of a trip on some kids, especially if they're all asleep and outta the way."

"And you didn't notice anything in particular about a red four-door Ford?"

"I was hardly more'n two, maybe three minutes away from here and I heard all *kinds* of noise and then I don't *know* how many cars came speeding and roaring outta here. I just took to the ditch so's they wouldn't see me and maybe run over me or something, they were all so drunk and so owly."

"You hid in the ditch."

"Damn sure I did. Halfa those people were crazy."

"They were in good company," one of the cops muttered, and Phoebe had to bite the inside of her cheek not to snicker. The cops knew. They might not know who or how or even when, but they knew, and knew too that they were up an alley with it all.

"Would you mind," Tammy said, very polite and ladylike, "if I start putting my kids to bed?"

"No, you do that, lady. You put the kids to bed."

A month and a half later, Darelle and Donny visited Isa and Carol for several days. Darelle was hardly talking, apparently having decided she could get through life with a vague smile and a few monosyllables. Donny, however, wanted to visit, wanted to establish contact, and actually tried to hold up his end of conversations. He covered the comings and goings of school, then had to look for other topics. With a vocabulary at least three years behind what it should have been, he filled Isa in on life in the bosom of the family.

"And Phoebe is mean," he confided, cuddling close. The smile on his face, and the comfortable slackness of his body as he soaked up the affection, was in stark contrast to what he was saying. "She locks us out of the place, even when it's raining, and she eats all the food. And makes me take off my clothes and get into bed and then she does things."

Isa felt cold. Her stomach was tight, her mouth dry. "What kind of things?"

"Oh, you know." The smile was fading, and Donny was dissociating, his face softening, going limp as he drifted off someplace where there were no questions he wasn't supposed to answer, no truths he wasn't allowed to tell. "You know. Things."

And when the kids weren't underfoot to see how upset she was, Isa once again phoned the Ministry of Social Services. She once again encountered the rule of confidentiality and, as an added bonus, was told her information was out of date and uncorroborated. But, she was once again assured, the Ministry very much appreciated the concern and interest she was showing for the well-being of the children.

9

Cindy's name drifted to the very top of the list and Gus rented a truck to move their few things. He wasn't exactly living with them, but he showed up sometimes and Cindy had his phone number for when she needed something. They moved on a Saturday because Dick was off work to help mule the heavy stuff, and by eight-thirty at night it was all in place and they were eating Chinese take-out. The place looked huge and too bare, and Cindy started talking about maybe bumming some money off someone so she could get some stuff from the Salvation Army.

"I don't like it that the kids sleep on mattresses on the floor," she said. "I'd rather they had real beds."

"Well, instead of bumming money all the time, you might's well break down and get a job," Tammy snapped. "You can make up to a coupla hundred a month over and above your welfare cheque without them docking you."

Cindy glared and chug-a-lugged her beer. "Don't you damn try to run *my* life!" she barked.

For an awful minute it looked as if they were going to scrap again, but then it passed. And when the kiss-my-ass stuff started up for good, it was two or three days later. Gus just laughed and said, "Take your ass off your shoulders, darling, and I'd be glad to try," and he left. Cindy went after him, calling him out for all kinds of an ay-hole, but he didn't slow down or turn back or stop to argue with her. So she went back to the new place and started getting dressed in her going-out-beering stuff.

Only Darelle and Donny were home the first time the strange woman knocked at the door, so she didn't come into the house. She just left a card with them and asked them to give it to Cindy when she came home. They did, and no sooner did Cindy look at it than she was on the phone, and when whoever it was answered on the other end, they knew something was about to come down or blow up, because Cindy was using her please-may-I-kiss-your-butt tone of voice.

When she was finished that phone call, Cindy phoned Tammy and fussed herself into a right fine stew wondering what was going on and why the whoofare was coming knocking at her door in the middle of the day.

"Maybe they were checking on why the kids weren't in school," Tammy suggested. So for the next few days it was out of bed with the birds, into the clothes, eat the cereal, and make sure your hair doesn't look like a squirrel's nest, then off to sit yawning in class, trying to appear to have some idea of what the teacher was talking about.

Then they were told to come home from school at lunchtime and they probably wouldn't be going back until the next day. With no idea what was going on, they headed home when the buzzer sounded. They had time for a peanut butter and raisin sandwich before the strange woman arrived.

George was in the kitchen too, but no sign of Georgie and Melanie, and they knew enough not to ask any questions. If people wanted you to know something, they'd tell you, and if they didn't tell you it was probably none of your beeswax.

George and Cindy sat at the kitchen table drinking coffee and smoking cigarettes they made by filling a metal shooter thing with tobacco from a green can. The ash tray was pretty well full, and both George and Cindy looked as if they were kids again, and about to hear the word about their report cards.

The woman went into the bedroom with Darelle and Donny and asked them some questions, most of them real easy to answer. Donny would have quite gladly answered—it wasn't often he had the answers to other people's questions—but Darelle sat right in front of him, giving him the shut-your-face-you-idiot look. Caught between the questions and the look, Donny felt himself slipping off to that other place, the one where the colours zipped and zapped and made designs behind his eyes, like pictures or something.

He was still off in la-la land when the woman left, and he didn't come back until George and Cindy had questioned Darelle about what she had been asked, what she had said, and what the Really part of it was. When Donny yawned and came back from what he thought had been a nap, he was sitting on Cindy's lap, on the couch, and she was holding him, rocking and weeping silently. Uncle George was on the phone and he was raising holy hell about something. Donny didn't want to know what, he just cuddled closer to his mother, fully enjoying the rare opportunity of her affection.

After supper, which George made because Cindy was in no shape to do it, Tammy and Dick arrived, but none of the kids were with them. Darelle protested when she was told she and Donny were both to get bathed and into bed, but her protest withered when George glared at her and said, very tiredly, "Don't get started, kid. I'm in no mood for it. Just scurry." She'd seen what George did to Phoebe last time he was in no mood, so she scurried, pretending she didn't mind at all. The snap-fizz of caps coming off beer bottles had already started.

Tammy heard what George and Cindy were telling her, and it took a moment or two for the full meaning to sink in. When it hit her, she stood up, her chair skittering and falling over backward. "Those damn kids!" she yelled. "They're always trying to get her in trouble! None of you are going to be happy until that kid is hanging from a rope in her bedroom!" and she started to cry.

"She won't hang from a rope in her bedroom," Dick answered, his words slurred. "She might string the rest of us up, but no way is Phoebe going sideways into the next life."

"It's all lies!" Tammy insisted, her sobs practically cracking her chest open.

"No it is not." Dick wasn't making a lot of noise. He even sounded as if he was trying hard to be real nice. "And what's got you so upset is you know it's true. After all, Barb dropped you the word not long ago."

"Barb's just a troublemaker, same as that damn Ruby!"

"Why, what did Ruby tell you?" Cindy asked.

"Ruby never told me nothing, nothing at all!" Tammy had gone past heartbroken to defensive rage. "The whole damn lot of you are just picking on that kid. What do you want me to do, beat her to death with a belt or something?"

"Oh, you and your beat beat beat, you make it sound like you tan their hides twice a week do they need it or not!" Dick wasn't bending over backward to be nice any more. "You don't *dare* hit her, she's big enough now she'll just turn around and clean your clock for you and you know it."

"Anyway, the whoofare woman said Phoebe isn't allowed to babysit my kids any more," Cindy said, sounding oddly satisfied.

That news was so welcome and so reassuring, Donny rolled over in bed and fell asleep with a smile on his face. He didn't know how anyone had found out, and he hadn't known anybody could do anything about Phoebe, but things seemed better than they had in a long time.

Gus moved in with them again. He said he'd been off working out of town, and probably he had. There was money for new bikes and money for giant-sized pizzas. He and Cindy were like lovebirds, sitting together on the couch watching TV with her head on his shoulder and his arm around her waist, and he could cook a lot better than she did. He got up in the morning before they did, and breakfast was ready when they came into the kitchen. This was due not so much to good parenting as the fact he didn't sleep well at the best of times. Gus made jokes about how his spirit guide was a big horned owl and how that meant he was more comfortable awake at night than asleep, and most of the time you could almost believe him.

Sometimes he went into the bedroom he shared with Cindy and closed the door, and a few moments later you could hear this sound, a low, droning wordless noise that intrigued Donny so much he once dared to open the door a crack and peer in. Gus was sitting in only his underwear, his legs crossed like an Indian in a movie, and he had his eyes closed. The sound was coming from his mouth, as if he was singing, only nobody Donny knew had ever sung a song with only one word, and that one *Ooooooooooohhhh*. Gus had also given up eating or cooking meat, which Donny thought was too bad. He didn't mind not getting any more eggs, though. The ones from the store tasted like fish and weren't as good as the ones Grandma got from her chickens. Donny liked the chickens, especially since Grandma had assured him they didn't have any teeth, so they couldn't bite him. He wished he knew what song it was Gus was trying to sing, and he wished Gus would stop singing it because it made Donny's mother very angry when she heard it.

Then Gus got a job driving the soft drink truck up and down the Island, dropping off cases of pop at just about every little store you could imagine. For some reason this had to be done at night, which was probably just as well for him, what with him being awake anyway. He got home at six in the morning, made a pot of coffee, drank some of it, then got breakfast started. Cindy didn't get up for any of it but both Darelle and Donny tucked in eagerly. Not just cereal, either. Some mornings it was pancakes with syrup, lots of times it was pretend bacon and eggs, which Gus made with stuff he got from the Chinese-food section of the supermarket. Gus called it toe-foo. He cut up onion, and maybe added some green pepper and maybe some frozen peas or something, then chopped up the toe-foo and put it in. Darelle said it was nothing but toejam and would make you go bald if you ate it. It didn't taste the least little bit like scrambled eggs, but it was good, no matter what Darelle said. And anyway, for all her talk she sat herself down and ate what was in front of her so maybe she was just teasing or something.

The phone rang just before supper one night and Cindy answered it. She didn't say much, she gasped one or two times and sort of whispered, "Oh no" and "Oh god." Then she hung up and told Gus to go down to the ferry terminal and pick up Georgie and Melanie. Gus said he wasn't sure he'd remember what they looked like, it had been so long since he'd seen them. Which wasn't true, but he was busy with supper. "Oh well, if that's how you're going to be," Cindy snapped, and she called a cab and got herself ready.

When she came back she had them with her, and their stuff, in big black plastic garbage bags. They both looked pretty well freaked out. They had no sooner set themselves down at the table to help pack away the supper Gus had waiting than the cops arrived. All Gus did was grin and say, "Hey, I'm just the domestic engineer around here, all I do is cook and throw clothes in the washer, no use asking me anything." Cindy did her usual number: "Gee, sir, all's I know is the phone rang and I got told to go get them at the ferry."

One of the cops started asking Georgie and Melanie questions, but Gus put a stop to that. Still smiling from ear to ear and with no sign of sass in his voice at all, he stepped behind the kids' chairs and put a hand on each one's shoulders. "Excuse me," he said politely, "but I understood that before you can question little kids, you have to have a couple of social workers on hand, to ensure the kids' rights are protected. Am I wrong in that?" The cop who had been asking the questions stared at Gus for a long moment, then moved away, his ears turning red.

Snugged down together in bed that night, Melanie told Darelle she didn't know what was going on. "All's I know is my dad showed up at school and said Come on, so we did. He had our stuff in the cab and took us to the bus depot and said we were to come here, and he'd let you guys know."

"Sure took his time about phoning! Hauled you out of school but didn't call here until just before your boat got in."

"Well, at least he remembered to call. My mom says for small mercies let us give thanks to god."

"What does that mean?"

"I dunno."

A couple of days later the postman brought a small parcel to the house. Gus didn't object to the money, but he was some ticked off about the pills. "That's just dumb, Cindy! All's has to happen is the cops to arrive and even if the damn parcel hasn't been opened, bang, they've got you."

"The cops aren't going to arrive. They've been and they didn't find out diddly-squat so you just calm yourself down, see. Anyway, I'm supposed to give 'em to Tammy."

"Then why didn't he sent them to her?"

"Because the money is for looking after the kids and she's not doing that, is why."

"Then send the money here and the shit there."

"Oh, will you stop nagging at me about it? I am not the one sent the damn thing! Keep it in your hat until you can yammer at *him*, okay." Cindy grabbed her jacket and muffed out of the house with her don't-give-me-any-crap look on her face. She left the money but took the pills with her.

"You better be back before I have to go to work," Gus yelled, which was as good as daring her to stay out all night. Which she did.

Gus stomped around for a while yammering about how he didn't feel good leaving all those kids alone but if he didn't go to work he'd lose his job and then where would they all be, and in the end he left them alone, which was what they'd been expecting anyway. Darelle didn't see that it made any difference, they were all asleep in bed before Gus headed off, and he was back with his coffee made before they were awake. Gus took the money with him and stuffed it in his pocket, muttering if he left it where it was it would wind up in the hands of the bartender.

Cindy didn't come in for three days, and when she did she brought Tammy with her, both of them looking defiant as they walked into the kitchen. But Gus didn't say anything, he acted as if nobody had even stepped out the door, let alone stepped out and stayed away for a while. Darelle and Melanie were doing up the supper dishes, Georgie was tidying up the living room and Donny was putting the Lego stuff back in its box in the bedroom he now shared with three other kids.

"I guess there's no supper," Cindy laughed, a harsh and uneasy sound.

"There are leftovers in the fridge, all you have to do is heat them up." Gus wasn't going to let anything get to him.

"Maybe later." Tammy walked to the big chair in the living room and plunked herself in it. "God, I'm tired, I tell you. This retail sales business is hard on the constitution. Besides," she tipped the recliner back and smirked over at Cindy, "person has to work fast or that one will have disposed of the profits before they've been made."

"Oh, you," Cindy answered. "You should talk, your feet haven't touched the ground for days."

"And I suppose you can remember everything that happened. I think not!"

"You be careful who your customers are," said Gus, too pleasantly to be believed. "There are more narcs in this town than there are ministers of the gospel. Which is probably why Georgie Porgie didn't come over and flog the shit himself."

"And I guess you know who they are?"

"Not all, but some."

"Maybe we'll have to take him along with us next time," Tammy yawned.

"I might go along, and I might let you know which ones I recognize, but I'm not part of the sales team, and you better know that for sure. I'm not doing time on a drug charge just to make things easy for your dipshit brother."

They bickered about it for a while, then Gus got up and warmed up the leftovers, and while the two women were eating the kids had their baths and got ready for bed.

They all woke up when the cops came. Gus was nowhere to be seen, he'd already left for work, but Cindy and Tammy were sitting side by each on the sofa, scared spitless, looking all eyeballs and asshole. The cops were busy searching the place, looking in the cupboards, on the shelves, in the drawers, even emptying the Tampax out of the box and looking in there.

"Lookin' for drugs," Georgie whispered to Donny. "They did that at our place, too. Even took the shower curtain down and unscrewed the rod and looked in there!" But Donny wasn't interested. He was sitting loose and lazy in a chair, his head back, looking as if he was watching a movie that was playing up on the ceiling.

"So, what are these?" one of the cops asked, holding up a clear bottle with a white plastic snap lid. In it were a few green and yellow capsules.

"They're mine," Cindy whined. "I've got a prescription."

"We can check on that easy enough," the cop warned. "And if you're making up stories it can mean real trouble for you."

"Go ahead, phone my doctor, his number's on the card above the phone!" and the whine was gone, Cindy sounded ready to do battle. The cop knew from her defiance she was standing on solid ground, and he just smiled mockingly, his insult hitting home and putting Cindy well and truly on the prod.

Eventually the cops left. The kids went back to bed, except for Donny. He moved from the chair to the couch and lay down on it, and Cindy got a spare blanket to put over him. Georgie didn't mind that, it made for more room in the bed for him.

When Gus got home, the place was still a mess and the search warrant papers were still on the kitchen table, but there was no sign of Cindy or Tammy. Gus woke up Darelle to find out what was going on, and she told him what little she knew, but she was so tired he sent her back to bed and didn't get any of them up for school. When they finally crawled out, they had missed breakfast but were in time for a big spaghetti lunch. They went to school for the afternoon, and when they got home, all hell was coming down between Gus and Cindy.

Tammy got into it, too. You could always count on her to contribute her two cents' worth. Gus told Tammy to go to hell, grabbed his jacket and was gone without making supper. Cindy and Tammy told each other over and over again that he sure thought he was someone, had this idea he was better than the whole damn world, and anyway nobody needed him, they'd get along just fine the way they'd been before they met him.

Tammy phoned the trailer to talk to her kids and they said Dick had just come in from work, so she talked to him too, then hung up the phone and started making supper. Dick showed up with Linda and Sandra, and a big carton of ice cream for dessert.

"Where's Phoebe?" Tammy asked.

"I haven't got any idea," Dick smiled easily. "If you want to know where she is or what she's doing, I think you're going to have to stay home long enough to find out for yourself, because she doesn't tell me a thing."

"Well, did she come home from school?"

"No, but then she seldom does, you know that."

"What time did she get in last night?"

"I don't know, I was asleep. IF she even came in."

"Whattya mean *if* ?"

"I told you. She wasn't in before I went to sleep and when I woke up I got ready and went to work.

"Well, when was the last time you set eyes on her?"

"About ten minutes after the last time I set eyes on *you*."

"I'll beat her ass raw," Tammy announced calmly, but nobody figured her for serious. Phoebe was two inches taller, and if she didn't weigh anywhere near as much, what Phoebe had was mostly muscle and what Tammy had was packed-on calories.

Georgie and Melanie stayed three weeks, then as good as vanished in the middle of the night. The kids had all gone to bed one night, same as usual, but come morning, Donny was alone in bed and so was Darelle. Most of Georgie and Melanie's clothes were gone too, except for a few things in the dirty clothes basket.

"Where are they?" Darelle asked.

"Gone," Cindy answered shortly.

"Gone where?"

"What you don't know, you can't tell the cops."

"Why would I tell the cops?"

"Well, someone told the whoofare about Phoebe," Cindy glared, and Darelle started to cry.

"It wasn't me," she wailed. "Why would you think it was me?"

"Shut up, Darelle, stop the whining."

"What did I do? All I did was get up and ask where Melanie and Georgie were and now . . . now . . ." She sucked in as much air as she could, all set to let rip and lay a good howl on the world, and Cindy slapped her.

"Shut up, I said!" And she raised her hand, ready to hit again.

Darelle stopped pretending to cry and raced to her room, sobbing.

"You keep that noise in there. From now on, you want to cry, you go to your room to do it. No need for the rest of us to have to put up with that crap!" She looked over at Donny to see if he needed a telling, too, but he was sitting at the breakfast table, spooning cereal into his mouth, so dreamy-looking you'd think he was half stoned. "You're a good boy, Donny," she told him, ruffling his hair briefly. "Never any trouble with you. Just as nice and quiet as can be, aren't you?" A small smile flickered at the corners of his mouth but he didn't say anything, just kept spooning up the alphabet and putting it in his mouth, chewing once or twice, then swallowing, seeming not to notice he had milk dribbling on his chin.

Just about all they got for breakfast these days was cereal. Gus hadn't come back. Well, he had come back, but only to pick up his stuff, ram it into a plastic garbage bag and huff off again.

"What's he got up his nose?" Tammy asked.

"Who knows?" Cindy pretended to be casually disinterested. "Who cares?"

Donny cared. He was trying hard to be Poppa's little man, glomming onto Gus as hard as he could. Darelle cared mostly at meal times. It didn't take long for a person to get sick and tired of the same old Crap Dinner or, worse, those cans of stuff the label says is Irish stew but smells like canned dog meat. That, on toast, was about enough to make a person go on a strict diet.

"Hey," Cindy would almost yawn with the boredom of it all, "I *hate* cookin', okay? You want something, figure out how to throw it together. A sammich is good enough for me." Maybe so, but it didn't take long for sandwiches to get dead boring, too.

Then, out of the clear blue, without any warning or clue, Barb arrived with her horrors. Billy and Bobby were mostly known as Ferret and Weasel, or Rat and Rodent, or worse. Dick insisted Billy was Vulture and Bobby was Buzzard. He also claimed the Department of the Environment had a bounty on the two, and anyone who could bring themselves to kill the little christers would get fifty bucks each and a medal for saving the entire country.

They just walked into the house in time for lunch, bringing with them two enormous take-out pizzas.

"Well, who you see when you don't got a gun," Cindy gaped. "You're about the last person I expected."

"Just goes to show ya, right?" Barb put the pizza cartons on the table and plunked into a chair. "No you don't, you keep your meathooks to yourselves until you've taken your packs to the bedroom. Take mine, too, your legs are younger and so's your backs. When that's done and you've washed your hands and face, you can have some pizza." She turned to Darelle and Donny and grinned, "If you get washed up first you can get a headstart on the grub." The two of them hurried to the bathroom and Barb sighed. "Well," she told Cindy quietly, "like it or lump it, sister dear, you're stuck with us for a week or so."

"Somethin' goin' on?"

"That fucker Real is what's going on! He's been drinkin' more'n'more all the time and gettin' owlier'n hell, too." She might have said more, but Darelle and Donny came back, scrubbed shiny. "Get the plates," Barb ordered. "Christ, do I got to do everything?"

Ferret and Weasel didn't look much cleaner when they came out of the bathroom than they had when they'd gone in, but they were undeniably wetter. They sat on chairs, waiting, faces eager. Darelle put out plates and Weasel reached for one. Barb slapped his hand. "Mitts off, mister. Mind your manners, okay?"

Barb opened the cartons, then looked at Cindy. "Which? Or does it matter?"

"One of each, I suppose." Cindy went to the fridge to get milk and the jug of juice. "Bobby, get the glasses."

"I don't wanna," Bobby answered tartly. Barb's hand flew, slapping him on the side of the face and almost knocking him off his chair.

He didn't even bother to yowl. He just moved fast and got some glasses.

"What, you can't count?" his mother glared. "Three glasses? How far is three glasses gonna go in *this* crowd?"

There was plenty of pizza for everyone, and even some for later. Donny didn't complain or argue when told it was his turn to help, so he could clear the table and put stuff away, but Billy had a fit about having to wash the dishes. "Why me?" he screeched.

"Because Darelle set the table, and Bobby got the glasses."

"A few glasses! That's nothing! I gotta do lots more'n him."

"Did you notice he got a crack on the side of the head to get him moving? You want one like it for yourself?"

Billy was so angry he felt as if he had been out in the winter cold without his jacket. That happened sometimes, when he was either just about ready to pound someone's head in, or when he was real scared. He just got colder and colder until he had goosebumps on his goosebumps. He stood at the sink scouring the plates with the blue plastic ball-dealy he found sitting in the mouth of the big green ceramic frog. He thought that was pretty stupid. Buying a big frog with a wide-open mouth just to keep your pot scrubber in. He knew the idea was your scrubber could drip dry and not just sit in its own puddle, but it had probably been four hundred years since Cindy had washed the damn thing, and the whole inside of the frog was slimed up with some kind of grey gunk. So he put that in the hot soapy water, too. God, if you're gonna keep your scrubber in there you could at least keep it clean. Fuck, Cindy prob'ly didn't give a toot, Darelle was too lazy to give a care and Donny, well, he'd lost some of the shingles off his roof and only Cindy hadn't caught on. "We'll be on our own," she'd said, "it'll work out fine," so what were they doing here? This bunch were as loopy as his old man, and for just about the same reason. Be on our own, eh? Tellin' people things that weren't true. It made him mad!

He supposed it wouldn't take his dad long to figure out where they were. How many places could they go, anyway? Well, he wouldn't even be out of jail yet, and when he got out they'd likely tell him to keep his nose clean, they'd already handed him a copy of the Peace Bond taken out against him.

They'd been drinking and playing Nintendo, sprawled on the floor sucking at long-necked brown bottles, laughing and teasing each other and then jesus, it was coming down all over the place. Bobby screeching and trying to get himself out of the way but somehow he got knocked to the floor and then Real tipped over the table and it come down and knocked Bobby cold as a clam. Billy had long ago figured out the best place to be when the balloon went up, right behind the bathroom door. When the door was open, the edge of the door hit the wall first, so up near the crack was this little triangle of space and he could hide safe in there and still see through the crack. What he couldn't watch directly he could usually see reflected in the great big mirror on the living room wall, the one with mermaids and seaweed all around the edge of it. Big correction, the one which *used* to be on the wall, because when last seen it was in bits and pieces and shards all over the floor.

So Bobby was under the tipped-over table and Real had Barb in the kitchen, backed into a corner with his rifle shoved under her nose, and Billy got so cold he thought he'd shiver his teeth right out of his head. Real was promising to do all kinds of gross things and Barb was scared, but telling him he might just as well kill her now, because he wasn't going to do any of that to her as long as she had breath in her body. The trouble was, she wasn't scared of Real any more. Things had been better when she was still scared stiff of him, he was more apt to quit sooner, then.

Billy had stood on the bathtub and slid the sideways window open, got himself up over the sill, teetered briefly on his belly, then sort of rolled himself out and fell into the tangle of fern, salal and Oregon grape that grew around the trailer-house. He had to stop and pee as soon as he got safely behind some trees, because it was ready to flood out of him, but once he'd got himself zipped up again he headed through the little fringe of evergreen to the neighbour's place. He pounded on the door, and when the cranky old guy opened up, Billy blurted, "My dad's drunk and he's got a gun."

Maybe the old guy wasn't all that old, because he moved fast as a cat to the phone. And the cops were there within minutes. There was a lot of shouting and yelling and then Real came out of the trailer-house with his hands in the air. Two cops ran in, guns drawn, then one came out with Barb and the other came out with the rifle.

"I'm fine, I'm fine," Barb kept repeating. "He just roughed me up, he didn't really hurt me, I mean I've got bruises, but no cuts or anything. It's my kid I'm worried about," and she sounded as if she had all she could do not to start crying again.

"Your son is fine," one of the cops said. "He's over at the neighbour's house."

"Not *him!* The other one," and she told them about the table and Bobby under it. Three cops raced back into the place.

The cops took Real to jail after they'd dropped Bobby off at the hospital. Billy and Barb went back into the trailer-house and went to bed in the same big bed. Billy didn't think he'd be able to sleep but he went out like a light, and when he woke up Barb was telling him to put on some clean clothes, they had to go to town. He had bacon, eggs and toast at the cafe while she was over at the courthouse filling out papers. "If he comes within half a mile of us," she said grimly when she got back, "he'll be behind bars so fast his goddamn head'll spin." She had a cup of coffee but didn't eat anything, and after she'd paid the tab they went to the hospital and got Bobby. He tried to brag about the jello on his breakfast tray but Billy shot him down. "In a cafe, dopey, a real cafe, and crispy bacon, too. Jello! Baby food, that's what that is."

"You got the dishes done yet?" Barb called.

"Almost." He was scrubbing at the frog, trying to get its face clean where all that old soap and stuff had gone hard. He could hear Barb whispering the story to Cindy and he wondered why she thought she had to do that. After all, he and Bobby had seen it, why couldn't they hear it?

"So Sunday, after I got the kid out of the hospital, we went back and packed our stuff. I was going to head out then but the lights on the damn car aren't all that good, so we waited until daylight and drove off, and . . . here we are." She looked over at the clock and laughed. "Numb-nuts is probably just goin' up in front of the judge now. They start at ten in the morning but the cop said he'd be one of the last ones. And," she sounded gleeful, "if he don't go up before closing time he'll have to sit in the Crowbar Hotel until the next court session on Wednesday."

"Serve him right," Cindy agreed.

Nothing would do but they phone Tammy, so when she got off work she had a message waiting on her machine. She changed and got Sandra from the babysitter's, then Dick was home from work and Linda home from school so they left a note on the door for Phoebe and headed in for a visit.

When Donny heard about them coming, he sneaked the cold pizza out of the fridge and hid it under his mattress.

Dick helped Tammy and Barb make supper, a huge pot of rice and about a half ton of stir-fried veggies. Of course the adults washed it all down with a river of beer. As soon as the dishes were done and put away, the kids were left on their own, with Linda supposed to be in charge and Darelle the second-in-command. That might have worked out fine, but Phoebe read the note on the door and got her friends to drive her over to join the get-together. The get-together had more or less gone by the time she arrived, so, with no adults to say otherwise, she brought her friends into the apartment.

They hauled the leftovers out of the fridge, they finished off the bread and the big roll of bologna, and they polished off pretty well all of the beer. Nobody could watch TV because Phoebe and her buds had the stereo on, cranked up so loud the next door neighbours pounded on the wall and, when that didn't do any good, they came over and yelled. Phoebe lipped them off so they said they were going to phone the police.

No cops arrived, but the threat was enough to send Phoebe and all her chums down the stairs to the noisy '57 Chev. They jammed themselves into it and roared off, leaving tire marks on the blacktop parking lot and yelling insults at the neighbours.

"Jesus," Linda moaned. "Look at the mess we get to clean up."

"I'm telling my mom," Darelle decided.

"And I'm telling mine."

Both Linda and Darelle had been expecting Billy and Bobby to raise hell and refuse to go to bed, and both of them were preparing to beat them up if they had to, but the boys were worn out by stress, travel and excitement, and once the noise of Phoebe and her friends had gone, they and Donny hit the pillows.

In all likelihood, Linda and Darelle telling their mothers wouldn't have done much good. But Phoebe did herself in, she came back to the apartment by herself just after midnight. She was half-cut on beer and pretty well tipped over the edge on pot, not enough to put her to sleep, but enough to bury any vestiges of good sense she had. She hit the fridge again, turning the kitchen into a disaster area. Linda and Darelle were so disgusted they got sleeping bags and lay on the floor in the living room, watching TV and pretending to be almost asleep. Which they did such a good job of, they both drifted off and were almost in dreamland when the smell got to them.

"Do you smell something burning?" Linda asked.

"Is that what it is?" Darelle sat up and looked around, but all she could see was Phoebe stretched out on the sofa, a half-eaten sandwich beside her. The smell persisted, and after a few minutes the girls got out of their sleeping bags and went looking. Eventually, they found the cigarette which had fallen from Phoebe's fingers and snugged itself between a couple of cushions. They had to roll Phoebe onto the floor and wouldn't you know it, she ground the damn sandwich into the sofa and then it fell down and glopped on the rug too. But they were able to pour water on the smouldering holes in the cushion and the body of the sofa. The smell became an acrid stink and before they could think of anything to do about that, the celebrants arrived home from the pub.

It only took one look and a sniff or two and the tantrums started. The kitchen was smeared with mayonnaise and margarine, Phoebe hadn't put a thing away, and there she was, snoring away in what was left of her sandwich, the cushion in the sink and the couch sporting a hole as big as a peanut butter jar. The adults were furious, and that before they found out about the vanished beer. In case anybody needed any more encouragement to fly off the handle, the next door neighbours arrived, still bent out of shape about the noise and the comments shouted from the '57 Chev.

"That's it," Tammy gritted. "By god, but that is *it!*"

"Ruined my chesterfield," Cindy whined. "There's no way I'm gonna be able to fix it."

"Thank god I only have boys." Barb dropped into a chair and looked down at Phoebe, then shook her head. "Gonna be up the stump in no time flat the rate she's going."

"Not on my dime she won't." Tammy was almost grey in the face and her eyes glittered, but not with tears. "I've had it with her and her plates of shit, a little bit of this bee-ess goes a long way with me."

"Ah, come off it." Dick tried to smooth things over and managed only to make it all worse. "They say everyone gets their own kids. You just don't like looking at her, she's too much like a mirror showing you what you're like."

Tammy spun faster than anyone believed she could, and the roundhouse punch caught Dick on the side of the face and knocked him sideways. He stumbled over a kitchen chair, lost his balance and fell to the floor, bashing his head on the chrome leg of the table, knocking himself cold as a clam. Linda ran, and put herself between Dick and the fierce kick Tammy was launching. Instead of getting him in the family jewels, she got Linda.

Darelle started crying. She couldn't believe what was happening to Linda's face. The right eye sort of inflated, like someone blowing the world's biggest bubble. Even before Barb could get out of her chair and over to help her to her feet, Linda's eye was shut and the swelling was spreading down her cheek and over to her ear.

"Why'd she get in the way?" Tammy wailed. "I didn't mean for to hurt her!"

"Sometimes you're fuckin crazy, kiddo, you know that, eh," Barb sounded so calm and mild, Darelle thought she was hearing things. "Just shut up, Darelle, you're only making things worse. Put your energy to something useful, like getting some ice from the freezer and wrapping it in a towel."

Linda didn't even cry. She sat on a chair at the table, her face white, one side of it so swollen you could hardly tell who she was. The more Tammy tried to fuss over her, the quieter Linda got, until she seemed more like Donny than herself.

"Jesus, baby, tell me you're all right," Tammy was crying, her hands fluttering uselessly.

"I'm all right," Linda said clearly. "But you better start doing something about your temper because you have a real problem." She focussed her good eye on her mother. "You're fuckin' crazy, you know that, eh."

10

Real sat in the pokey for almost ten days, then went up in front of the magistrate and was given a lecture on guns, bad temper, and generally unacceptable tacky behaviour. When the scolding was finished, he was let out on his promise he would show up for the real trial two months down the road.

The cops gave him back his gun, his belt, his shoelaces and the stuff they'd taken from his pockets, then turned him loose. He went home to an empty house, got a bottle of whiskey from the cupboard and tossed back a few solid swallows before getting on the blower and starting his telephone search for Barb. It didn't take much phoning before he was talking to her, and it didn't take much talking before she had agreed to come home. She was so reasonable about it he was surprised into agreeing she should leave the boys with Cindy for a week or so, "to give us time alone to work things out," she told him.

She wasn't in the house more than four or five hours and he was into re-runs. This time there was no kid to go out the bathroom window, but at the sound of the first holler, the neighbour was on the phone. The cops arrived so quickly you'd have thought they were parked just down the road, waiting. It took them half an hour to talk him into handing over his rifle and going with them, but once they had him convinced, he went meekly enough.

Barb didn't ship out immediately. She actually managed to catch a few hours' sleep on the couch, then had coffee and a long hot shower, put on clean clothes, and drove into town in Real's old beater pick-up. She went to the bank, checked on some business there, got the safety deposit key, checked the box, then went to the car rental company. When Barb drove home she was driving a maxi-van, and Real's beater was parked in a No Parking zone on the main street.

What she hadn't bothered to tell him was she already had an apartment rented in the same subsidized housing complex where Cindy and the kids lived. She also hadn't bothered to tell him she was registered with the welfare, had no intention of moving back in with him, had known he was drinking and would undoubtedly blow his cool, and had come only to get the furniture she wanted. And that she knew two arrests for the same BS holds more water in court than just one.

She packed the Nintendo, the kids' beds, all their clothes and toys, her own clothes, the stereo and tape collection, the TV, the photo albums, the framed baby pictures and most of the bedding and towels. Every pint of pickles, preserves, relish, chutney and jam she had made and stored in the spare room went into the maxi-van. She also took the pots and pans, dishes and cutlery. And to drive her point home as clearly as she could, she took two tubes of Liquid Steel and poured it into the mechanisms of every gun Real owned, starting with the pellet gun and working up through the .22 to the 12-gauge shotgun. She couldn't chemically weld his 30.06 because the cops had taken it from him when he walked out of the trailer-house to surrender.

"Fix you, you owly son of a bitch," she muttered as she drove away for the last time. "Had enough of your wing-nut goings-on."

Tammy and Cindy helped her unpack the maxi-van and carry her stuff into the apartment. Some of the neighbours stood around looking suspicious and even a bit proddy, but Barb wasn't upset. Everyone knew city people took a while to warm up and relax.

The apartment still looked bare, but Barb figured she could get a decent living room setup from either the Sally Ann or the Goodwill, and the stuff she'd left behind wasn't fit for much more than the municipal dump, anyway. The built-in nook thing in the kitchenette would do. She had everything she needed to cook meals, although she did wish there'd been some way to move the freezer and its contents.

Well, she could get another freezer and maybe go back when Real was in camp. Then watch out, there wouldn't be a package of peas left behind when she was through.

Tammy had Sandra with her, so when she, Cindy and Barb headed off to the bar, Darelle was left in charge at Cindy's apartment. She didn't have any trouble at all with the toddler, but neither Billy nor Bobby would do a thing properly. They wouldn't even come inside when it started to get dark. They whooped and hollered and hung off the railing of the second floor walkway, they slid down the banister to the parking lot and whipped around between the parked cars playing some mad version of tag. Donny chased around with them for a while, but once Darelle had Sandra asleep, she called Donny and he came in willingly. He didn't want to get ready for bed, but at least he sat quietly on the floor, his back against the chesterfield, contentedly watching the Eight O'Clock Movie and eating saltines spread with peanut butter.

Billy and Bobby came in long enough to drink most of the juice and snitch a bunch of grapes, then they got away from her again and tore off outside to drive the neighbours crazy. Darelle wished Linda was there to help her, but nobody had gone out to get her so she was in the mobile with Dick. He'd phoned and asked if Tammy was there, and when Darelle said no, she was out with Cindy and Barb, Dick just sighed and said, "Right, and I guess the balloon will go up in about two or three hours. Is Sandra with you?"

"Yeah, but she's asleep on my mother's bed. Are you going to go looking for them?"

"I've got work in the morning," he replied. "And anyway, I don't feel like being the only drake with those three ducks. If you need anything, you get on the phone and I'll get there as fast as I can, okay?"

"Billy and Bobby won't do what they're told." Darelle was all set to cry, but Dick just laughed and said Oh hell, when did they ever, don't sweat the small stuff, kiddo, and hung up the phone.

The celebrating trio had a few beer in the Queens, and a few more in the Neon Peacock, then went down to the Riverside to drink beer and watch the line dancing lessons. Gus was already there, sitting at a round table with a slender blonde who looked like a low-rent copy of Farrah Fawcett.

"Nothing to her but a mop of hair and enough damn teeth for two people," Cindy muttered, so jealous her eyes were nearly turning green.

"Well, go over and put the run on her," Tammy dared.

"How am I supposed to do that?"

"You just go over and tell her to keep her meat hooks to herself. If you want him, of course."

Cindy didn't go over right away. She sat sullen as a soaked cat, watching as Old Hair'n'Teeth tried to talk a half-packed Gus into getting up to dance. He just kept laughing softly and shaking his head no, until the poor White Princess started to get pee-oh'ed about it. About the time her flirtatious mask began to slip, Cindy drained an entire glass of beer, got up, and marched over, threading her way among crowded tables, pushing past chairs, avoiding the waiters with their trays of draft.

"Ho-boy," Tammy laughed gleefully, "this could be fun."

"Troublemaker!" But Barb turned her chair so she could watch too.

Cindy leaned over the small terrycloth-covered table, put her face practically up the nose of the Low-Rent Princess and tapped her index finger on the table top. "Listen," she said coldly, "it usually isn't very healthy to mess around with someone else's husband, if you get my meaning."

The young blonde woman opened her mouth to speak and not a sound came out. Gus laughed softly and lit a cigarette. "Don't be stupid," he told Cindy. "I'm not your damn husband. I haven't even seen you for months."

"I'm not talking to you," Cindy said. "I'm talking to her." A passing waiter slowed, as if sensing trouble was about to break loose in his section, but Cindy just sat down with Gus and the blonde and took a sip from one of the extra glasses of draft in the middle of the table. "I don't want any trouble," she gritted, "but you might want to think about how much you want this guy. You want him enough to risk a thick lip? You willing to have mosta your hair ripped out?"

"Gus, what the hell is going on?" the young woman asked.

Gus laughed and shook his head. "I'm not married to her," he said. "I lived with her until a couple of months ago, is all."

Right about then Tammy and Barb came over, bringing their jug of beer and their glasses. They sat down at the table and smiled cheerily. "Well, hi, Gus, how's my favourite brother-in-law?" Tammy asked.

The blonde stood up, took her jacket off the back of her chair, forced a smile and spoke directly to Cindy. "Hey, I'd love to stay and chat, but," and she tipped her head at the dancers, "I want to get in some dancing, too. See you around sometime." She moved away quickly.

"So there," Cindy said smugly. "See how far you got!"

"Rough and tough," Gus mocked. "Hard to bluff, and mean and cruel and vicious," and he laughed yet again.

No sooner did the blonde leave than two young guys walked over with a fresh jug and some glasses. "Mind if we join you?" the taller one asked, looking directly at Tammy and smiling widely.

"Can you behave yourselves?"

"Yes ma'am, I'm good. Very good." He put the jug on the table and sat on the chair next to hers. "In fact, where beautiful and exciting women are concerned, it's safe to say I always do exactly what I'm told."

"Not me," said the shorter one, sitting down beside Barb. "I don't always take orders. In fact, sometimes I like to sort of . . . improvise."

"Adventurous little soul, aren't you," Barb laughed. She took a cigarette from her package, then offered it to him. He took a cigarette, at the same time pulling a lighter from his pocket.

Gus sat in his chair watching the sparring and smiling, until Cindy couldn't take the silence any more. "So what you been up to all this time?" She nudged him so he'd know she was talking to him and not to the table at large.

"Me? Nothing much. Same old thing."

"Where you been staying?"

"Oh, here and there, you know how it is."

"You still working?"

"Yeah. Different job, though. I'm driving a gravel truck again."

"Is it, like, you know, an okay job?"

"It's pretty damn scary if you want the truth. Bad enough when they're scooping up the stuff and dropping it by the ton into the back and you're sitting there wondering will they miss and pour the whole shiterooni down the back of your neck, and the truck feels like a bloody barrel going downhill once it's loaded. But then you get where you're going and you have to dump, and jesus, when that load starts to shift! I have to keep swallowing all day just to get m'damn heart down outta my throat and back where it belongs."

"Barb walked out on Real. She just moved into a place near mine. She's gonna get a job and I'm gonna look after the kids."

"She gets the best of the deal," he laughed. "Christ, if it was a choice between a job eating garbage with a dirty spoon or lookin' after those two sad little farts, I'd take the job, too."

"They aren't sad, they're laughin' all the time. Runnin' around yellin' and hollerin', scootin' up and down the stairs, go go go from the time they wake up until they fall asleep in their tracks." But Gus just laughed again, as if what she'd said was funny. "So what else you up to?" she tried again. "You still doing that singin' and eatin' that funny food?"

"No." He shook his head as if he felt sorry for her. "No, I'm studying music, though. Bought a twelve-string guitar and I'm taking lessons on it. And I've signed on for computer stuff at the college. I'm not the least bit interested in computers as a job of work, but I do like learning about them. It's like a whole other language."

"Twelve-string, I guess that's hard, eh."

"No, not really. I've been kind of thinking of trying classical, too. I suspect there might be more challenge in that."

"Oh. Well, I wouldn't know." She was starting to feel very strange. Everyone else seemed to be having a real good time and here she was trying to get a conversation going with a guy she ought to feel at home with, and didn't. Anyone watching would think they didn't even know each other.

Darelle was still awake when the lot of them arrived home. She heard Barb holler, and heard both boys yelp, then race up the stairs and along the outside landing to their own apartment. When the adults came in the house, Darelle was sitting on the sofa with a cushion hugged to her belly, her face beet red, tears slickering from her eyes.

"I'm sorry," she sobbed, "I tried but they just—"

"You stop crying, Darelle." Cindy patted her on the head and even stroked her cheek. "It's not your fault. Barb'll take care of the little suckers, you just go wash your face and go to bed, and don't worry about a thing."

"Donny was good, though," Darelle sniffed bravely. "He was real good."

"Donny ain't got sense enough to not be good," Tammy muttered.

Darelle brushed her teeth and went to bed, still sniffling, still feeling hard done by. She lay awake for a while listening to the faint wisps of conversation she could hear from the living room. Barb and her friend Herb said they were going over to the other apartment to make sure the bloodsuckers were actually in bed, but they'd be back soon. Cindy and Gus drank beer in the living room with Tammy and her friend. Darelle half expected to be roused out of bed and put in a sleeping bag on the living room floor with Donny snoring next to her, but she fell asleep anyway. Barb and Herb weren't back before Darelle dropped off, and when she finally woke up again, just before noon, Tammy and her friend were sleeping together on one opened sleeping bag with another one draped over them. And still no sign of Barb and Herb. Or of the two boys.

Tammy's friend left within a half hour of waking up, saying he had to get back to his place, shower and change and get himself over to pick up his kids for his weekend visitation. Tammy told him to take care, have a good time with the kids and not work too hard, he probably needed a rest. He grinned and said he would probably need a chiropractor, and everyone laughed softly, even Darelle who understood zip-all.

Barb and her friend Herb came over for coffee at about one-thirty. Billy and Bobby were with them but were much quieter than anyone could remember. Darelle couldn't tell whether they were tired or Barb had really taken a round out of them.

Their improved behaviour was a bit late, though. The super showed up at suppertime with a typed up piece of paper which he handed to Cindy without so much as a how-d'ya-do. He left as soon as her hand closed on the notice and was halfway down the steps to the sidewalk by the time she'd read it.

"Well, thanks for nothin', ya asshole!" she yelled. "It wasn't even my kids!"

She was still telling him chapter and verse when Barb came out of her unit holding a second paper. They looked at each other, both of them insulted and angry. "I just bloody well moved *in!*" Barb glared at her sons, standing sullen and frightened in the doorway. "Boy what a pair you are," she sighed. Then she looked at Cindy, and suddenly they were both laughing.

"T'hell with it," Barb decided. "I was lookin' for a place to rent when I found this one, I guess I can just keep on lookin'."

Gus laughed and laughed and laughed but wouldn't tell anyone what the big joke was.

"Pay him no mind," Cindy said bitterly. "He's halfways round the damn bend at the best of times," and Gus laughed even harder.

11

The voice coming through the phone sounded both happy and excited. "Hi, Mom?"

"Yes," Isa answered out of habit, knowing full well whoever was calling, it wasn't *her* daughter.

"It's Cindy. You know, Gus and Cindy."

"Oh, sure. Uh, how are you?" Isa supposed she was about to be hit up for money again, and she supposed she'd say yes even though they were now up to fifteen hundred with no sign of anyone paying any of it back. Carol had told her a dozen times she had rocks in her head for digging into her jeans whenever there was a phone request for forty or fifty—or sixty or seventy—dollars to "tide us over" or "see us through." Part of Isa agreed, and wondered what the hell she was trying to buy when she sent the money. Another part of her knew that directly or indirectly, the Bingo hall would get the bulk of it. But the part of her she always responded to was the one which thought of the kids, empty fridges, no milk or bread and a big pain in the little belly.

"I'm fine. We've got some great news for you."

"Yeah? Did someone get a job?"

"Better than that. You're going to be a grandmother again."

Isa almost said what do you mean *again*, neither of my kids has kids, but self-preservation made her hold back. Besides, she saw more of Donny and Darelle than most grandmothers got to see of their out-of-town grandchildren.

"Surprised you, huh?"

Isa stalled for time. "Tell me again."

"I *knew* you'd be flabbergasted! It's true, though, Gus'n'me's going to have a baby." Cindy's tone changed slightly. "Aren't you happy?" she asked.

"Cindy, to tell you the honest to god's truth, I think my brain has stopped dead. I hardly know what to say!"

"I *knew* you'd be happy. I told Gus you'd be right out of your mind with it. Didn't I, Gus? Maybe you'd like to hear it from him."

"Oh, not yet." Isa felt as if her brain had come to pieces, with each little chunk scurrying around looking for a home. "Tell me how you are, have you seen a doctor?" She wanted to ask, Have you thought of quitting the booze? But again she held her tongue.

Cindy chattered on about how happy she was, how happy Gus was, how happy Darelle was, how happy Donny was, how happy her sister Barb was. There were so many happy people in her world you'd have thought something uplifting was going to happen instead of another little life coming into a world of violence and damage.

"You be sure to take your vitamins, now," Isa said, making herself sound suitably mother-in-law-ish and concerned.

"Oh, I am already. And I've joined Building Better Babies, Gus told me I had to. They do, like, pre-natal stuff, you know, films and stuff, and they get speakers in to talk to you about nutrition and stuff. The last one I went to, last night, they talked about how anything I eat, the baby gets, and how if I get real excited or upset, the baby does too, because the adrenalin stuff affects it. And they said if I take fluoride drops in my juice, the baby gets the benefit, but not to take too much or it'll mark its teeth when they finally come in. Isn't that something? I mean it doesn't *have* teeth, right, it's just a little blobby thing no bigger'n a frog, but what I do now can affect its teeth when they come in. Kinda scary." She paused. "I guess maybe you're wondering about, well, the partying and all, right?"

"Well . . ."

"Yeah, they talked about that at the very first one I went to, and they said if I have a beer the baby gets the effect of it. I didn't know should I believe that or not, people's always coming up with wild stories so's to make other people quit drinkin' or smokin' or whatever. Anyway, Gus had already said that and I didn't believe him, but then they said it and, well, even if I didn't believe it at first, by the time they were finished the meeting I did because they had a film about kids who, like, can't learn? Because of drinking before they were born? So what I wanted to tell you was I'm not doin' that, okay? I quit beering and I only drink, like, 7-Up or ginger ale or something, and I cut way back on cigarettes. So you don't have to worry, okay?"

Don't have to worry? Isa worried. It sounded as if Cindy had been to maybe three Triple-B meetings. Put that together with the fact the baby was due in April and you were left with about three months between conception and the time she heard the news about alcohol. That first trimester is the most crucial. But don't worry about your first grandchild having fetal alcohol syndrome or maybe worse, fetal drug syndrome. Or both. Hell no, we've seen the light and of course it'll be retroactive.

When Carol came home from work, Isa was lying on the couch with the TV tuned to Oprah, watching homeless teen-agers talk about why they were living on the street, getting their food out of dumpsters.

"Why are you watching that trash?" Carol blurted.

"Oh, I'm just trying to get myself prepared for the coming generation," Isa said, tears slickering down her face. "No sense suffering from Future Shock, right?" and she told Carol about the phone call.

"It could be worse," Carol said. "The kid could be due in February instead of April. After all, the entire population of the West Coast is suicidal in February. Combine that with post-partum depression and you've got the makings of a real horror show."

"I wonder, with all the money she has, if Oprah Winfrey will think to set up these kids on her program in an apartment or something? It could be a tax write-off for her, she probably needs them, and she's getting two one-hour programs out of them. Maybe she'll get Meals on Wheels to go around with food, and get them into trade school or something."

"Sure, and maybe there really is a pot of gold at the end of every rainbow. Come on, Lily Lump, up off the couch, blow the nose, wipe the eyes, I'll take you out for pizza."

But Isa was too upset to go out for pizza. Carol phoned the

restaurant, ordered a take-out and sped into town to pick it up and get it home again before it was stone cold.

"It's the most heartbreaking thing I've heard in years," Isa sobbed. "The poor little bugger ought to at least be welcome, I ought to at least be willing to love it, and instead, here I am, and I'm right in the middle of an Oh woe is me, Oh woe is you, Oh woe is all of us deep-blue bummer! Her third kid, for crying out loud, and *now* she learns about substances crossing the placental barrier. What in hell did she think people meant when they said You're eating for two?"

"You stop that!" Carol snapped. "You're so busy being the White Queen, worrying about everything before it happens, you aren't even eating your pizza. Chill out, Isa, before I get cross."

"Oh, fuck, as if you getting cross was the most I had to feel sorry for myself about! The way those people live we'll be lucky if the coming blessed event doesn't turn out to be another Clifford Olsen!"

"The Clifford Olsens of the world don't all come out of trash-town, you know. And everybody out of trash town doesn't necessarily end up a menace to society. Look at yourself. The kid won't even be here for five months and already you've got it grown up, wing-nut, and a serial killer of little kids. When you get morbid, Isa, you get all the way morbid. And to watch *that* program after you get *that* news . . . you're just plain stupid, is what you are."

"Yeah? I love you, too." Isa reached for another slice of pizza. She even made herself straighten up and get a grip. "You're right, I know it. Look for the silver lining and all that, right? Maybe it'll be Toulouse Lautrec, crippled legs and all, but hell, look at that kid colour with his crayons."

"This is how you cheer yourself up? We could hire you out to be stand-up comic at a convention of undertakers. What is it you told me your grandmother always said? Something about Sufficient unto each day is the evil thereof?"

"I shouldn't have told you that. Now I'm shacked up with my own grandmother. The shrinks would have a heyday with that one."

"They're all their own best patients, anyway." And Carol shifted from the big chair to snug in close to Isa, still eating her lukewarm pizza. "I'm not your Gran, anyway," she whispered conspiratorially, "I'm actually, if the truth be known, a total love slave, a veritable pulsating package of pulchritude who lusts after your meat constantly." And they laughed softly together, each of them feeling as if the shittiest stick in the history of human endeavour was being used to paint the horizons of their life.

Isa went down to the city for a session with the producers, the story editor, and the aging maven said to be one of the best script surgeons in the industry. They met in his hotel room, and right at the beginning Isa figured out he hadn't read the script. She considered standing up and announcing she was leaving and would come back when Hizzoner had at least done that much. Instead, she sat with the others, waiting for room service to bring the coffee and croissants. And the gin and tonic for the Expert.

"I want you to *tell* me this story," he said, leaning back in his chair facing Isa, his pelvis tilted slightly so that she would be sure to see the erection pressing against his expensive slacks.

Was she supposed faint with shock or swoon with lust? Once upon a time Isa had known how to cope with such unspoken dynamics, but she was years out of practice and even longer past any interest. She had a mad impulse to stand up à la Lady MacBeth and shout, "is this a dagger which I see before me, the handle toward my hand?"

The producers had seen the lump too, and looked at Isa helplessly. She shrugged. The script surgeon saw the shrug and interpreted it the wrong way. Or perhaps the right way. He straightened in his chair, the boner vanished in the redistribution of his corpulent form. Infantile pettishness flashed across his round face, and was covered quickly by phoney friendliness.

"I find it very helpful to *hear* what each of you thinks relevant and salient in the film before I actually *look* at the pages. A sort of intellectual show and tell." He looked directly at Isa, who rewarded him with a carbon copy of his own fake smile.

"I think maybe the producers and story editor should be the ones to start," she said smoothly. "They'd be the ones working from the pages, and that's what's going to sell the project."

"Isn't it your story?"

"Yes, it is. But if I haven't managed to put it on paper . . ." She leaned back, and brought out her cigarettes.

The coffee and croissants came; the session continued. Isa sipped, smoked and looked out the window at the concrete Lego sitting at the base of the mountains. She longed to tell the Expert to jump in the air and bite himself on the ass, but he would only turn the clock to payback time and slander the script he hadn't even read. How many others had wasted hours of their time stroking the old bastard for the same reasons? How had he got himself into such a position of power?

The story editor had pages of notes and some excellent suggestions. He asked Isa a couple of questions and while she was answering, room service brought another pot of coffee and another drink for the Expert. One of the producers asked the story editor to clarify something. He did. The producer asked Isa if she agreed with the story editor. She did. The other producer wasn't sure. The four of them talked it over while the Expert went to the sideboard and mixed himself a third drink from his own supply. Lunch came and lunch went. The expert managed half a sandwich and two more drinks.

When Isa stepped out on the tiny balcony for some fresh air, the Expert joined her. "What is that building?" he asked, moving closer to her and pointing. Somehow, when he lowered his arm, his hand wound up on her shoulder.

Isa turned slightly and the hand fell. "I don't know," she said, her tone easy. "I don't live here."

"I thought you were from the West Coast," he smiled, flirting.

"I am, but this city isn't the entire Coast, it's just a little pimple on the face of the place."

"But you live out West full time."

"Yes. Twenty-four hours of every day."

"You're married?"

"God, no! I was, but only in my youth, before I got smart and bought my way out of it."

"But you have a relationship?"

"I have several."

She went back into the room and suggested they wind up the session. "Let's give our surgeon time to think about what we've discussed," she said, "and to *read the script.* Should we meet again tomorrow?"

"We could meet for dinner," blurted the Expert, "and then, oh, I don't know, take in some of the night life together?"

"I'm going to beg off," Isa said firmly. "I hate to break the flow. I'm going to spend the night pounding in some of these excellent suggestions."

But she didn't spend the night with Jen's computer keyboard. She tossed her notes into her suitcase and closed the lid.

"So, kiddo," she said to her daughter, "what's the best Szechuan place in town?"

"Already have reservations," Jen told her. "How was your story session?"

Gus was waiting for them at the Szechuan house, a wide smile on his face. Isa was happy to see him, and even happier to see he was alone. She wasn't ready to deal with the whole fam damily. Social ritual demanded, however, that she at least ask about the others.

"Oh, they're visiting with her sister," he shrugged. "I'm not sure when they'll be back."

Isa let it drop. With Gus it was easy to tell which things could be pursued, which should be left alone. Besides, she wasn't very interested.

"What's this I hear about you becoming pater familias?" Jen sounded as if the entire idea was just too funny for words.

Obviously Gus didn't find it so funny. "I guess so."

"You *guess* so?"

"Well, Cindy's pregnant, for sure." He shrugged again. "As for the pater part, only God and the angels know."

"Gus!" Isa blurted before she could bite her tongue.

"Hey, remember our agreement," he laughed softly. "You can shit your friends, and I can shit my friends, and our friends can shit whoever they want, but we don't shit each other."

"I thought—"

"Mom, there are things in this mess that are unfinished, and because they are, I'm not ready to pack my bags, move off and stay moved. But that doesn't mean moon-June-croon-love in bloom, okay?"

"But—"

"No buts. It's all up in the air. And until things become more clear, they'll stay the way they are, and that's not clear at all."

"What do you intend to do?"

"Well, for one thing, I intend to pig out on Szechuan. And I intend to have a good time and not ruin the evening by trying to solve things, most of which I don't even understand, none of which I have any control over, or even a lot of interest in."

"Or in which I even have a lot of interest," Isa teased.

"Right. And if you see me heading out with my participle dangling, please let me know, okay?"

"Ditto the split infinitive," Jen agreed. "So what about the pepper chicken?"

They ate hugely, talked freely and laughed easily, especially during Isa's tales of her story session with the Expert. Gus told jokes and teased Jen about her job, and she teased him back. "All this going here and going there in search of yourself . . . what are you going to do when you find you?"

"Probably sit down over Szechuan and ask me why I was so damn hard to find. I mean, what have I got to hide, right? Maybe I've done something tacky that I don't want me to know about. Won the lottery and forgot to go pick up the money."

"Or joined the RCMP and you're too embarrassed to let anyone know, even yourself."

"I thought of that once," he said, not joking. "I even checked it out. What you need by way of education, stuff like that. But," and he was joking again, "it was like a gentle breeze passing over the surface of the still pond which is my mind, and the ripples were gone, leaving not a trace."

"Why not think of taking the real estate course?" Jen said.

"I thought of that, too. Thought about it a lot, in fact. But I couldn't see myself doing it. Well, that's not exactly true, I could see myself doing it, and getting so sucked into it that it wound up the only thing I was doing. And that's not who I want to be. I'm not like you, Jenny. You seem to be able to see it as a job. Me, I'd get pulled into it as a life."

"For sure, there's guys who get sucked into exactly that. They wind up with pots and pots and pots of money and no home life, social life, or . . ." Her tone changed back to teasing. "Poor buggers, eh, nothing to do but drive around in their sports cars, talking on cellular phones, making reservations for a month in Cancun or the Virgin Islands."

"Right," only Gus wasn't joking, "and in the meantime there are more and more and more people every day eating out of dumpsters and living on the street, sleeping in underground parking lots with old cardboard boxes for blankets."

"Oh jesus, Gussy," Jen sighed. "Don't get started on that, please. What can I do about it? I pay my taxes, in full and on time. I give a good whack to the food bank, I give another to the downtown shelter. Are any of them going to be any better off if I quit my job and join you doing whatever it is you've decided to do this week? You talk a lot about those poor people, but what do you do to make things better for them?"

"What can I do?" he shrugged. "If you can't figure out what to do, how do you expect me to? But maybe if enough people stopped supporting the system that not only allows but condones that kind of crap—"

"Except what you're talking is utopia, and it isn't going to happen. It would be nice if it did, but let's be realistic, okay?"

"You ever wonder what you were in a past life?"

"Past life? Gus-boh, I've got all I can do to deal with my present life, I don't have the energy to start coping with previous incarnations. Or the possibility of future ones."

"I do." Isa sipped her green tea. "I've decided in my next life I want to be tall, strong and athletic. I think I'll be born to very very *very* wealthy parents. That way they can underwrite my forays into, oh, horsey things and such. I think I'll pass on the downhill skiing and anything else that might break a bone or two, and concentrate on safe things, like sunbathing and weightlifting. Not heavy weights, god knows what would happen if you dropped one of them. Little weights. Two-pounders, nobody much bothers with them, they might welcome the attention."

"And what are you going to do with all that tall strong athletic money?"

"Nothing. A life of sloth, please. Sloth and leisure. And, of course, intense satisfactions. I might," she declared, "grab Reba McIntyre's voice, and her hair, too, and be a C&W star."

"I'll be your manager and bean counter," Jennet offered. "And I'd invest your money in real estate. Probably huge condo developments."

"I could drive your bus," Gus put in, "maybe play guitar in your band. We'll get Carol to come along and keep us all organized and maybe even once in a while sane."

"Sane?" Jennet wasn't joking, and they all knew it. "Gussers, there's not one of us would recognize sanity if it was shoved up our noses. I mean, really, talk about endangered species."

Darelle and Donny arrived on Boxing Day, stepping off the ferry with big smiles and backpacks in their hands. Donny was wearing a ratty pair of sneakers at least three sizes too big for him, the laces passing under the sole and tying on top, which held the things together marginally. Darelle's sneakers were in better shape but were cheap, thin-soled canvas and rubber jobs more suited to the beach in summer than the sidewalk slush of winter.

"Did you eat on the ferry?" Carol asked.

"No," Donny whispered, shaking his head. "Mom didn't give us no money."

"Good!" Carol put her arms around him. "I'm glad. Because we thought we'd put the packs in the trunk, head up to the store, let you pick your Chrissy prez stuff and then go to Mr. Mike's. Does that sound like something to do on a miserable cold day?"

There were cheaper sneakers in the store, but Isa was so upset by the way the kids were rigged out she was ready to mortgage the farm if need be. When she took Donny's shoe off to try on the new ones, she saw his sock was worn out and soaking wet. "Oops!" she tried to make a joke out of it. "Best we get some new ones before we start stuffing our toes into shoes we haven't paid for."

She got three packages of socks, heavy cotton-blend jock socks with stripes on the top, three pair to a package. Under his dripping sock, his little foot was wrinkled and bleached white, and had obviously been wet for hours. Still making herself behave as if it was all a great and exciting party, Isa pulled the warm dry sock on his foot, then tried on the new sneaker. "Stand up, dumpling," she told him. "Let's see if this thing fits or not."

"It fits!" he blurted. "Really it does."

In fact, it was two sizes too big. When she took it off his foot, he sagged as if his only chance was leaving. Isa went back to the display of sneakers and found a pair of leather high-tops with bright purple inserts, like the ones she saw on the treasured middle class kids in the mall. She slid it on Donny's foot, got him to stand, and then she nodded. "Well, that's the size all right," she told him. "Now it's up to you to pick the colour you want."

"That one!" It was like putting a sandwich before a starving person.

"Okay. You've got it, guy. Now we have to get farm gumboots, too, because there's a lot of mud at our place."

"What about Darelle?"

"Carol's with her. Carol and Darelle *love* shopping. I hate it. I get itchy when we've been ten minutes at the tee shirts, trying to figure out which goes with what and what goes with which and if and should we or could I or maybe . . ." and Donny was laughing, yarding off his other worn-out shoe and grisly sock, eagerly pulling on the new ones.

She took him to the underwear bin and got him seven pair of shorts, not just white ones, but brightly coloured ones as well. Then tee shirts, some warm sweatshirts, a couple of machine-washable sweaters and four pair of new jeans.

"Costin' a lot," he warned.

"Hey, mister, I've been wandering around in this damn mall for weeks looking at things, asking myself Will my guy like this or would he rather have that over there, counting the days until you got here. Indulge me, okay?"

"What's that? 'dulge?"

"It means please be a nice guy and let me play this little game we're doing. Please?"

She nearly choked when she saw the price of the new jackets, but what's it for if not to spend. Loaded down with paper and plastic bags, they found Carol and Darelle still consulting each other about the jeans situation. "Donny and I are going to the washroom so he can rig himself out in some of his new stuff, then we're going to Mr. Mike's. Wait there for you." And she handed over the credit card. We got," she hinted, "four pair of jeans and a new jacket."

"Yeah, how are they for prices on those things?"

"As close to a hundred as you can get without bumping your head."

When she stripped Donny down in the toilet cubicle and started hauling on his new clothes, she saw the stripes on his butt. "Someone use a belt on you?" she asked softly.

"Auntie Barb got mad at me," he admitted. "She said I was bad."

"Yeah? Why'd she think you were bad?"

"I don't know. She never said."

Togged out in his new stuff, strutting proudly in his new high-tops, Donny looked like any other kid from the comfortable end of town. In fact, he was better looking than most of them. After all, the new clothes effectively covered the belt marks on his butt and the bruises across his shoulders. Isa's own skin burned, and the memories embedded forever in her flesh squirmed, demanding attention. That night, before she pulled Donny's new pyjamas on him, Isa smeared camphorated salve on the marks. She knew it wouldn't heal them or even stop them from hurting, but she wanted him to know that someone other than himself thought it important that he'd been walloped so severely. Someone should at least bear witness.

Several times in the days the kids stayed with them, Isa felt as if what she really wanted to do was prowl through the bush until she found a place she could sit down, put her back against the bole of a large second-growth fir or cedar, and howl like a lonesome hound. Coming as it did hot on the heels of another script session with the gin-sodden old fart, the kids' visit explained to her why she kept putting up with the cow cack and heifer dust. All she had to do was evade the gropings of the old lush and follow the protocol, writing what they said they wanted and getting paid by the draft. Then she could take her whore's wages to Wal-Mart and buy some clothes to keep the little jiggers warm and dry. Maybe, somewhere along the line, some good would come of it all. At least Donny was no longer hang-dog and ashamed of the way he looked. And wonder of wonders, Darelle hadn't blubbered one single time. Yet.

Jennet came for a holiday visit and took the kids out touring in her fancy car. "I'd like a car like this," Darelle announced, "and nice clothes like yours, and some of that perfume."

"Tell you what." Jen sounded as if it could happen. "You work hard at school and graduate from grade twelve and all that good stuff, and I'll pay for your real estate course."

"I'm not all that good in school," Darelle admitted.

"Just have to work a bit harder is all. It can be done. You're not a dim-wit, Darelle. If your cousins can get on the honour roll, so can you. I have," she lied with a huge smile, "every confidence in the world, darlin'."

Later, when she and Isa were alone, Jen had a minor tantrum. "It's a damn sin, Mom, and you know it. Darelle is heading for twelve and she can barely understand what she reads, and Donny, my god, heading for grade—what, two? Three? And he can't read at all. He doesn't even know his fuckin' alphabet! Where's the welfare at, anyway? I thought they were mandated to scoop kids if they were demonstrably at risk?"

"If I had an answer or even a clue, I'd share it with you."

"Well, *fuck*, Mom, do I got to do it all myself?" And then Jen, who was on the verge of weeping, grabbed onto that streak of tough that was her survival instinct and forced herself to find a joke in it somewhere. Because when you're laughing, at least you aren't scream-ing. "Life's a bitch," she said, "and then you're dead. And the poor bloody Buddhists have to turn around and try 'er again."

12

The funding came through, the producers made all their cross-collateralization deals, satisfied all requirements, went public and sold shares in the film. Isa cashed her last cheque from them and heaved a sigh of relief. No more alky-old fart! Thank you, sweet lord.

All that sitting in front of the glowing screen, travelling to and from the city and perching for hours at a time on a sofa with a binder on her lap had kicked her back into an absolute shitfit. Her physician took one look at the dark rings under her eyes and the tight-drawn skin of her cheeks and throat and upped her medication. He also gave her some new pills, large pink ones with a kick like an army mule.

About all she could manage was to stumble and lurch her way through the morning and evening barn chores, and once in a while go out to visit with the mares. They seemed to realize there was something different about her, something frail, maybe even helpless.

The rest of the time she spent on the sofa, watching TV or staring without comprehending at the pages of books or magazines. She wondered if this was how things looked to Darelle. Each individual letter was recognizable, but what they were doing lumped together like that was anybody's guess. Unable to focus, Isa let her mind wander into some ridiculous places. Some of the ideas she hatched for making a living seemed so logical and reasonable, and so far from sane, that when she recounted them to Carol in the evening, they both wound up helpless and giggling.

At some time in the not-too-dim past, some nameless body was said to have started a frog leg farm on Texada Island. He imported some humungous commercial frog species from France and turned the seed stock loose in a large lake. A year later he started harvesting the offspring. As the story went, he killed the frogs, removed the legs, packed them in cans with some garlic and parsley and a dab of farm fresh butter, then he canned them the same way just about everyone on the coast canned up salmon in the kitchen, and shipped them to Europe by the case.

He made a whack of money. So much of it he lost all interest in work and took off for parts unknown, leaving the big frogs to their own devices. Some withering wit caught some and transferred them to Cranberry Lake in Powell River. And now everyone knew someone who had seen at least one great gronker with the legs of a duckling poking out of its grinning mouth. Some people insisted they knew someone who had seen one of the mammoths with a grown adult snow goose half swallowed.

Catching them, killing them, and exporting canned frogs legs seemed like a fairly good idea, but as with any good idea, modifications and improvements could be made. "We don't kill the frogs," Isa told Carol, who was already red in the face and trying hard not to guffaw. "We just amputate the legs. That will leave us with an abundance of legless frogs. Now every year in the States, somewhere, they have this frog-jumping competition. Tens of thousands of people go for the three-day festival. Our frogs wouldn't have a hope of winning without legs. *But,* every toy box in Powell River is littered with wheel-less cars and car-less wheels. We collect them and get unemployed people to make little wheelchairs. Then we challenge everyone in the world to a Handicapped Olympics, three days of wheelchair races. And of course our frogs would win because they'd have more practice. Be a real boost to the local economy."

"What about the other three hundred sixty-two days a year?"

"Abalone. We get a government grant to start us up. Business development, something like that. Get the government to lease us some foreshore, buy us a few boats. We put the abalone seed in the ocean and sit on the foreshore drinking beer and going for the occasional boat ride. It takes seven years to grow abalone to market size. And these government grants pay your wages until your first harvest."

"How are you going to harvest them?"

"Not going to. An abalone is nothing but one great big foot in a shell that's just waiting to be made into buttons. And they're *always* flying those damn jets from Comox too low. So we tell the federals the jets scared the abalone and they're all just a footin'er off into the deep and uncharted brine. Maybe even get a second grant, another seven years of free money. Be just about time for new boats, too."

She and Carol both knew the crazy schemes were Isa's way of fending off the demons of past, present and future, her way of not thinking about the day-by-day inevitability of the birth of yet another kid to be walloped with belts or knocked on the ear or left alone or sent out into the world with someone else's worn-out sizes-too-big sneakers on its feet.

Just before Isa cracked up entirely, her physician put her on Prozac. It was a month before she began to feel the effects of it, but at least the screams got stuffed deep enough inside her she didn't have to think up mad schemes to keep her brain from shredding.

She also started a new film script. After all, with another little mouth to feed, another body to clothe and keep warm, a dose of money couldn't do any harm, and her back was about as bad as it could get anyway. On her own, she would have wound up with a script that was heavy, dark and compelling; with the help of Prozac it turned out light-hearted and meaningful. And she had no problems with the new story editor the producers found.

The first time Isa saw her grandson she felt so weird she was afraid to hold him. She felt, in fact, as if she was going to pitch face forward to the floor. Something was buzzing in her head, and she could feel cold sweat starting on her back and chest. Her hands shook and she could taste that sulphur-egg-wotzit that means it's time to call on Ralph at the porcelain altar.

Gus and Cindy were all smiles and hugs. A casual observer would have thought the entire scenario was from this month's edition of Traditional Family Values. But Isa knew all too well the giveaway signs, Cindy sounding as if she had a bad cold and Gus like a flea in a fit, bopping around to make coffee, coming back to grab jackets and coats, heading back to the coffee maker, and talking machine gun fast. Isa figured Cindy had a hangover and Gus was working overtime to try to cover it up, not realizing he was somehow making it worse.

Isa had never in her life dropped a baby, she hadn't even come close to dropping a baby, but she nearly dropped her first-born grandchild. She sat on the sofa feeling as if the world was getting ready to spin away from her, and she finally had to plop the kid on the sofa next to her. By god if she fainted, she wasn't going to land on eight pounds of soft flesh.

A look of insult or anger flickered across Gus's face. He probably thinks I don't even like his kid, Isa thought. "I'm too excited," she said, which wasn't exactly true, but which might keep Gus from one of his sulks. He turned and looked at her, not fully believing, until she held out her hands and he could see the trembling all the way across the room. "I'd hate to drop him," said Isa. "I didn't shake like this the first time I held my own kids, I don't know what's come over me."

But she did know. What had come over her had to do with ratty sneakers and grubby worn-out jackets, what had come over her had to do with babysitting cousins who did weird things and were as mean as garbage dump rats.

The baby lay on his back, swaddled in a new blue and white blanket, staring at her. Isa didn't dare look at him for long, she was afraid she'd start to cry. She stole glances at him, and when the coffee was ready she took her mug as if it were a lifeline thrown by the Coast Guard after her leaky tub had given up the ghost and plunged to the bottom.

Two cups of coffee and several cigarettes later, Isa relaxed. It was as sudden as the onset of whatever it was had come over her. One minute she was sure she was going to collapse or leap to her feet screaming, the next minute she was fine.

She handed her empty mug to Gus, put the ash tray on the floor, reached over and picked up the baby, who was still wide awake and staring. She didn't say a word to him, she just held him in the crook of her left arm and let him grab onto the pointy finger of her right hand. They stared at each other. Then he stared at Carol. Then he closed his eyes and snuggled against Isa, yawning.

"Well," Carol said softly, "there's someone has been here before and knows who's on his team."

Isa's grandmother had told her any time a baby younger than a month old smiles, it's because he or she is talking to the angels who have come to visit the one who so recently lived among them. And who knew, maybe that is exactly what is happening. Or maybe those people are right who say it's gas. But Isa knew the smile her grandson had turned toward Carol was more than all of that.

"He's agreeing with you," she said softly. "Want to hold him?"

"Not yet." Carol rose from the sofa and took her mug to the coffee maker. "I'm having too much fun watching you two. You might not know it yet but you've been in each other's lives before and it was a great, tight relationship."

"So, little boy, who did you used to be?" and the baby opened his eyes again and stared at her. Isa felt as if she was about to start crying.

"They say that when a soul comes back," Carol said, "it comes back the opposite gender of who it was the previous time. So who did you know who was female and very *very* important to you? Someone who's been dead for quite a few years."

Isa knew Carol was only acting calm, leaning against the counter, sipping coffee. She knew Carol was trying hard not to screech with the visions of the future which were hammering at her brain.

"My grandma," Isa said firmly. "My grandma and the Old Woman."

"So which is he?" Gus laughed nervously.

"I don't know. Maybe both. Does *he* have a name?"

"Steve," Cindy said smugly. "He was married to my sister, see, but he got killed in the bush, and all she's got is girls, so there wasn't any boy to carry on his name, and so I thought it might be nice to kind of, you know, keep it going." She didn't bother telling Isa it was a good way to flush Tammy's damn toilet at the same time, grind her face in it that Cindy had two boys and Tammy didn't even have one to name after a guy.

Isa and Carol stayed two days, sleeping on the pull-out couch at night, feeling out of place and overcrowded during the day. Darelle and Donny trailed off to school each morning and came back in the afternoon showing no interest or enthusiasm for the place they spent so many of their hours. They came in the door, took off their jackets, hung them on hooks, put their backpacks on the floor under the jackets, then went to look at the baby. If he was awake, they played with him like a toy; if he was asleep, they sat on the floor in front of the TV and watched soaps and situation comedies until suppertime.

Isa and Carol went grocery shopping and came home with enough to fill the cupboards. Isa did the cooking and Carol organized the kids to help with clean-up. Gus did the laundry and tidied the house while Cindy sat sipping endless cups of tea and smiling contentedly, waiting for the baby to get hungry so she could undo the buttons on her blouse and nurse him. Isa wasn't sure how much nourishment the kid would get with his mother on a steady diet of tea and cigarettes, but she said nothing. It would only sound like mother-in-law bitching, and anyway there's no sense saying anything unless it will improve the situation.

She was so glad to have the farm as an excuse to go back, she blessed each and every critter on the place. And so glad to leave that without knowing she was doing it, she sighed deeply, repeatedly.

"Rough, huh?" Carol patted Isa's knee.

"Jesus. The poor little christer!"

"Well, at least Gus is there. He can at least organize poached eggs and toast."

"For now," Isa sighed again. "I'd bet the longest he's stayed there at one time is a few weeks, a month or two at most. And yet, I have to tell you, it's longer than I'd be able to manage. On the other hand, I'd never have got involved in the first place."

"Yeah, but if all you were looking for was a brief encounter or two with a good-looking body . . . because she is good looking, you know."

"She's past dumb, she's *stupid*, Carol!"

"Maybe he wasn't in the mood for intellectual stimulation. Come on, be honest, haven't you ever embarked on a short-termer for strictly lustful reasons? Be honest, Isa."

"Yeah. And I guess it was either shithouse luck or the constraints and restraints of biology that saved me from starting a new life. That's something the moral majority ought to consider before they build their ovens and get ready to shove in all us queers. At least we aren't adding to the population explosion."

"Well, maybe when Gus takes off again he'll take the baby with him."

"No chance." Isa wasn't going to fool herself about that one. When Gus moved, he moved fast and light.

Melanie didn't see why Darelle and Donny ought to be the ones with a new baby. Why couldn't she have one, too? After all, her mom was back home again, and she knew her own mommy would do a much better job than Cindy. She said as much to Georgie. He stared at her for a long time, shaking his head slightly, and she thought he was thinking about it, but then he told her No way, Mel, no way at all, and when she asked why, he told her. What he told her upset her so much she couldn't talk to anyone for two days. What could she say? Every time she looked at her dad or Georgie she was reminded of what she'd been told and shown. They wound up with a little dangly thing that looked as if their pee-er had been ripped right off them, leaving only this little bit of a thing like the head of a turtle. A blind turtle, who didn't even have any eyes. A birth-defect blind turtle. When she looked at her mom she thought about how she had actually let them put their deformity into her pee-er to get a baby started. It was all just too gross for words, Melanie didn't like any part of it. If that was what you had to do to get a baby, well, she'd pass on it.

Anyway, she could play with Stevie as long as she wanted to because Darelle and Donny had to go to school every day and she and Georgie didn't. They were just visiting, taking what her mom called a mental health break. Melanie had no idea how long they'd be there, she hadn't even had much warning they were going. Dad came home and took Mom by the arm, led her into the cubbyhole that was supposed to be a kitchenette, said something to her that made her sigh and shake her head, then they came out and told the kids to pack up as much as they could as fast as they could, they were going on a mental health break. And poof, there they were, into a cab and down to the bus depot and it was comic books and Mr. Big bars to keep them occupied on the trip.

While the other kids were in school, Melanie played with Stevie and sat with ears like vacuum cleaners sucking up everything said by everyone. Maybe she would find out why it was she and Georgie were always on the move from here to there and then on to somewhere else, when Linda and little Sandra had been living in the same place for just about as long as Melanie could remember. How come some people stayed and others went?

George came home after supper one night with a wide grin on his face and a wad of money which he hauled out of his pocket. Then, making sure everyone saw him do it, he divided the money into two piles. One he put back in his pocket, the other he left on the table to, as he put it, "help out a bit." The next day he went off with his half and came home even happier than he'd been the day before, and then wouldn't you know it, out came the black plastic garbage bags and stuff stuff stuff, and into a cab and into a furnished apartment near the main drag.

It was nice. There was a little balcony thing and you could stand out there and look out at the water, watch the little boats zipping around, or the seaplanes taking off or landing. Nice too that there was no suggestion she or Georgie go to school. When she asked her dad about it, he said no, then looked at her as if making up his mind about something.

"C'mere, baby." He sat down in one of the big chairs and patted his knee. Melanie went over and leaned against the warm bulk of him. "I think you're old enough to understand, but if you aren't, don't worry about it, you'll wake up one morning and it'll all be clear as a bell. Trust me?"

"Yes."

"Okay. There's a misunderstanding going on right now, and it involves the cops, me, your mom and some of our friends. And we don't have enough money for a good lawyer. So we've moved here and your mom will join us later. There's more work for her in the city than there is over here in this little bit of a town. She and I are going to work really hard to get money for a lawyer, and when we have enough, we'll be able to prove to the cops that we didn't do anything wrong, okay?"

"What do they think you did?"

"That doesn't matter, we didn't do it. So these guys are all in it together, anyway, you know that. Cops, whoofare, the whole bunch, and if you and Georgie go to school they'll check up with their computers to see where you were before and poof, there it is and we're up to our noses in fuzz and us without the money for a lawyer. So," and he blew a horse laugh into the curve of her throat and made her giggle, "your mental health break might seem like a very long summer holiday, okay?"

She didn't understand, but she didn't mind not going to school. Some uncomfortable place inside her knew it wouldn't last, and that at any time at all she and Georgie could wind up in another foster home or receiving home, and as soon as they did it would be school and tutors and fuss fuss fuss. But until it actually happened, she for one wasn't going to worry about it.

She could leave the apartment, go down in the elevator, cross the lobby and out the front door, then in less than three minutes she was on the beach. Entire afternoons could vanish in no time flat just walking up and down the wooden walkways looking at all the boats, everything from prawn boats to fish boats to cabin cruisers. She could sit on a warm log with the concrete apartment buildings and busy highway behind her and ignore it all completely, absorbing herself in the lap of the waves, the squacking of the shit hawks, the scuttle of crabs of all colours. Sometimes the tide washed in big tangles of bull kelp and she could spend hours sorting out the mess, pulling the bullwhips into neat rows, pretend all kinds of silly things, like maybe the whips were a herd trying to go somewhere. Invaders from outer space, maybe, or refugees from a dying planet.

When she thought about it, she figured it was probably a good thing they didn't have a baby. If the cops could track you down through school they could probably track you down through a doctor, and it seemed as if Cindy was at the doctor's every week with Steve. He didn't look sick, but Dad said Cindy could make a big deal out of anything, even a pimple on the ass.

It was really gross to think of Cindy and Gus and how they'd got little Stevie. And gross to think the poor kid wound up with the same name as a guy who was dead. She had asked her mom, asked right out if she herself had been named after a corpse, and her mom hugged her tight, the scent of her perfume making Melanie feel all happy inside. "Jesus lord, baby, no way! You're a whole new person and we gave you a whole new name. Why?"

"It seems . . . gross, you know? I mean . . . I'm glad I'm not named after someone as got their head ripped off. I'd have nightmares!"

"You're like me," Maria agreed. "The whole thing seems just about unsalted crackers to me, too. But one thing you have to know, sweetheart, when it comes to your dad's family, there's not a one of them has all the bricks you need to build a wall, okay? The whole bloody lot of them is potato salad with no eggs or onions."

"Spaghetti without the sauce." Melanie loved this game. They only played it when her mom was in a real good mood.

But that was Before, when they were living together. Somehow it seemed as if no sooner would her mom come home than something would come up and she'd be gone again. There were times Mel would take out the bottle of perfume she'd swiped from Maria's dresser top, loosen the lid and sniff, and the scent would fill her with the strangest combination of feelings. Part grief or sorrow, but most of it a yearning, an excited feeling in the very pit of her stomach. Other people had moms who looked like moms, kind of unfinished or even ratty, with those pull-on polyester slacks that go baggy at the knees right away and those awful sweatshirt things that are all little balls the first time they're washed and put in the dryer. But Maria never looked like that. Even when she was in what she called her sloppin' around stuff she looked great. Her jeans always fit just like another skin, and her tops were every bit as good as the stuff Auntie Cindy thought was steppin' out clothes. Maria never had rundown or scuffed-up sneakers, and she wouldn't be caught dead in those cheap canvas things with the white rubber soles. Maria's sneakers were LA Gear or Nike, with purple or pink inserts. Never catch *her* chewin' her nails, never catch *her* with split cuticles. And she'd probably jump off a bridge before she got caught with her hair looking like it had fallen out of a bird's nest and landed on a person's head, like sometimes happened with Auntie Barb, who, even if there was no baby to prove it, was probably doing with Herb what Georgie had said big people did. Sick.

Barb and Herb went over to Cindy's place after supper, taking a two-four pack with them. Both Billy and Bobby were glad to go visiting, anything that got them out from under the eagle eye of old Herb for a while. Didn't miss much, that Herb, and he didn't take any guff, either. You wouldn't even hear him coming and thuh-*whack*, right on the butt. Especially those nights when he decided he wasn't going to work, because then he was home right up until bedtime and even after, and no jacking around if Herb was home. It was bathtub, jammies, teeth, bed, lights out and dead silence *or else*. And Mom happy to let him run herd on them, too. But if he was sitting at the table with Cindy and Gus playing Rummoli or, better yet, Trivial Pursuit, he wouldn't pay much attention to them.

Herb had this mad simmering anyway, because of the 'viction notice and all that stuff. They didn't get any ref'rence from the landlord, so the place they rented was pretty crummy and Herb just out and out blamed Ferret and Weasel. Darelle and Donny'd had to move, too, but they had Gus to get the place so there wasn't anything marked down anywhere about him bein' a bad tenant. Still, Cindy was miffed about how much the rent was. His mom had talked about that to Herb and said she didn't see what Cindy was bitchin' about, she had full welfare for herself and three kids, plus the money Gus brought in from his job. Herb just shrugged and said Gus was a fool handing over the whole thing. Catch me doin' that, Herb had said, laughing. I'll pay my own way but damned if I'm pickin' up the tab for someone else, especially someone else's goddamn rug rats. And then his mom said something about not dropping any hints, she knew how things were, just the same as they'd always been. And Herb had said you're damn right about that.

Things were changing, though, because when Ferret tried to get Darelle's goat she didn't even snivel, let alone start crying. She just shouted over to the adults. "Uncle Herb, Ferret's trying to bug me and he's gonna get the baby crying if he doesn't stop," and just like that Herb was up from the table and hauling his belt out of his jeans.

"I'm not doin' nothing!" Ferret blurted.

"Okay, asshole, the belt is off, right? And it's gonna hang over the backa my chair, right? And the next move on your part mister is gonna have that belt wrapped right around your arse with the edges overlapping, do you get my meaning? Well? Do you?"

"Yes, Herb."

"All right, chrissakes. You're only gonna make it rough on you, fella, not anyone else."

They watched *Star Trek* and Ferret fumed. Didn't seem to matter what a person did, someone was always yammering on about behave, behave, behave. Or else, or else, or else.

Before they'd made their way through their third beers, they had all come to some kind of agreement. Or at least Cindy and Barb had come to one and Gus and Herb decided to like it or lump it. Anyway they were all in such a good mood Ferret dared to give sleepy Donny a good punch on the shoulder. Donny yelped and, off-balance, lurched against Darelle. That woke up the baby, who started to cry, and before anybody had time to tattle-tale, Herb was up and moving.

"I saw that!" he roared, scaring the baby into even louder yells and squalls. "Never happy, are you?" And he grabbed Ferret by one arm, dragged him down the hallway to the bathroom and then it was hell to pay. Jesus *christmas* but Herb could hit!

"And you can just fuckin' well sit in that corner there, all by your damn self, with nothing to look at but the toilet bowl, and you can stay here and leave everyone else alone." And Herb was gone, back to the kitchen. Ferret could hear him griping and bitching, still madder'n a wet hen. "Attention Deficit Disorder with Hyperactivity my *arse!*" Herb snarled. "All what that is, is a licence to act like a goddamn asshole."

"Well," Barb said mildly, "no sense yammerin' at me, sweetheart, I'm not the one came up with that idea. It was because the school said he couldn't go back unless I took 'im to that goofball doctor or whatever he was, and he's the one said deficit wotzit. So don't *you* start in on me."

"It's all bullshit. If it was something medical like that you know full well they'd have a pill for it. And you better believe, if they had a pill for it I'd ram them pills up his arse four at a time. Now where were we?"

So when Cindy and Barb went together on renting a big old house together, Herb insisted there had to be one room set aside for what he called the Arseltart Treatment Centre. There was nothing in that room. Not a thing. And no way you'd be able to open the window and shinny out either, because Herb and Gus nailed a strip of some kind of metal along the top of the bottom window, so you couldn't raise it. Ferret had a feeling he was going to see an awful lot of this room, and he had no doubt so would Weasel. And what a drag of a room! Blah blue walls, grungy white ceiling tiles, and the rug on the floor looked like something that had died and it hadn't been worth digging a hole to bury it. Something kind of greyish with brown blotch-things on it. Maybe a whole bunch of greyish things had croaked and once they were dead they poisoned the brown things. And a big bolt on the door, but on the hallway side so whoever was in here couldn't get out.

Well, that might be okay. If you had the door half open, say, when dipshit Darelle came swanning down the hallway as if she was Somebody instead of just who she was, you could give 'er a shove, send 'er into the room, slide the bolt shut and eff off, leaving her to holler and screech all she wanted. If you did it right, and if you did it fast enough, she wouldn't know who had done it. Maybe try it out on Donny first. Except he prob'ly wouldn't screech, he'd just do that nutty thing where all of a sudden it was like he took a plane to Hawaii because he sure the hell wasn't here. Prob'ly just sit down in a corner and pee himself or something.

The rest of the house was okay, though. Lots better'n that place they'd been in for a while. Big, real big, with lots of room for everyone. Or there would be for as long as nobody else moved in with them, but you could just about bet someone would. Built from the ground up, so what was a basement wasn't really, because it wasn't in a hole in the ground and didn't have scrunch-over and creep ceilings, they were probably higher than in most houses. A room for the furnace and the hot water tank, another for the freezer, then three rooms with nothing in them yet, but Herb, he wanted one of them for what he called a workshop. What would he work on? He didn't seem to do much. On the main floor the big kitchen with the 'lectric stove and what his mom called More damn cupboards than you could shake a stick at, thank god. They ate their meals there, on a big table that used to be a door before Gus rigged up a couple of leg frames.

The living room was big enough you could have played on your roller blades, if you had any, and there was room in it for both their sofas and all the big chairs, too. And still lots of floor space. Sometimes, if you looked real careful, you could see how that one big room could have been two rooms, but maybe they'd tooken out the wall or something. When he asked Gus about it Gus said there used to be sliding-shut wooden doors that fit into the dip-in spot, but that was dumb, how could the whole door slide in? Gus told him to go by the furniture store and look at the roll-top desks, but a desk was a desk and a wall was a wall. Gus had some pretty screwy ideas sometimes. Across the hallway from the big living room were two bedrooms, and at the end of the hallway a big staircase going up to the top floor, which was where the Hell-Hole room was, and if you didn't use it for a Hell-Hole, it could have been another bedroom.

All the kids slept upstairs, with Cindy and Gus in one of the main floor bedrooms and Barb and Herb in the other. "And the buncha you better behave or we'll just nail shut the top'a the steps, y'hear?" Barb warned. "And I'll tell all you boys right here and right now, there is no reason at all, none whatsoever, for any of you to at any time be in Darelle's room. I mean it. Don't bother tellin' me she invited you in, or you were only lookin' for something or any of that guff. I find you in Darelle's room and you are guilty. Do you hear me?"

"What if she does invite us in?"

"You say No thanks, my mom will whip my ass if I do."

"Well, what if—"

"No, or your mom will whip your ass. There is *no* reason, *none at all*, and you'll get your ass whipped. Period."

Every now and again you knew she meant it. Some of the time you could get around her, some of the time you might or might not catch hell, but every now and again you knew flat out that you might as well just bite your tongue and do what she wanted. Herb could hit, and Herb's hits hurt, but it was nothing, nothing at all compared to what happened when Mom blew her cool. And anyway, who'd want to be anywhere near drippy-eyed Darelle if you didn't have to be?

Gus was working again, driving the pop truck up and down the highway, but his shift had been changed so sometimes he worked days, too. Must be a lot of people drinking an awful lot of pop! Herb thought Gus was a drip. He'd suggested Gus could deliver more than case after case of pop, and make way lots more money doing it, too, but Gus said count me out, I don't use that shit and I don't deliver it, either. Nothing anyone said would change his mind, and he wouldn't even agree to let someone else ride along with him and do the other delivery. Herb talked about how it was the perfect cover and the last thing the cops would suspect, and Gus said he didn't really give the first part of a good goddamn about anything anyone said, he wasn't going to be part and parcel of anything like that. Herb told him he was a dweeb and a loser and Gus shrugged and said he wasn't concerned one way or another what Herb thought. Funny about that, because old Herb could probably beat the spit right out of Gus without even half trying, but he didn't do it. He didn't even get mad about Gus saying no, he just shrugged and said well, it's you who's gonna wind up with empty pockets, not me.

Herb went out most nights, but now he waited until Billy and Bobby were in bed before he headed off, usually with Barb. Lots of the time Cindy went with Barb, and sometimes Gus if he wasn't working. But if all four of them were going to be gone Linda usually babysat, and when Linda babysat, usually she brought Sandra with her, and then Tammy and Dick went out too. Lots of times everyone got ready to go out except Gus, and he didn't so much babysit as just be in the house, usually at the kitchen table with a raft of books and a whack of paper. If it was Gus at home a guy could relax, because as long as there wasn't any noise or any rough-housing, Gus didn't mind if you didn't go to sleep right away. Some nights it was next to impossible for a guy to go to sleep, no matter how early he'd got up or how much running around he'd done that day.

Linda was no fun any more, though. She kept track of how many times a guy got out of bed, and how long he was up for. If you sassed her back she wrote down on the paper what you said, word for word. Then when the others got home she handed over the paper and Herb took care of it, right away. And if there was anything much worse than being jerked out of bed, jolted awake and given a shellacking with a leather belt before you even knew what was going on, Billy didn't know what it was, and he figured Bobby didn't either. Gus had told Herb it was probably one of the reasons it was so hard for a guy to go to sleep, because he was scared of being jerked awake that way. Herb said in that case all a guy had to do was make goddamn sure he didn't pull any stunts, and the best way to make sure of that was to stay in bed, lip zipped.

Linda didn't mind if Darelle stayed up for a while, they'd sit with their backsides on the floor, leaning against the front of the sofa, drinking tea like a couple of old grannies, talk talk talking away as if they actually were someone. You could pretty much bet Donny'd conk out as soon as his head tilted sideways, before he even hit the pillow. And little Stevie, well, who cared when he went to sleep? He didn't have school or anything. Sometimes he fell asleep halfway through supper and didn't wake up until who knew when, and a bottle stuffed in his face would put him back to sleep again. Other times he woke up and screeched until someone lifted him out and took him down to crawl around in the living room in front of the TV. Little dork, anyway. You even looked at him and someone was climbing your back. Baby Creepo could stay up, yammer, chase his toys, do what he wanted, nobody said a word about it. But just let Bobby or Billy so much as start down the damn steps and it was rah rah screech screech yap yap and good old Herb in the middle of the night with his belt.

Tammy got a new job, one she said she didn't mind too much at all. For the first month or so it was okay, but then the Ay-rab who ran the place started to presume, and there's nothing much more tiresome than someone who presumes. Mind you, if he wanted her to get up from her sewing machine where she was turning out gym suits and go make coffee, she'd do it, she got paid by the hour and if his coffee was worth six-fifty an hour to him, fine, no skin off her rosy red one. She didn't mind a change from sitting there guiding that goddamn grey-coloured fleece-lined polyshitzit stuff through the machine, the needles zipping like bees trying to sting something to death. And if he thought it was worth six-fifty an hour to have her sweeping floors or washing the damn windows, fine, she'd do that too. Mind you, if he had her doing windows all afternoon and then suggested they were behind on orders and maybe she might come in of an evening for some overtime, well, he could think again. She knew what was really on his little mind. God, they must all think they're Tom-freakin'-Cruise, all they have to do is smile pretty and every woman for a hundred miles is flat on her back, already panting. All you had to do was look at the guy and you knew you were dealing with another prickless wonder. Little half-bald dome always kind of gleaming, his hair carefully combed over the top of his head, as if that hid something instead of making it just that much more obvious. Little potsy belly as if he'd swallowed a watermelon seed. Probably had to have a string on the end to find it and pull it out to pee. And he thought he could get her to go in for some overtime on the fabric piles? Did he think she was hard up or something? A couple of times she just smiled and said she couldn't manage it, and then, finally, she said something about her children, making it sound as if they were all drooling on their chins with dummies stuck in their mouths. The bugger looked sympathetic and said It must be very hard, your husband gone and all. She nodded and looked as if she was about to bust into tears, and he backed off a bit. The heartbroken widow and all.

But she knew her job wasn't going to last. They act so bland, as if there was nothing going on, no undercurrent, zip-all, but as soon as they realize there isn't going to be any hump hump hump they fade back and wait, and the first excuse they have, they pay you back. With some of them, money is the final weapon, so if you don't pretend all you really want to do is fuck, well, goodbye job hello pogey. And that'll show you. Bitch.

If he thought he could make her feel as if she'd blown her one chance in life, he had another think coming. His wasn't the only place where you got the chance to sit on a lousy chair with a cramp growing in the small of your back, feeding fleece through the serger. In fact he was pretty small potatoes. Besides, the fish plant paid closer to eight bucks an hour, and if the work was stinky and miserable, well, so what, lots of people in the world were stuck with lots worse than that, and at least you didn't have to open your legs on a pile of polywotzit.

Without telling him a thing about it, Tammy went around to the other clothing places, looked them over, asked a few questions at personnel, and then, only partly because it paid more, she checked out the fish plant. It was cold. The workers wore jeans, heavy bush shirts and jackets or insulated vests, and they stood in heavy socks and gumboots on a wet concrete floor, shoulder to shoulder on both sides of the conveyor belt, filleting frantically. The more they did, the more they got paid, and those up near the head of the line had more chance to make money because they got first pick of the fish as they moved down the line. She figured she'd start at the bottom end, and why not? She hadn't done this in years and would need some time to get back her speed and skill. But she figured there was no way short of total paralysis she'd make less than she was making sitting at the serger getting a crick in her back while Chummy walked around fantasizing about his world-class woody. And she could afford to make less for a while anyway, because the Compensation pension was a sure thing, you could pretty much guarantee it would come on exactly the day it was supposed to come.

Every now and again, especially when the crap is falling thick from all directions, the great goddess waves her well-tanned hand and sends a good chortle your way. Tammy had been home from work an hour or more, had supper on the table and doing its magic disappearing act into the mouths of the kids, when the phone rang and the manager of the fish plant asked if she'd be able to come into work the next morning at six.

"I'll be there," she said pleasantly.

"You can buy your knife here and pay for it off your next few cheques. They're expensive." He sounded as if he was apologizing. "But the health inspector insists on it. No wooden handles or whatever for germs to hatch, these knives are moulded in one piece, handle and all, and they're made outta stainless steel. Take a helluvan edge, so watch yourself with them."

"Sure. Thanks a lot."

She stopped by Chummy's sweat shop on the way home from the fish plant. Of course he got nasty and said that since she hadn't given him any notice he was going to dock her two weeks' pay, but when she said she was sorry he felt that way, and that of course he had to do what he thought best, but she was sure he'd understand she had to do what she thought best, too, and if he docked her pay she was going to have to go to the Labour Relations Board and put in a claim. She knew he couldn't afford even a cursory examination. He was playing sloppy with too many rules and regulations, the least of which were fire regulations. When he angrily handed over her cheque it was all there, every penny, even her accumulated sick time and holiday pay. She smiled her widest and most winning smile and told him it had been a real pleasure working with him.

Shifts at the fish plant were the most hellatious mess you could imagine. Everything depended on everything else. When the boats came in, how much they off-loaded, how fast the off-loading happened. All of which was dependent on the weather, the tide and whether or not it was pitch bloody black or bright sunlight. But Tammy didn't have to worry about babysitters, because if push came to shove and the neighbour woman couldn't take Sandra, Tammy could always drop her off at Cindy and Barb's place.

They didn't mind having Sandra around. She was company for little Stevie, and she was one of those kids who more or less look after themselves. Lots of times you could almost forget she was even in the house. More than once they'd become aware of the quiet and started looking, and there she'd be, lying on someone's bed, thumb in her mouth, sound asleep, usually with little Stevie cuddled up beside her. With Tammy busy at her latest job, and that job all over the clock, a person could have wound up in a big confusion around babysitting. If, when, for how long, and was it or wasn't it overnight. But who needs any kind of fuss? Besides, it wasn't like you had to run after the kid, and anyway Dick was usually there as soon as he was off work, and he scooped her up and took her home with him. Made a person suspect she was *his* kid, even if she didn't look the least bit like him. Well, who knew *what* he looked like, anyway. It had been so long since anyone had seen him without that damn shaggy beard, they'd all sort of grown fuzzy on his appearance. But then even if he shaved it off he'd look different than before. He'd only grown it to hide the big jeezly scar Tammy had put on his kisser when she blew her cool and laid him out with a full bottle of beer. They'd stitched him up at the hospital and done a good job of it, too, but the scar was there, no way you could not be aware of it, so when he started growing fuzz they were all sort of glad of it. They didn't have to look at the evidence of Tammy's temper all the time.

Barb privately figured if they could get Tammy to calm down a bit, there'd be less trouble with Cindy. Tammy was younger than Cindy, but you'd think she was older, the way Cindy tried so hard to imitate what Tam did. Like the way she was starting to act toward Gus, treating him more and more and more the way Tammy treated Dick, as if he was a servant or something, a guy you could take for granted. More and more and more it was Gus who wound up doing what was supposed to be Cindy's share of the cooking. He'd always been the one to do the laundry and all. Now when he was home he got the babysitting, too, because he'd no sooner come into the house than Cindy'd have her coat on, ready to head off to Bingo. She spent so much time at Bingo she'd probably bought her own table. And she didn't win very often, either, although she could have if she'd paid more attention. It was as if they called the numbers too fast for her to keep track of on her cards. Someone would yodel Bingo, and then later Cindy would sigh Oh shit, and there it would be on her card too, only she was too late. The story of her goddamn life if you stopped to think about it.

Herb, now, he must have been born with horseshoes up his yingyang. Hand him a pair of dice and he'd rub them slowly against the palms of his hands, hold them up and blow on them a few times, then his eyes would glaze over for a moment or two and when that had cleared up he'd grin happily and seven times out of ten he walked away with new money in his pocket. Sit him in on a poker game and he would quietly and steadily rake in enough to make anybody happy, but not so much the other players got steamed. Take him to a pool hall and it was different, only the smart arses who were hungry for recognition would go up against him, because the regulars knew they didn't have a hope in hell of winning. Barb had asked him why he didn't go to Vancouver or Victoria for some of the big games, and he looked at her as if he didn't recognize her.

"That's not what it's about for me," he said. "I'd prob'ly lose it if I got that serious about it."

"But you could win big money."

"I don't need big money, I'm doin' fine the way things are." And that, as they say, was that.

Well, they were doing fine. She had her whoofare cheque, and

Cindy had hers, and Gus brought most of his pay home most of the time, and Herb was always quick to throw money in the pot, and since the whoofare didn't know dick-all about Herb or Gus there were no deductions from the cheques so it was all like free money anyway.

For sure Barb was way better off than she'd been when she was living with that crazy coot Real. Now if only she could find a way to keep the silly bugger from phoning all the time and bleating into her ear about how much he missed her, how much he loved his kids, and how much he didn't understand why she'd hoofed off, as if some dumb shit pointing a loaded gun at your nose wasn't ample reason to scurry toward the horizon.

Then Cindy went off to Bingo and didn't bother to come home. Gus acted as if there was nothing out of the ordinary. He went to work same as usual, came home same as usual, looked after the kids same as usual, and smiled until a person wanted to throw a jug of water in his face. It was okay when he was home, but when he went off to work everything came down on Barb's head and she didn't appreciate that at all. The first few days she didn't mind too much, but then it started to drag on and on, and the whole thing started to pick her arse.

"Jesus, Gus, why don't you go lookin' for her?"

"If I did I'd prob'ly find her," he laughed. "And if she isn't ready to be found she'll get owly. And if she gets owly I'm apt to need stitches. So I think I'll just let her find her own way home."

"What if she's in trouble?"

"She can't be, or I'd have heard from her."

"She could be lyin' up by the dam with her throat slit, for crying out loud."

"Well, if she is, no use me going looking for her, is there?" and he walked off, smiling.

A person with that attitude is really flirting with quick and early death. In fact it's one of the most enraging things a guy can pull on you. But no use trying to get a rise out of Gus, he did things his own way, squirrelly as that way was.

"Well, if it was my old lady, I'd sure the hell know where she was." Herb made it sound like an insult.

Gus stared at him for a long time. Then, just before Herb got mad,

Gus smiled. "What it is, Herb, is she isn't 'my' old lady, okay? I didn't buy her in a pet shop, or win her at Bingo, or have her given to me for my birthday."

"You're a real bad case of pussywhipped, boy." The insult was out in the open, and still Gus didn't take offence.

"How come you put up with it?" Tammy asked.

"It's exactly the way it's always been, Tam, you know that."

"So why do you hang on?"

"I'm not hanging on. If I was hanging on, I'd be out looking for her, right? I thought things were one way at first, and when I found out they weren't, well, that's the time I should have called it quits. I'm the one read things the wrong way. Besides, it's no skin off my nose one way or the other."

"Yeah? And what about this past life connection thing? She act like this in your last lifetime?"

"Maybe I'm the one acted like this. Why do you care, anyway?"

"Jesus, boy, not only are you pussywhipped, you're out to lunch," Herb guffawed. "You sound like you really believe all that shit."

"And you sound like someone who's afraid to believe it."

Then, more than a week after she vanished into outer space, Cindy came home again, pretending nothing out of the ordinary had happened. She came in when Gus was at work, which was probably no accident. Barb would be go-to-hell if she asked and Cindy had no intention of telling, so it all wound up as if nothing had been different.

When Gus came in off work, he barely looked at Cindy and didn't say a word to her, he just went into the bedroom, stripped off his work clothes, pulled on his tatty housecoat and went to the second floor bathroom. They heard the shower running same as usual, heard the water stop same as usual, heard him pad barefoot down the hall and the steps, and go in the bedroom, same as always. He was in the bedroom long enough to get dressed, and then he came out, hair combed, everything slicked in place, and a big black plastic garbage bag in his hand. Barb knew he'd been packed and set to go for days. Without a word to any of them, not even Stevie, Gus grabbed his jacket and walked out of the house.

"Hey! Hey, you!" Cindy hollered, but you'd have thought he was deaf or she was mute, because he didn't even shrug, he just kept on a-hoofin' it.

That put Cindy in a total fury. She went flying out of the house after him, yelling every step of the way. At the bus stop she caught up to him, standing there as if he hadn't a care in the world, just waiting for the bus, no problemo. People on the street turned to look, shake their heads and move on, uneasy, and Gus acted as if there was nobody out there but him. Cindy swung at him and he caught her wrist. She tried to kick him and he moved out of the way. She screeched and yelled, and he pretended to ignore her, even as he warded off her slaps, punches, and attempts to scratch his eyes out of his face.

The bus pulled up and the doors opened. Gus casually crack-the-whipped her so she spun away from him, lost her balance and fell flat on her prat. Gus climbed the steps, the bus doors closed, the bus pulled away and Cindy got to her feet raging, looking for rocks to throw.

She came back in the house still half out of her tree with fury, and stayed that way, sullen and slit-eyed, smoking one cigarette after the other, her lips moving sometimes as she muttered to herself. She wouldn't come to the table for supper, and a body would have thought she didn't have any kids depending on her either. Barb just flat-out refused to get Stevie ready for bed, god knows he wasn't *her* kid, and Darelle quietly got up and took over with the baby. She even washed the little guy's hands and face, put a dry disposable on his bum, and put him to bed with a bottle of milk.

Cindy watched it all with a look on her face that would have made you think she hated Darelle for being able to do for the baby. Well, jesus, someone had to! She muttered something about Trying to show me up, then she was into her bedroom, slamming the door. Came out twenty minutes later dolled to the nines and headed for the door.

"Oh no you don't!" Barb screeched.

"Up your nose with a rubber hose."

"You been gone damn near two weeks and I wind up with mosta the load, and now Gus's gone and I won't even have him to help me. So you needn't think you're effin' off."

"What are you, my mother or something? I go where I want to go, when I want, and with whoever I want and no way you give me orders."

"Listen, bitch!" Herb yelled. "There's five kids in this house right now and three of 'em's yours. I don't know who'n'hell you think you are but you're nobody special, okay. Smarten your damn self up or you'll be good and sorry."

"And who the hell are you," Cindy laughed, "other than some do-nothing go-nowhere next best thing to a damn bum! The day you give an order and I take it is the day pigs'll do the ballet on TV. You're fuckin' nothin', little guy." And she swanned out the door as if there was a limo waiting for her instead of a half-block stroll to the bus stop.

Herb was so mad his lips went colourless and his eyes glittered like little bits of ice. He gave Barb a look that scared her so much she decided maybe she'd just make herself as scarce as she could. He slammed into the bedroom and Barb whipped out of the house and hurried to catch up to Cindy. By the time Herb knew she was gone, the bus was halfway to town.

Neither one of them came home that night, and neither did Herb. In the morning Darelle got Donny ready and sent him off to school with Ferret and Weasel, but she was pretty sure they'd never make it there, probably wouldn't get past the first alleyway. She couldn't go because someone had to look after Stevie. Then, as luck would have it, Tammy dropped by to drop off Sandra and pitched a total fit that nobody adult was in the house. She was so mad she said a few things, Darelle started to cry. That made Tammy so mad she gave Darelle a good slap on the side of the face before scooping up Sandra and leaving the house, slamming the door behind her.

Darelle was still sobbing when the phone rang.

"Hi, baby duck," Isa said. "Why are you so upset?"

"Because Auntie Tammy hit me real hard in the face, and she swore at me and scared me."

"Where's your mom?"

"I don't *know!*" Darelle bawled, and the hysterics she'd been getting ready to have since Herb had raised hell the night before came on her, and she stood sobbing and blubbering into the phone, barely able to speak.

So of course Isa phoned the Child Help Line. They contacted the

Ministry of Social Services, and they in turn sent a worker to the house. By then Darelle was so unnerved and frightened, she couldn't think of any lie at all, let alone a good one. When the worker asked where her mother was, Darelle said she didn't know. When the worker asked how long her mother had been gone, Darelle told the truth.

Ferret and Weasel were put in one foster home, Darelle and Donny in another, and Stevie in a third. When Isa arrived, he was still raising the roof. She found him sitting on the polished linoleum of the kitchen floor, mouth open, roaring and red-faced. "Hey, there, Bubba," she said quietly, "no need for all that noise." He whirled, glaring, then saw her. The glare vanished and he crawled toward her, already reaching for her hand.

Isa had to sign more papers than she could believe, but once they were signed, she had the permission of the unwieldy bureaucracy to take Stevie with her. She drove to the foster home where Darelle and Donny were staying, and visited with them briefly.

"But why?" Darelle wailed. "Why can't we?"

"Darling, I'm sorry." Isa wanted to sit down and wail, too. "But they say we aren't blood relatives."

"What does that matter? I don't want to stay here!"

"Well, you have to. They won't let me take you home with me. But I'll tell you what. You calm yourself down so they don't get a bad impression of you, so they can't say you were fine until I showed up. We don't want them to be able to prove we aren't good for each other. And I'll keep working on it."

"Where's Gus? Why can't we stay with him?"

"As soon as he gets in touch with me, I'll tell him where you are, and then we'll see what he can do. I promise."

"And will you phone me?"

"I'll phone you, and you can phone me. I promise."

She had to stop at the mall to buy an expensive government-approved car seat for Stevie. She got him strapped in and then handed him a sandwich. "Here, guy, get this into you. I'm sorry we can't stop and dine at Chez Pierre, but we've got a ferry to make. If you get thirsty, there's fresh milk in your bottle. And apple juice in the other one."

He looked at her and smiled, so relaxed she could hardly believe he was the same red-faced roaring horror she'd found at the foster home. She was glad she'd listened to Carol, who had advised Isa to make the trip down at least a couple of times a month, to visit. "You never know," Carol had warned. "The day might come when you have to go get him, and everything will go much easier if he knows you."

Well, here was the day. It had come. Thank Carol, and thank all the deities the kid felt comfortable with her.

Too bad he didn't know where Gus was. Too bad he didn't know where his mother was. On the other hand, maybe it was a damn good job he didn't.

13

Phoebe was looking for a photo or snapshot of Steve, something she could put on her wall and look at when she felt that odd sensation that was so much like emptiness. They hadn't got along, but he was her dad, and now that he was gone she could see his side of it a bit. If he hadn't had his head ripped off like that, maybe they could even be friends now. Part of her still hated him, hated the memories of the beatings and harsh words, but part of her could remember other things, before the arguments and yelling had started. He was the one taught her to swim, and he was the one took the big sliver out of her hand that time, just let her cry and when the sobs slowed, he sat on the steps beside her and pulled out his little pocket knife and told her what he was going to do. Then he slipped the thin blade under the protruding end of the big splinter and tugged. It hurt, sure, and it bled, but out it came, and then he took her into the bathroom and put peroxide on it and made jokes about how the bubbles were going to wash the cut so clean she'd have a white mark on her hand. She cried, remembering that, and wished with all her heart she'd been better behaved. Maybe if she hadn't been as stubborn as he was, maybe if she'd been nicer, maybe it wouldn't have happened. What if he'd been thinking hard, trying to figure out how to mend things, and that was why he was just standing there when *snap*, and him too preoccupied to even know.

How come things are okay and then they aren't? Why does it happen so fast, and why can't we figure out how to put a stop to it?

Why couldn't she? Like the thing with the rope. Ruby knew how to stop that, and Phoebe had done what Ruby said, and it worked. On her own, she'd have died before she would have even thought to pretend to be sorry. Even though she really was sorry. But it worked, poof, like that, the head-butting was over. How many other big uproars could have been avoided if Phoebe had only known how to stop them?

There was a big trunk in the storage room, and so what if it was locked, it didn't take long with a turkey skewer to pick the lock and pop it open. There were some picture albums, with photos of people wearing old-timey out-of-date clothes. Some of the pictures had Steve in them, but Steve a way lot younger than Phoebe had ever seen him. She began to realize how much older he was than her mom. Way lots older. Of course, with him bein' dead her mom would eventually catch up to him, unless she croaked choking on her own bad temper.

There were loose leaf binders too, and in them were neatly typed pages Phoebe quickly realized were stories. They were starting to take story writing in English, and it hadn't interested her. But now, sitting on the floor in the storage room, reading her dead father's typed pages, it seemed different. She'd had the idea stories were written by people who lived somewhere else, other people, like university professors or high school teachers or something. But here were these ones, and all her dad had been was a high-grade logger, so did that mean *anybody* could learn how to do this? Well, why not. Gus said his mother did, and god knows she was nothing but an old biddy. Always going on about the well-being of the kids, the kids, the kids, you'd think she was Mother goddamn Teresa the way she went on. And who was it phoned the whoofare about that thing one of the kids had said? Snooping around, question question question, as if it mattered, as if anybody got hurt, which nobody did. But at least it took Phoebe off the hook for babysitting the little buggers. Didn't mind that, not one bit. You'd think she was Cinder-fuckin'-ella, do this, do that, scrub scrub work work. Not likely.

There were lots of letters in the trunk from publishers, rejecting the stories Steve had sent out. At first Phoebe couldn't understand why, the stories were just perfect. Then, bit by bit, she began to get a sense of how to make the stories better. There was something not quite true or real about them. No use asking the English teacher, Shakespeare's Ghost. Sure as hell he'd never had anything published, the dimwitted twit. Too busy wandering lonely as a cloud that floated on high o'er yon pulp mill tra la la la de da.

If there was one thing Phoebe could not abide, it was not knowing at least as much as everybody else around her. Sometimes her mom or her aunties called her Miss Know-It-All, in a tone of voice suggesting disapproval or even insult. Phoebe wasn't insulted, and if they disapproved it was no skin off her nose. Maybe she didn't Know It All, but by god she was going to Know More by the time she was eighteen than they'd ever find out in their whole ridiculous lives.

She read the stories and re-read them, then started experimenting. She didn't so much steal the stories as just try to make the endings more believable. Happily ever after didn't always work. And some of them, she was sure, didn't need any "real" ending at all. Life doesn't have them, unless you count death, and what way is that to finish off a book? You can't kill them *all* off, for Pete's sake. Unless you're Shakespeare.

She knew her first dozen or so attempts were no improvement. In fact they weren't even as good as her dad's endings. But at least they were more real. That's what she wanted, something real.

The work changed her approach to reading. She had never cared much for the paperbacks Shakespeare's Ghost recommended, what he called young adult novels. In Phoebe's opinion most of them were downright gorpy. She had passed them by in favour of the kind her mom read once in a while, romances, usually set in England. But they weren't any more real than the stuff Steve had written.

She tasted here and tasted there and then found Elmer Kelton. She devoured his work, then she dove into Larry McMurtry. Even if they weren't writing about the same kind of place, they were writing about people like the ones Phoebe knew.

Her English marks got better and better. She was so engrossed in what she was reading and writing that most of the family fuss and hoo-rah passed over her head unnoticed. Some of it, though, refused to be ignored. There was hell to pay when Barb got home and found the notice the welfare had tacked to the door. Barb blamed Tammy because she was the one who had slapped Darelle and pitched her into such hysterics she had spilled her guts when the whoofare arrived. Barb was pretty sure it was the next door neighbours had called the fuzz, probably because Darelle was howling and wailing so much they thought she'd been half murdered. Tammy said she damn well had not, it was probably that goof Herb had blown the whistle, just to pay Barb back for taking off after Cindy. But Herb was as long gone as Gus, and couldn't, as they said, be reached for comment.

Barb went up in front of a magistrate and gave him a song and dance about how she hadn't left her children unattended at all, she'd left them in the care of her sister Cindy, and a friend, Herb, and she hadn't expected either of them, let alone both, to leave the kids alone. She must have sounded convincing because she got them back almost immediately, with only a stern warning that next time she had to leave the kids left with someone reliable.

It took Cindy longer to get her kids back. They had it down right in the computer that this wasn't the first time. Cindy blamed Barb *and* Tammy, which was pretty stupid since she knew Barb wasn't at home with the kids, what with her sitting at the same table in the bar.

"Don't give me no static about it," Tammy raged. "I'm not the one left 'em all alone."

"No, but you slapped Darelle and pitched her into crying."

"Damn kid cries all the time, you know that. She's as big a blubberguts as you are."

Phoebe listened to everything she could overhear and made notes. But when she worked it all into a story and handed it in, Shakespeare's stupid ghost gave her an F-minus and a lecture about how writing was supposed to elevate the human condition, not denigrate it. Dumb tit. How was anything supposed to be elevated if people didn't even know what was going on? Did he think everyone lived in four-bedroom split-levels in brand-new subdivisions, going to the office every day and living sober and righteous lives?

Another loser, happy to spend his life in dreamland. He'd eat it one day. And you could lay bets it would be Phoebe who fed it to him. Wait until she knew enough and was good enough at what she knew to get published. What was it she'd read just last month? Revenge is a dish best eaten cold. In other words, Don't get mad, get even. F-minus my ass.

The whoofare put out its hoops and Cindy jumped through them, took her substance abuse course and her parenting course and must have kissed foot often enough, because eventually she got Darelle and Donny back from the foster home, and they told Gus's mother to drive Stevie back home again. Phoebe was there when Isa showed up with Stevie and some new clothes and stuff she'd got him. You could tell the old fart didn't want to bring him back, but she didn't have any choice. She tried to be nice, had a cup of tea and some of Robin's donuts, and then left. It was pretty awful the way Stevie cut up, though. When he realized she was gone he just about raised the roof. Well, why not, she'd probably spoiled him half rotten the whole time he was there.

Personally speaking, Phoebe thought they were all just about too stupid for words.

Barb was in the bar, waiting for her chance at the pool table, when Herb walked back into her life. He didn't even mention her being gone, so she didn't mention anything about him being gone, either. When the bar closed, he went back home with her, and life settled back into the same old routine. Cindy wasn't talking to Herb, and he wasn't too interested in talking to her. She blamed him for not being home when the welfare arrived, and he made no secret that he thought it was entirely her fault.

And three weeks after Herb moved back in, the same stuff came down on their heads again. Only the more minor circumstances were changed. Herb went out first, and Barb joined him after Ferret and Weasel were settled. About two in the morning Herb suggested Barb should head home, that he'd catch up with her later.

"No reason to go home," she said. "Cindy's there, let her see what it's like to ride herd on the whole bunch of them for a change."

"That airhead?" he sneered. "You wait and see, you'll be sorry."

When they got home it was almost time to get the kids out of bed and ready for school. And there was no sign of Cindy at all. Herb waited until the four older ones were gone, then he turned and very casually slapped Barb's face. "I told you," he said coldly. "She left them alone, just like I said."

"So what?" Barb blurted, holding her cheek. "What business is it of yours, anyway?"

Herb slapped her again, and left. Barb waited until Darelle got home from school so there'd be someone with Stevie, and then she left, too. The next day Darelle had to stay home from school. Isa phoned at seven-thirty, and knew immediately something was going on, because Darelle was once again speaking in monosyllables. So once again Isa phoned the Child Help Line. And the next morning she phoned the worker to tell him the kids had once again been left alone.

Isa's phone call to the welfare went into the bureaucratic grinder. And languished. Barb was back home before a social worker arrived two days later.

"What?" Barb shook her head wearily. "Come on in and have a coffee while we try to sort this out."

"Is, uh . . ." The worker checked her notebook. "Darelle at home?"

"She's in school. They're all in school. Except for Stevie and he's a baby. What's this all about, anyway?"

The worker followed Barb into the house, sat at the table and accepted the mug of coffee. She checked her notebook again. "Would it be possible for me to talk to Darelle's mother?"

"No reason why you can't if you can wait until she gets home. Her boyfriend had some trouble in the family, you know how it is, and she's gone to see if she can help in any way."

The worker knew this one was going to be touchy. She didn't say who had phoned, in fact she left the hint of an indication Darelle herself had somehow been in contact with the office.

"One thing you've got to know about Darelle," said Barb, tired to the bone and close to giving up. "That kid is, well, she's high-strung or something. You so much as look at her, she's bawling. Ask her to do the dishes and she'll do them, standing at the sink with tears dripping off her chin the whole time, as if she was the only person ever had to wash a plate around here. She doesn't get to choose the TV program? She cries. She gets sad, she cries, she gets mad, she cries, she cries for just about every damn thing comes down the pike. And she figures she should be front and centre number one no matter what's going on. So her mom gets the word, right, and she's getting ready to go and Darelle takes it in her head *she* wants to go, and when she gets told no, well, guess what she does. She cries. And she pitches this big fit."

The social worker did not believed or disbelieve. She just made notes in her little book, drank her coffee, shook hands and left. When the kids came home from school Barb gave Darelle a look that promised her all kinds of holy shit, but Darelle didn't know why. She went to her room, lay down on her bed and wept.

She was still there, face down on a damp pillow, when Herb arrived. He hadn't been home since he'd slapped Barb, and none of the kids had expected to see him again. He had Cindy with him in the cab, and she looked awful. Either she'd been sleeping in a wind tunnel or she hadn't been sleeping at all. Her eyes were red and swollen, her hair defied description and her clothes were crumpled and stained. She practically lurched toward the house, and when Herb shoved her through the door she aimed herself at a chair, plopped into it and sat shaking. Donny looked over at her, then turned his attention, such as it was, back to the TV.

"And ain't you just a pair of bloody sweethearts." Herb sounded as if he was about ready to pull the house apart.

Billy and Bobby nipped quietly through the side door, hoping out of sight was out of mind. Stevie, the front of his tee shirt covered with spilled cereal and evidence of a can of what Donny called shapgetti, scuttled over to Herb and held up his arms.

"Lookit him," Herb dared. "Little bugger is totally helpless here. He depends on what's supposed to be adults to do for him, and he looks like he ain't been washed in weeks. Come on, toad, Herb'll fix you up."

He scooped up the toddler and headed off for the bathroom. Cindy looked at Barb, then looked away, stumped for anything to say. But Barb wasn't stumped. She had lots to say, and said it in an angry monotone. Cindy just nodded her head, miserable, working into the godmother of all hangovers. She felt just about sick enough to find a corner, lie down and die.

Herb came back with a clean Stevie. "When did he last get something decent to eat?"

"He had his lunch." Barb was defensive and frightened.

"He had his *lunch?* At what time?"

"Lunchtime, a'course."

"Well, in case nobody around here noticed, what with the mad social whirl and all, lunchtime was about four or five hours ago. So see if you can haul that hunka lead outta your ass and give this kid some solid food. And I mean solid food, not a goddamn bottle of milk stuck in his face to keep him quiet."

There was no sense expecting Cindy to do anything, she would drop anything she touched. So Barb did it. She made Kraft Dinner, enough for the other kids, too. Just looking at his face, she knew Herb had no intention of eating, and she knew too that if Herb didn't eat, no other adult in the place would. The balloon still hadn't gone all the way up.

Herb left the kitchen and headed to the bedroom. Barb hoped he'd just lie down and go to sleep, but it was a dim hope. She called Bobby and Billy in for supper, went to the TV to get Donny and even went to get Darelle, who took one look at Auntie Barb's face, got out of bed fast and hurried downstairs to eat her supper.

"Why's she been bawling?" Cindy asked, puzzled and hurt, as if Darelle's blubbering was an insult to her.

"Who would know?" Barb spoke very quietly, and almost pleasantly. "I don't know how come she cries so much. She takes after you. You cried all the time, too."

"Not *all* the time!"

"Close enough to all the time it doesn't make a difference. Billy, so help me god, if you get out of line here I'm going to turn you over to Herb, okay?"

"You figure there's something wrong with that kid? I mean, don't you think that by now he'd have caught on that when you start in on devilment and buggery you get walloped."

"Too much like his dad if you ask me." Barb couldn't have told anyone why her hands were shaking. "I don't know who Donny takes after, half the time it's as if he isn't even on this planet!"

"At least he's quiet. He's my good boy, aren't you, Don?"

Billy didn't want to get turned over to Herb. There was something just a bit snaky about Herb at the best of times, and this was shaping up to be not one of the best of times. He concentrated on his Kraft Dinner, hardly bothering to chew, stuffing it into himself as fast as he could.

They heard the bathwater running, heard Herb moving between bedroom and bathroom, heard the zizzybuzz of his electric razor. Nobody was speaking, except Stevie who was cooing and laughing and eating as if he knew this might be his last meal for months. They all sat hypertense, adrenalized without knowing exactly why, every little sound Herb made coming to them as if through loudspeakers.

Without being told, the boys cleared the table and got busy with the dishes. Bobby washed, Billy and Donny dried, Darelle put things away, and when everything was clean and where it belonged, Donny took the wash cloth and made sure the table and countertops were clean. He even remembered to wash the top of the stove. Then they all went into the living room and sat side-by-each on the floor in front of the TV, their supper in a lump in their little bellies.

Cindy sat at the table, hands shaking so bad Barb had to light her cigarettes for her. Barb's hands trembled too, but not out of control. Both of them waited for Herb to come in the kitchen and tell them what was on his mind.

He waited until seven-thirty, then walked in freshly shaven, still flushed from his bath, and dressed in clean clothes. He didn't sit at the table with them, he went over to the kids in front of the TV.

"Darelle, get two bottles for Stevie, then take him up, change his bum, and put him to bed. When he's in bed, you go to bed. Billy and Bobby, take a hint. And no wrestling, no bullshit, not one single solitary sound from you or you might wind up in the fuckin' hospital tonight, get my meaning. Donny," he spoke gently, even reached out and touched Donny's hair, "you be Herb's good boy, okay? Time for bed."

Donny smiled. He was the first one up and moving.

Herb leaned against the wall, waiting and smoking a cigarette until the kids were all in bed and the house so quiet they could hear the clock ticking. Then he moved, fast as a snake, and both of Cindy's arms were pushed up her back so far her shoulders made cracking noises and the pain was like fire. "Listen, bitch," he said softly and calmly. "Next time you pull one of your tacky little stunts around me I'm gonna break your fuckin' neck and take your body up to the dam. You know where the lake empties down the sluiceway and the water shoots out the end like outta fire hose? Well, that's where I'll dump your cold meat. And you'll go down the goddamn sluice, over the edge, down the hundred-foot-drop waterfall and if they ever find you, which I doubt very much, they'll know you were fuckin' drunk and they'll figure you fell in and bust your scrawny dirty neck when you went over. Now just haul your festering ass outta here, get into your bedroom, and remember what I told the goddamn rodents. You can wind up in hospital tonight. *If* you're lucky! I'm damn near ready to put you in the morgue."

Then Herb made a pot of tea and brought it to the table, poured a mug for Barb and one for himself, then sipped quietly. He seemed so calm, so under control anyone who didn't know him would think everything was just fine.

Barb thought different. She sat across from him waiting for the balloon to go up. The hard lump in her stomach swelled until she was short of breath, and inside her head it felt as if she was about to be hit with a migraine. She knew he knew exactly how terrified she was. If he pulled a Real and beat on her, it would almost be a relief. She'd survived beatings before, and anyway it didn't really hurt after the first wallop. The fear and adrenalin blocked the immediate pain. Of course you ached and throbbed and were stiff for days, but that was nothing compared to this growing terror.

"Why'd you hoof off?" he asked quietly. "Didn't I tell you to stay with Stevie?"

"I knew you were mad. I mean, you slapped me and all. I thought the best place I could be was out of the way altogether."

"So because I was mad, you did something to make me even madder? Jesus, Barb, that makes no sense at all." He smiled and she almost vomited with the fear. "A person would think you were bloody suicidal or something."

She couldn't say anything. All she could do was sit with her hands clasped together on the table, her fingers gripping so tightly her knuckles were white and her nails bit into her palms. She could feel terror filling her from way down deep all the way up to her throat, and she knew if she swallowed she'd hork, if she opened her mouth to speak she'd hork. In fact, she was afraid just sitting there trying to hold it all together would start her horking.

"I've got some stuff I have to look after, babe." He rose from the table and stretched his arms above his head, yawning slightly. "No rest for the weary."

She nodded. Even that took an effort of heroic proportions. He smiled, went for his jacket, came over and gave her a kiss on the cheek and left by way of the front door. She could hear his heels clicking on the cracked cement walkway, she heard the gate squeak and click shut, and only when the sounds faded did she dare get up and go to the window to make sure he was gone.

14

The relief of Herb leaving was so overwhelming, Barb knew the only place to be was in bed. She didn't fall asleep immediately, and by the time she did she had convinced herself she was being a goof, scaring herself silly like that. After all, the man had barely even raised his voice, and when he did it was at Cindy, not at Barb, and the saints in heaven knew there were times she'd like to yell in Cindy's face until the sheer noise forced her sister to break down and take a reality pill.

She fell asleep relaxed and full of good intentions. She didn't hear Herb come home, didn't hear the front door close, didn't hear him come to the bedroom. She didn't stir when he sat on the edge of the bed, removed his shoes, then stood up to take off his pants and hang them over the back of a chair, unbutton his shirt and fold it before placing it on the seat of the chair. He took off his watch and put it on top of the shirt. Then, wearing only his jockey shorts and his socks, he knelt on the bed. Barb was asleep, curled on her side. Herb reached out and lifted her head from the pillow so gently she only fluttered her eyelids. Holding her head tenderly in his left hand he let loose with a short vicious jab with his right fist. In a fraction of a second, Barb went from being sound asleep to being unconscious.

When she came to, it was morning and she couldn't for the life of her figure out what was wrong with her. She didn't think she had ever in her life felt worse. For a start, she could barely see. For another thing, everything she had throbbed.

She forced herself to a sitting position, and that's when she saw the blood soaked into her pillow and pillowcase. There was blood on the sheets and blankets, too, even blood splashed on the wall behind her side of the bed.

Herb was curled up with his back turned to her side of the bed, sleeping like an innocent baby. She almost woke him up to ask him what had happened. Something, possibly a vestige of self preservation instinct, stopped her.

She got out of bed and hobbled to the bathroom. When she looked in the mirror, what she saw was so horrendous she thought she was going to lose control of her bladder. Her first thought was Oh god don't pee on the floor, her second one was Get to the hospital before something worse happens.

The cab driver took one look and snapped her gaping mouth shut. She didn't say a word on the ride up to the Emergency, and Barb didn't offer any explanation. Why bother? Anything anyone needed to know was on full view.

The minute he saw Barb, the physician on call in Emergency spoke quietly to the nurse at the desk and within minutes, Barb was admitted to hospital. While the physician was assessing the full damage and already planning what he would have to do to even begin to fix it, the operating room staff were preparing for facial surgery.

Barb was under anaesthetic a full three hours, then got wheeled to the recovery room. When she began to stir, she was taken to a semi-private room, and by the time she wakened, she felt only a strange sort of stiffness and no pain at all.

Mind you, she had to drink through a straw because her nose was packed and her top lip so swollen and laced with stitches she couldn't manage a glass or a cup, and when she looked in a mirror she almost started shrieking. But as traumatized as she was, she knew she had actually got off lucky. She could just as easily have died during the night as survived, and it was a miracle she had got herself to hospital.

By the time Cindy got her brain in gear and realized there was one person missing in the troupe, Barb was asleep in her semi-private with an IV running into her arm. Herb was sitting in a big chair watching the sports network and making notes in the little coil-top pocket binder where he kept track of how much he'd bet, and with whom, on what.

"Where's Bet?" Cindy asked him.

"Prob'ly in hospital," he said. "You'd better go and change the sheets'n'stuff on our bed."

"Me? On *your* bed? Why'n't you do it your own self, I'm not your slave."

All he did was turn his head and look at her and the same kind of helpless terror which had turned Barb to jelly hit Cindy, and about twice as hard. Wordless, she rushed off to do as he had told her. The condition of the pillow and bedding only added to her fear.

"What happened?" she blurted, her hands shaking so hard the bundle of bedding wobbled visibly.

"I don't think you need the exact particulars," he said, ice dripping from his words. "Just take a good look at what you've got in your hands and know, beyond any shadow of doubt, that it's about half what I'm nearly ready to visit upon you. Get my drift?" She nodded, her mouth feeling full of cotton batting. "Now," he continued, "put that stuff in the washing machine, then find some place for that little guy for the next while."

"Why?"

"Because you, bitch, are going to be busy looking after two litters of kids, and that's going to be more than a full-time job for a dipshit like you. The little guy is more than you can handle."

"But he's my baby."

"You want to see tomorrow, or is this morning the sum total of your ambition?"

She knew he meant it. Jack had been prone to swatting her around, but at no time had her bed looked as if someone had cut up a deer on it.

She hopped to it and did exactly what the snake-eyed wonder wanted, even to phoning Isa and asking if she could come down and take Stevie to her place for a week or so. "Something has come up," she stammered. "It's my sister, she's been in a car accident and she's in the hospital and," she heard herself sobbing, but it was as if it was someone else doing it, "and I have to look after all the kids."

"I'll be there as soon as I can," Isa promised. Cindy managed to stutter her thank-you's and hung up the phone, so frightened she couldn't even make herself look at Herb. When he took off to do whatever it was he did that made him feel so important, she whipped out, caught the bus and got up to the hospital for the last bit of evening visiting hours. When she saw Barb she couldn't think of a single thing to say.

"The good part is," Barb mumbled through her swollen lip, "I don't remember any of it and I didn't feel a thing. He got me when I was sleeping."

"Hey, listen, you've got to get rid of this guy."

"He didn't even seem ticked at me when he went out. You think I'm gonna put the run on him and give him a reason to be mad? If he can do this when he's calm, you think I want him all revved up? Give your head a shake."

More than Cindy's head got a shake. Just about every part of her got turned downside up and arse over appetite, and that from just looking at her sister and realizing how systematic the battering had been. It wasn't exactly like taking that reality pill and it didn't add anything to the loaf between her ears, but it sure did stir her to some kind of action. She didn't want the serpent mad at her any more than Barb did.

Isa enjoyed the month and a half Stevie spent with her. And Stevie seemed to grow enormously in the experience. He even started trying to talk, something he'd shown no inclination to attempt before. He put on weight, lost the dark half-circles beneath his eyes and got some shine in his hair. Then, of course, just about the time he was fully settled in, it was time to go back to what the voting public at large would refer to as his home.

Gus was back by then. He slipped back into the loose weave of the family ties as easily as he had slipped out, and Cindy was too relieved for words, because no sooner was Gus back in the picture than Herb took a couple of deep breaths and eased off. Barb was out of hospital, and if Gus wondered at the new pink scarlines on her lip and eyebrows, he kept his questions to himself. He just smiled and joked, took over most of the cooking and fit in so well a person would have thought he'd never been away.

But then there was so much else going on that you could have slipped in a battalion of Princess Pats and had it go unnoticed. Georgie and Melanie were staying in the big house while Maria and George both served time in the recreational resort known as the Crowbar Hotel. Cindy wasn't sure what they'd been nipped for, or at least claimed she wasn't, but she was nursing a big grudge against the police, the prosecutor and the judge. What right did any of them have to suggest she was lying? They might not believe the alibi she and the others had concocted, but no need to put it in no uncertain terms for the reporters to smear all over the front page of the local rag. Personally, she thought they'd managed to come up with a really good, really believable alibi and she thought it was unfair of so many people to disbelieve them just because some of the clever-ass cross-examination had got her mixed up and stammering. Anybody would get mixed up with them asking the same question six different ways, making it sound like something else so the answer wasn't the same. Besides, everyone knows those guys all stick together anyway.

Georgie was openly teed off about having to stay with all the others in the big house, and didn't even calm down when they explained to him that nobody had a choice. His mom had made the decision to have them "children in the home of a relative," and that was only fine as long as nothing disturbed the situation. If something did, the whoofare had a backup solution, and it was called Foster Home.

"And I don't think you want that," Barb said darkly.

"What I want is to be with my mom and dad."

"Well, unless they start puttin' kids in the pokey, there's no way that's gonna happen. You've got a choice, boy, and it might not seem like much of a one to you but it's better than no choice at all."

"What choice?" he screamed. "*What choice?*"

"Like it or lump it. Agree or kiss yer own arse," she snapped. "And if you're in a bad mood don't take it out on us around here. We're only doing as much as we can to help out."

Georgie assumed an air of detachment and went about his own business his own way in his own good time. T'hell with 'em all. *He* wasn't sittin' around for years'n'years in this squirrel cage with this pack of dozey losers. One way or the other there had to be something else, and almost anything else would be better. He'd heard enough from his parents and their friends to have a pretty good idea of where to go and who to contact, and he wasn't going to lose out because he was too busy doing nothing.

He let himself out by way of his bedroom window, then padded quietly across the roof to where the branches of the big old apple tree made spider web designs against the starry night sky. He got back in basically the same way, except for the one morning he was late getting home and had to think fast.

"What'n hell you doing out here?" Herb demanded, scowling.

Georgie stalled for time. "Nothin'."

"Don't give me nothin', you tell me what you're up to."

"I couldn't sleep," Georgie said sullenly, hoping Herb would think he was dragging the truth out of the kid inch by inch. "And I didn't want to lie in bed while those three idiots snored and farted until you couldn't breathe in that room. So I got up and got dressed and sneaked out here."

"When?"

"A while ago."

"And what you been doing?" Georgie didn't answer. Herb grabbed him by the collar. "Speak up, guy," he whispered.

"Smoked a cigarette," Georgie blurted, suddenly quite honestly frightened.

"You just make sure when you swipe smokes you don't swipe none of mine. You keep your thievin' little meathooks offa *all* of my stuff, y'hear?"

"Yes, Uncle Herb."

That night, when he went out the bedroom window and across the roof, Donny climbed out and followed him. Georgie almost sent the little dumbbell back but he figured Donny would argue so much the whole house would wind up awake. So he took the bean-brain with him.

That worked out really good. Donny not only acted years younger than he was, he looked it, too. And he loved the attention, the flattery and the presents. By the end of two weeks, Georgie had more money socked away than he could have managed on his own in two months. And, since Donny'd never been what anyone would call a ball of fire, it didn't matter he was as apt as not to fall asleep at the drop of a hat.

It didn't occur to anyone he was missing sleep, they all just thought he was a bit quieter than usual. Even the teachers at school, wearily accustomed to evidence the kid was dragging himself up, thought nothing of it when he put his arms on his desk, his head on his arms, and went to sleep. He contributed nothing but his smile anyway, and while he got passed from grade two to grade three, from there to four and then five, nobody even pretended he had learned anything. He was quiet, he was amiable, he was always eager and hungry for a cuddle or gesture of affection, and he could always be counted on to amuse, entertain or occupy the time of one of the pre-schoolers. Little kids thought Donny was the nicest of the bigger boys, and Donny was very much at home with them. And if he fell asleep because of the circumstances at home, well, he wasn't bothering anyone.

Tammy didn't much care for the job at the fish plant. It was cold, and she had to be super careful when she got home and showered because the fishy smell clung to her hair and skin. Sometimes the only way she could get rid of it was to rub herself with lemon-scented dish detergent, then stand under the shower, cursing inwardly as the water sluiced away the suds which left her skin tight and dry. Seemed like no matter what you did, if you were using dish detergent, you wound up with some of it in your eyes, and it stung like fury. The alternative, however, was to go around smelling of fish.

She had other things on her mind beside the aroma of dead seafood. She didn't have any idea at all what to do with Phoebe. Dick, god knows, wasn't much help. He just shook his head, a hint of a smile at the corners of his mouth, and told her there was no way he was going to get joe'd into being Godzilla. "I don't think hammerin' on a kid does anything except make them nurse grudges. The time to lay out the rules is when they're small. Well, you didn't do it then, so don't even bother trying now."

"Damn it, she comes and goes around here as if she owned the place!"

"When didn't she?"

"Linda isn't like that!"

"Linda don't have to be like that. Phoeb's bein' like that for her, and all she has to do is hold back a bit from what Phoeb did and she looks like the angel of all time. If Phoeb wasn't out there goin' a hundred percent you'd notice Linda was busy with seventy-five percent herself."

"Well, can't you gimme a hand here?"

"I do give you a hand. I bring home my paycheque, I do my share and then some around the house and with Sandy. You got no grounds for complaint and you know it. But I am *not* going to take over with the slammin' around, beatin' up and tyin' down like what Steve tried. It don't work with that kid. It don't work with *any* kid, but especially with that one. And if you try it, she'll up and dump you flat on your keister and you know it. That's why you want me to do it, she can't dump me on mine. But I'm not doin' it Tam, you might's well get used to the idea."

"She hasn't been home for two nights," Tammy said, and hot tears slipped down her face. She wiped at them angrily, and blinked rapidly to stop any others from betraying her.

"She'll be back when she's ready and not a minute sooner. And when she gets back, if there's a big go-round and hoo-rah, she'll stay gone longer next time."

"You want I should pretend it's okay for her to just tara-diddle off like she was grown up and on her own?"

"How old were you when she was born?" And he laughed out loud, laugh lines fanning from the corners of his eyes. "Jesus, babe, think on it. She's older now than you were when you were breastfeeding her! I know it, you know it, and she knows it. Think on it. What would you have done at her age if someone yammered at you the way you yammer at her?" He went over and put his arms around Tammy, holding her gently, stroking her back, rocking her. "They say everybody gets their own kids. And you got yourself in your oldest so pack 'er in and salvage what you can. The last thing you need is to send that kid angry out the door because does she ever go like that, you know Phoeb, that'll be it for the next fifty years. She is a right-roarin' ramblin' bitch, just like her momma."

When Phoebe finally came home, Tammy ground her back teeth together and forced what she hoped would seem like a cross between casual interest and genuine pleasure. "Well, hello there stranger." She was pretty sure she had her voice under control too, even if her throat did feel as if there was a tight rubber band around it. "Will we have the pleasure of your company at dinner tonight?"

"Yeah." Phoebe cast a suspicious glare which Tammy chose to overlook entirely.

"Good. In that case, maybe I'll whip up some of my Swedish meatballs. You always say they're your favourite."

"Since when does anyone give a poop about my favourite?"

"Oh, listen to you, Grumpy Guts herself. You don't fool me, you aren't really the curmudgeon of all time. You're just trying to pretend you are."

Phoebe figured Tammy was up to something, she wasn't sure what. But no skin off her nose, she could play along with just about anybody at all, whatever their game. More and more now she had to agree with some of the things her dad used to say, like the time he said people were really something, they could be the most disgusting piles of crap breathing air and then turn around and do some of the most beautiful acts of kindness. She supposed she would never figure it out. At times she felt so absolutely weird when she compared herself to other people that she wanted to sit down and cry. Other times the differences only made her feel angry and defiant. Who's to say they are right just because there's so many of them? After all, probably just about that same percentage of the population didn't give a shrug one way or the other how many Jews went up in smoke and no way anyone would convince her *that* was right. And how many of those oh-so-nice people gave the first part of a fart how many people lay dead under the hot sun in Africa?

Sometimes she felt so old and so tired. Nobody else she knew seemed to feel that way. Just another example of how weird she was. Sometimes the other kids teased her and called her Cynical Phoeb, probably for the same reasons Tammy had called her Grumpy Guts. Other times they shook their heads almost admiringly and said she spoke aloud the things other people thought but kept to themselves.

She was getting kind of tired of a lot of stuff. Bored, maybe. Like with guys. For a long time it had been nice to cuddle, stroke and smooch, and if it went farther than that, so what. It didn't hurt and it made them feel good, which meant she got the snuggling she enjoyed, fair exchange is no robbery. And maybe it was just another example of how weird she was but weird or not, nothing had been quite the same for her since the time she and Kurt were getting it on and, by accident, she looked sideways and saw them in the mirror on his bedroom wall. It was nighttime, and they'd made jokes about the moon being so bright a person better be careful about moonburn. The light coming in the large half-open window to her right back-lit everything so that in the mirror to her left she could see Kurt's hard round butt rising, falling, rising, falling as he worked himself from Christmas to New Year. She had nearly burst out laughing, not just then, but practically every time since. Not just with him—whoever she was getting it on with she'd have this mental picture of the bare butt pumping away, and any passion she'd been feeling was gone, pop like bubbles from a kids' pipe. Sometimes her inner imaging got even more graphic. She would envision the hair at the base of the spine, a pimple or two on the backside, and so many of the guys had zits on their shoulders and backs she'd given up reaching under their tee shirts to stroke them, god, if you knocked the head off one of those oozing volcanoes you'd probably puke.

Maybe you've only got a certain amount of whatever it is. She'd found out about birds and bees and the not-so-sweet mystery of life when she was what, seven? Seven or eight. One of those damn parties Tammy used to throw all the time, with half the beer parlour showing up after closin' time and drunks passed out in every place and position including upright in the corners. Phoebe had been asleep, and then she was awake and that creepy arseltart with the dark beard streaked with white was curled behind her, his hand over her mouth, his dick pushed between her legs. That's all he'd done, worked his load off against the soft skin of her pressed-together thighs, but at the time she hadn't had a clue what it was he was doing. He put his finger inside her, but it didn't hurt, it just felt distinctly odd and not too pleasant. He puffed and huffed, then did something and his hanky was between his thing and her skin, then he cuddled her and stroked her and told her she was a good little girl, his little girl, his special one. She fell asleep and in the morning when she got up, he was in the kitchen drinking coffee. He smiled and patted his knee, and she went over to sit there and take little sips of coffee. He showed up not too often but halfways regularly for a while, and then, with no explanation, he didn't come any more. Maybe he'd left town. Maybe he'd found another little girl. Who knew? And by now, all this time later, who cared? But at the time she had cared, and cared a lot, even hated the unknown little girl who might have replaced her.

There were others, too. Mr. Jones, for one. Now there was one weird and creepy dude, good old Mr. Jones, friendliest neighbour in the trailer park, I think not! Funny thing about that, when she told Tammy she didn't want to babysit the Jones kids any more, Tammy gave her a long, long look.

"Got a reason?" she asked.

"Yes, I do," and Phoebe got set for a real argument.

But Tammy nodded and said, "Fine then, you want to tell 'em or you want me?"

"You," and that was that. Nothing more said but she was off the hook. Better yet, the hook was out of her!

By the time she'd started letting the guys from school get it on with her, she was pretty well schooled by the finger-fuckers and pussy-petters. The girls' counsellor at school gave them all these idiotic talks about how giving out will lose you the respect of the boys, and what you do now might seem like nothing but when you're older you might regret, and rah rah la de dah. Well, Phoebe didn't feel cheap or used, and the boys didn't seem to have any less respect for her than anyone else, which was probably zip-all at the best of times. Nobody judged anybody by the scorfing anyway. It was like marbles or tiddlywinks, everybody played, some better than others, some more than others, and those who practised more played better, same as softball or anything else.

So it wasn't any of the Methodist madness the counsellor yammered on about, it was just, well, like the joke. Been there, seen it, done that.

So maybe a person is born with only a certain amount of—what?— and maybe if you start using it early, and use it with lots of guys, maybe you use it up, and from there on in the equipment is there, but the driver's inside drinking coffee. Or maybe it was like chocolate bars. Phoebe absolutely *loved* Molly-Oh bars, one was never enough. In fact, she'd been known to gorp down three at a sitting. But she was willing to bet if she had them for breakfast, lunch and supper every day, in a week she wouldn't give a pip if she never set eyes on one again.

Linda, now, there was a horse of a different garage. Sometimes Phoebe thought Linda was the very best friend she had ever had or ever would have. Other times she could have happily poked Linda in the eye with a sharp stick. It wasn't that everyone thought Phoebe the black sheep and Linda the little white lamb. No, stupid as they might all be, they knew Linda was no such thing. She just never went as far with anything as Phoebe did, like she'd been born knowing the limits and boundaries. Linda saw what happened when Phoebe stayed out until two in the morning, so Linda was home by eleven-thirty without having to be told. When she was out bombin' around in cars and yelling along with the tunes, turned high as the speakers could handle, Linda was as wing-nut as anyone and as quick to take a risk as Phoebe. And Linda had done some making out herself; she just approached it in a different way, was all. Phoebe couldn't put her finger on what the difference was, but she was willing to bet Linda would never feel bored and indifferent.

If you asked Linda, she'd laugh and say, Oh pooh, Phoeb, you just chew on things too much. Turn off your head, relax, and stop trying to figure it all out. Most of it makes no sense anyway.

Talking like that, a person might think Linda was an airhead. Well, if more people were that kind of airhead the world would be up to its ears in geniuses. Sometimes Phoebe felt as if she was about to fall flat on her arse when put face-to-face with something newly discovered about Linda. Like she'd known Linda came home on the bus with everyone else, and she'd known Linda didn't bother watching TV, and she knew, the way you know your shoes are on the proper feet, that Linda got her homework done before supper or immediately afterward. But it had just about set her on her ear to find Linda sprawled on the floor poring over Phoebe's own notes.

"What the hell . . . ?"

"Do you mind? It's okay, isn't it?"

"Sure, but . . . what are you doing?"

"Well, I guess I'll have to know this stuff next year so, well, I thought I'd get a jump on it."

"How can you even make sense of it when you haven't had the background for it yet?"

"I read ahead in my text book," and she smiled up at Phoebe, making her feel as if she wanted to scoop Linda up like a baby and cuddle her. "Jeez, Phoeb, you do this stuff every day? I'll die. It makes my head feel as if I've got flies buzzing in there."

"Flies buzz around dead meat, dough-head."

She sprawled on the floor next to Linda and put in an hour bridging the gaps as best she could. "One thing's for sure," she grumbled, "we know the last damn thing I'm gonna do is be a teacher!"

"Yeah? What *are* you gonna do?"

"Run away, join the circus and become a lion tamer," Phoebe laughed with no trace of bitterness. "Hey, after this mad pack, lions'll be easy!"

Linda laughed too, but wondered why Phoebe had to respond to everything with a joke or a putdown, some of them cruel. Why couldn't she just up and say Oh, I don't know for sure, or Maybe I'll go in for nursing. Was it the kind of thing some of the old people had, where you weren't to say what you wanted in case the Snarkies heard and went out of their way to make sure you didn't get it?

"Come on, Phoeb, you must have some idea. You're only a year and a bit away from finishing. Surely to god you aren't gonna just waltz out and get a job slinging hash or standing next to mom on the line in the fish plant."

"Slit my throat with a rusty table knife first!" For a minute Phoebe looked desperate. Then she pulled it together and was very quiet for a brief time. "If you laugh," she promised, "I'll pound you silly."

"I won't laugh. Even if I feel like laughing I won't laugh."

"There's this course a person can take, and it's hard to get in and hard to stay in, but I betcha I could handle it easy. Easy! They teach you about drivin' truck. Takes about five or six months, eh, and then you're licensed to drive the smaller ones. Do that for a while and you can work your way up, level by level, until you're driving the big ones."

"So why would I laugh?"

"Because it costs a couple of thou and where am I gonna come up with that? If I get a job it'll be something like waitress. Hell, you can't even work as a bartender until you're past nineteen! And on those wages I'll be so old when I finally have a couple of thou squirrelled away they'll turn me down for bein' deaf and blind and havin' no teeth."

"Ask Mom for it."

"Shake your head, Linda. Then do it again. Where is she supposed to come up with that money? They're paying what, eleven or twelve bucks an hour at that fish plant? Figure it. Fat chance."

"You could ask."

"And have her laugh in my face? Shake 'er again, kidlet."

So when there was nobody in the house but Tammy, Linda put it to her.

Tammy just stared at her. "Why didn't Phoebe ask me herself?"

"She doesn't even know *I'm* asking. She figures you'll laugh in her face because of all the hell-raisin' and all."

"Jeez." Tammy looked as if she was going to sit down on the sofa and bawl. "Jeez, my own kid and she thinks . . . boy, every now and again a kick in the teeth comes flyin' out at you, usually from the last direction you'd expect it."

First chance she got, alone in bed with Dick, Tammy told him, and with him she dared to let her misery show. "I know it's been an uphill battle," she mourned, "but my own kid? Does she think I don't remember what it's like? Everybody telling me to give 'er up for adoption, go back to school, pretend Steve didn't even exist, and when we did get married, they all acted like we were provin' to the world just how crazy we were. So what ought to have been a real happy time wound up bein' like a damn fight or something. I remember how that feels."

"So do you want to talk to her, or do you want me to do it?"

"Would you? If I just go straight to her she'll get her back up."

Dick bided his time, and when he felt everything was ripe and prime he cracked two beer and handed one to Phoebe. "Don't tell the cops," he grinned, "or they'll have me up for contributing to the delinquency of a delinquent, or something."

"I'm not a minor." She took the beer and smiled her thanks. "I never set foot in a mine in my life."

Linda didn't need a ton of bricks to fall on her toes. She grabbed Sandy and went outside with her to the little play yard where the swings were. Sandy could never get enough of swinging. And it left the other two some privacy, something in short supply at the best of times.

Dick and Phoebe sat sipping beer and staring at the TV without paying any attention to it.

"Truck driving school, huh?" he said softly.

"She squealed," Phoebe sighed.

"She loves you, ding-dong."

"She still squealed."

"Yeah, I guess so." He sipped his beer, drawing it through his teeth and swishing, enjoying the taste and the feel of the bubbles in his mouth. "You know your dad got killed at work, huh?"

"Of course I know, what y'think, I'm dim?"

"Gimme some time here, this is what they call delicate work," and he nudged her with his elbow. "I'm tryin' to relate to a very prickly personality, okay?"

"I'm not prickly."

"Sure y'are. And a good thing, too, it's the only defence we have sometimes." This time he didn't nudge her, he just patted her knee. "Well, your old man was a lot older than your mom, and he had this thing about dyin'. You know how they say someone is like old enough to be her father, for crying out loud, well, with your mom and dad that was true. He could easy have been her dad. And he had this thing about how he'd go first and she'd be left on whoofare. So he had insurance of every kind right up the old gee-gaw. On top of which, he got snuffed at work so there's the Compensation pension fund. And on top of that, I can easy work overtime the next six months or so and whack that money into your course and you mom said to tell you she had some cash squirrelled away in a jar under the trailer."

"Why didn't she tell me?"

"For exactly the same reason you didn't tell her."

They sat quietly for long minutes, then Phoebe leaned to her left and put her head on Dick's shoulder. "God damn, but we are all of us crazy, right?"

"You got 'er, kiddo." He put his arm around her and held her gently for a moment, then straightened, drained his beer and stood up slowly. "So I think what I'll do is just make myself scarce and give you some private time to think things over and maybe have that cryin' jag you're tryin' to fight off, okay?"

"Thanks. Better stay gone at least an hour."

"Yeah, I'll take Lin and Sandy with me. Maybe go get ice cream or somethin'."

"Sure." Phoebe made herself sound as if she was teasing him. "Just like the rest of the creeps in my life. Go get ice cream and leave me here alone, same old crap, it never stops, let's ditch Phoebe, we'll get ice cream and she won't, right guy, and thanks a heap." She even made herself smile, and if it wasn't convincing, it was at least a good try.

15

The second growth fringing the periphery of the pastures looked dark brooding blue rather than green, and the fresh spattering of snow caught on the heavy boughs was so clean, so beautiful, it looked false, as if some kitschy-craftsy had been busy turning the place into a postcard. The sky seemed caught on the tips of the trees, dark grey, heavy and full, and the snow fell in little twenty-five-cent-sized flakes.

The horses had ruined the effect in the orchard. They had rolled so many times there were large patches of dirty smeared stuff, and their running back and forth, tails up and streaming behind them, tangled manes blowing, had churned what wasn't flattened and made it look old, especially compared to the untouched blanket in the upper pasture.

The cows were in the lower one, standing quietly, jaws working, chewing their cud and looking thoughtful. The snow was marked where they'd walked into the barn for their morning feed of hay, then walked back out again to stand loosely grouped, gnaw gnaw gnawing. Their backs were coated with a fine layer of white, and the heifer seemed to be the only one the least bit excited by the change in weather. She stalked around sniffing, sniffing, then blowing, her breath a fog around her head. The older cows just stood, bored. Hey kid, we've seen lots of this before, don't get your water hot. But she did have her water hot, and managed to look both endearing and stupid.

Isa would have preferred to stay in the house and ignore the whole damn mess, but instead, here she was with her light green toque pulled down over her ears, her white woollen scarf wound around her neck, and her hands in lined leather gloves stuffed into the pockets of her heavy jacket. She stood watching, smiling, wiggling her toes in her warm lined boots, watching as Stevie came down the driveway hill on the plastic garbage can lid. He was bundled for the weather, his cheeks red with cold and exertion. She could hear his laughter, see his happy face, and she wanted to scoop him up and squeeze him tight. But she didn't. There was still that place inside her that was afraid to let go, afraid to dive right into her emotions and wallow in her love for him.

She hadn't wanted to get this involved. She knew the only thing that could come of any of this was more lines in her face, more grey in her hair, more tension in the muscles up the back of her neck and across her shoulders. Bloody Cindy, bloody Gus, both of them too self-centred to be able to do half of what that kid needed. Where do people get this idea that they are terminally unique anyway? Absorbed in their own little miseries, which are mostly their own fault, convinced nobody in the history of humankind has ever had to cope with such staggering loads of pony puckies.

"Yook!" Steve screeched. "Yook, G'amma," and he lurched himself off the garbage can lid at the bottom of the driveway, then stumbled, slid and ran to a fresh patch of snow, flung himself to the ground and wallowed like a puppy, sending lumps and dry flakes of it flying. "Come do. You do, too."

He ought to be talking better than that. He sounded like a slow two-year-old when in fact he was working himself toward four. Maybe that's what happens when nobody talks *to* you but only *at* you, do this, don't do that, come here, go there, get ready for bed. Too bad they hadn't also taken the time to show him what a toothbrush was for, and then told him to go do that too. She'd bought him one with Mickey on the handle and he'd been as awkward with it as a year-and-a-half-old would have been. His wonder and glee at bubble bath told her he hadn't had much experience with it, and the way he first stared, then tentatively tasted, then dove into and stuffed himself with waffles had made her feel both pleased and grief-stricken.

Isa had no idea what was going on. Something, for sure, but she was being treated like the family mushroom—keep it in the dark and feed it steer shit. First Gus with any number of intensely frequent phone calls, each time insisting everything was fine, just fine. Then the call from Ucluelet and the offhand information that he had, yet again, split up with Cindy. This time, he said, he wasn't going back before they'd had a chance to really talk things out and make some changes in the way they did things. Fresh from several different college courses where he had studied and earned extraordinary marks in psychi-psycho studies of one sort and/or another, he had the vocabulary memorized. He used terms like co-dependent, enabling behaviour, abandonment issues, and he talked easily about dysfunction, dysfunctional, dysfunctionality and generational maladaptability. Or something close to it.

"He's crazy!" Isa knew she sounded totally exasperated. "I knew he was a nut, but I didn't know he was crazy, too."

"Oh, darlin'," and Carol laughed easily, "you're so damn out of touch! I thought you pop-cult artistes stayed on top of everything. He's not crazy, he's just a sensitive new age guy who is working hard on his enlightenment," and she guffawed loudly.

"Stay on top of everything? Babe, I can't stay on top of anything. I've been snowed under since the age of nine or ten. So what do you think, after all these years, do you think we love each other or are we just caught up in a sick, neurotic, pathological, destructive mutual co-dependent and inter-dependent unhealthiness?"

Looking down at Carol laughing up at her, Isa felt such sheer joy she didn't know if she would be able to hold it in. Not too often, but every now and again, she would say something that hit Carol's funnybone, and that look would start—part surprise, part admiration, and then the laughter would bubble. The fine crinkles at the corners of Carol's eyes would accordion shut, her face would pinken and her eyes fill with light.

Not a month later, Cindy phoned, and it was all too sadly clear that she was up to her top lip in hot water again. Mind you, she'd rot on the cross before she would say what was going on. She much preferred to sling the BS until your mind was so weary of picking through the contradictions, you lost interest in the whole subject. Amazingly, this time it wasn't money she wanted. This time she wanted Isa to come and get Stevie and keep him "for a while."

Isa had wondered more than once if a while meant a day or two or until Stevie had finished university. But off she went to get him. He was all set, too, with his little fourth or fifth-hand Goodwill backpack right by the door and a black plastic garbage bag a third full of something sitting next to it. "Yet's go, yet's go!" he shrilled, jumping up and down, and Isa wished she could think of it as eagerness instead of something heavily touched with frantic.

"Don't I even get a cup of coffee?" she grinned. He kept shrieking he wanted to go, right now, and Cindy and Barb were so edgy Isa realized they, too, wanted her to hurry off before . . . what? Did they have an inside tip the earthquake of all time was about to hit? If so, you'd think they'd want company while the roof fell down around their ears.

"He's been driving me crazy," Cindy whined. "He got up early this morning and was ready to leave before he was dressed. I guess he'll just drive you crazy if you don't head off soon."

Of all the options open to her, Isa could have named seven dozen preferable to the idea of sitting down and having a cup of coffee with this all-too-well-matched pair. "I think you're probably right about that," she said. "Would you mind if I loaded him and his stuff and just whipped off? Maybe he'll agree to stop for fish and chips or something."

"Yeah, we'd all go nuts if he kept on at us for long."

Barb just nodded, her smile tight and false. The two of them were about as graceful as a pregnant sow on a sheet of glare ice, and Isa was glad to get away without having to spend much energy on either of them.

Stevie didn't want to stop until over an hour later. He was like a flea in a fit, looking through the back window as if expecting the Phantom Mutant Ninja Penguin to come flying from the sky to peck holes in his head.

"So what do you want, fish'n'chips, hamburger or Kentucky Fried?"

"McDonald's pizza." He sounded uninterested, but once they were seated at the table with a pineapple-decorated pizza between them, he relaxed, so quickly and noticeably it gave Isa a start. He smiled up at her. "Sanks," he said shyly.

"You're welcome, sir. It's my pleasure. Nothing I like better than to dine out with my main man."

He ate pizza and swilled milk until she thought he'd burst at the seams, and she wasn't on the road again for more than five minutes before he was sound asleep. His hair was long and shaggy and had no shine to it at all, the dark brown half moons were back under his eyes, and his hands twitched as he slept. His nails were long and dirty, and his face cleaner now than it had been before Isa had taken him to the bathroom to tidy him up for lunch. Jesus, he looked as if they'd stood in line outside the mission and got him some clothes from the grab bag. Nothing fit, everything was shapeless and covered with those odd little balls.

By the time they had got back to the farm, done the evening chores and had supper, Stevie was too tired to bother with a bath, and Isa let him go to bed just as he was, jeans and all. So it was the second night before she got him stripped down and ready for the tub.

"Where did you get that?" she said, gently touching a big black bruise on one cheek of his baby backside. He shook his head.

"Sweetheart." She knelt then and put her arms around him. "Any time anyone does that to you, *they* are the ones doing wrong, not you. *They* are doing the bad thing, okay?"

He nodded, but his face was stiff, his expression guarded.

Isa was so angry she wanted to put him to bed, wait until he was asleep, then get in her truck and head down to the pigsty where that pack of rejects were squatting. But talking would do no good at all, yelling would do less good, and she had a lifetime habit of at least trying to be law-abiding, so blowing them all to smithereens with her shotgun wouldn't work either. It wasn't that she was unwilling to do the crime, but she was very unwilling to do all that time. You could count on it, the damn law would send her off for twenty years the same as if she'd wiped out decent human people. You can head into the bush and blow the shit out of a quiet, nonthreatening, minding-its-own-business bear and there's no penalty, but eradicate a pack of child-battering arseltarts and they pour hot water on your head.

Her rage was so deep, so hot, so hard to control, she didn't even tell Carol. If she uttered even a few words about the bruise, or the red strips criss-crossing his bum, lower back, and even his bony shoulders, marks that could only have come from a leather belt, she would flip right out. And the last thing she or the kid needed was for her to lose it.

She spent a night from hell, unable to sleep, glad for the first time that she and Carol had separate rooms. She would never have been able to hide what was going on if she'd been sharing a bed. Her body thrummed, her eyes felt hot and dry, and the mental movie just kept playing. Things she hadn't thought about for years were suddenly there, incidents she must have made herself forget were played and replayed, sounds echoed, sometimes several scenes jiggled and twisted at once, individual soundtracks blending, layering, weaving, and his anger-contorted face was like a superimposition or a scrim through which everything else was seen. Isa wanted to sit up and scream and scream and scream and scream, and she knew that was absolutely the worst thing she could do. Besides, she was terrified she would never be able to stop. They'd said the truth shall set ye free—eyewash! When it surfaces, the truth can send you mad all over again. It would make a great film script, the woman who learned the truth and destroyed civilization because of it. It wasn't diamonds were a girl's best friend, it was amnesia. Except no matter how well you boxed it, sooner or later something would happen that ripped off the lid and let the devils out to dance up and down your spine.

She survived Hell Night. She was first one up in the morning, weak as a dishrag but marginally under control. Carol was almost ready to leave for work when Stevie woke up and came into the kitchen. Isa made him his favourite breakfast, instant oatmeal, the peaches and cream flavour. All she had to do was get the kettle boiling, open the package, dump the processed whatever-it-was into a bowl, add boiling water and stir. A minute later, she would pour on some of Pansy's cream-rich milk and, just to put a spark in Stevie's day, dribble some candy sprinkles on top. It didn't take much to make him happy. He packed it away quickly, then had cinnamon toast too.

After Carol left, Isa dressed Stevie and took him with her to finish the morning chores. And as soon as she thought the ding-dongs at welfare had bothered to open the office, she phoned. This time, by the lord Harry, someone was going to get her head out of her arse and do something.

Barb wished she could win the lottery so she could dump the ferret and rodent into a military boarding school for the next twelve or so years while she climbed onto a cruise ship and let the world take a pass. She felt as if she'd been painted into a corner and didn't dare step out, not because she was afraid to leave tracks on the floor, but because the paint was poisonous. Each step she took would only bring her that much closer to something awful.

First Herb told her he was leaving, he hoped there wouldn't be hard feelings, he wanted them to be friends, he just didn't want them to be in a relationship. "It's too much like marriage, white picket fence, all the stuff I've worked overtime to not have to contend with," he said. She might have believed him but she'd lived with him long enough to know him better than she wanted. There hadn't been any beatings as bad as that first one. He had her trained, and trained well. He even had Ferret and Weasel convinced they should behave when he was around. Even Cindy knew enough not to pull some stunt that would tick him off and light his short fuse. No, Barb was being dumped was the long and short of it, and the longer and shorter was she was glad. She'd have dumped him if she wasn't afraid he'd kill her for it.

But she didn't hop up and cheer. That might have made him mad. Instead, she just nodded, her face as grave as she could make it. She hoped she looked as if she'd been given some bad news.

"You gonna be okay?"

"Yeah."

"You mad at me?"

"No," she lied convincingly. "Nothin' is forever, right? From the start we said no strings, no chains, right?"

She even helped him pack the few things he'd kept at the house. Managed what looked like a wan little smile as he climbed into the cab. And when it was out of sight she went back into the house, went to the blessedly solitary bedroom, flopped on the bed and grinned from ear to ear. One less lug nut to put up with, thank God.

Except that no sooner was the dust of Herb's leaving settled, than who came up the pike except that crazy bastard Real.

"No hard feelings," he told Barb, as if she was the one had been outrageous and he the one put-upon. "We can work it out," he said, and "Can't just throw it all away." He also told her, "Try it for the kids' sake," and "We had it good for a long time."

He seemed to think he could just walk into the house and he'd be back in the bosom—and bed—of the family. When Barb made it clear she not only wouldn't start over with him ever again but would call the cops if he tried to go into the bedroom, let alone the bed, Real got a bit slit-eyed. And the next thing any of them knew he was drinking, which was never good news.

Nobody quite knew how to get him the hell out without kicking off World War Four. Maybe if they acted as if he was as welcome as springtime, maybe if they acted as if it was the most natural thing in the world for him to show up to visit his kids, maybe, just maybe the whole thing would simmer down and they'd escape a huge scene. And maybe pigs will learn to fly.

They thought they'd aced it when he lay down on the sofa, kicked off his shoes, yawned and dropped into a drunken slumber. Well, no wonder, it was past three in the morning and he'd been boozing for hours. Barb and Cindy even felt safe enough to go to bed. Together. In Cindy's room. With the door shut and locked.

Darelle got up first and put boxes of cold cereal on the table, got some bowls and spoons, put out the milk and had her own breakfast before the others came swarming from their rooms. Stevie was the next one awake. She got him fixed up with breakfast, then the others came down, quarrelling and bickering. "You better shut up," Darelle hissed. "Real's sleeping on the sofa and you know what he'll do if you wake him up."

The arguing and pinching stopped. Ferret and Weasel sat cowed, shovelling their breakfast quietly. They hadn't seen their dad in so long they barely remembered what he looked like, but the memory of the strap, the swat, the wallop and the kick were as fresh as the day.

Stevie finished his cereal and got down from his chair. He went to the fridge and got out the juice, poured a bit into a glass and put the container back in the fridge.

"Me too!" Billy shouted. "Don't be a pig."

"I want some!" Bobby screeched.

And Real opened his eyes, glared, sat up and winced as his head asserted itself.

Stevie ignored the noise and clatter from the table. Most of the time he acted as if he was as good as alone in the house. He drank his juice and put the plastic glass on the counter near the sink. Bobby and Billy, who could have got off their chairs and got their own drinks, continued to harass Stevie, while Darelle tried in vain to get them to shut up. She could not believe they would lose control so soon, when they knew better than anyone else how ticked off Real could get.

Stevie left the kitchen, one hand hauling up his pyjama bottoms, which were hand-me-downs and too big for him. Besides which the elastic at the waist was just about dead.

Darelle grabbed Bobby's arm. "You shut *up!* Jeez, Bob, use it for more than a place to put a hat, okay?"

But even the presence of Real, even the memory of his anger, weren't enough to stop the usual Billy and Bobby behaviour. It was as if once started, the furor had a life of its own. They argued, they teased Donny as he sat smiling and spooning cereal into his mouth, milk dribbling down his chin, and they both flipped their wigs and got into a big shoving match over which of two cartoon channels they were going to watch.

The TV noises weren't helping Real's head. He got up from the sofa and headed through the kitchen to check on the possibility of crawling into bed with Barb. He opened her door, a big smile on his face, then felt anger welling when he saw the bed, made up, untouched, empty. He went to Cindy's bedroom door, tried to open it and found it locked. Well, jeezly aitch, who do they think they are, Princess Anne and Mother Teresa?

Stevie passed Real in the hallway and ignored him, not knowing who this guy was, let alone know who he used to be.

Neither Billy nor Bobby had bothered with the juice until they saw Stevie come back into the kitchen, dressed in jeans and tee shirt, carrying his socks in his hand.

"Can you help me?" Stevie asked Darelle, holding out the socks. She sat him on a chair, then expertly got the socks on his feet.

"Steve's a pig, he hogged the juice," Bobby whined.

"Wouldn't give any," Billy nagged.

"Thinks it's all his."

"Shut the hell up about the goddamn juice, okay?" Real barked from the doorway.

Both his sons started tattling, blaming everything on Stevie, who still hadn't spoken to either of them.

"There you go, bubba." Darelle patted Stevie on the head. "Go get your sneaks and I'll lace them up for you, okay?"

Stevie got off the chair and padded sockfoot toward the fridge. Maybe he intended to get juice for Billy and Bobby, maybe he intended to get more for himself.

"You stay the hell outta the fridge, y'hear!" Real snarled.

Stevie stopped dead, turned slowly, looked at Real for a long moment, then turned away and went to the fridge door.

And that's when Real kicked, knocking Stevie sideways against the sink. Darelle gasped and froze. For once in her life she was unable to take hysterics. She was paralyzed with disbelief.

Real's left hand reached out and grabbed Steve by the back of the neck, while his right hand hauled the big leather belt from the loops of his jeans. Stevie gasped, and yelped, then couldn't make any sound at all because of the shock and pain. Time and again the belt connected with him, and finally, his legs gave out and he fell to the floor, moaning. Real gave him a few more good wallops with the belt. Then, still cursing and threatening all sorts of dire things, he replaced his belt and went across the kitchen to make coffee.

Darelle moved then. She picked Stevie up and carried him to her bedroom, lay him on her bed and cradled him. His face was chalk white, his eyes round with shock. His body shivered as if it he was naked in a snowbank in the arctic mid-winter. He retched, and Darelle raced to the bathroom, got a basin and made it back just in time to catch the cereal and juice as it came hurtling back up again. When there wasn't a thing left in his stomach, Stevie lay down and went to sleep so quickly Darelle was convinced he had fainted.

Donny sat at the table, staring at the spot where Stevie had been beaten. There was no smile on his face and no light in his eyes, but anyone with half a brain would know something was going on in his head.

And still Bobby and Billy pushed it. Real had no sooner finished his first cup of coffee than they were rolling in a ball on the floor in front of the TV, flailing at each other in yet another argument about who was going to watch what. Real threw his mug into the sink, smashing it. Once again he hauled off his belt, and once again he started swinging. The boys screeched and yelled, scampered away from him and raced for the outside yard.

The uproar wakened Barb and Cindy. When they got to the kitchen they found Real in a totally rotten mood, pouring another mug of coffee.

"What's going on?" Cindy asked.

"Bloody brats," Real glared. "Never a minute's peace."

"He beat up on Stevie," Darelle said from the hallway. "He kicked him and knocked him around and beat him until he couldn't cry and his legs wouldn't hold him up. And Stevie puked." She looked from Cindy to Barb. "And it was *your* stinking kids caused it, not Stevie."

"Beat up on—" Cindy whirled and headed down the hall and up the stairs, looking for Stevie. When she found him she lay down on Darelle's bed, holding her youngest and weeping helplessly.

"What the hell is wrong with you?" Barb screeched. "Jesus, you're gone from our lives for years and we're doing fine and then the first time you hoof 'er back in, you make a great big stinkin' mess!"

Real muttered something and went to sit at the table with his coffee. Barb told him to drink it fast and eff off, and he said he'd be bloody glad to do just that. They were exchanging opinions of each other's characters when Donny left the table, put his half-filled bowl on the counter, opened the hell drawer, took out the scissors and sunk them into Real's shoulder.

"Fucker," Donny yelled. "Stinkin' fucker! Hittin' my baby!" Just to be sure the message got through, he stabbed again, one of the blades going deep into the muscle from Real's shoulder to his neck.

All hell'n'frenzy broke out then. Blood gushed, noise came from all concerned and Cindy shrieked down from upstairs where Stevie was still either asleep or passed out.

"He stabbed me, he fuckin' stabbed me!" Real squealed repeatedly. "The goddamn little retard stabbed me!"

"He ain't retarded!" Cindy screamed. "You're the one is retarded!"

"Break his neck if I get hold of him."

"Oh shut the hell up and get into the car! I'll drive you to Emergency. And tell them to sew your troublemaking mouth shut in the bargain." Barb gave Real an unsympathetic shove toward the door. He stumbled and lurched outside, past his sons, who gaped at the blood, then grinned widely.

"Oh, Donny, Donny, my baby." Cindy knelt and put her arms around him. "Oh, Donny, the cops're gonna come now, and they'll take you away and lock you in the kids' loony bin."

Donny bit her. Then he started hissing words at her she hadn't known he knew. While she sobbed, he told her his opinion of everything that constituted his stunted little life. Billy and Bobby came in yammering about their dad and the blood and asking what was going on, and Donny went at them so fierce and so far over the edge he managed to beat up both of them and send them, terrified, up the stairs to the bedroom, where they locked the door behind them.

"No more!" Donny shrieked repeatedly. "No more!"

Gus was supposed to come at noon to pick up Stevie for the weekend. Cindy wasn't the least bit in favour of it but the judge had told her she was in violation of a court order and could be sent to the pokey if she refused again. Contempt of court, he called it. But she figured she'd have a better chance of talking herself out of going to the pokey for not letting Gus have him than she would have if Gus got him and saw the mess he was in.

When Barb came back from Emergency to pack Real's things and send him on his way, Cindy had Stevie's stuff packed and the arrangements made. Barb drove the still groggy little boy out to Tammy's place. When Tammy saw the bruises and welts, and the traumatized look on the kid's frighteningly pale face, she began to shake. "Well, good for Donny!" she said firmly. "And you tell that ay-hole if I ever set eyes on him I'm going to kill him."

Dick didn't say anything. He just got in his car and headed to the Emergency, where Real was patched up and waiting for Barb to come back and collect him. "You've gone too far," Dick told him. "You go back where you came from and stay there. Show your face here again and I'll fix you for good. Understand me?" Real nodded. Dick drove him to the bus station and stood waiting, grim and menacing, while

Real bought his ticket and climbed on the bus. He didn't even raise the question of his stuff. Dick stood watching until the bus left some twenty minutes later, then he got in his car and followed it for a good ten minutes more, just to be sure that the ding-dong was gone.

"And how'n hell'm I supposed to get his stuff and his damn car to him?" Barb protested. "I don't want nothin' of his here, he'll be back for it."

"I'll get it to him," Dick promised.

So when Gus showed up, Stevie wasn't there. Gus raised hell on the doorstep, then went home to mutter to himself all weekend. On Monday morning he went to see his lawyer.

Stevie stayed a week and a half at Tammy's place, watched over by whoever was home. Those times when nobody was home, Stevie was at the neighbour's place.

Then Gus's lawyer made contact with Cindy's lawyer, who phoned her to tell her either she make the kid available or he couldn't do anything to protect her from a contempt charge.

"Well, he's been yammering at me to let him go see his grandma," Cindy stalled, "so why not tell numb-nuts to go up there with him and have a real good visit." And when she had hung up from talking to her lawyer, she phoned Isa.

16

sa took Stevie to the police station and showed them the bruise on his butt and the welts and belt stripes on his legs, belly and back. One of the constables wrote on a form, but Isa knew there were too many questions she couldn't answer. She had no idea who had hammered on the kid, no idea when or where it had happened. She wasn't surprised when the constable phoned later to say there wasn't much he could do about it. He didn't use those words exactly, but that's what he meant. Isa figured someone had started sending the cops to the same school of euphemism and indirect talk where they sent social workers.

Then she phoned the Ministry of Social Services and told them about the marks. The woman to whom she spoke promised a worker would come out to the house to see Stevie and talk to Isa. Well, no, she didn't think much would be served by Isa taking Steve to the office. The worker would be there as soon as possible.

By the time Gus arrived, the stripe marks were gone and the bruise faded. Isa had used half a roll of film taking pictures of the boy's body, but she wasn't an expert photographer and the photos didn't show enough to be used as proof in or out of court. The welfare worker didn't show up until after Gus had phoned them and had the next best thing to a psychotic episode. And even then, Isa could tell by the look on the woman's face that there wasn't enough proof left on Stevie's butt and back.

"If you'd come when I first called," she said hotly, "you'd have seen them clearly."

The worker mumbled something about how busy they were, then mumbled something about how Stevie's principal residence was in a different jurisdiction, then, looking everywhere except at Isa or Gus, euphemized at some length. Isa interpreted the bureaucratic jargon to mean grandmothers didn't count in the scheme of things.

Stevie refused to talk to the welfare worker. He just stared at her, then looked at his dad as if the chair on which he was sitting was at least half empty, then spoke to Isa. "Not s'posed to talk to cops," he said firmly.

"She's not a cop," Isa told him.

"She's a cop," he insisted. And that was pretty much that.

Gus stayed four days, then had to leave. He had exams to write and a job interview waiting. "I'm doing what I can," he told Isa defensively. "I try to see him. Half the time there's nobody home when I go to get him. I'm sick and tired of waiting in lawyers' offices and in hallways at the courthouse, and I don't think it does him much good anyway. If I do force the issue and see him, she's off on another of her episodes. She tells him I'm going to steal him and take him far away and he'll never see her or Darelle again. She tells him all kinds of shit, most of it at the top of her voice. It's better for him if I just leave him alone."

"Jesus, Gus! You know what goes on."

"I give her money!" His defensiveness was turning to chippiness. "There's every chance in the damn world he isn't even my kid!"

Isa could feel herself getting close to the boiling point. She wanted to yell *So what!* but had the sense to bite her tongue.

"Listen, please," Gus pleaded. "Those are Cindy's kids. Even my own lawyer has made that clear to me. They're *hers.* If I fight hard enough for long enough I can force her to allow me visitation and access—to Stevie. Not to the others. I'm doing everything I can legally do."

Isa felt like slapping his face. Fine for him to say. In the meantime, here was a kid who was, to put it mildly, at risk. Isa had hoped and prayed for years that Gus would distance himself from Cindy. She had prayed he would wake up and fall out of lust as rapidly as he had fallen into it. Well, be careful what you hope for, you might not like it when you get it.

Otherwise Gus was doing well, and it showed. No more driving pop trucks, no more driving gravel trucks, no more talk of karma and bulgur wheat, and he had a new girlfriend, too, a single mom with two daughters. Isa hadn't met them, and that suited her fine. She figured if one more kid called her Grandma she'd start screaming.

And at least he was voluntarily sending money. More than ninety percent of all separated, divorced and otherwise absent fathers didn't, and more than ninety-five per cent of all court orders for maintenance were forfeited within the first year. Next to nothing was done about it. Isa could imagine what would happen if ninety-five percent of the population neglected to pay income tax or car insurance. Once again the army would march, and this time it wouldn't be against five-year-old Mohawk children with gun barrels shoved up their noses.

Isa waited to hear from the local Social Services office. Failing that, she expected to hear from the office in Stevie's jurisdiction. When she heard diddly-hoop from either, she started phoning. The calls brought her no satisfaction at all and a bill at the end of the month which was right off the map.

So Isa wrote letters. And in return she got such mind-elevating epistles as We thank you very much for your letter and the information contained therein . . . Your concern for the child is very much appreciated . . . The laws of confidentiality do not allow us to share with you the decision regarding possible investigation . . . Please feel free to contact us in future.

Isa fumed, Isa raged, Isa lost ten pounds she could ill afford to lose. She went back to the police and showed them the photos, and what they told her boiled down to Stevie was too young to testify in court, especially since he wouldn't even speak in their presence.

So there it was. She could eat it or not, but she couldn't change the way things were. Phone calls didn't help, letters didn't help, cops didn't help and the welfare was as much help as a cold wet toilet seat in winter. She left the police station even angrier than she had been when she went in.

Then she took Stevie to the mall, to see the big motorcycle display. "When I'm big," he vowed, "I'm havin' one," and he stood next to the huge gleaming Harley, gazing at it the way pilgrims gaze at the relics of saints.

"Hey, li'l buddy." A huge, shaggy guy, who looked a step and a half from the apes, reached over, picked up Stevie and set him on the seat of the new bike. "How's that?"

"Good," Stevie beamed.

"Did I hear you to say when you were big you were going to be a biker?" If the guy's voice was any lower it would have rumbled below the range the human ear can hear.

"Yep. I'm havin' a red one."

"Red, huh. You could call her Scarlet O'Harley. You'n'me could go on trips, your red one, my black one. Have us a great old time, eh, li'l buddy?"

"Yeah. Or you could ride me on yours."

"I could, eh. Well, soon's you get old enough to wipe your own chin I'll take you for a ride. Then maybe send you out to trade horses for me. You're a silver-tongued little rug rat, I'm tellin' you."

When the huge gorilla lifted Stevie down from the bike and set him on his feet, Isa reached for the boy's hand. "Come on, dumpling," she said. "Let's go for a bite."

Ten steps from the motorcycle display, with Stevie practically walking backwards so he could get another eyeful of his dream, something clicked inside Isa's head. The sensation was physical—she not only heard the click, she felt it. She thought hard while Stevie was packing away a fishburger and fries, and when he was stuffed full and yammering on about how he wanted to go back to see the murdersickle again, Isa said okay and ordered two coffees to go. Then, while Stevie perched on the leather seat of the gorgeous black bike and dreamed something the biker understood completely, Isa and the biker sat together on a bench in the mall, sipping coffee and talking.

With Herb gone and Cindy off on a tear, Barb had a week or two of relative peace and quiet. Once the kids were home from school, life assumed the proportions of an air strike on a tiny village, but at least from the time they left in the morning until zero hour when they returned, Barb could find a quiet corner and sit there and think. She hoped if she got enough time and sat thinking long enough, she'd figure out why she kept getting tangled up with head cases. It would also be nice to know why Real didn't scare her but Herb left her spitless.

She would also like to know what the sam hill was going on with Cindy. Ever since Real blew his cool, walloped Stevie and got stabbed by Donny, Cindy had been weirder than an outhouse rat. Barb didn't get it. Crazy as he was, Real wouldn't let the cat out of the bag at the hospital. When they had asked him what happened, he told them he fell.

"Fell?" The young doctor stared, incredulous. "Onto something that put four nasty holes in you?"

"Hey, I feel stupid enough, okay?" Real really ought to have been in Hollywood helping Charlie Bronson make explosion movies. "The light bulb burned out in the kitchen. So I get the stepladder and go up it to change the bulb. My wife is at the sink finishin' off last night's dishes." He turned to Barb as the nurse rinsed his punctures with peroxide."If you'd'a done them damn dishes last night!" he growled. She looked away, as if she'd heard it too many times already. "So she's got the cutlery drawer open, and she's drying stuff and putting it away, and then the damn dog ran under the ladder and the next thing I know I'm *in* the cutlery drawer. I don't know what stabbed me, but damn, it hurts! I shoulda landed on the damn dog instead. Maybe I could have squashed it flat. And dead."

"It's a good story," the doctor agreed. "Not the best one I've heard, but it's up there on the short list."

"What? You don't believe me?"

"I'm just saying," the doctor grinned, "that one is shortlisted."

But when she told Cindy not to worry, Real had covered things up, Cindy ranted and raved about how it was all Real's damn fault anyway, and sooner or later someone was going to get snoopy and show up and drag Donny off to reform school. And after having to hide Stevie out so Gus wouldn't see the marks, then getting the phone call from her lawyer and having to send Stevie up to stay with the old bitch, Cindy got downright hard to put up with. Close to impossible, in fact.

"I can't have my baby with me because of that damn Real," she mourned, "and I have to have Donny out at Tammy's for the very same reason, and it's not fair. If it wasn't for Darelle I wouldn't have anybody."

"You don't have to have Donny out at Tammy's. I don't know why you ever got that idea in your head in the first place."

"Because if he's out there, then when the snoops come here to find out about him stabbing people, he won't be here, will he?"

"I guess you think that explains something."

"Well, why'd you have to go and marry a nutbar like that?"

"Why'd *you* let him into the house? It was *you* answered the damn door."

"Was not!"

"Was so!"

"Was not!"

"Was *so!*"

Cindy was so upset after the argument she went to her room, had a good cry, then slept for several hours. Barb recognized the signs and wasn't surprised when Cindy took a promenade after supper and wasn't back at breakfast time. She phoned Tammy, but Cindy wasn't there. So she phoned Frank and Ruby, but they hadn't heard from her either. Frank was mildly concerned, but Ruby didn't seem to give a hoot one way or the other.

"Any excuse is better than none," Ruby said, "but if none's all she's got, it'll do fine, too."

"I didn't phone to talk to you, I want to talk to Frankie!"

"Fine, I'll put him back on the line, but I want you to know right here and now there's no way we're coming down to hold anybody's hand. She's done this before, she'll do it again, and you know all you can do is check out all the bars until you find her, or sit tight and wait for her to limp back home."

"Boy, aren't you all heart."

By one in the afternoon Barb was going from bar to bar looking for Cindy, asking the regulars had they seen her, did they know who she was beering with, had there been a house party after the bar closed, where was it. But she might as well have been looking for angel dust. She went home long enough to make tuna casserole for the kids, then headed out again, going from pub to pub, from bar to bar, even checking out the lounges. But while several people said they had seen Cindy the night before, nobody remembered if she was with anyone.

Melanie and Georgie were together in a foster home, and as much as they could, they enjoyed it. The foster mom didn't seem to be too hung up on the things their other fosters had found vital, they had plenty of privacy, and there wasn't the usual rush to head off and get their hair cut or their clothes replaced so they'd be acceptable to the neighbours. All they were expected to do was get up in the morning, make their beds, get dressed, have breakfast and get off to school, in whatever order they preferred to do it. They went straight home after school, not so much because the foster mom wanted it that way as because they didn't know any other kids yet and weren't ready to start exploring. They had chores to do at home, but just the usual things you'd wind up doing anyway. There was a bit more emphasis on homework than they were used to, but all in all it wasn't a bad deal and they were allowed to use the phone whenever they wanted, as long as it wasn't long distance.

"So where is everyone, then?" Melanie asked.

"My mom is 'out' and Auntie Barb's looking for her," Darelle said. "Same as usual."

"I tried to phone Aunt Tammy, but I guess nobody's home because the phone just rang'n'rang, and nobody answered. I thought maybe they were at your place."

"No. Nobody here but me right now. The horrors are outside somewhere, probably doing something gross. How're you and Georgie doing over there, anyway?"

"Good. The foster mom said maybe next month we can have someone spend the weekend with us. You want to do that?"

"You mean, like, sleep over?"

"Sure. You want to?"

"Yeah. You want me to?"

"Yeah. Maybe make popcorn?"

"Yeah. I'll bring some with me."

They yattered on for a while, and for some reason it made them both feel better.

"Well, if there's nobody out at Tammy's place, where are they?" Georgie fussed.

"Maybe they're just down at the park or something. You worry too much."

"And you don't worry at all! People can just disappear and you pretend nothing has happened. Everybody's gone, Mel. Cindy's nowhere to be found, Barb's trying to find her, nobody's home at Tammy's, and you're not worried because you actually got to talk to Darelle!"

"Oh, calm down, Georgie. You know where I am, and I know where you are, and if anything happens Darelle will let us know. Just simmer down, Pete's sake."

Georgie tried, but simmering down was impossible. He didn't mind the foster home, and he'd had time to get his poke from where he'd hidden it, so he had plenty of money if he needed to take off. But he couldn't leave Mel behind, and he knew she would never agree to leave. She'd had enough of moving from place to place, had enough of uproar and uncertainty. When he'd talked to her about hoofin'er out of there, she'd given him that look that was equal parts of love and pity.

"Georgie, for cryin' in the night," she'd said, sounding so much like their mother it almost made him weep. "We're kids. There's no place in the entire country that's gonna let kids rent an apartment. We can't even check into the Sally Ann to sleep, they'd call the cops in a minute. We've got no way to make money, we can't get jobs, and why should we take off from here when we know we'll get caught and sent to another foster place, and it might be worse than this one. Stop dreamin', Georgie. Give your head a shake and get real."

"But Mel—"

"No, George. I don't know how you got all that money, but you didn't get it working! And just look where Mom and Dad are because of not working. I'm not going there. Not now, not ever. And if you're smart, you won't either."

Georgie didn't know what to do. Well, he knew what he had to do, he just didn't know how long he had to do it for. If he didn't hit the road now, if he just stayed here with Mel and waited for George and

Maria to get out, hell, there'd be no use running away. By the time they saw the daylight again, he'd be as good as finished school and ready for a job. If something even worser didn't happen.

His dad was sick. No doubt about that. A person doesn't go from being built like Van Damme to looking like a stick without there being something really really wrong. And if George had it, you could just about make book on Maria having it, too. He just couldn't put a name to it. He wanted to run and run and run, get away from it, away away from all of it, away from the fear it was partly his fault Donny was wing-nut, away from the fighting and yelling and lying and going to jail and getting sick. Sometimes he wanted to just sit down and cry. But he had to take care of Mel, and if he started crying he'd scare her, and then she'd never feel safe again.

He didn't know that Mel was holding back her own tears because she didn't want Georgie to think she was too weak to take care of him. If she couldn't actually be strong, she had to at least look strong. Otherwise something—she wasn't sure what—would start to unravel, and they'd wind up with that thing Momma joked about, a legless stocking without a foot.

Cindy didn't know half the family was on the prowl looking for her. Cindy didn't know if she'd been pinned, folded, stapled, punched or bored. She was drunk, and had been since about two and a half hours after she took her hike. She didn't know whose apartment she was in and she didn't much care. She couldn't remember the names of most of the other people there, some of whom were even drunker than she was, and she had no idea what kind of pills she was taking whenever someone handed one to her. But she knew Herb, and she knew he was there. Not only there, he was often the one handed her one of those pills.

Funny, she wasn't afraid of him now. She'd been uneasy around him for so long, actually terrified for a few weeks, but he seemed fine, just fine, right here, right now. She was too drunk to figure out the reason he seemed so nice was he was the only person she recognized.

Cindy didn't really want to go into the bedroom with all these different guys, but each time Herb asked her to be nice, she went along with it. After all, it wasn't as if it was a big imposition, it wasn't as if it was hard to do. Sometimes she had the dim feeling there were other people in the room, in the bed, on her, in her, but as soon as she got restless or uneasy, she saw Herb's face, and he was smiling at her, asking her if she was ready for another drink or another pill. Once he asked her if she wanted anything to eat, but food was just about the last thing on her mind, so he brought her a drink instead.

She half came awake when he lowered her into the bathtub and started soaping her, and she got the giggles when he washed and rinsed her hair, but he laughed with her, as if they were brother and sister, for sure and for real, and had been easy with each other for years. Some woman she didn't know blow-dried her hair, and Herb told her she'd never looked better. He told her she had to eat something, so she did, a hamburger and fries brought from some-where by somebody, then she had a couple of cups of coffee and might even have started to sober up, except Herb handed her two itty-bitty pills. She started to say no, then changed her mind because he was frowning and she didn't want him anything but damn happy. And soon after she swallowed the pills, the blurring started up again, with a whole bunch of different people arriving to party.

Donny liked being at Tammy's place. He had Sandra to play with and the older kids to make sure there were sandwiches and stuff on hand. Dick helped cook real meals and even Phoebe was easy to get along with, which Donny hadn't expected. He couldn't remember why he had this uneasy feeling when he thought of Phoebe, because she was acting just fine toward him. She had even sat next to him on the floor, in front of the sofa, and put one arm around his shoulders and given him a squeeze. When he looked at her to try to figure out what she wanted him to do this time, she just smiled and said, "Good for you, Don. Good for you for letting that ay-hole have it when he hit Stevie." She didn't try to smooch him or anything, just gave him that one great hug and smiled. That was nice. He hoped she would do it again.

Tammy brought home quarts of oysters and packages of filleted cod, and Donny loved sitting eating oysterburgers with plenty of fried onions and mushrooms piled on them. Sometimes Tammy traded

quarts of oysters for quarts of prawns, and a guy could sit at the table
as long as he wanted shelling and eating to his heart's content.
Nobody asked him why he'd let Uncle Real have it. Nobody asked
why he'd had a temper tantrum and cursed out his mom. It was
almost as if they not only understood but in some way agreed. Auntie
Tammy sometimes sat in the big chair at night with both Donny and
Linda on her lap, and she talked softly to them, cuddled them, said
they were her own dear darlin' babies and the bestest kids in the
world. Bit by bit the flashing lights and images in Donny's head
calmed, the reds, oranges and bursts of bright white light were
replaced by cool blues and greens, and he was able to lie down and go
to sleep without falling into a big black hole. Sometimes Dick would
put the sleeping bag on the sofa, get Donny zipped into it, then sit
beside him, stroking his hand until Donny settled, and drifted off
instead of plummeting into sleep. Maybe he wouldn't mind just
staying there. No Billy to pinch him or Bobby to trip him, nobody to
swipe his stuff or call him retard and tease him until he wept. He
wasn't going to school, but the kids had lots'n'lots of crayons and
stuff, which was about all Donny ever did in school anyway. As
everyone headed off to work or school or the sitter, Donny could
settle down in front of the TV. He could crayon or play with his
matchbox cars, he could watch TV or play the video game, and he
knew when it was time to eat the lunch someone had made him
because the dinger on the stove would sound. Donny knew how to
turn it off before going to the fridge and bringing out the brown paper
bag with sandwiches and cookies, an apple and some juice to drink.
When he'd eaten it all, every speck of it, he knew to turn the TV to
number 31 where there was a movie. He didn't always understand it,
and most of the time he fell asleep before the middle of it, but Donny
didn't mind being asleep, as long as there was no Ferret or Weasel to
dump cold water on the front of him so it looked like he'd peed
himself when he hadn't.

Gus was so mad when he found out Cindy hadn't been seen for the
most part of a week that he too went looking for her. Not because he
wanted any part of her, but because until he knew where she was and

what she was doing there was no way his lawyer or hers could do anything. He didn't mind Stevie being up with Isa and Carol, he just wanted a few things settled. Otherwise, first thing you know, she'd make it to second base before he did, and everyone knows it's the one who gets there quickest has the most chance in front of the damn family court judge.

17

Tammy didn't come home until close to four in the morning, and she was half-packed when she arrived. Phoebe sat up in bed and listened to the noises, the stumblings, fumblings and lurchings. She shook her head, lay down on her other ear and went back to sleep. Linda figured there wasn't much going on that involved her, and she too went back to sleep. Sandy didn't stir. She lay belly down, her butt stuck up in the air, one thumb in her mouth. They were supposed to get out of bed and check her and slide the thumb out, to wean her from it, but both of them figured she wasn't their kid, it wasn't their responsibility. So Sandy just kept sucking her thumb, and her front teeth were beginning to show the effect. Tammy called it an overbite, but as far as Phoebe was concerned the kid was out and out buck-toothed. Or would be, if someone didn't get on top of it.

Dick wakened and knew immediately what was going on; Tammy was drunk and trying to make herself a cup of tea. It was beginning to sound as if, before she could do it, she first had to hammer a kettle out of a sheet of steel. Not all that long ago he'd have got out of bed, gone into the kitchen, smiling, and made the tea for her. But he was getting just a tad fed up. Sandy or no Sandy, kids or no kids, things were just pissing him off, and he was less and less inclined to let everything drift. Tammy was boozing from about the time she got home from work until bedtime, except on nights like tonight when she didn't come home from work at all and didn't seem to know there was a bed, let alone a time to get into it. Her dipshit family was in yet another huge go-round, everybody out looking for the stray lamb, the prodigal hoofer, the wandering pain in the arse. By him, they were already doing enough looking after poor little Donny, who was curled up in bed next to Dick because he'd been having nightmares alone on the couch. Asleep, Donny looked absolutely normal, a good-looking little guy now, old enough the tell-tale facial differences no longer showed.

Funny, if anyone, doctor included, had known way back when what the entire population of the country seemed to know now, they might have been able to put enough pressure on Cindy that she would agree to get Donny into an enrichment program. But who knew? And now it was probably too late. They'd laughed and said he was a pixie, an elf, and his passivity had seemed to be gentleness.

Dick tried to go back to sleep but the noise in the kitchen was starting to enrage him. Maybe Tammy had already been to bed, maybe she'd already been to sleep, god knows it didn't seem to bother her to come in at the crack of dawn, pack a lunch, shower and change her clothes, then head off to work and put in a full shift. Roundheels, the lot of them, born with a congenital foot deformity.

So he got out of bed and went out to the kitchen to give her a piece of his mind. Five minutes later the entire household was wide awake, and in all probability the neighbours were beginning to rouse too.

Cindy woke up in bed with someone she had never seen in her life. She lay rigid, trying to piece together the flashes and images darting in her head. She felt as if everything in her brain had been taken apart, like a jigsaw puzzle, and she could only see patches of it, not the entire picture.

The burly, hairy-bodied guy with the half-bald head sat up, stretched his arms, yawned, then checked his wrist watch. Cindy could focus enough to realize the watch was making a persistent *ding ding ding,* which she'd thought was just another part of her headache. The guy smiled, leaned over, kissed her on the forehead, said something she didn't understand, then got out of bed. Naked as the day he was born, he padded from the bedroom. Cindy closed her eyes, about ready to pray she would die. And soon.

Whoever he was, he came back a few minutes later with two cups of coffee on a tray with a bowl of sugar and a container of cream. Cindy managed to sit up and drink about half a cup, then her stomach started doing loop-the-loops and she rushed to the bathroom and just let 'er rip. The cramps in her stomach were awful, and she was shaking from head to foot. What scared her most, though, was that she had known where the bathroom was. How the hell had she got here? And when?

The nausea passed and she went back to bed after rinsing her mouth with warm water, then swishing some minty-smelling green mouthwash. There was a fresh cup of coffee and two slices of buttered toast waiting for her.

She didn't even look at the toast, but the coffee was welcome. To her amazement it stayed down. But her shakes got worse, her stomach cramps were agonizing, and when she started to pour sweat, the big burly guy with all the body hair got out of bed, got himself dressed, then wrapped her in a housecoat she didn't recognize and took her to the Emergency.

Time telescoped in and out, some things seeming to take forever, others passing in the blink of an eye. And then Cindy felt a needle slip into her arm, and with a deep breath, she was asleep again. When she came out of it, she was alone in a room and the big fuzzball was standing by her bed with a flowering potted plant.

"How you feeling?" he smiled.

"Lousy." She didn't care if she sounded bitchy.

"Small wonder." He put the plant on her bedside table.

Cindy looked at it, then looked at him. "Who the hell are you?" she blurted.

He laughed. "Boris." As if that would explain everything, including the black hole theory. He pulled a chair to the side of the bed, sat down and settled himself for a visit. "You can drift off again," he said. "I can look after myself. But I'll be back, so if you wake up and I'm not here, don't worry, just wait a bit."

She was going to ask why he thought she'd worry if he wasn't there, but the gabby bugger would probably answer, and she didn't care to listen. Whatever they'd poked into her arm began to wear off again, and she felt the growing aches and pains, the stiffness and discomfort, the start of stomach cramps. Tears slid weakly from her eyes and Boris wiped them for her with a hospital tissue. "Easy, babe, easy, it's all going to get better, way way lots better."

Isa tried to phone Tammy to check on Donny but there was no answer, the phone just rang and rang and rang. So she tried phoning Cindy. As soon as Darelle answered, Isa knew as much as she needed to know, more than she wanted to know. She chatted briefly with the kid, not saying that Darelle ought to be in school, not saying she knew the entire damn pack was busy boozing, not saying anything because it would be met with evasions or downright lies.

Darelle knew her grandma knew, and Darelle also knew her grandma wasn't going to ask. The whole situation made her so sad she wished she could just sit beside Isa and pour it all out, but everyone else in the family warned her to shut up and say nothing to the old bitch, and Darelle knew better than to disobey. Bad enough having one of them mad at you. To have the whole lot of them mad was more than she could begin to bear.

Billy and Bobby weren't in school either. They'd been racing around the house all day, fighting, arguing, making a mess like you wouldn't believe. Peanut butter all over the cutting board and counter, jam and jelly smeared everywhere, even on the side of the toaster, milk slopped on the table, cereal spilled on the floor, and Darelle was sick and tired of cleaning things up. She was just going to leave the damn mess so other people would know what had gone on. She'd already tried to clean up twice and what good had it done? At least they were marginally quiet now, and not hanging off the phone cord screeching so hard she couldn't hear what Isa was saying to her.

"How's Donny doing?" Isa asked. "Is he there with you?"

"No. I think maybe today was the day they were going to start him in school again. Some kind of special school, I don't know what kind."

Billy and Bobby came tearing down the stairs, faces white, eyes like holes burned in a wool blanket. Darelle knew right away something was up, and it was bad news.

"What are you guys up to now!" she yelled. Neither of them

answered, they just slammed out the front door and kept on running. She hoped they'd run until they fell off the end of the earth.

"What's wrong?" Isa asked.

"Oh, those *boys!*" and Darelle was sobbing. "They act like alley cats and the place is a mess and—Omigawd, Grandma, there's *smoke* coming down the steps, I have to go!" and she slammed down the phone.

Isa had had enough. She hung up the phone, got out the book, checked the numbers and called the Child Help Line. It had never helped before, but you never knew, every now and again St. Jude takes a hand.

Darelle ran up the steps and along the hallway to the boys' room. The curtains were burning and coming apart, bits of flaming cloth drifting in the hot upwards draft. One of the bits of flying flame, a hunk no bigger than a sheet of writing paper, had landed on the bed and started a fire there. Darelle knew the fire was past the point where she could put it out. She slammed the door shut and raced back down the steps, through the kitchen, out the door to the front sidewalk and over to the next-door neighbour's, screeching.

The fire trucks arrived and the firefighters jumped off, connected hoses to hydrants and went at the blaze. Just before they got to the house, the red plastic five-gallon can of gasoline went sky high. Billy and Bobby had swiped it from the garage and taken it to their room, where they had poured just a little bit of it in the empty lid of a tobacco can and set it alight to watch the pretty blue flame.

A gallon of gas has the explosive force of more than a hundred sticks of dynamite, and this was five gallons. The blast was incredible. Bits and pieces of window flew, not only from the big house but from neighbouring houses. When it was over, there wasn't a whole helluva lot of the top floor left, and what there was blazed furiously.

By the time the blaze was extinguished the house and everything in it were pretty much gone. The cops were asking questions, the welfare was on hand, and Darelle had collapsed in a heap on the neighbour's sofa, sobbing she had no idea what had happened, she was talking to her grandma on the phone, find Billy and Bobby and ask them.

The police found Barb sitting in the Halfway House nursing a beer and trying to find out from a grinning Herb where Cindy was. Herb was having too much fun laughing at her to tell her anything the least bit helpful. When she saw the two Mounties moving toward their table she had a hopeful moment, imagining Herb getting arrested for something that would put him behind bars for at least ten years. Then she realized they weren't looking at him, they were looking at her.

Tammy was just getting off work when the Mounties caught up to her. "Donny? He's prob'ly at home, asleep in front of the TV, why?"

"You left him alone in the house?"

"He wasn't alone when I left for work," she stalled. The cops looked at each other, then looked at her, and she didn't much care for the expression on their faces. "What's goin' on, anyway?" she demanded.

Boris left the room when the welfare people arrived. He went down the hall to the smoking lounge, went inside and turned on all the fans, then sat down to enjoy one of his hand-rolled smokes. He restricted himself to no more than ten a day, and was aiming to get down to five soon, so when he did light up, he liked to settle down and actively enjoy every puff.

Even that far down the hall with the door shut, he could hear Cindy when she started screaming. A large part of him would have liked to go down and reassure her, but when the whoofare and or the cops showed up, Boris had learned to be so low-profile he didn't get noticed. He couldn't afford to be noticed. The last thing he needed was to get noticed. The worst thing that could happen to him was to be noticed. Besides, Cindy wasn't going anywhere. She'd still be there when the damn officials left, he could calm her down then.

Cindy heard what the whoofare workers told her. She knew Darelle had got out and gone to the neighbour's, knew Don wasn't even in the house, didn't give the first part of a good goddamn what happened to Ferret and Weasel. But she'd been waiting a long time to screech like hell, sometimes it seemed like she'd been waiting all her life, and this was the straw that broke the poor old camel's spine. The fire was going to bring the whole shiterooni down, falling apart, with welfare, cops and who-knew-who crawling all over her life. "Oh my *God!*" she screeched, "oh my dear *God!*" and then the words were gone and there was nothing in all the world but the sound coming from her belly, coming from lower than her belly, filling her head, filling the world, and still it wouldn't be enough.

Isa strapped Stevie in the car seat, then climbed in her truck and headed off, first to the bank for some money, then to look for Darelle and Donny. Trying to get the welfare to tell her what was going on with the kids was a lost cause. All she heard was one version after the other of the regulations concerning confidentiality, one dispassionate voice after another telling her to wait patiently and one of the children would call. Well, Isa had about had it with confidentiality and patience, and she was pretty much at the limit of civilized respectability. After all, civilized respectability had sat on its overeducated duff doing zip-all while a kid she didn't know personally was admitted to hospital more than twenty times with suspicious injuries. Broken bones, huge bruises, and so underweight he looked like someone who had just come out of Birkenau. Time and again the hospital reported to the welfare, time and again the neighbours reported, time and again the welfare worker made reports about the growing rapport they were establishing with the family, and they were still passing inter-office memos around like the golden fleece when the kid was killed. And then the representatives of civilized respectability fudged the records and even down-and-out dirty-dog double-damn lied about it. Isa figured if she sat around being one of the nice people much longer, chances were Stevie would hit the front page too. There are those in life who get their arses kicked and there are those in life who kick arse, and Isa was not interested in being the first. If any arse-kicking needed done, well, she was in the mood to do some of it.

She checked into a motel, took Stevie for supper under the golden arches, then drove to Tammy's place, because the smoking heap of rubble couldn't tell her much and the firefighters still pouring water on the charred remains wouldn't tell her anything at all.

Tammy looked like someone had dragged her through a prickly hedge backwards. "Jesus, I don't know, it's more than I can figure. Mounties showing up at work, whoofare showing up at the house, they haven't found those two horrible little buggers yet, and they just transferred Cindy from the hospital to the detox centre. You want a cup of tea?"

Stevie was happily playing on the floor with Sandy and a half dozen small plastic cars, so Isa opted for a pretence of normality and sat at the chrome table with a cup of tea and some peanut butter cookies. Phoebe and Linda were finishing the dishes, but there was no sign of Tammy's boyfriend, wotzisname, Dick.

She was on her second cup of tea when the front door of the trailer opened and Real stomped in, roaring that he wanted to know where his goddamn kids were. "What's this about a house fire, anyway?" he shouted. "What'n hell's goin' on?"

Stevie was on his feet, a wet spot spreading on the front of his jeans, a loud mindless wail coming from his open mouth. Isa started up out of her chair to grab him, and Real turned to Stevie and hollered that he had better shut up or he knew what would come down on him. Tammy threw her mug of tea at Real and it splashed on his shirt, spattered on his chin. He asked her, at the top of his lungs, who the hell she thought she was, so she told him in no uncertain terms who had bought and paid for the trailer.

"And that's *my* front door, you useless ape, and you don't come through it without an invitation, so just take off."

"Oh yeah? And I suppose *you* are gonna make me?"

And then Phoebe stepped into the trailer with Dick's hunting rifle in her hands.

"Get out of here," she said coldly, "or someone will carry you out."

"The bitch is crazy!" Real was backing for the doorway. "Someone oughta do somethin' with her."

Isa scooped up the still-screeching Stevie and sat down with him on her lap as he clutched fistfuls of her shirt. "Easy, easy," she soothed, "easy on little guy, I've got you."

"Honest to god!" Tammy shook her head tiredly. "Some days if it isn't one goddamn thing it's another. Phoeb, put the gun away, will you? It scares hell out of me."

Darelle could hear Donny raging, the sound coming up from the basement through the floor vents. The evening shift was having no easier a time with him than day shift had, he was bouncing off the walls and hollering mindlessly. From time to time he would shut up, and just as fast as someone switching off the light he'd be asleep, white-faced and exhausted. No more than a couple of hours later he'd come awake with a shout of fury, and the whole thing would kick off again.

Darelle had tried to calm him down but he'd charged at her as if he'd never seen her before, and she knew the best thing she could do for herself and for him was to butt out. Already he'd grabbed a compass from a geometry set in the kids' room and stabbed one of the group home workers in the leg. When he got hold of the scissors, they'd managed to get them away from him before anyone got hurt, and now they had him in a room where there wasn't much of anything at all, let alone something he could use to hurt someone. He just kept yelling, over and over and over yelling, I'll kill you bastard I'll kill you bastard I'll kill you bastard, sounding as if he would never stop saying it, I'll kill you bastard.

Darelle sat on the floor in a corner, her forehead resting on her jack-knifed knees, her hands clasped on the back of her head, tears dripping miserably. They'd said her grandma would be coming to see her first thing in the morning, but that was a lifetime away. She was afraid by the time Grandma got there, Donny would be right over the edge and unable ever to come back again, I'll kill you bastard. And why wasn't she allowed to phone Georgie and Melanie, why wasn't she allowed to phone Tammy, why was the only phone in the place locked in the room they called the office, the one with the thick glass around it, like one big window, from her waist to the ceiling, and how come Gus hadn't shown up like he used to do, and where for god's sake was her mother?

Melanie and Georgie saw the wreck of the house on the TV news. They looked at each other, eyes wide, and grinned slowly. "Want to bet it was Ferret and Weasel?" Georgie asked. Melanie just shook her head. No doubt about it, no use to bet, you'd only lose. "Boy," she sighed. "some people's kids, eh?"

"Hey, there's Darelle. And guess what?" he laughed and she joined in, each of them pointing at the TV screen. "*She's cryin'!*" they crowed.

18

Isa drove home, her nerves on edge, her eyes burning. She felt as if she ought to find out where that damn Gus was, go there, and beat on his head with a rock. Fine for him, he was as good as out of it, but what in hell had he dragged her into? What do you say when a kid who has known no other grandmother but you looks up with tear-filled eyes in a terror-gaunt face and wails, "But if you're my grandma . . . and they're my cousins . . . how can you say no?"

Well, the long and short of it was she couldn't. So Darelle was allowed to go with Isa and Stevie to visit Melanie and Georgie in their foster home. They waited until the kids were back from school, then drove over and asked for permission to take them out for supper. Isa was beginning to feel that if she had to sit at one more green plastic table and eat one more mass-produced hamburger with dry-stick fries she'd declare war on the world, but the kids loved it. They were overjoyed to see each other. In fact the whole thing would have been quite pleasant except they all kept calling her Grandma. It was Grandma this and Grandma that, and Grandma maybe you can come and watch Georgie's basketball game, he's on the school team. Melanie wasn't into sports, but she belonged to the school photography club and if good old Grandma bought the film, Melanie could probably take real good portraits of all the kids and then Grandma could have, like, her own collection, a gallery. Grandma here and Grandma there and Isa feeling increasingly trapped. And yet, what do you do? Tap the table to get their attention and then tell them she wasn't their grandma, tell them the only grandchild she had was Stevie? She couldn't do it.

For most of her life, Isa had leaned in the direction of "when in trouble or in doubt, run in circles, scream and shout," but there were too many others running, pelting, shambling and limping in circles and spirals, screeching, yodelling, moaning, whining and blathering mindlessly. Anything she could do would be so puny in comparison it wouldn't be noticed. So she kept her mouth shut, smiled until her face ached, and tried to give the impression she was having as much fun underneath the arches as the kids, only one of which was biologically related to her, all of whom seemed quite comfortable with the idea she was their grandmother.

She and Stevie spent a second night in the motel, then left first thing in the morning to return to the farm. Just to ensure she in no way got sucked in any further, she didn't contact any of the older ones until she was back home and caught up on her chores.

Stevie trudged through the choring with her, helping toss flakes of hay down to the cow mangers, carefully measuring grain into feeders, checking the bathtubs to ensure the animals had plenty of water, feeding and fussing the horses. Coming back from collecting the eggs, he found yet another treasure, a dark grey rock, almost black, with a strip of white encircling it. Happy as a piglet in mire, he wiped the rock clean on the front of his jacket, then put it carefully in his pocket. He kept it there until they were back in the house, then he pulled it out, looked at it and smiled, a pint-sized Midas with his gold.

"See?" He held it up for Carol to examine.

"Oh, wow, another one. I never knew anybody to find as many lucky rocks as you, fella. Want to wash it clean in the sink?"

In washing the rock, he also managed to get his hands and forearms clean, and after he had taken his new find into his bedroom and added it to the scads of others on the little table under the window, Isa got his face clean, too.

He packed away a good supper, stuffed himself with two desserts and went into the living room with Isa and Carol. While they watched the news he played with his Etch-A-Sketch, but he was flagging, his eyelids drooping, and Isa had no trouble getting him to go to bed early. She didn't even bother with the jammies, just hauled off his jeans and undershorts, then pulled his NHL hockey quilt up under his chin.

The house was dark and the farm quiet when Stevie's screams jarred both Isa and Carol wide awake. Isa ran from her room, Carol ran from hers, and they nearly collided in front of Stevie's door. Carol flipped on the light and Isa rushed to grab the terrified kid. He sat upright, stiff as a piece of plywood, eyes wide open, staring unblinkingly, and from his mouth issued a wail of such total hopeless horror, both women felt nauseated.

Nothing Isa said or did got through to him, so she finally gave up and went to the bathroom to run a tub of warm water. She sat Stevie in it, socks, tee shirt, undershirt and all, and lay him on his back, his head supported by her hand. "Easy, my guy," she crooned. "Easy, easy. See, you're in the bathtub, in the bathroom, in the house, on the farm. See, you're safe and Grandma and Carol are both here. The dogs are in their shed, the animals are all safe and asleep and you're my darling little boy." Over and over, variations of the same reassurances, trying to focus him, trying to centre him, trying to bring him all back to where he was.

And bit by bit the hopeless wailing eased until he lay quietly, eyes open, tears pouring, looking too much like Donny.

"What is it?" Carol asked softly.

"Monster," he managed.

"What does it look like?"

"A rock," and the stiffness was gone, he was limp and hiccuping his sobs. "It looks like a rock, but it isn't. And it comes up out of the dirt and it sits on me and it says," his eyes widened with terror, the voice coming from his throat deepened until Isa would have said it wasn't Stevie's voice but that of a grown man, "it says *you're gonna diiiieeeee,*" and he was clutching at her, shaking and weeping.

Isa got his wet clothes off him, rubbed him dry with a thick soft towel, then soothed and crooned him into his jammies. There was no question of him going back to his own bed. The nightmare was too fresh in the room, the rocks too visible. She took him to bed with her, holding him close, stroking his back. Carol crawled into bed with them and they sandwiched Stevie between their two warm bodies. He was asleep so fast Isa was almost scared.

"God," Carol breathed. "When your all-time treasure turns into a monster, things are getting rough."

"Can't trust a damn thing these days," Isa agreed.

Carol didn't sleep the rest of the night. She lay awake and alert, her mind running on overdrive. Times like this she really wondered what it was about Isa had attracted her in the first place, what it was that kept her connected in spite of the roller coaster crap that just kept coming down, disrupting everything, nudging and noodling her into situations she had never imagined, let alone wanted.

A woman has to work hard and be careful not to have kids. Any woman over the age of thirty who doesn't have any children and doesn't have a biological challenge making pregnancy impossible, has probably taken a degree of time and trouble to have things work out that way. Getting pregnant is one of the easiest things in the world for women. Beautiful women get pregnant, brilliant women get pregnant, forceful women get pregnant, executive-type women get pregnant, ordinary-looking women get pregnant, women in nursing get pregnant, women in offices and banks get pregnant, ugly women, stupid women, unpleasant and even disgusting women get pregnant. All kinds of women get pregnant, and too many of them don't think about it or the consequences at all.

But Carol had made sure she didn't have kids. She ignored her mother's disappointment and endless hinting, and she grinned off hopeful questions from her aunts, cousins and other rellies. Once in a while she would shake her head and laugh softly, Oh no you don't, just because you got yourself caught in a leghold trap you don't have to talk me into it, too.

And then she met Isa and it was skyrockets from the get-go. Isa who made no secret of the fact she had grown up in something so messy the word "dysfunctional" was an understatement. Isa, who had said up front she didn't know if she'd get involved with someone like herself. "I don't think I know what a relationship is supposed to be," she had said, as if she was confessing to a string of gore-smeared murders. Isa, who when asked why her marriage had ended looked almost embarrassed and said, "I was bored to death. He wasn't a bad guy, he wasn't a louse, he wasn't a drunk or a child beater or much of anything at all, really, except all the things they'd told me to look for—you know, stable, kind, considerate. They hadn't told me all of that could bore you to the point you wanted to slash your skin open just for the chance to do something different."

Carol knew Isa came with strings attached. Grown or not, there were kids in the picture. Kids who were still struggling with their own conflicts around their father and his behaviour after the split, their mother and her behaviour after the split. Kids who would someday have more kids.

And Carol knew that life with Isa would also involve more dogs than it made any sense to have. Not pedigreed, registered, puppy-producing cash machines, not noble hounds or elegant best-in-breed. In all these years, with all these dogs, there hadn't been one that looked like anything but a vet bill waiting to happen, a big drooling mouth which wanted unbelievable amounts of food and a collection of assholes which left mounds of muck all over the yard, invariably right where you were going to put your foot. Townspeople seem to think those who live on farms are just panting for the chance to have some starveling dropped off on the property. And so they limped down the driveway, lurched across the pastures, hobbled toward the house, the three-legged, the one-eyed, the brink-of-deathers, and each time Isa found yet another makeshift food bowl and dished out the kibble. Carol had always thought she liked dogs, but after a while enough becomes too much. When she protested, Isa looked as puzzled as a six-year-old confronted for the first time with what adults call logic. "They want to live as much as we do," she said. And what can you say to that?

Not just dogs, either. Carol had no idea how many cats were living in the garage and the barn. She did know Isa got two quarts of milk a day from the neighbouring farm and put most of it out for the cats. She had no idea how much dried cat food was being devoured, but she had a fair good idea of how much cat shit was being produced because it all seemed to wind up in the garden, where the digging was easy, and most of it seemed to be under a spatter of dirt just exactly where she wanted to plant tomatoes. "They aren't all mine," Isa said, probably thinking she was providing an explanation. "We only have two cats. The rest . . . I don't know whose they are, where they come from or how they got here."

"*We* don't have any cats at all. *You* have them," Carol said firmly. "So if none of those other fat lazy things are yours, why not just pop 'em off with the .22?"

"You want them shot, you shoot them. I can't," and that was that because Carol had probably never fired a gun in her life and had no more intention of doing that than she had of getting pregnant and giving birth to quintuplets.

She had never wanted kids. But here she was, cuddled up to Stevie, alert to his every twitch, and there was nothing in the world she wouldn't do to guarantee his safety. People had probably converted to oddball religions and cults on the basis of less emotion than Carol felt for Stevie. And what she felt for him was about half what she felt for Isa. The weirdest part of it was she didn't feel the least bit trapped.

Cindy was glad they were giving her some kind of nerve pills in the treatment centre, because by the time the whoofare bitch had left, Cindy needed all the help she could get. So that was the way it was going to be, huh. They would hold off on the court crap until she had herself under control, then it would be up in front of the judge. But that part was a formality, it was already decided. Darelle would move into the same foster home as Georgie and Melanie were in, and Donny, her darling little Donny, her cuddlebug and teddy bear, was going to a special hospital for kids who couldn't be trusted not to hurt other people or themselves. And she could either take this damn treatment voluntarily or be placed here by the judge. If she did it voluntarily it would only be a couple of months, but if she got put here by the judge she could be here until some snoop decided she had learned whatever the fuck it was they thought she ought to learn.

And Boris. Who knew what that was about? She didn't even remember how she'd met him, for crying out loud, yet he was like a burr stuck to her, even though he hadn't complained when the bitch in the office told him that for the first three weeks Cindy wouldn't be allowed visitors or phone calls.

And wasn't *that* a slap in the face with a dead codfish! No contact with her kids, her sisters, her brothers, nobody. Just her. Her and the stuff in her head. The same stuff that was making her feel as if she was going to come out of her skin and splat on the floor. Ought to report them to the human rights people, calling it treatment when it was really torment. And they wanted her to donate money to some group butting its nose into the business of foreigners, agitating for the release of political prisoners. Well, she might not be political as she understood the word, but she was a prisoner. And they called it a free country?

Tammy was so bummed out the only thing she could do was go to work, do the best she could there, make money and take it home to the kids. What a friggin' mess it all was. Some in jail, some so far outta town you hardly ever saw them, kids in the bin, kids in group homes, kids all over the place, Cindy in the treatment centre and Barb, well, god knows where in the name of shit she was. Her or those firebugs she had spawned. Sparky and Flash, what a freak pair they were. And dumb! By jesus they were too dumb to be believed, playing with gas and matches. Bloody wonder they hadn't sent themselves sky high along with the house.

The neighbours said they had seen Barb standing on the sidewalk with her two torchers, one on either side, hanging onto her hands and snoffling miserably as they looked at the ruin that had been a house. One of the neighbours headed out to invite them to stay with her until they got themselves properly set up again, but before she could get there they had moved off down the sidewalk, and when she hollered for them, they didn't even turn. She figured they hadn't heard her. And since then, nothing.

Well, by god, if any of her kids had torched a place and nearly incinerated themselves and Darelle, she'd hit the old lonesome trail too, and move on to someplace where the cops didn't have descriptions of the little buggers and orders to pick them up on sight.

Damn cops. Well, they might have thought it was godawful shocking to let Donny stay home by himself with plenty of food and a clear understanding of his limits, but they'd only made things worse when they scooped him. Even with Darelle in the same place, Donny had spun off the rim. They'd come back fast enough, asking Tammy if she'd please go with them and try to calm him down. She had. Not for them, though, they could all go to hell in an Easter basket. She went because Donny needed someone.

But either he hadn't recognized her, or he was so out of it he didn't care. They told her he was "acting out." They hadn't said he was violent, but that's what it was. Violent. Wild. Mesatchie. Crazy. He had yelled and cursed so much he had next to no voice left, and as fast as they put clothes on him, he ripped them off and threw 'em at them. He had bitten one of the staff so hard he had drawn blood, and whenever anyone spoke to him he turned like a savage dog and snapped at them, his teeth clicking together.

"See what you did?" Tammy told them. "I sure hope you're proud of your damn selves," and she turned and walked out. Donny didn't know her, didn't see her as any different than any of the others. If he bit her or turned his rage on her in any way, her heart would crack right down the middle. So best to just get the hell home. If they'd a just left him, quiet and feeling safe, he'd still be there, colouring Porky Pig, eating sandwiches and watching Sally Jessy Raphael. But no, scare the spit out of him, put him in a cop car, send him completely wing-nut, then expect Tammy to wave a magic wand and make him sane again. Jesus, and they went to school to learn how to run other people's lives?

She probably could have pushed them hard enough to let Darelle stay with her, but Tammy didn't feel up to that. All she'd need at this point would be for Darelle to start blubbering. And where had that bloody Dick got himself to, anyway? What was he up to? Taking a page out of Gus's book, maybe, pulling the old fade trick. A man's gotta do what a man's gotta do. Well, piss on him, he wasn't the last one God had made. And if Cindy gave her any static about not taking Darelle, Tammy was going to let her know the train had stopped and it was time she got off and joined the real world. Should never have let that kid get away with all that damn snivelling in the first place. Didn't do any good to cry. Didn't clean up any messes or solve any problems, just gave you a damn headache and made you feel worse. Whatever kind of pain in the ass Phoebe had been, she was past it now, and you'd rot up to your knees in garbage before Phoeb would give you the satisfaction of whining or bawling. Linda, too. And by the lord god Harry, Tammy was going to make damn sure Sandy grew up every bit as tough as the others, because crying never solved a damn thing.

And that fester-brained Real, hadn't he showed up at just about the worst time a person could imagine. The old bat might have had suspicions, but that's all they'd been until old bucktooth himself came waltzing in as if he had a right. Some people think doors don't mean anything. And then Stevie freaked out, and any suspicions the cranky old thing might have had got solidified. Well, more than just cranky. Tammy had long ago recognized a streak of—something—in the old biddy, something Phoebe and Tammy both had. Something that could go from indignant or angry to downright bloody-minded and vengeful. Slit your damn throat in the dark of night and then go home, go to bed, get up in the morning same as always, and sit down to a plate of sausages and eggs. Be lucky if whoever it was had pissed her off didn't wind up *in* the damn sausages. You coulda recorded it, the click in the old bitch's head when Real walked in and Stevie started screeching.

Well, you couldn't blame Stevie, that's for sure. Tammy had seen him after old bravery himself had got through with him. Probably should have been taken to the hospital before he got taken to the trailer. She couldn't believe what she had seen, and couldn't believe old stinkfeet had dared show his ugly face again, not after the way Dick had put the run on him. But there he was, as if it was all water under the bridge and everyone ready to forgive and forget. Wanting to know where his kids were. He could have 'em! With any luck he'd find them, and they'd all move in together and then, while old snaggletooth was sleeping or passed out cold, whichever came first, maybe the two horrors would find something even more intriguing than gasoline—nitroglycerine, maybe—and do another of their science projects. Couldn't they just hatch tadpoles or something? If they were so freakin' interested in scientific experiments, couldn't they wait and do it in school?

Good job Donny hadn't been in the house at the time. He'd have frozen rigid, gaping at the flames until he was part of them, and Darelle would never have got him out. What a mess. Seemed as if all her life if it wasn't one thing, it was another. Tammy was tired of it. Surely to god there had to be another way to live.

Isa and Stevie went into town at ten in the morning, when the banks opened. Isa withdrew a thousand dollars from her account, then went up to the mall. She bought a package of double-sided high-density disks for her computer and paid for them with a fresh fifty, then went over to the hardware store and got new furnace filters. She paid for them with another fresh fifty and put the change in her wallet with the rest. At Workwear World she bought a pair of work gloves and some thick wool socks. At Shoppers Drug Mart she got a package of cigarettes. Store by store, small item by small item, breaking the fresh fifties into smaller bills until there would be no group of them in any one place, no sequence to the serial numbers. Then she went back to her truck and got Stevie into his car seat and her purchases stowed on the floor.

She drove down to Beverly Anne's Cafe and parked in the lot out back. She helped Stevie out of the truck and stood for a moment, holding his hand, looking out at the blue-grey waves slamming against the wet boulders and rocks. Two million dollars' worth of view, waterfront property that would be worth its weight in gold in the city, and here, in this backwater, it was an unofficial parking lot.

They locked the pickup and walked up the rise to the cafe, went inside and found a booth. Stevie caught sight of the burly biker who had let him sit on his Harley, and he wanted to go sit with him, but Isa said no, the man was busy reading his newspaper. "We'll stay here," she smiled, and brushed Stevie's hair from his forehead. "It isn't polite to interrupt people."

She wanted to tell him it wasn't polite to hammer on little guys and it wasn't polite to burst into other people's trailer homes, either. And it certainly wasn't polite to terrify children so bad they were pitched into screaming fits and wet their pants. But for now, the idea of not interrupting people who were reading the news of the world, would do.

Stevie wanted a hot dog and fries, Isa wanted only coffee. She didn't even want coffee, actually, but she had to have something. You don't just take up a booth and buy nothing. While Stevie munched fries and ate the wiener out of the bun, Isa took her wallet from her left rear pocket and openly counted her money. The wallet was stuffed with twenties, tens and fives, and she placed the bills in piles on the table in front of her, twenties here, tens there, fives here, twos over here. Twenty, forty, sixty, eighty, one hundred, twenty, forty, sixty, eighty, two hundred. She got the nine hundred dollars neatly stacked and wrapped a serviette around it before sliding an elastic band around it. The rest of the money went back in her wallet. She left the wad on the table top.

Mountain Man Personified finished his toast and coffee, paid his bill, left a tip, replaced the paper on the pile by the cash register, then moved toward the door. He stopped beside Isa's booth. "Hey, little buddy," he rumbled. Stevie looked up, saw his current hero, and smiled. "Here, gotcha something," and the chunk put a key ring beside the plate of hot dog bun and smeared ketchup. The disk hanging from the key ring showed an eagle, the eagle everyone on the continent would recognize.

As the chunk moved on, his hand closed around the wad, and before he had made it to the door the money was in the pocket of his grungy leather jacket. Isa may have been the only person in the place who saw the switch.

"You could put that in the hole in your zipper tab and wear it on your jacket," she suggested to Stevie. He grinned, and nothing would do but that she get the thing fixed in place right here and now.

When they left the cafe Stevie was strutting proudly, his keepsake bouncing on his chest with every step. They went back to the pick-up, got in and drove to the supermarket, where Isa stocked up on groceries. Then they drove home, put away their purchases, hauled on work clothes and went out to visit with the critters.

Isa watched him stomping in the mud with his gumboots, splashing the thick goo onto his jeans. One of the scad of cats jumped out of the way of a splash and Stevie swooped on it, scooped it up, held it tight against his chest, his face buried in the short hard fur.

"It's Helen," he told Isa.

"How do you remember all their names? I can't."

"Helen," he repeated. Then he pointed. "And there's Jessie, and

Christopher's in the tree, and—" He looked around. "The others must be busy," he decided.

"Well, we know they aren't busy catching mice or rats, they don't do that kind of thing."

She went into the house, took off her muddy boots, changed from her work clothes to the ones she had worn into town, and started thinking about what she would make for supper. She got a chicken in the oven to roast, scrubbed her vegetables and put them in salty water to wait until it was time to cook them, then went to her hell room and turned on the computer. She called up the script she was working on and reviewed her notes. She heard Stevie come into the house, heard him rummaging in the bowl of treats, knew he was getting biscuits to take out for the dogs. The dogs who probably thought the kid had come equipped with pockets full of treats for them.

She wasn't going to bother to phone the welfare, she wasn't going to waste time, effort, energy, electricity or recycled paper calling them or writing to them. She was going to do her own version of Pontius Pilate and wash her hands of them. All they did was take her taxes and use them to hire others just as useless as themselves, so that more and more of them sat in brand-new offices doing less and less of what their mandate said they were supposed to do, while their salaries went up and protection for kids went down.

What she could do that would be useful was work steadily and make money, because those with enough of it could patch holes in safety nets, and those without any could go to hell. It wasn't exactly true that money talks and bullshit walks. Money talks, sure enough, but bullshit puts on an expensive suit and sits behind a brand new desk in a government building.

"Grandma?" Stevie stood in the doorway, an orange in one hand. "I can't peel it."

"Bring 'er here, sweetheart." Isa pushed her chair back from the desk and patted her knee. Stevie climbed up, handing her the fruit.

"You got stories in there, huh?"

"Yeah."

"You workin'?"

"Why?"

"You got games in there?"

"Sure," and she finished peeling the orange, handed it to him, then stored her script and called up the games. "But not until you've finished your snack and then washed the juice off your fingers. These machines don't like mess, and they can get really snarky if you get them dirty."

The motorcycles drove down the highway, turned off onto the side road and, engines purring contentedly, made their way to the driveway, where they turned off and slowed. By the time they got to the house, they were gliding to a stop. They parked side by side, angled slightly, the chrome glinting in the moonlight.

Real didn't hear a thing. He wasn't aware there were others in the messy house until they sat on the sides of his bed and tapped him on the chest, hard. Then he came awake. He sat bolt upright, his eyes bugging.

"Need to have a little talk with you," one of them growled through his bushy beard. "About our little buddy."

"Jesus, man, I ain't done nothin'!"

"Well, actually, guy, you have."

"Don't hurt me! Jesus, don't—"

"I said we were going to have a little talk." The big guy held up his hand and Real had enough survival skills to shut up. "And this time, that's all it's going to be, a talk. Which I hope you'll pay attention to, because we won't talk again. So what's this about you using a belt to beat a little guy senseless?"

"Oh, hey, guys, listen, I was drunk. You know how it is."

"If that's what you do when you're drunk, then best you climb on the wagon and stay there."

"That was weeks ago. Months, maybe. Listen, I ain't been back since."

"No and you're not going back ever again, either. If you go anywhere near our little buddy we're going to get very upset." He rose and the others followed suit. "Now you just go back to sleep and when you wake up in the morning, you think hard on what we've talked about." He smiled, and Real nearly puked with fear. "And don't make the mistake of thinking this is a bluff, okay? Any more bullshit from you and you're dead meat. I promise."

Herb walked out the back door of the club and paused under the streetlight to hitch up his collar against the chill wind. Miserable bloody weather, it was enough to make a person think about places like Arizona or Nevada. Or Hawaii, or Fiji. Anything to get away from this unending howling wind and raindrops the size of bloody nickels. He had enough money socked away he could go to Mexico for six months and still not be in a bind when he got back again.

The bikers moved quickly and Herb swallowed hard. Jesus, were they going to steal his money? They stood in a loose group around him, and he didn't know if he was smelling them or tasting his own fear. He licked his lips and swallowed several more times.

"Like to have a little talk with you," one of them said quietly.

Isa stayed in the small pool with Stevie, but not trying to teach him how to swim. All she wanted was for him to feel at ease in the water. His new fluorescent pink water wings bulged like muscles on his skinny arms, and his lifesaver floater belt wouldn't stay at his waist, it floated up almost to his armpits. But he trusted his gear and was having more fun by the minute. He could even put his face in the water now, and blow bubbles.

The small pool was warmer than the big one, but even so, Isa was starting to feel chilled. Stevie's lips were turning dark. She was sure he had been in too long, but when she had suggested they go home, he shook his head and looked as if he was all ready to burst into tears.

"Want to go for a bite?" he asked suddenly. "We could, you know."

"I'd love to go for a bite. You going to help me up the rampway out of this pool? I'm an old woman and I get tired trying to keep up with you."

He wanted to go to Kentucky Fried, so that's where they went. Isa even ate chicken nuggets and chips. Stevie packed away two drumsticks, then ate his chips and half of Isa's. When they left and headed to the pick-up, his keepsake jingled. But the first flush had worn off. He hardly even noticed he had it any more.

He stopped before they got to the pick-up, bent over and picked up an irregularly shaped chunk of greenish stone. "This is a real good one," he told her. Isa nodded and smiled agreement.

She strapped Stevie into his car seat, locked his door, then moved around to her side, unlocked it and got in.

"I'm going to take you to Eva Bryson's place," she told him, and he stared at her, his face suddenly gone serious. "I've got a pack of work to do on the computer this afternoon and Eva said you could stay at her place and play with the kids. Carol will pick you up on her way home from work."

"You sure?"

"Sure I'm sure," and she made her voice sound easy, relaxed, almost casual, knowing it was the most profoundly serious conversation the two of them could have. "You know we'll pick you up," she teased. "You know I wouldn't ditch you."

"Okay," he said. Then he reached over and handed her the green stone he had found. "Here, you can have it," he said. "'Cause it's real good luck."

"Well, thank you." She put it in her pocket, started the truck and pulled out of the parking lot. "We could use some real good luck."